THE REDUNDANCY
OF COURAGE

ABOUT THE AUTHOR

Timothy Mo was born in Hong Kong in 1950 and educated there and at St John's College, Oxford. His novels have won the Geoffrey Faber Memorial Prize, the Hawthornden Prize, the E.M. Forster Award from the American Academy of Arts and Letters, and the James Tait Black Memorial Prize.

He is now based in South East Asia after more than twenty years in London.

Also by Timothy Mo

The Monkey King
Sour Sweet
An Insular Possession
Brownout on Breadfruit Boulevard
Renegade or Halo^2

The
Redundancy
of Courage

TIMOTHY MO

Paddleless

The Redundancy of Courage

First published in Great Britain 1991 by Chatto and Windus
This edition published in 2002 by Paddleless Press

Paddleless Press, BCM Paddleless, London WC1N 3XX
email: timothymo@eudoramail.com

British Cataloguing in Publication Data
A catalogue record for this book is available from the
British Library

ISBN 09524193 4 3

Printed and bound in Great Britain by Cox & Wyman

PART ONE

ONE

I DON'T WANT THEM FORGOTTEN: Rosa, Osvaldo, Raoul, Maria, Martinho, Arsenio. It would be easy to say in the glib way of those who can lead uninterrupted lives in placid places that such oblivion would be a fate worse than death. No fate is worse than death.

My first sight on that day, and the strongest picture still, stronger than all the bad things which came later, was of parachutes dropping; drifting as if they were thistledown or broken cotton-pods: silent and smooth. By some freak of weather the sky was cloudless that day, freakish for it was the monsoon season – the 7th December to be precise – and the falling chutes appeared almost as a natural phenomenon against the blue, in the place of clouds. There was nothing, it seemed, out of the ordinary about them, certainly nothing that could be conceived as a danger – the sky suddenly blossoming with a thousand canopies. (It was a reinforced battalion, as I now know.) At the time I was shaving in the yard. I did not cut myself. I rinsed my neck, towelled carefully, slapped my cheeks with some cologne. In those days I could be fastidious about my toilet. Our monkey ran at me, chattering and grimacing, showing his yellow teeth. Poor Chico. I flicked some foam and sent him complaining up the jack-fruit tree to the end of his tether. In the hotel I put on a fresh singlet and starched white shirt, then stepped outside to where I had left my Yamaha parked under the shade of the jacaranda. I didn't lock the office. The guests had long since deserted the place and I had nothing to hide from old Carvalho, the gardener.

The sky was still full of dark green down as I buzzed round the corner, then slowed to pick my way through the ruts in the beach road. I noted with pleasure the trunks of the palms which I had had painted white to a uniform height of one and a half metres. Something to set us apart from the rest. Even at that distance I could see the storm of dust in the

7

town; it hung like a thick mist over the centre, and was nothing more than what the wheels of traffic had summoned up. In the territory we had no sealed roads. One cottage hospital, a seminary, a barracks, two airstrips, two hundred metres of street-lighting, and ninety kilometres of unsealed roads which the rains washed out every year – that was the legacy of four centuries of colonialism. Nevertheless, the size of this storm was unusual. It meant the whole town was out. Still the seeds drifted in the sky. I twisted the accelerator, not noticeably improving the speed of the puny machine, but sending a jar through my spine at the next bump. There were people now, but they were proceeding in the opposite direction, away from Danu. These were townspeople, with suitcases. I recognised a man from the waterworks, a minor bureaucrat to whom I had once paid a bribe. He wore a white suit; under his right arm he carried a tennis-racket. My own dust-trail enveloped him. Coming over the steel bridge, pride and joy of the penultimate governor, I glanced through the gantries to where the first of the cotton-pods were falling on the hill behind the airstrip. The bridge shook, lifted with a great thump, as if a giant hand had seized it. Then I was off the smooth planks and bumping again over the dirt. Only then did the bang of the explosion reach me. Later, I was to become knowledgeable about explosives, but then I was the merest neophyte. And in quick succession came six or seven more, each prefaced by a convulsion of the earth. The line of dirt fountains ran parallel to our runway. In the sky high above were three silver insects. I do not strive to be poetic. That was exactly how they appeared. I stopped the Yamaha. They banked to come in over the town. Much lower now, they appeared as the machines they were. Undistracted by any fire – there was not a single dedicated anti-aircraft weapon in the hands of our garrison – they came in side by side, one slightly behind the other. Gouts of flame burst from the wings, as if they *had* been hit, then streaks of fire shot towards the centre of the dust-storm. Briefly, there was orange blossoming; then, merely more dust, tinged darker by smoke. They made four more passes before turning towards the bridge. I had been standing as if I was some privileged witness, outside the events I was observing, with, I admit, some degree of interest. Now, as I came to a sense of myself, I kicked the Yamaha into life and lurched down the track. Too late, I realised my mistake. The aircraft, too, were following the road on a collision course with myself. The nose cannon began to wink light at me. I found myself on my back on the grass bank, the Yamaha still bawling, on its side. Puffs in the road; splinters along the bridge's planks; sparks and ringing as the shells struck the girders and with a terrible howl the jets were over and gone.

I turned the engine off. In the sudden silence I could hear a bell ringing in the town; too tinny to be the Cathedral's monster and rung far too insistently, it baffled me until I identified it as coming from the fire-tender. Well, they would have their work cut out with that venerable machine. From the distance there came the sound of what, in ordinary circumstances, I would have called a car back-firing. I wanted to hear it as such. Certainly, it was no unusual sound in Danu. What it was I already knew perfectly well, even before what would have to have been a fleet of such ramshackle vehicles added their flat reports to the score. And, following these single reports, the long stuttering of an automatic weapon, enthusiastically but amateurishly worked, though I was not to know that then. Probably an invader – our people knew how to fight, had been well-trained by their colonial officers, and hardened to battle in our own Civil War. Just how ill-disciplined the *malais* were did not become apparent for a while, although we were to suffer the consequences soon enough.

The Yamaha did backfire, and I jumped out of my skin. Had I been with someone we might have laughed to break the tension. Being by myself, I trod on the starter again with some reluctance. There were no more refugees along this part of the road and within five minutes I was on the seaward outskirts of the capital. Capital! That was a joke. None of the gun emplacements or machine-gun posts was manned. As I found afterwards, Arsenio Remedios had given orders to his men to move out and not resist the landings – a typically shrewd decision which preserved his resources and enabled the struggle against the invaders to continue, on the terms he bequeathed. But, at the time, right then, it was easy to mistake it for pusillanimity. Some bombs had fallen in the main square on the military barracks and caved in the roof of the guard-house. I am now inclined to believe the hit a matter of luck but at the time it appeared frightening accuracy. FAKOUM soldiers, the only detachment left behind, played their hoses on some smouldering rubble. They bore their G3 assault rifles slung across their backs. But now a jeep came across the square and I recognised Arsenio Remedios, FAKOUM's top commander, in reflective sunglasses, beside the driver. There was a heavy machine-gun on a sturdy mount in the back, manned by one of Arsenio's two permanent bodyguards. However, it was to tell his troops to drop their hoses and beat a retreat that their commander had come. The jeep reversed, at a typically excessive speed, and went through one of the big Praça's narrow exits, at the south end. In a little while, I was the only person standing in the square, the square where just a short time ago FAKOUM had held their celebration of Independence. Only, there was the sound of water in the gutter. The discarded hoses writhed like eels but soon the pressure dropped and even they stopped flapping. It was reasonably quiet in the square. The sun beat down. Again I had the sensation of being dissociated from what was going on around me. I did not want to be part of it. The Yamaha's exhaust echoed in the square, and as I circumnavigated the statue of the Infante Henrique I noticed that his right hand was missing. Three mangled pigeons floated in the fountain.

I was going to follow Arsenio's jeep out of the south street; at the last minute I thought better of it and went round again, a whole circuit almost, to the lane leading to the water-front. Now I got the Yamaha up to a snarling pace, whipping past the sugar-cane and ice-cream stalls (dry ice we possessed!), and the morning fish-stands.

Except no one was there.

The barge that had brought relief supplies from Australia lay by the wharf, and tied up on the end of the jetty was the Governor's launch, which had been commandeered by FAKOUM. In the distance, within the reach of the naked eye, was Toro island and, I knew, the Governor himself, kicking his heels in the corvette the Home Country had reinforced him with far too late. They would sit this out: he, his suite, his wife and son, the boy's tutor, and his bodyguard of paratroopers. The paras, veterans of the African wars, *they'd* have liked to have fired their guns but they never got the chance.

More glittering insects appeared, from seawards this time, to repeat the earlier bombing and rocketing. Again, I had the sensation of being an invulnerable witness inhabiting a third dimension. The planes flew off, far out to sea, well away from Toro island. I now proceeded with a circumspection that surprised the objective, witnessing part of myself which I had surmised to be in command, for I found myself going back into town by cautious ways that did not leave me exposed along the quay.

All changed. I had arrived in the Chinese quarter; that is, the district of the stores and repair shops. It was thronged with people, almost all of my own race. They didn't want to leave their businesses unattended, were far more conscious of the risk of looting by the Danuese than of any threat posed by the invader. They – we – had been the ones who'd had the most to lose by Independence. Most Chinese didn't give a damn about politics, independence or dependency, it was all one and the same to them. Except that the colonial regime offered peace and stability, the given framework in which they could prosper without worrying about big things. And we were resented by the Danuese, of that there could be no doubt. Exploitation was the name of the game. We'd always done it and were cheerfully continuing the tradition of our ancestors. Rip-off didn't begin to describe it. We held a stranglehold on the economy: transport, meaning the trucks which roared up and down the awful roads; the distribution and export of the coffee-crop; the retail goods we hawked up-country at inflated prices. Whole villages were eyeball deep in debt to a Chinaman. No, we didn't want self-government. The natives, and that included the *mestizo* leaders, half-castes like Remedios and his friends, were determined to get their pound of flesh from us. Which will now allow you to understand why the metal grilles were pouring down over store-fronts. The quicker, and the more fearful, were already padlocking the shutters to rings in the ground, a characteristic local way of securing. The cans of corned beef, the sweets in their jars, the galoshes, the saws, the plastic watering-cans, the transistor radios, disappeared from sight.

The general exodus was to a large warehouse called the Toko-ru. This had originally been the Tokyo Rose, so-named by the liberating Australians after the Pacific War, for it had been the Japanese military brothel during the four years they were in occupation. Now it had lost both its old function and the sense of its name, as the Danuese bent the unfamiliar sounds to what was easiest for their tongues. The Chinese owned it co-operatively, used it to hoard stock off the irregular cargo-ships, while the two upper floors were rented out as accommodation to single Chinese men. People were leaning out of the upper windows, fastening a large multi-coloured strip of cloth to two balconies. I recognised it as the flag of our neighbour.

'Aiyee! You've got it upside down!'

Hysterical laughter from everyone, in which I found myself joining. The men, nevertheless, leaned over at some peril to exchange corners with their counterparts on the other balcony and it was at this point that João Wong fell over the railings, seven metres into the street below, landing badly on his hip and elbow. He was a good mechanic and we didn't have too many of those in Danu. When I got to him, I thought he was dead. But he had merely fainted. He opened his eyes. He didn't groan but his chest rose and fell rhythmically; he appeared to be concentrating very carefully on going on living. We carried him into the darkness of the warehouse. I had just put down my end of the plank when there came three explosions, one after the other, not as impressive as the earlier bombing. Someone shouted from the flat roof: 'Ships! It's ships firing at us!' Instead of seeking shelter we all ran up the stairs. We couldn't see anything, flashes let alone ships. But there was a rumbling overhead, not unlike the street-cars in San Francisco (Calif., not São Francisco, the miserable hole of a fishing village on our own Mangrove Coast), before the shells exploded harmlessly in the suburbs. This was the area known as Colonia where, in the old days, the administrators from the Home Country had made their residences. Some of the foreign journos had rented places there but they'd gone by now, all except for Bill Mabbeley, the crazy Australian. I am ashamed to say there was laughter, back-slapping. The next salvo trundled over, beyond the houses. The following salvo burst in the oil storage tanks. I now suspect that they had a forward observer spotting for them, perhaps some of their paratroopers, more likely an agent with a radio on a roof, much like ourselves. Well, that did it. The cornet of black smoke, sometimes orange at the centre, sometimes embroidered with the flame at the sides, kept on rising into the blue of the sky. I asked myself, and it was a measure of my state of mind, if it would have cast smuts onto the parachutes. And that was the second sight of that day – the fiery pillar straight out of the Old Testament, to go with the parachutes, the falling manna of the early morning. That brooding column – it seemed too big, too grand, out of place on our little patch of ground. The group was sobered.

I decided to return to the Hotel. It was at this point, I think, that I no longer felt outside the events of that day; that I felt in a great danger. But the Yamaha had gone. This, too, made me feel strange. Theft among ourselves was virtually unknown. Pilfering was reserved for the tourists, mostly for the Australians, who were as mean as they were monied by Danu's standards, and by general consensus deserved it. Taking the Yamaha was a spectacular crime. But there was nothing for it. While the others busied themselves with yet more of the invader's flags, I hurried on foot out of the quarter, past the blank shops and garages. There wasn't a person or a vehicle to be seen. Odd shells, from seaward I judged, began to fall again on the waterfront side of the town, making passage there perilous. Harassment and interdiction is the military expression, I believe. I abandoned the idea of a retreat to the hotel – scurrying along the shore, as vulnerable as a rat pelted by boys. My steps took me towards the Marconi Centre, located on a well-forested hillock on the edge of the park belonging to the old Governor's Residence. It got hard to see where I was going, with smoke and dust mixed, hanging in the still air. The morning sun was getting all the time hotter but its rays barely penetrated the gloom. This had been the most heavily bombarded area, the centre of the rocketings and cannonade. In the immaculate turf before the Governor's mansion were four large holes, the grass scorched at the edge of the craters. They were all on a line, as if a giant had raked the earth with dirty claws. It was extraordinary, that. The desecration, the wanton vandalism of it. And once again the sense of unreality, of alienation from the actual, descended upon me. Piles of bodies in the streets – which had been conspicuously absent – burst water pipes, none of that would have had the same effect upon me or, I think, any other resident of Danu. It's the small things which can bring about the greatest sense of violation.

The Marconi Centre was untouched and so was its dish. It was a low, modern building, well-constructed by the island's standards, and the company had taken the trouble to soften its outlines with some well-placed creepers. They'd flourished in our jungle conditions. I liked that: the little touch, the bit of extra care lavished, just like my whitewashed palm trees on the avenue to the hotel. This was unusual for Danu, I'll tell you. I now believe that the Centre must have been a prime target for the pilots, more important even than the airstrip or the oil tanks, but their rockets still missed. Privilege and high pay were theirs, not to mention the American instructors, and they still missed. Inside, the atmosphere was a strange mixture of tension and calm. Say, rather, of a sustaining but still artificial professional coolness

14

on the part of the operators and near panic where everyone else was concerned. I recognised three FAKOUM committee members, including Pedro Ribeiro. Ribeiro, dressed in the olive greens that were *de rigueur* for FAKOUM, looked jumpier than anybody I had seen on that day. The buzz of static, the shouting of the FAKOUM people, did not quite blot out the calm voices and measured procedures of the trained operators, but it was still a scene of the greatest confusion. In a corner, scribbling into a notebook, was Bill Mabbeley, the Australian journalist. He was the most absorbed person in the room, the busiest and the most disinterested. Ribeiro was calling up Darwin, but he was getting impatient with the operator. Finally, he snatched the mike from him. He was screaming now, sweating and shouting in his heavily accented English. 'This is Danu calling, Danu calling the world. We are under attack. We are being attacked by air, sea and land. Repeat – Danu is being attacked by armed forces of her neighbour – army, navy, air force, and paratroopers. We ask the world to come to our help. The invaders are massacring our people, they are killing everyone in sight. This is Danu alerting the world to planned atrocities.'

When he'd finished, his army shirt was soaked across the chest and back as well as under the arms. 'Broadcast that,' he said. The operator, who was not as excited as Ribeiro was and who had not neglected to note his message, read it back to him. *'Bom,'* said Ribeiro. He turned on his heel, the olive entourage following him through the baize doors. On the way he nodded at me. 'You people,' he said, 'are in this as much as us.'

When they'd gone, Bill Mabbeley glanced up. He grinned. 'Bullshit to the end,' he said.

That surprised me. I knew Mabbeley sympathised with FAKOUM. His reports for his newspaper, one with a large circulation and surprisingly liberal views, though not as left-wing as those of the journalists it employed, had been uniformly sympathetic not only to the Independence movement but, which was much more unusual, to the acts of the FAKOUM administration itself in the few months of its life.

All the other journos, most of whom had been staying at the Club Lusitano in the town – do not, I beg you, suspect me of trade jealousies – had caught their planes long ago. They'd known what to expect from the *malais*. The clumsy executions of the Australian and New Zealand TV crew the *malais* had caught as they came over the Border seven weeks before had been lesson enough. I didn't blame them; in fact, I thought Mabbeley foolhardy. But what I said was: 'You tell them the truth, Mr Mabbeley. Tell the world what's happening.' I was embarrassed for myself as soon as I heard the words issuing from my mouth, though Mabbeley, who was a leathery, tough old fellow, but vain like hell, said: 'Thanks, mate.'

I waited awkwardly, but he was frowning at his notebook again. One of the operators winked and gave me a thumbs up sign as I left. I didn't want to leave the Marconi Centre – the companionship, the link with civilisation, the illusory air of calm, of technical competence, made it seem the sanctuary it wasn't. It was probably the most dangerous place to be in Danu. Outside reigned the most perfect silence, strange after the squawkings and hissings of the radio, with not even the roar of the cicadas which usually infested those trees. Only the rocket craters gave the lie; without them it would have been hard to have believed there was anything out of the normal happening. In that hallowed spot, I mean; the rest of Danu was a different place altogether.

In fact, the invasion hardly took us by surprise. We'd all been expecting it. The weeks, months, of move and counter-move, the destabilising, the broadcasts of our neighbour, the marching songs, the relentless playing of their anthem, the incessant messages of support for the Amalgamationists, that is the party who favoured integration with the larger neighbour, the incursions over the mountains, the burning of villages and crops, had evoked a popular mood of near-hysteria. We'd been waiting for it, sure, but when it came it was still a shock. Like being struck in a bar if you're a peaceful person: even as you know the shock of the blow, you cannot acknowledge it has been struck, refuse to believe in the enormity.

16

Coming out of the Marconi Centre that morning, with Ribeiro's plea still in my ears, what was being done to us in the name of the crusade against international Communism, I less than half-comprehended. I began to run. It was something in the air. And coming from behind a shack in which garden tools were stored, I saw them for the first time. *Malai* elite troopers, distinctive in their crimson berets. Their cherry berets. They flitted from place to place, tree to car, to crater, to bush, all the time covering the approach of those who were moving until it was their turn to glide again. They were long-legged, spry men, not the stocky, brutish specimens of my, and I dare say our collective, imaginings. I think we thought we were being invaded for a second time by the Japanese. Copying their example, I, too, looked for cover and found it on my belly behind a half-eaten watermelon, noisome with flies. The *malais'* faces, as they now came closer, struck a terror into me. No pity existed in those faces. They were implacable. I won't say bent on cruelty, because that came after, inflicted on the defenceless, and was a kind of weakness, an insanity, whereas now they were themselves vulnerable; they expected resistance and could afford no indulgences. Behind those eyes I dare say they were frightened.

There was a sheet of newspaper, full of black melon seeds someone had spit out. My whole world had come down to tiny things. The flies, the seeds, a few blades of grass, a couple of pebbles. They started to assume a momentous significance for me. I looked to protect, to conceal with what I could. The witnessing part of me might have found pathos in these feeble efforts. I fully understood the old saying about a drowning man clutching at straws. Without any sense of distaste, I placed the half-transparent newspaper before my face. The flies still buzzed around the seeds. I hoped I looked like a corpse. The figures were so near now that I no longer dared look.

It was at this point that Arsenio Remedios, in his jeep, with additional FAKOUM troops seated on the sides, facing outwards, their boot-heels dangling by the tyres, came coasting down hill to the Marconi Centre. He was almost certainly looking to escort Bill Mabbeley to safety, probably on the instructions of Martinho Oliveira. Mabbeley was as valuable to FAKOUM now as three tanks or a jet-fighter; maybe more valuable. With the gears in neutral Arsenio caught the *malais* by surprise but he was equally unprepared. The two sides summed each other up for the briefest moment, then the shooting started. There was not a man without an automatic weapon. The FAKOUM troops had an abundance of guns, inherited from the colonial arsenal, fairly modern equipment – thanks to the Home Country's NATO obligations – from German-patented assault rifles and general purpose machine-guns to rockets, mortars and the odd recoil-less rifle. FAKOUM were not shy to shoot. As I said, after the Civil War, they were more used to shooting and, still more relevant, to receiving fire, than even the elite units of the *malais* who were being used in this invasion.

But it was the *malais,* with more hormones in the system at that moment, who recovered from their surprise quickest, and the first burst of fire killed Remedios. Arsenio! The best commander FAKOUM had; the winner of the Civil War; the planner of their strategy; the man of method who also knew when to be rash; and, above all, despite his toughness in battle, among the most moderate of the Central Committee – the one who had counselled clemency in victory and reconciliation with those losers of the Civil War who hadn't already fled to the *malais.*

That was the terrible irony of it. Within half an hour of the invasion FAKOUM had lost one of its best and most visionary commanders in a squad-level action.

I saw from behind my sodden newspaper the bullets strike Remedios down. Even as he pointed to direct the fire of his bodyguards, he was hurled back against his seat, and the blood poured out of his neck. I thought I saw his lips move, say 'Son of a bitch'. But his shades stayed on. As he slid down, his knees coming to meet his darkening chest and his hand falling outside the chassis, the .50 calibre machine-gun on the mount behind him opened up on the *malais*. The noise from this was deafening; it sounded like a cannon. Even in the day you could see the flash from the muzzle. It was that piece which settled for the *malais*. The gunner just kept the butterfly of the trigger depressed and worked the heavy weapon round, the bullets gouging great sods from the park, smashing down the heavily burdened *malais,* knocking their radio operator, set and all, a metre in the air, before putting him on his back in a wrestler's bridge. Some of it came my way, too, but all overhead, misses at the *malais,* while I pulled my newspapers over my head and tried to wriggle into the ground.

Arsenio's men put their jeep into reverse, the gunner still firing at the surviving invaders to cover their retreat and they roared backwards over the brow of the hillock the way they'd come, taking with them their dead or dying commander. By a truly special irony, he was the only man in the jeep hit.

The silence was absolute. I was numbed with terror. If the cherry berets found me now I was a dead man. I was always potentially a dead man, of course; what I mean is that, following the deaths of their comrades, I feared the unusual degree of cruelty which might accompany my demise. However, they were too preoccupied with their own condition to look around much. They seemed as dazed as I was. None of the six or seven hit seemed to have survived those terrible bullets but the remaining five dragged away by the arms one who must still have been alive. I watched them depart with a relief which was not spoiled by worry about what might lie around the corner. I just lived in the moment. I lay still for a while, luxuriating.

A few minutes later Bill Mabbeley came from the same direction I had, proceeding with a caution which was ludicrous, considering I was watching him the whole time. He tiptoed across the grass, looking around and stopping a couple of times. My right cheek and eyelid kept twitching for a while after I'd finished tittering. Mabbeley went on out of sight, now and then staring back at the *malai* bodies. When he'd gone I made my own move, which was back into town.

I was effectively driven back down there. I didn't fancy heading on into the outskirts and running into troops advancing from the airstrip. Never mind that I was putting myself into the jaws of a closing trap. Remedios, were he still alive, or even Ribeiro, could have told me the safest plan would have been to advance as far as possible and meet the *malais* where their line was extended across the greatest distance and then slip through the gaps. But, like a poor, frightened fish, I did the natural thing, the wrong thing, and ended up netted.

I was to learn later that their marines had by now landed from fast inflatables, much like the one which bobbed by my hotel jetty. They'd chosen the identical spot, a rocky point just west of town, where the Japanese had landed in 1942; doubtless a source of some hard amusement for those who remembered.

My steps took me back towards the Toko-ru – we gravitate towards our own in a crisis, do we not – with the sounds of shooting growing louder every moment.

Three teenage boys came racing down a cobbled alley at right angles to me. They were native boys, the kind who lounged around the waterfront with nothing to do – the kind I sometimes chose. They were scared out of their wits. As he turned too sharply, one lost his rubber sandal, the ones Australians call 'thongs', and a moment later he staggered, clutched his leg, ran a little, fell, crawled, got up, and with the clatter of the burst still re-echoing, dropped again. His friends kept going. I saw the bullets chip the masonry of the buildings after them and I think they got away.

I flattened myself against a doorway. From my position 1 could see one of the boy's legs; it appeared unwounded. There was the tramp of boots – they were well-shod, the *malais* – and three came past the mouth of the alley. Before I stood to attention, my head pushed back up against the door and the hairs on the nape of my neck actually prickling, I saw they were identically equipped to the ones who had shot Remedios, except that they were wearing purple berets. Violet berets! They were their marines, though I didn't know that then. I didn't give much for the boy's chances. My curiosity was stronger than my fear. I stole a glance. The soldiers walked round the boy. I now saw the ugly wound to his thigh. One of them kicked him. With those excellent boots. The boy didn't scream. I waited for the *malais* to shoot again, finish him off.

But they didn't. They walked on, down the street. When I came out he was unconscious; very pale, bleeding to death probably. I think the *malais* were conserving their ammunition in the knowledge that they'd killed him already. There was nothing I could do for him. I arrived at the Toko-ru without further incident. I don't know whether I'd have done better to stay where I was. I guess I'm still alive and telling the story.

There were some very anxious-looking heads peering out of the top floors of the Toko-ru. By now, they had the *malai* flag stretched out as big as they could without actually tearing it in half. And when I entered I smelled cooking. They had gas flames going, with the big Chinese pans sizzling on top. It was ludicrous, but touching. The Chinese, always cooking up some tasty mess or other, reverting to type now. I guess a Frenchman would have been found smoking, an Englishman drinking a cup of tea, an American chewing gum. But they weren't frying for themselves.

It was for the *malais*.

Someone was ripping the polythene off cases of beer. It seemed to me that to inflame those troops with alcohol would be to throw petrol on to a fire. My expostulations went disregarded. They took tables outside. Up went bunting, streamers, mini-flags, and a sheet still wet with the paint of running characters which read: '*Welcome* to *our heroic neighbours and liberators.*' Had he been alive Arsenio Remedios would have shot the bunch of them on the spot. I doubt even if the *malais* could have read their own language with ease, at least not the enlisted men.

I decided to remain inside.

Fierce firing – it sounded like the very next street – did nothing to change my mind, but I went to the smallest

21

window on the first floor. It belonged to the 'bathroom', a noisome place, I'll assure you, but the stinks were as nothing at that moment to the hotelier who owned ten of the fifty flush toilets in Danu. The Chinese were still fiddling with their streamers when the first *malais* appeared at the end of the street. I saw them well before anyone else and, again, enjoyed all the sensations of the voyeur, with my countrymen busy about their hospitableness, unaware for some time of the flitting at the top of the street. For men who, unlike the cherry berets who'd run into Arsenio, had encountered nil rather than minimal resistance, these *malais* were notably cautious. So, I understand, are even the largest sharks who will circle their prey many times before attacking. They covered each other in turn, sprinting for corners and doorways, while the Chinese arranged their buffet-table. At last one of our younger Chinese saw them. He didn't speak, but grabbed the arm of the man beside him. By some voiceless mutual accord the others then realised the *malais* had arrived. They stayed quite still, some with plates and glasses in their hands. The leading group of *malais* were about thirty metres away, most of them kneeling on one leg, with their rifles levelled. Behind, as far from them as they were from us, two lay on their bellies with a light machine-gun on a bipod, not as formidable as Arsenio's jeep-mounted monster. Unfortunately, I slipped at this moment, my shoe sliding off the criss-crossed concrete pedestal on which the squatter was meant to perch to do his business, with the result that I fell into the discoloured white porcelain of the pit. It would, would it not, be difficult to imagine a more inelegant or unhygienic predicament. When I looked out again, it was to see the Chinese walking towards the *malais* with food and flags in their hands; their faces contorted into the false and ready smile of our race. The *malais* reacted without hesitation and seemingly without needing to be ordered. The machine-gun opened up, knocking down the line of advancing Chinese from right to left, the impact of the bullets flinging them two or three steps backward, jerking their limbs like puppets, one man sent skidding on his knees,

22

then toppling sideways, blood patches blooming on their white shirts, and all in a chaos of falling cutlery, smashing plates, and splattering food. Before the burst got round to them, two old men at the far end of the line made it back into the Toko-ru, the last bullets kicking up street dust and then sparks and stone chips from the stairs behind their retreating heels. The riflemen hadn't fired, nor did they as the two with the machine-gun got off their bellies and ran past to cover the riflemen in turn as they conducted their mortal game of leapfrog. At the open door of the Toko-ru they placed themselves left and right. In went a hand-grenade. It took a very long time to explode. During that interval, one *malai* looked upwards, right up my nostrils, and exclaimed. I paid the price of the nosey-parker. He fired vertically, straight up at the sky, and back I went. This time I fell completely and utterly into that awful hole, smearing hands as well as pants. Shortly after, the grenade went off. That might have been my salvation. A burst of fire followed, then the *malais'* boots on the staircase. Presented with the choice of dying in the rest-room or the corridor, I decided to confront my destiny in the open. My smell was terrible, worse in the unpolluted corridor. There had been no more shots. I stood against the wall, with my hands raised in that universal gesture of surrender. Two *malais* came up the staircase and didn't shoot me. They went into a room and brought out three Chinese. These they placed against the wall next to me. I kept my hands up, standing, while the others squatted. After a while they moved slightly away from me. The *malais* emerged from the rest-room and drove us downstairs, without brutality, other than a shove in the butt with a boot-sole. I fear his boot got the worst of that particular exchange. They then marched a dozen of us down to the water-front. On this journey I did see three civilian bodies although I was unable to identify them. We found more Danu people on the dock, sitting cross-legged with a few *malai* sentries by them. After we had joined the group other prisoners were brought. I remember thinking that's what we were, prisoners. Altogether we numbered a little more than 70 people. Now

23

that the immediate threat of death was past I began to wonder what they wanted with us.

An hour or so later, at about half past two (one cannot be more definite because they had taken our watches when their officer wasn't looking), a line of civilians appeared on the water-front, then were marched out along the jetty. Even at that distance it was possible to see that their hands were bound behind their backs and that many walked with difficulty. When we joined them, it became obvious that several had been badly beaten. At midday the blood on their faces had dried quickly. These people were guarded by green berets. We were put on our knees this time, just behind the latest arrivals who had to keep standing.

Ten minutes later a woman and two children, guarded by a whole squad of greens, came at gun-point down the jetty. It was Sonia Ferreira, the mistress of Osvaldo Oliveira, who was the real driving force behind FAKOUM, its true as opposed to titular leader. So they had the next best thing to the chief of FAKOUM himself.

Her appearance was the signal for proceedings to commence. A member of the Amalgamationist Party (PA), in other words a Danuese, was accompanying the red berets and now walked along the standing ranks, pointing at those who struck his fancy, among them a late middle-aged woman of undistinguished appearance, who was both President of FAKOUM and Arsenio Remedios's aunt. I shall explain this unlikely conjunction in due course. These unfortunates the cherry berets seized, invariably by the hair, dragging them to the edge of the jetty and forcing them to their knees. Little imagination was required of us to envisage what would happen next and the reality of their situation was not lost upon the victims. They began to cry out, those waiting also, begging for mercy. But they could have saved their breath. The soldiers wore the same look as the *malais* I had seen near the Marconi Centre. They'd have shot their own brothers, then.

As the green berets withdrew to bring more to execution, cherry berets shot dead the first trio of victims. They used

24

single shots from the Soviet-pattern assault rifles which their deposed President had bequeathed them. The cracks of the shots had not died away before the greens brought the next three. But these had to wait a while for their turn. The shots had smashed the victims down dead, face-first, but they had not fallen into the sea. Now they lay in great streams of blood. I was surprised how much blood. The *malais* did not want to soil their uniforms. Accordingly, the three citizens of Danu who were to die next were made to throw the bodies over the jetty. One of them was known to me – Danny Xaneros, a policeman. He was the brother of Xavier Ray Xaneros, who had built my hotel and was to play a great part in my later life. He still had his leather holster but they'd taken his pistol. He was ordered to sit with the other two right on the edge, their feet dangling over the water.

The splashes followed the shots, with a second's lag.

This was convenient, but insufficiently dramatic. Now the *malais* took to shooting the victims one at a time. And for each man we were made to shout: *one, two, three*. The funny thing was, eager to please, we all shouted with great vigour. It sounded quite a cheerful sort of chorus. You'd have thought we'd been at a basket-ball match. We'd got to thirty-one when there came a pause in the proceedings. Did the *malais* feel the shootings were losing their effect? I personally knew several of those killed, but after the first few the executions ceased to have the same impact. I felt as if I'd been hypnotised. The *malais* knew all about this. They'd killed hundreds of thousands in their own country: communists, socialists, liberals even.

This was the moment the captain had been waiting for. He produced Sonia Ferreira. With her small son and daughter. I have to record she was in terror of death. You will judge for yourselves but I know they wouldn't have got a word from Osvaldo Oliveira, her lover; however, she was a normal woman. We could hear her pleading. She begged for mercy, for her children, for herself. He was like stone, that *malai* officer. He was seated on a bollard, with a clip-board, on which he was recording the names of the executed, bare-headed with a crew cut, so I never knew whether he was a violet, green, or red beret. A red, I'd have said: they were the true killers. Two greens were trying to get the crying children from their mother but that thin woman in her thin frock wouldn't let them go, even when a cherry beret drove his rifle butt into the small of her back. In the end they would have beaten her unconscious but then Arsenio Remedios's jeep appeared, driven by *malais*.

Where Arsenio had sat was a man much stouter than the FAKOUM army commander, dressed in a blue safari-suit and white shoes that flashed as he dashed up the jetty, with a cherry beret officer doing his best to follow. I think the cherries considered bayoneting him there and then, but for the senior officer behind who was of far greater rank than anyone on the ground so far. The stout man was N.J. Pereira, a FAKOUM CC member. The only reason he was alive was that he was also the son of a *pro-malai* Amalgamationist chieftain and the brother of the PA's military commander, who in other words were closest kin as well as political foes. He also happened to be Sonia Ferreira's brother-in-law. Such was the nature of things in Danu. We were a small place and, as with all civil wars, brother had fought brother, son father, cousins their uncles. Pereira was waving his hands a lot and shouting, which inclined me to suspect he didn't have a lot of real influence with the *malais*. He pushed past the captain with the clip-board and strode towards the end of the jetty. That was a very dangerous thing to do; it was a brave action. Or maybe he hadn't seen much so far. Those cherry berets were unpredictable. The senior officer came with him. He was more worried for Pereira than Pereira was for himself. But then he knew his men.

Sonia Ferreira surrendered her son and daughter; the children went willingly to their uncle. He carried the small boy, while the daughter held his hand. With an inclination of the head he tried to indicate to Sonia that she should follow him as well but then, without warning, one of the *malais* who had been doing the killings felled her with a back-handed slash of the gun-butt against the jaw. It was brutal, much more so than the firing. It was that which brought Pereira to a sense of how things really stood. The senior officer shook his head at the men, as if to say: wait, rather than, no. Then his expression changed as he turned to Pereira, to a smile, one of great kindness, of manly solicitude, shrugging as he spread his arms. I warmed to him. He took the little girl's hand – she seemed to trust him – and they went off to the jeep. The son turned to look at his mother as they drove off. We all felt a little less safe when they'd gone, which was absurd.

They shot Sonia Ferreira just like they'd shot the others, but we spectators failed to take up the chorus properly and, in a rage, the captain with the clip-board shouted 'Thirty-two' at us.

The work proceeded by threes again, and the process of simple arithmetic finally left two men, not three. I'd worked it out before it happened. These were shot with the rifles on full auto. That used up the second magazines they'd fitted. Long after their bodies had splashed into the water, we were kept waiting in the sun with only the urgent scratching and bursts of words on the *malais'* radio to break the silence.

It became evident we were not to be executed; our function was something else.

At length arrived the *pièce de résistance*. This was in all senses. It was Bill Mabbeley.

He was cursing his captors, calling them every name under the sun and, though his hands were tied behind his back, he kicked viciously. Did I say he made a little affectation of wearing the FAKOUM-issue military boots? The *malais* had the guns, they would shortly murder Mabbeley, but for the moment they were helpless against his shrewd and angry kicks: they didn't want the task of carrying him in the hot sun which they would have faced if they'd tied his legs and, for the same reasons, they didn't want to shoot him on the spot because of the mess and nuisance. The body of an Australian journalist would require special disposal. And these *malais* were lazy to their core, as well as blood-thirsty amoks as the mood took them. Mabbeley, too, had

27

surrendered to his rage. He was shouting, rather hoarsely now.

'Bastards, ratbags. Your mothers were screwed by pigs. You're scum. Fuck you, you miserable collection of pig-fuckers.' He had all the command of invective of an Australian and was, besides, verbally quite inventive as a journalist – I suppose – but after a while he started to repeat himself. The words didn't mean anything – he just wanted to defy them, though the constant references to pigs reflected his basic knowledge that eighty per cent of the *malais* were Muslims. If you could say, as a generalisation, that all Malays are idle, you could also say all Australians are brave, or at least non-respecters of authority. I was mean-minded enough to hide my eyes as Mabbeley went past. I didn't want him recognising me. His captors were sufficiently near to their chosen spot now to feel free to retaliate in kind and kicks and blows from their weapons made Mabbeley stagger. He kept shouting at them, though. Finally, he ran head-down to butt a cherry beret in the stomach and this was when they lost patience and stabbed him in the side. His mouth opened at that, but he didn't go down until they'd kicked him in the legs a few times. He dropped heavily on to his knees, but his head was up, despite the blood widening around his waist. The officer gave his clip-board to a cherry beret, unbuttoned his holster, and cocked and presented the pistol to Mabbeley's temple. Mabbeley wasn't looking at him but straight ahead, down the jetty to the mountains – maybe wondering at the last sight of his life – and he said in a calmer tone than before, maybe because it was the end at last, or maybe because he was faint with loss of blood: 'You really are a bunch of bastards.' And then: 'I hope the whole world...' But what Bill Mabbeley hoped of the whole world was cut short by the shot which pitched him dead on his side.

The *malais* were quiet after that. I think the way Mabbeley had died did that to them. You couldn't have shouted 'Forty-four' after that. You could say he'd imposed his sense of himself upon them, that he wasn't just something falling off the edge of a jetty, a corpse before it had hit the water. Of course, he was white, which helped.

The *malai* officer went to the jetty's edge to peer over. What he saw seemed to satisfy him. He still had his pistol out but holstered it again. Not just from that, I could tell the killing – organised killing – was over for the moment. What they required of us now was to clear up for them. Some of us were sent to the Toko-ru and other warehouses to get weight – chains, iron-bars, bricks, to tie round the bodies after they'd been fished out. Meanwhile, they burned Mabbeley. We weren't trusted with this task. The *malai* officer did it himself. While I tied a rusty car-part around the corpse of a mountain man I hadn't known – probably he'd had the simple misfortune to be in town selling durians on that day – I saw the *malai* from the corner of my eye, sprinkling petrol. He was doing it at arm's length, with great care not to wet his own clothes and having some difficulty with the heavy jerry-can. It wasn't as easy to light as one would have imagined, unless I wasn't seeing the flame in the bright sunshine. But finally it went. There was no doubting that. The officer got a cherry beret to throw more petrol on. Along with smoke, a horrible smell came. People wrinkled their noses with disgust. It was funny. They were pulling sodden corpses out of the water, most with terrible facial injuries, and yet it was really only the smell which was insupportable. I, too, hurried down to the end of the jetty, dragging my mountain man with his heavy weights. Mabbeley appeared to have sat up, the corpse shrinking into a semi-foetal position and quite black now in the centre of the flames and oily black clouds. And as I looked away and down into the water, I saw riding in on the flood, the incoming tide which would keep many of the inadequately weighted bodies bobbing in the harbour until long after dark, shoals of giant white and dark-green jelly-fish. They hung in the clear water like ghostly canopies, suspended above the blue void in a fall they continued to suggest but would never make. The salty manna to go with the pillar of fire.

TWO

YOU ARE PROBABLY WONDERING ABOUT ME. I don't blame you.
When a man writes, you get the core of him. If I were
religious, I could say you get his soul. That is, you are
presented with his essence, but essence is clear stuff. Race,
culture, quirks, physical appearance, they've all been boiled
away. After all, when the souls go to the Day of Judgement
will God differentiate between us as Americans, Africans,
Indians or Chinese? As tall, short, thin, fat?

My name is Adolph Ng. Please laugh. To pronounce it,
imagine you have been constipated a long time. Now strain.
There you have my surname. You know I am of Chinese race
and you may surmise that in despite of my occupation of
hotelier – if you are given to snobbery, or are merely realistic
– I am an educated man. I am a man of the modern world.
The world of television, of universities, of advertising, of
instant communications, made me what I am. It made me a
citizen of the great world and it made me a misfit for ever. I
was offered the glorious things of that realm, and when I was
tempted and said: yes, give them to me, I was thrown down
and when I awoke I was abandoned and lay in a desolate
place, yea, and the air was full of the sound of wailing and
the gnashing of teeth. But the rending of one's clothes and
the flaying of one's flesh with his fingernails start to pall
quite quickly as diversions, if he is a sensible fellow. And I
think I have that much of the Chinese pragmatism in me.

My father, who had made money from his up-country
cantina and trucking business, sent me for an education. He
sent me to America. Where else? Except it was Canada. The
poor old man thought Toronto was in America. But who are
we to scoff at him? The ignorant assumptions of the
uneducated can be a kind of blunt wisdom. Of course
Toronto is in America. My Macao Uncle, my Vancouver
Cousin, part of that complex, extended family network, the

30

reliability and efficiency of which could never be doubted for a moment by any of its members, assisted in those details which were beyond my father. I'd already benefited from their intervention with the private high school in Macao which I had attended from the age of sixteen. Travelling expenses, immigration procedures (also a vital part of that modern world I aspired to join: they were the bouncers at the club door), examination qualifications, college admission, these were matters about which the old man never had to give himself the least concern. They just told him the cost; then he'd send instructions to the Bank of America in Guam (like most of his compatriots he was too wily to leave more than a few escudos with the Banco Ultramarino). I was the lucky one, of that there could be no question. Some of the *mestizos* might get sent to the Home Country, to either the decaying old seat of learning in the capital or to the blank concrete monstrosity in a provincial town which the Fascists had built in the 1930's. The Dictator had been a Professor of Economics! Truly. Neither institution could be said to provide an efficient or a modern education. The affluent Chinese preferred something more cosmopolitan for their junior generation. Some might contrive to slip a son into an Australian University, though this was frequently a case of so near, yet so far, for although the Northern Territory was less than an hour away by air, the immigration difficulties were notorious. For reasons which will become clearer, I prefer Australians to Americans. Nevertheless, for those who'd made money, or for those who saw learning as the key and were prepared to make sacrifices, the US was possible. Not easy, but possible. The garage-owner had a son at Berkeley; the woman who ran my father's *cantina* (not a bar but a general store) had a boy at Pomona. California was popular – only one ocean to be crossed, even if it was the Pacific. But for me it was not so convenient. There were several changes of aircraft. Going over those Pacific thermals, I'd been sick. The big jet flapped its wings like a bird.

In the transit lounge at LA things got a lot worse. I had no paper sack in which I could put my homesickness. To be honest, it was simple fear. Having all those cases to look after, while I fingered the string bag of oranges which had been my father's parting gift, made me feel like a refugee, rather than a traveller. But that was the low point. Afterwards, I never felt so bad again – not until the day of my return.

The university was good. Suffice to say that my studies were both stimulating and rewarding. I think I am entitled to say that I derived more from my courses than the home students. Those were wonderful years. To be given the leisure and the opportunity to become acquainted with the great thinkers of the past and the *savants* of the present was to be granted the freedom of an enchanted city. This didn't seem to be an opinion shared by those born into that world, who took its resources for granted. I gained an unenviable reputation as a worker. I was told later there were under a thousand books at the Danu seminary. When I walked into the college library at Toronto I was struck dumb, like Aladdin, before I began to plunder the cave of its stored treasures. The incense of the books, the light hum of the air-conditioning, the candle-like glow of the desk lamps, the bowed heads of the worshippers at those separate shrines, the discreet ministerings of the librarian-acolytes and their murmurings in that huge hush, and every now and again a telephone's single 'ting', conspired to produce reverence in my breast. As I worked, as I committed sentence by sentence the wisdom of the west to my tablets of paper, I made soft clicks of pleasure in my throat. One morning I was made vaguely aware of my neighbour, not by noise but – in the parlance of the youth of that time – by vibrations, 'vibes', 'aura' (another catchword of the day). These were not particularly friendly, though he was grinning. He was imitating my collecting sound. I blinked and got on with what I was reading. When I came to myself an hour later he'd gone. They didn't stay long, those Canadian boys and girls. Another day I was copying a saying of Blaise Pascal (and allow me to translate for you). I believe it was, *'If the whole universe were to fall on a man and crush him, he would be killed but not destroyed, for he would be conscious of his end but the universe would not.'*

I had run out of paper but had written on a scrap the girl beside me had left – a petty meanness of the third world from which I was not immune. I turned to continue with another Pascal *pensée* on the other side, and read, *'Hi, I'm Mike. How about coffee?'*

Mr Burnett, a Balliol man, encouraged me in my strange diligence. Like myself he was something of a fish out of water. He reserved a certain aristocratic disdain for the New World. His favourite film was the one where Chaplin comes as a European king to Madison Avenue. Nevertheless, Mr Burnett was quite capable of reconciling this fastidiousness with continuing to accept his large emolument and residing in Toronto. He was flattered by my enthusiasm and the way I copy-catted his vocabulary and mannerisms. In turn I was glad for guidance with my reading. I needed a map.

I remained four years without returning home; that would have been inconceivable, not just on grounds of cost. I made a few friends. Real ones, I mean, not Pascal. I didn't allow myself to become like some of the overseas students. For instance, there was an Ethiopian who spent twenty-two hours of the day in his room with the curtains permanently drawn. There was gossip of witchcraft. When he left for the cafeteria he'd walk close to a wall with his eyes on the ground. His manner was sullen. He would eat with ferocious concentration before returning to the room with its closed curtains. I wasn't a weirdo. I belonged, briefly, to the China Society and to 'North and South', one of the multifarious clubs for those who took an interest in the 'emerging' nations. Unfortunately, I was the wrong kind of Chinese. At that time the Mao badge, the blue tunic, that red plastic book, were all the rage. There was a group, of young Canadians, who aped all that, dressed the part and, for all I knew, ate rice out of enamel dishes. It was too absurd. I expect they are investment bankers now; no, in advertising. It was style they were interested in, after all. The third worlders' club wasn't much better. It was heavily frequented by, of all people, Jamaicans. These boisterous fellows aimed to have sex with the earnest Canadian girls who attended. It has to be said they enjoyed a high rate of success. The society received some kind of government grant and its members would have long discussions as to whether or not they were abetting an instrument of Canadian government foreign policy. It was pretty clear they were, but it didn't stop them attending.

There was a friendly girl who took me up. We'd drink instant coffee and listen to Joan Baez in her room. Once she shared a marijuana cigarette with me, a joint. Wincing as I drank the harsh coffee, I told Annie Laval about the prize arabica beans of Danu.

'I'll get in some Jamaican Blue Mountain for you, Adolph.' For a moment I thought it was a brand of dope. She giggled. 'Wouldn't it be neat if they could grow grass in Danu, too?'

'Of course they could, Annie. It would grow like crazy. Drugs are the best third world cash crop. Everyone knows that.'

She liked me, I think, for not being solemn, like the other overseas students, if we forget about the Jamaicans, though she professed to be shocked by my twenty-year-old's 'cynicism'. Once, we kissed but some of her thin brown hair got into my mouth. I wasn't that interested and I think she was being kind. Afterwards I went to the men's room at the railway station and had a shorter but more satisfactory encounter with a Turkish cab-driver. Do I startle you? Annie Laval wasn't shocked. I told her, you see. She was a girl who strove to be understanding.

'All good things have to end, Adolph,' she'd say as she finished the brilliant cherry on her drug-store sundae and, sure enough, my student years drew to a close. By that time I was ready and equipped for a career in the big, bright world I've talked about. I'd tried not to think too hard about what lay at the end of it all and in this respect I was as cossetted from the real world as any of the Canadian students. My Vancouver Cousin wasn't very helpful. In this, he was not disowning any family tie but rather reaffirming it, beyond any personal liking he felt for me: my duty was to return home. To become a Canadian, to get that coveted blue passport, isn't too difficult if you are wealthy, but as with all these things there exist procedures more or less irksome. For me, the possibilities were not open. Leaving behind my Hair and Che Guevara posters – no one is immune from the times – I packed my Bantams and Penguins. Right up to the moment I buckled my seat-belt in the jet, I didn't believe I was leaving the big world. A sense of being in a dream settled over me, my way of evading the struggle, minimising the disappointment, much as it would three years later when the *malais* invaded Danu. The reality of it, return to what I could only see as barbarism, the small, broken-down settlement at the back of beyond, only came home to me as I got on to the small prop plane that took me from Darwin to Danu. Then I felt numbed. I felt lost. It was not the home-sickness I'd felt in LA four years before, when I'd been bewildered and intimidated by uncertainty, the challenge of finding a niche, making an identity for myself in a vast, strange, and complex society. This was the sickness, the vertigo, and familiar nausea of knowing to a certainty that there was *no* place for me in the simple community to which I returned and that the man I aspired to be did not exist there. Could not. As the small aircraft buzzed over the ridiculous sea, turquoise over sand, purple where it was deep, scarred with the dark carbuncles of the reefs and the passing blotches of the clouds, I leaned my head for relief against the vibrating plastic of the window. The covers of *Esquire* and *MacLean's* mocked me. I stuffed them into the webbing of the seat in front. The plane was full of Australians – a few hippy tourists, geologists, and a couple of engineers – as well as some of the colony's administrators, European, but distinctive by their black hair and swarthy or olive complexions. I'd tried talking to the Australians but their manner had dismayed me. To them I was clearly not a citizen of the greater world. As we circled the mountains to line up on our approach to the airstrip – not the one near the capital

35

which the *malais* were to bomb, but at Bacalhau where Raoul Garcia was to give the great performance he'd always craved – my morale dropped with the altitude. I hoped we'd crash. I was last off the plane but the hippies were still being grilled by officials as I got into the stand-up truck for Danu. A policeman, who had nothing to do with it, leaned over their papers as well, hand on his pistol butt. Even then I thought this sergeant had a particularly nasty face and manner. I was mean-spirited enough to enjoy the predicament of the long-haired Aussies after they'd snubbed me. And so I returned in a welter of discreditable sensations: of destroyed hopes, of self-pity, and a vicious glee in the misfortunes of others. They say that as the planes taxied off forfeited airfields in Vietnam, the abandoned ARVN troops began to shoot at their luckier comrades and to try to lob grenades on to the wings. Well, I'd become one of life's grenade-throwers.

But not quite.

The island to which I'd rebounded wasn't even a whole island. We were confined to the eastern half. The malais owned the western portion. There existed no single, prominent physical feature to mark the ragged boundary – no Rio Grande – and the maze of jungle paths and mountain-tracks which wound with sublime unconcern from one side of the border to the other and back again made a mockery of the customs-post with its counter-weighted barrier. This accident was one of those quaint inheritances of empire: sweating teams of rival, compass – and theodolite-armed white men trying to post-rationalise the impromptu annexations of junior officers and the bargains struck around the mahogany conference tables of Europe. The reality bore no relation to the map. The market-town where the western, malai-governed population sold their produce lay in our territory and there was a regular exodus and return on Sundays. And, if you can credit it, we possessed an enclave in the heart of the malai half, with its own portion of coast for access, a kind of beleaguered, tropical Berlin.

The *malais* and ourselves had been parts of different empires. They were not Malayans, by the way, governed by the British in the old days and become independent as Malaysians. Although there were similarities in language and culture, their old Dictator had fought a war against these Malayan cousins. *Malai* was a Danuese word, meaning stranger or foreigner; but, happily, it also sounded like Malay. Our *malais,* our scourge, had been colonised by a crew of flaxen-headed burghers and herring fishermen from the North and ourselves by a gang of swarthy wine-growers and olive producers from the very south of Europe.

After them we'd had our own Asian imperialists in 1942, in the shape of the Japanese, who'd shown us that the white regime wasn't so brutally oppressive as we'd thought.

Not much had happened after the Liberation in 1945. The Home Country had concentrated on preserving its African empire. It was a poor nation, with a glorious past, and the budget hadn't left much for Danu. A frigate showed the flag once a year. Otherwise, the roads and bridges rotted in the sun and rains. For the conscripts and administrators it was a hardship posting – two years of going out of their minds with boredom and heat. They could have had rope-burn on their palms from all the jerking-off they did. Many would have preferred being shot at in Africa. We did have a few independence-minded hotheads of our own, mostly among the better educated *mestizos,* but the secret police treated them with kid-gloves. No electric shocks in basements or any of that kind of stuff. A year's exile in Africa was the maximum penalty, where of course they'd be infected with the very latest in extreme revolutionary ideologies, bringing home a whole trunkful of Fanon, Mao, and Fidel past the customs on their return.

But in the end Independence wasn't won. That was the problem. It was given to them on a plate. And they fought over it – to borrow Raoul Garcia's picturesque expression – like hungry dogs.

THREE

FOR A WHILE I SULKED. It was nothing more than that. Melodrama was what I craved. If my life was to be thrown away, then I'd waste all of it. I didn't want to save a scrap. I'd forfeit all: an early Christian attitude, but it didn't last. I tired of getting up at midday and ignoring people on the street. There was a cafe on the main square of Henry the Navigator where the iron tables spilled out on to the Praça, and this was where the youth met in the cool of the evening. My steps took me there. After a few solitary evenings I recognised at the big table where there had been energetic and frequently heated discussion the face of a fellow alumnus from the liceu in Macao. When he waved me over, after he'd made an O-shape of surprise, I found myself glad to cross. They weren't unfriendly, but I'd forgotten about the half-mocking familiarity which characterised exchanges between the island's youthful elite. There could be a barb in the most innocent statements. In this there existed a trace of fidalgo-ism, something of the crackling southern Chinese wit, and maybe a pinch of the peppery native temperament. So, after the mono-dimensional geniality of the North American continent – the most hidebound people in the world behind the bland and regimented casualness of their manners, formality expressed through informality – my reception was astringent. It did me good, took me down a peg, as Mr Burnett would have said.

'So this is the *Yanqui* who reads *Time* magazine by himself,' said a very thin Chinese girl.

'And drinks cappuccino instead of having it black in a glass like everyone else,' from a short, very dark young native woman with a shock of hair in a beret.

'That's because he's got used to milk shakes,' said a small *mestizo* in glasses. 'I am Raoul. Let me get you another cup of froth, my friend.'

Although the reception took the form of a baiting, it was a welcome nonetheless. Because of my surprise, I was not as quick myself as I would have liked. And, again, I needed some surprising.

They all became my friends.

The man who had drawn out a chair for me had not taken part in these sallies. He was older than the others, in his late thirties, quiet, but with an intelligent and humorous face in which kindliness could also be read. He, too, had the frizzy hair and beard of the *mestizo*. This was Martinho Oliveira, an ex-seminarian, as was Raoul, the younger man in the glasses. Raoul was one of those who'd never had any intention of entering the priesthood. Like so many others, he'd used the seminary on the hill as an education, Danu's equivalent of a good high school. But Martinho Oliveira had really thought he was going to be a priest; only at the very last moment had he decided not to proceed with the vocation for which I, with many others, believed he was ideally fitted. There remained something of the clerical dignitary about him but he lacked the haughtiness of the Roman Catholic priest. They all have it. When the hand is extended, I make a point of shaking, never kissing, it. With Martinho you wanted to kiss the stubby fingers, his ugly, almost Papuan face radiated so much benevolence and fun. Raoul Garcia, a small, slight person, was at the other extreme. When his steel-rimmed spectacles flashed, the sharp, dark face of an Iberian grandee assumed the severity of the Inquisitor. He fancied himself as something of a poet. He was a clever man – his father had been a Communist journalist exiled to Danu in the 1930's by the Fascists – but honesty compels me to say that he was an atrocious versifier. I am sorry, Raoul. Before a meeting of our Literary Society some months later, I had decided who he reminded me of (apart from Torquemada) and I informed him. He then frowned. 'A character from Thomas Mann?' I wondered if I'd offended him before his habitual severity of expression was cracked by the grin which exposed the white teeth in the goatee. 'Do you mean the beautiful young boy in the sailor-suit? I suppose I should be flattered, Adolph, though I didn't know you were interested in me in that way.'

It was my turn to laugh. 'I am sorry to say I meant the Jewish Jesuit in *The Magic Mountain*. The one who shoots himself.' Unfortunately Raoul was not acquainted with the work and I don't believe he had actually read *Death in Venice* either, but had taken in the movie in Lisbon.

He'd studied at the university with Rosa Soares, the young native woman in the beret. If you'd deduced left-wing sympathies from this item of Guevarist headgear, you'd have been on target. Rosa had been christened Maria but had, of course, found this insupportable. She was stocky, pugnacious, and obstinate. It is not redundant for me to mention this last in connection with pugnacity, for while the native tribes were fiery, as the colonialists had reason to know from the constant uprisings of the early century, they lacked perseverance. They weren't faint-hearted; they just lost concentration. Rosa was descended from a tribe of reformed headhunters from the central mountains of Danu and, though she was a pure-blooded native, I'll persist in saying she possessed a steadiness not normally associated with the tribal character. She was, however, a great chewer of betel, which, even at her years, had blackened her teeth and rendered her gums a startling colour. I never liked to ask how she'd made provision for her habit while in Europe but no doubt she'd taken her little betel basket with her. I very soon realised she wasn't interested in men, which made for a bond between us: I who was interested in them.

The skinny girl with Rosa, and it is not an adequate description of a formidable person, although that was all I immediately saw, was Dr Maria Nolasco da Silva. Utterly Chinese in appearance, with an extremely dark skin and the typical cheekbones and eyes, as well as the purple, bee-stung lips of many attractive Chinese women (which are less frequently remarked physiognomic traits) she flaunted this proud name which appeared at odds with her evident ancestry. Again, it was one of those quirks of empire. Macao was full of people like her. Liberal intermarriage had been one of the instruments of colonisation – it had made our empire unique – but in the end like reverted to marrying like and the European infusion was quickly diluted to the point of invisibility. She'd qualified as a physician in the Home Country, in paediatrics, and now worked in the Danu hospital, mostly excising conscript servicemen's ingrown toenails. It was her great ambition to get the funds to open her own children's hospital. She operated a voluntary travelling clinic to the outlying districts on Sundays. There was nothing in the least maternal about this intense, breast-less, and sarcastic young woman. Her politics were the least conspicuously held of the group but, of them all, her life, I should have said, was the most faithful expression of those ideals. Not that the others were hypocrites. But I've noticed that behaviour gets in the way of beliefs, if I can leave it as vague as that.

On that first evening we fell to chatting about this and that in our circular way. The agenda was a mixture of high-flown, generalised discussion about the Home Country, Africa, and world affairs and, taken up with equal seriousness, intensely trivial, salacious gossip about friends and local personalities. The same weight was attached to both topics. They were all intelligent, well-informed people – far better acquainted with what was happening around the globe than, say, their equivalents in Denver, Colorado – and they didn't lack a sense of proportion either. They'd have laughed in my face if I'd accused them of parochialism. 'No, no, you do these young people an injustice,' Martinho Oliveira would have remonstrated in pseudo-clerical tones (typically assuming that he, Martinho, wasn't subsumed in the criticism). And Rosa Soares would just have blown a raspberry with that startling tongue of hers. Raoul's spectacles would have flashed and Dr Maria might have given me a smile full of friendly malice. But the give-away was the very intelligence with which they dissected each other and deduced, often with amazing accuracy from the smallest clues, who-was-sleeping-with-whom. The vehemence and rigour of the

41

analysis was the same whether they were speculating about that intensely absorbing, endlessly recurring subject, or analysing the social composition of the liberation fronts in Angola or Mozambique. Blowing the spume off my coffee as the ancient motor-bike exhausts battered the overheated air in the square, I felt much bigger than the others. I looked down on their petty, circumscribed horizons with amused scorn. I've read that look – about me – on other people's faces before and since. And, of course, inevitably, naturally, within a month I was gossiping away with the rest of them on subjects which had become of fascinating moment to me, too.

It was the two girls who were to become my particular friends, although I reserved the greatest esteem for Martinho. It's a bit of a trial after a while, excessive respect, though, and it's not what we look for in our friends, is it? Easier, even, to despise them a little. Besides, Oliveira was quite a bit older. The best part of it was that there was nothing sexual in my friendship with Rosa and Maria. With men there was always the prospect of that, or they felt a slight unease in my company, especially when alone. What was I going to do? Rape them?

I believe there to be something inherently exploitative in any carnal relationship, where gratification is sought in another's body. Perhaps that's the vestigial influence of the Church upon me, but I think it's true. There is no special difficulty in being a homosexual Catholic priest. The vow of celibacy encompasses that, too. I was as good as a priest to the girls and they were more relaxed in my company than they would have been with a padre. Rosa the militant atheist! We were not in thrall to each other, that's what I'd say.

I mentioned this to Raoul, when I had drunk too much. He said: 'That's how normal men feel about each other.' I was tart. I said waspishly, like any offended queen: 'A poet would normally choose his words better.' There was always the shadow of that between us. And when I was sober, I was still angry.

With the two young women things were clear, our friendship was limpid. Even with Mrs Goreng later things were not awkward. At this time Rosa, in common with the other over-educated colonials (to which category I relegate myself), was 'under-employed'. That was a good expression. There were plenty who had no employment at all but they didn't make it to this category: villagers in the inaccessible mountain hamlets of the centre, those who had to sleep outside at night in the town, the cripples and the blind. Under-employed is a word of UN bureaucrat-economists, themselves grossly under-employed. I've often thought that the Home Government could have made things easier for itself by 1. Not educating anyone 2. Only training engineers, doctors, chemists, agronomists, and architects. Maybe not the last two – they are also taught, in a suspect way, to think of wider things. To bring back people like Rosa as sociologists was asking for a lot of trouble. They were left kicking their heels with nothing for them to do but talk. And talk and talk they did. And talk's dangerous. The *malais* knew that; under them there was no discussion. And if our European rulers thought talk was a safety-valve, they were wrong. The talkers encouraged each other on beyond what they'd individually have dared.

But that's a little way in the future.

Rosa began by running a crèche! This was in a place where married women didn't work, where – if they did – they had servants, or a mother in the same house, where the social conditions of Toronto, or London, or even Lisbon did not yet exist – those agglomerations of unattached individuals in their separate cells of the honeycomb.

'Rosa,' I said, 'this is an absurdity.'

We knew each other well enough by then for her to realise that I jibed her for being a Comrade, not as what she was. She punched me in the ribs, not so playfully. I was then treated to a lecture on 'combined and uneven development in the backward societies'. She was a Trotskyist, of a kind. Trotsky, Bronstein, Bernstein, the Russian Jew, on the lips of a headhunter's granddaughter! She might have been walking

43

proof of her own theory. She ran the crèche to bring the women together. That was all, she said.

It was a crèche with a difference, I thought: the mothers were present with their children; only the minder was often absent. 'Union is the point, Hitler,' she said. (She had this unamiable habit of referring to me in this way, or, worse, as *mein Führer*, despite the fact that I'd learned in Canada to pronounce my given name with the long 'a' of A-1 as opposed to the short 'a' of apple: thus Ay-dolph and not Ah-dolph. But never mind.)

'These women have to be concentrated together,' Rosa went on, warming to her subject like any ideologue and starting to sound as if she was reading from a book (probably the tattered Lenin on *Imperialism as the highest stage of capitalism* which she kept by her hard wooden-bed with its grass mat). I was treated to further discourse on how in 1917 the 'backward' Petrograd workers were actually concentrated into larger-scale units of production than those of 'advanced' Western Europe. 'Just for these women of Danu to be together in a group is a revolutionary act of solidarity,' Rosa concluded triumphantly. 'Just for them to talk will give them a political consciousness.'

'They are certainly talking,' I agreed.

It was easy to mock, and, indeed, I do not believe I have succeeded in expunging a certain unwanted superiority of tone from my account of that rainy season afternoon more than a decade ago. Behind the phrases, the formulae, the inappropriate analogies between small and large, there was the grain of truth in what she was saying. Knowing Rosa as I did, I don't doubt that she'd have turned up her flattened nose at such a task anywhere else. She needed something to do in Danu, to dissipate her enormous energy against. The revolutionaries of the history books were lucky enough to have walked on to a bigger stage, but Rosa could have played a part on it. And if Krupskaya, Kollontai, Luxemburg had been women of our society, of Danu, what would they have done? They'd have begun with a crèche, of course.

44

There was no ambiguity or embarrassment about Dr Maria's work. It was necessary and no one else would or could have done it. I mean the voluntary work she undertook. She'd go up into the hills at the weekends with a nurse and a chest of bandages and medicines. Rosa Soares drove the jeep, which the Commissioner of Customs lent to Dr Maria. Maria herself, as one might expect, was caustic about her own part and dismissive of any results. 'It's a waste of time, all of it,' she'd snap as Rosa crunched through the gears on the steep road out of town. I had taken to riding with them, at Maria's invitation. She was quite egalitarian, that woman doctor. She was dedicated; she was efficient. But she never pulled rank on us. We were treated as equals in the endeavour, which patently we were not. On the other hand, subordinates would not have been quite so subject to the lash of that sarcastic tongue.

The road climbed six hundred metres in five kilometres. That was just the beginning of the adventure. It levelled out for a spell after that. You turned left and the town was spread out below you, looking strangely neat. That's one of the things about backward places, places that have been willed into existence on the fringes of where they should not be. There's been no natural growth, steady development from the inside, buildings from different periods co-existing with each other. These places have been made overnight, from the outside, it seems, pre-fabs erected along arbitrarily straight routes. The thoroughfares weren't there before, people had no business which would bring them there. The highway was created just by making houses face each other. I've seen it since, in Brazil, in a light manufacturing township in the middle of the jungle. Danu had a past, of course. I've told you about it. Some older buildings survived. Close-up, living in Danu, they impressed you disproportionately with their solidity and significance. But at a distance, with a downward perspective, you saw the place for what it was.

It depressed me, always. On my companions it had the opposite effect. At this point, Maria and Rosa became gay, started to chat and, in the end, to sing. How they could sing, those Danuese women! Rosa had the voice of her people, sweet, lilting, but strong, saved from perfection by being just a little nasal. Two of them together could sound like a choir of angels, reedy angels. I'd pay them the compliment. 'There are no angels, *mein Führer*,' Rosa would retort. Sometimes she'd take her hands off the steering-wheel to clap in time and then sway her whole body to the song. On Danu's roads, and on such mountainous terrain, it was incautious, to say the least, as the jeep's wheels would swerve out of the ruts and we'd head for the precipice with a crazy lurch, the valley already seeming to be rushing up to meet us, until Rosa swung the wheel again and, undeterred, continued with her honeyed and wild refrain. Needless to say, there were no fences at the sides of the sheerest and most awful drops. Thus Rosa's ancestors must have returned from their raids, chanting songs of war, with their bundles of heads knocking, a living captive or two trussed and carried swinging on a pole, their eyes rolling – like mine – as the inverted landscape of eucalyptus gums, gorges, thorns, water-falls, the mist-wrapped peaks and rocks, bounced dizzily past: all upside down. By travelling a few miles you'd get whole new landscapes: the thin coastal belt with its mangroves and palms, the varieties of bushes changing as you climbed, extensive plateaux of savannah, with grass as high as a man and gum-trees everywhere, much like the Australian outback. Then the real mountains, heavily rain-forested on the lower slopes, becoming quite bare as you went above two thousand metres.

It would not be often we got that far. Danu distances were deceptive. Ten miles could take longer than five hundred on a North American freeway, and leave you more exhausted. In one sense it was a small island; in another it was very large. We'd stop at the same village, Boa Vista, on the way out on Friday evening; continue early on the Saturday morning until lunch-time when, depending on the date, we'd fan out to one of four villages in rotation. The villages weren't that far apart, but people going to them to see Dr Maria could be from settlements that were days apart. She'd thought it out well.

The District Administrator at Boa Vista had dinner for us at his Residence: fried pigeon he'd shot himself, sweet-potato, spinach, tomatoes, and home-fermented wine. 'Vinho Verde', that fat and jolly man called his brew. I slept in a hammock, under a mosquito-net, on the verandah with the stars above and the sweetness of the Administrator's pipe-tobacco and vines in my nostrils. On those nights I was better reconciled to Danu.

With the local coffee penetrating our bowels like a liquid sword, we'd start before dawn and be up out of the savannah by eleven. The children, the healthy children, would be out on the path, a quagmire or dust-bowl depending on the season, miles out from the village. Then Rosa would slow down, the kids would lope beside us for extraordinary distances, the bolder endeavouring to leap on to the sides but carefully prevented from staying by me. We'd pass the men in the fields with their six-foot digging-sticks. They barely scratched the soil with these, and the primitive ploughs pulled by the ubiquitous water-buffalo weren't that much better. No one could get them to change their habits. They were incorrigibly inept. If the season turned out clement and regular they could just get by, with a little to spare. If the rains were late or unusually long and heavy, then they went hungry. Everyone went hungry except the buffalo. Once every three years they'd slaughter one of these venerated specimens, the whole village gorging on the unaccustomed feast. The affair wasn't quite the bloody shambles it appeared – custom allotted a specific cut of the carcass to every person in the village, from chief to newest child. As far as I was concerned, it was one of the few instances of custom operating rationally. Dr Maria, though, was surprisingly respectful of custom.

The first time I accompanied her into the mountains we drove straight past the headman's house, which even I knew was a clear breach of protocol, and went on to a large, open-sided lean-to with the usual straw-roof. A fire smoked on the dirt, with a cauldron bubbling above it. A boy on crutches hopped towards us with a big grin on his face. Four or five

47

others lay on the ground. Maria greeted the boy. In his position I would not have been grinning. I relieved Maria of her heavy black case, for which she promptly thanked me. I could now see that all the people were young cripples, except for the old man stirring the cauldron. He'd stuck a ladle into this, and I should say that the thick, lumpy brown paste resembled nothing so much as boiling vomit. Under the approving eye of Dr Maria he began slapping his sludge on to the legs of his cripples. They were good patients, I'll say that. It must have scalded. Not a sound escaped the lips of even the youngest boy, though their faces said it all. I waited for Maria to do something: pour cold water on their legs, push the old sadist into the fire, anything. Instead she entered into a long discussion with the fellow and if he'd been wearing a white coat and suit instead of being in his raggedy-ass shorts and wide bare feet her manner might have been that of conferring with a senior colleague. She let him scrape the congealing goo off the cripples' legs with a banana-leaf before undertaking a close inspection. On all of them, the skin was red with heat. One boy had a grotesquely crooked leg, the others' limbs just seemed swollen up. When Maria pushed the flesh of a boy's calf it quivered horribly, like jell-o, with no will of its own. I looked to see what Rosa made of all this, but she was rolling betel with some old woman on the fender of the jeep. As I returned with Maria, I said: 'He's done some damage in his time, that old charlatan.'

There is more than a touch of the toady in me, you may have gathered by now, but I prefer to be indirect about it. Maria looked genuinely surprised. 'He has done a lot of good.'

'He is the next worst thing to a witch doctor. They are damn lucky you have come up.'

'They'd get well without me.'

'That I venture to doubt, my dear Dr Maria.'

'You're a fool, Adolph. He has got people to walk that hospitals in the Home Country would have given up on. And he's the best re-setter of bones I've ever seen.'

'Oh, yes,' I sneered, no longer sucking up to Maria, 'and the bubbling shit is better than penicillin. '

'It's part of his treatment. Heat is the best way of stimulating blood-flow, you know. Any medic would tell you that. It doesn't have to be like Dr Kildare, you know, Adolph.'

By now we'd got back to the jeep. I tossed Dr Maria's bag into the back, causing Rosa to lift an eyebrow. After 'lunch', a disgusting meal of gritty rice and root vegetables, Maria saw the children. And this was where she truly came into her own. The three principal ailments which afflicted the people were diseases of the eye, the skin, and malaria. Those living higher than 1500 metres avoided the worst of this last, the most awful scourge of the Danuese, although Maria said they all had developed some natural resistance to it. Nevertheless, some of the children's skins had to be seen to be believed: parasites, boils, scabs, fungoid growths. Believe me, scabies was the least of it. And this was where Western medicines beat the traditional poultices of the witch-doctor out of sight. 'It's just a matter of dispensing,' said Maria, dispensing. She'd call out the names on the bottles and packets to Rosa, who'd hand them out from the chest and instruct the mothers. Provided the people carried out orders to the letter, and they mostly did, the results which she secured in this area could be impressive. I had the evidence on my second visit. Eyes were trickier. The cataracts of the older people were something Maria didn't undertake. But she could alleviate irritation for the children with eye-baths and droplets. It was the fires they kept in the center of the huts, with only a hole in the thatch for the smoke. Ten minutes with the headman and you left feeling you'd been tear-gassed. That was Rosa's analogy. She'd confronted the riot-police on the streets of the metropolitan capital.

As for malaria, it was in the bones of the people – or, should I say, their blood. They'd sweat, shiver, and that would be it – until their next bout. The colonial government would send officials to the villages. They'd explain how the disease was communicated; posters would go up, showing the larvae breeding in stagnant water, even inside a broken flower-pot. But to get the villagers to drain their ancestral ponds, or to spray sweet water with kerosene was another matter entirely. Maria took only a small supply of tablets with her. She insisted religiously on our own prophylaxis. But this generosity did not extend to the natives. That was how I saw it at first. She sighed – we were bumping back down to Danu in second gear – 'It's not that, you know, it really isn't.'

Rosa scowled at me while Dr Maria continued. 'You have to think of their situation. No. 1: they wouldn't take them at all. OK, not too bad. No. 2: they lose them or they take them a few months and then get impatient and stop. Disaster. We have malaria cases on our hands and a parasite that's on the way to becoming drug-resistant. No, the solution is treatment, not prophylaxis. Even half a tablet can get one of these people over the symptoms. You have to be cruel to be kind.'

That was the trigger for Rosa. The rest of the journey was spent in an argument over ends justifying means in which she became so vehement that I feared for our safety on the road.

I was not the founder of the Literary Society of Danu; it had already been moribund when I left for 'America'. But I took it and changed it into something else. Which is the same thing. For a start I rendered its name into English. I won't say that made it instantly fashionable, but from that moment it was a different creature. I kept the old leather transactions book, with its brass lock, but the minutes soon became more contemporary reading. The papers on Shakespeare, on Machado de Assis, on local history (the sandalwood trade and the Black Portuguese of the seventeenth century), were superseded by lectures on André Malraux, George Orwell, Franz Fanon, Gandhi. The old membership, such as it had been, ceased attending, all but one retired coffee-grower from Europe and his wife. You know, I think the old fellow was deaf. He only came to life in the refreshment break. But I didn't mind. He was a useful cover and, unlike some others,

I was no bigot or paranoiac. The scuttlebutt that he was a government spy served only to fuel the self-esteem of the membership. Even Rosa could see the joke.

We met at Raoul's – he being theoretically the Hon. Sec. to my Chairman – but the price of invading his house was to submit to readings of those execrable poems at what seemed overly frequent intervals, though the minutes book shows it was less than three times a year.

'Ha-hum, ha-hum,' Martinho Oliveira would go, rising to face the company of sometimes as many as thirty people, holding his hand up in demi-priestly fashion and getting silence more rapidly than anyone else could from that gang of loquacious atheists. 'Welcome, welcome to one and all. Tonight we are to be edified by a paper on *Mao Tse-tung and...*' looking at his prompt card, '*...the Returned Students Clique* from the pen of our distinguished Chairman. But first...' and this would be the signal for tittering and suppressed groans '. . . we are additionally privileged to hear, the first to hear, the newest compositions of our host and talented author, Senhor Garcia.' Some of the comments were extremely rude and, indeed, I think someone once deliberately farted in the middle of Raoul's declamation, but Raoul never seemed to hear the hecklers. Strange for that proud little man, with more of the Iberian grandee in him than any of the others. He could be touchy about anything less than an unambiguous compliment about his verses when it was uttered in private conversation, but on taking the lectern his hide became a lot thicker. Of course, the deafness was politic; he heard every word, every titter – and, for sure, the fart – but had to behave as if nothing had happened. What were the alternatives? Tears, suicide, running amok into the audience?

On the occasion of my paper, his reading was merely mediocre – we were spared those scorching love poems (he had no lady friend, by the way; he'd written the verses just for the sake of writing them) – and the audience had been instructed to behave itself. This was to *my* disadvantage, as the Chairman's paper was not received with quite the attention and respect the Chairman had hoped: coughs, shuffling of feet, whispers, marred the reading. But one thing. At the end, whoever's paper it was, there was never silence, never the need for the chair to put a pre-contrived question to bridge an embarrassing pause. Such had been my brief experience of the Canadian university's societies. We weren't play-acting. The intellectual level was sophomoric – what was worth more was passion. The subjects meant something real to the members. All right, the Chairman was play-acting. No one else was. In the nature of it, the proceedings could become lengthier than was to my taste. Once the topic was thrown to the floor it was a free-for-all. People would stand, orate for twenty minutes without repeating themselves – one of the more demanding drills of the North American classroom, I am told. Hands would be shooting up before the speaker was finished, eyes desperately trying to lock on to mine. Believe me, it was a nice change for male eyes not to be sliding evasively away from my own! And in the end it would be my task to close the meeting. The throat-clearing of Toronto, the turn of the wrist with its watch, were not effective on the debaters of Danu. But protocol was observed. When I closed the debate, I was obeyed. And the meetings stayed terminated – no matter how feverish the debate, how loud the groans of disappointment when I raised my voice and hand, the discussions never continued informally. Rather, argument was replaced by small talk, which could go on at the tables of the Praça until the early hours. It was as if a need had been met, a boil lanced.

Of course the success of the meetings was not due (solely) to the force of my own personality, nor was it accidental. Eighteen months before my return the Governor had closed the seminary news-sheet.

This had been an organ of far broader appeal than its title might suggest. It had been edited by none other than Martinho Oliveira. Under the ecclesiastical imprimatur had reigned an amazing liberty. The most subversive opinions had been aired with apparent impunity. It began with religion. At Easter there had appeared a reproduction of a drawing done by one of the students, originally captioned something like, 'Our Lord endures his sacrifice between the two thieves.' One of Martinho's godless crew, not he himself I'm sure, altered it to: 'Jesus Christ (centre).' From blasphemy they moved on to sedition. Martinho got away initially with reports of petty maladministration or corruption, heavily oblique where the reader had to supply a good deal to go between the crooked lines of smudged type. This in an organ where Ignatius Loyola and the Council of Trent had been contemporary news under his predecessor. Lack of retaliation encouraged Martinho to publish readers' letters of complaint, at first pseudonymous and many written by himself, but later perfectly authentic. From here he got up the nerve to print real sedition. Extended critiques of imperialism, calls for revolution, loads of that purple, rhetorical stuff (which was still a good deal less violent in tone than the letters on tainted water supplies, non-collection of garbage and complaints about roistering soldiers). Oh yes, and there was also a letter about the appalling crèche situation from a 'Maria'. In a different class from the other contributions was a penetrating analysis of the coffee trade. Martinho showed the article to me with a quiet pride, which although not misplaced, had led me to suspect that he was its author. It was signed 'Nicolau'. I thought his modesty excessive, but in character (not for a moment did I imagine he was trying to conceal his true identity from fear – we didn't think like that then). 'Very good, Martinho,' I said, 'but really excellent. The Vatican lost a superb economist.'

He smiled, which made his snub Papuan face look doubly ingenuous. 'Oh no,' he said, 'the author of this article has even less of a vocation than myself. A shedder of blood even.'

'I believe you do him a serious injustice,' I said, enjoying the ironies of our little conversation all the more for employing one of Martinho's pet phrases.

Martinho smiled innocently. He was savouring not the

double irony I imagined we were sharing, but a triple. The writer of the article in question was his younger brother, Osvaldo, as I was later left to discover. That misunderstanding presaged the nature of my relationship with Osvaldo; it wasn't a good start but it was an appropriate one.

What brought the news-sheet down in the end was opposition from within. I don't think the Bishop looked at his complimentary copy, and I'd have been surprised if the Chief of Police or Governor were even aware of it. The trouble was the mixed nature of the seminarians themselves. They were the wildest collection of incompatibles. As I've said, it was Danu's only opportunity for an education that went beyond high school. Who could blame a bright boy, with no inclination for the priesthood, if he pretended to have a vocation? It wasn't unknown for ex-seminarians to enlist in the army – certainly the military valued the instruction and discipline of the Fathers. Time at the seminary was worth at least a year's service on the way to corporal and nearly all those who made it to sergeant had been aspirant priests. Some, like Arsenio Remedios, even became lieutenants in Africa. Unfortunately there were flies in this ointment of secular advancement: those youths who actually had religion for real. The minority of seminarians with priestly ambitions resented Martinho's high-handedness, his hijacking of their house journal. There were a round dozen of these zealots, who were promptly dubbed The Apostles by the news-sheet faction. Of course, Martinho didn't publish *their* angry letters. He was no democrat. Indignation rose. The ecclesiastical minority took to worshipping on the left-hand side of the Church ('The *left*, Martinho?' 'My dear Adolph, the irony was lost upon them.'), while the news-sheet faction occupied the pews to the right. ('Singing the Internationale, no doubt.' 'I am *not* an atheist.') Separate tables in the refectory, it goes without saying, and rival basket-ball teams on the quadrangle when the Apostles, mostly taller than the radicals and spurred by a far greater hatred, invariably scored the most. And, in the end, as was bound to happen with high-spirited youths, particularly when denied access to sexual release – women in most of their cases – it came to blows. In a public place, with an army-bound radical for once getting the better of the Apostle. They were brought before the Bishop. He was shown the red rag. Within twenty-four hours there were mass expulsions, a new editor, a replacement Dean of Discipline (I translate his title by the Toronto equivalent) and a new post of Censor (which is precisely what they called him). It was Martinho's lack of connection with the institution which so incensed His Grace. More than this, much more than this, his invulnerability to chastisement. There was nothing they could do to him. He'd left long ago – they could hardly throw him out of an institution to which he didn't belong. And as he wasn't actually a priest, he couldn't be exiled to a malarial parish or defrocked. Excommunicate? Listen, His Grace would have liked to have put him on the *rack*.

'Marxists on a hill,' that was how Martinho related the words of the Bishop to me. There was a glint in his eye, which indicated to me that he wasn't entirely unhappy with the description or the storm in a teacup he'd caused. After that, the Apostles themselves went too far. Starvation diets, floggings, a mock crucifixion, were only part of the penances they imposed upon themselves. The Bishop had to cool them down, and the next year's intake purposely contained as many unholy corporals as always.

FOUR

I'D BEEN LIVING OFF MY FATHER for the eighteen months of my return. The wizened little man from Hainan island had made possible Pascal and Mr Burnett. He made possible the Praça and the papers on Mao and Ho Chi Minh. He also made possible my sulks and depressions. If I'd had feeding myself to worry about I wouldn't have enjoyed the luxury of self-pity. Now, consulting my convenience to the last, he died. I went, dry-eyed, to the funeral. I found the grief of his best friend and gambling crony faintly ridiculous, excessive. As I looked at the coffin, I exulted in my own immunity from feeling. That night, brushing my teeth and seeing his bald brush, I surprised myself by my shaking shoulders and wet cheeks. But it was just the body betraying me. In my heart I felt nothing. Am I too honest to you?

It became clear to me that running the up-country businesses was beyond my capacity, even had I been able to supply the inclination. Keeping the trucks running looked the worst part of it. I sold out to my father's weeping friend: sorrow hadn't blunted his appetite for a sharp deal, I noticed. His first offer was almost insultingly low. I demanded a fortune. We met in the middle. He smiled for the first time since the funeral.

The capital I put on deposit in the Banco Ultramarino. Father would have had a fit. But that was only a temporary home for the escudos. I had plans – for the hotel, of course. There was already the Hotel Turismo in the centre of 'town'. Ill-named establishment. It was a concrete box businessmen used if they'd been bumped off an overbooked Darwin flight. Once in a blue moon, with ill-grace, the aircrew would also have to avail themselves of its hospitality. And there was the Hippy Hilton, a wall-less shelter by the harbour. Of a true hotel of tourism there was no trace.

I wanted to build a real resort-hotel. Umbrellas, swimming-pool, tennis-court, coffee-shop. Of such stuff are dreams made. Who had I thought I was when I mocked Rosa's vision of a crèche? I had no idea of the absurdity of my own ambition in the context of Danu. I was blinded by the desire to make. The futility of my existence was a daily mockery. There is that in the entrepreneur as well as the simple appetite for cash; it's not ignoble being a capitalist. Wicked, maybe, but not ignoble. This opinion I did not share with my radical friends.

There was a decaying great house, nine kilometres outside town. The owner had hoped to revive his family fortunes by harvesting copra. He'd planted palms in regular rows all over the grounds. Most still stood, some grotesquely bent in

56

the direction of the prevailing wind – sensible trees – but a few had rotted and fallen, this small number sufficing to spoil the symmetry of the arrangement.

It was raining the day I went over. I trudged along the beach, sheltered only by the red baseball cap of my Canadian college, carrying my rubber sandals by their thongs. The wetness of the sand from the falling rain seemed distinct from its wetness from the sea, grainier. With the sea on my left, the palms on my right, the crunching white highway before me, despite the lowering sky, I felt as cheerful as I had in Danu. Not in the way of quiet contentment, as on the DA's verandah at Boa Vista, when I accompanied Dr Maria on her field-trip. This gaiety was hysterical.

Hopping over a broken fence, I came to the out-buildings. These housed rusty machinery, the specific purpose of which was to remain obscure; no doubt something to do with husking nuts. The sight sobered me: corrupting iron, that was all that was left of a vision of the mind that had been perfect in its insubstantial state: the nightmare skeletons of someone else's dream. There's something about the tropics which seems to doom these schemes to perdition, to tempt men to such lush fantasies, extravagant declarations and beginnings which have this way of petering out into ... nothing. I've seen it since, too, in the Caribbean and the Americas. And there's always some mouldering monument to folly left. As the rain-drops trickled off my visor, I felt the need for a cigarette. For a moment my fantasy began to dissolve but then the sun came out and my earlier cheerfulness on the sand returned. I strode round the mansion, making notes, startling roosting birds in the big room on the second floor which would become Major Rebus's. The building looked older than it really was. I knew it as a fact that it had been built shortly after the First World War but it seemed to belong to the previous century. They'd built well, though; it wasn't yet the age of corrupted iron; it wasn't a jerry-built fantasy. The dilapidation of the main building, as opposed to that of the machinery in the outhouses, was cosmetic, more a question of blistering paint, broken panes, and dirt than anything structural. The roof was water-tight. You could cut out the rot on the ground floor. And it had sewage. God knows where the shit went to, feeding the fish just fifty metres out to sea for all I ever knew. All I cared was that it should never come back.

You wouldn't believe the price I paid for it. Even in escudos – one of those grandiloquent Latin currencies where sums run into the figures of astronomy for the price of a box of matches – it looked absurdly low. It would have got you a seedy room in Manhattan for a couple of weeks. And still nodding heads said I'd got burned, making business more difficult for the whole Chinese community!

X. Ray Xaneros didn't think I was a fool. He was never a man of a great many words – unusual in FAKOUM – but the way he puffed on his pipe was enough to reassure me as to the wisdom of my purchase. He was a little more violent with my property than I thought was fitting, tearing strips of paper off the walls, digging cracked putty out of windows with his fingernails, and chipping a perfectly good, if stained, toilet-bowl with a kick from his steel-toed boot. But that's the forthrightness of the professional, so bold and careless to the layman. No, I make excuses for him. He shouldn't have kicked the john. I think he read my face and after he bounded up the stairs was gentler with the upper floor. Or maybe it was just in better condition. We bumped back through the palms in his little open pick-up, a coconut suddenly thudding into the sand a metre from his elbow. It would certainly have killed him, had it landed on his head. 'Dead tourist,' he said between his teeth, the pipe in the side of his mouth. As I said, he wasn't the greatest conversationalist. I made a mental note to have the trees castrated. It was the word which came to mind when I looked up at the tight bundles of nuts. We stopped by the police-station to collect his brother. They were both *mestizos* with the shock of frizzy hair which no official cap could subdue. Police Sergeant Danny Xaneros was going to help X. Ray at the weekends, which was good. There'd be no nonsense with permission and regulations. The X, by the way, stood for Xavier. Nobody ever made fun of him and I reckon his father had been unaware of the modern implications of the initials. In fact, I'm sure of it.

By the standards of Danu the building work proceeded frenziedly. That is, the men worked from six till ten a.m., instead of from seven till nine, from five to six p.m. instead of not at all, and during the morning limited themselves to four betel breaks. I was there plenty, hanging in and doubtless making a nuisance of myself, but what else did I have to do? I milked the project for all the interest it had. I got a yellow hard hat from X. Ray. This was more so I could enjoy my sandwiches with a back against a coconut tree than to guard against accidents in the building. I thought the macho headgear rather became me. 'Hey, can I keep it, X. Ray?' I asked my contractor. Although taciturn he wasn't insensitive, and he picked up the earnestness of the request behind the frivolity. My voice had come out a shade camper than I'd intended. 'Senhor Ng, it is yours,' he said – he could be surprisingly courtly in his sparing way – but I could see in his eyes that he was thinking of a way to hide the item in the final invoice. The fact was none of his workmen wore them – what, *safety* consciousness in *Danu?* You have to be kidding. The hat was a symbol of authority. Only X. Ray, his foreman, and João the electrician, the men least likely to be struck on the head by falling tools or masonry, wore them.

About half-way through the restoration, I noticed a change come over the men's attitude to me. Up till then I'd been a licensed clown. I did my best to keep the labourers happy; to make myself popular I wasn't above distributing free cigarettes. But as the building came back into the twentieth century, so I became distanced from the work-force. The men didn't laugh at me any more; they kept to themselves in the betel break; they pocketed my cigarettes instead of smoking them with me. Even Xavier Ray's limited conversation dwindled into monosyllables.

It was odd. It wasn't a personal thing; of that I felt sure. Man to man, there was no animosity. And when I scrutinised my actions, I could find no cause.

And then I had it.

I had become a Chinese.

Up till then I'd had no place in the society of Danu; I was uncategorisable. There was this difference from the mental compartments you got put into back in the West, the drawer the Aussies had slotted me into on the Twin Otter from Darwin, where it was all done on appearance, on your foreign face (until they got to know – give the Aussies that): in Danu it was different – more a question of what you *did*. The sun had made me quite dark, anyway, and my perm could make me look Malay at a distance (though never *mestizo!*). Now I had found an identity, a place in the little society of Danu. It was not quite what I had desired, but there was no question that was how I was seen. I was a Chinese entrepreneur with capital. I was an exploiter. I was a provider of work. I was a parasite. I was hated. I was to be appeased. I was vulnerable. I was powerful. This was interesting.

And my left-wing friends? They respected me for my position and evident means. In Rosa and Martinho especially I detected a new consideration. I'd like to think it was because I'd proved myself a doer, not because I was the owner of property. But you never know.

The architectural effect, overall, was surprisingly pleasant. I should best describe it as one of ramshackle graciousness, quite different from the shining modern edifice of my daydreams. The bedrooms, twenty-one of them, were spartan by the standards of Conrad Hilton but they were cooled by the sea-breeze and protected by mosquito screens. We had our own electric generator. It was a small, infernally noisy Kawasaki but it never let us down. As the lights over the bay in Danu flickered, dimmed, and eventually died, so the Kawasaki would roar into life and the Hotel Oscar Tango X-Ray (my little pleasantry) would sparkle in a blaze of light, a beacon of efficiency and private enterprise in the benighted gloom of collectivism. (Power cuts were to be a lot more frequent and longer enduring under FAKOUM than they had ever been under the colonial regime.) The public rooms were quite different. The black and white marble floor came up beautifully from under the grime of years and when I had the (false) pillars painted white and gold, it looked like a little palace. Okay, a palace designed by Cecil B. De Mille. Then there were the old flowering trees and the palms, the ones whose lower trunks I had whitewashed, and Chico the monkey. Chico was an African. I bought him from a Muslim, a negro man, an emigrant from one of the old Indian Ocean colonies who lived in the squalid Islamic enclave by Danu harbour. We built Chico a little house of his own – a replica of Government House. Martinho and Rosa split their sides over that. There was no swimming-pool. Xavier Ray set a price so high that I knew at once it was beyond his capabilities – he would have been reasonable otherwise. By then I knew him well enough.

So, no pool, no tennis-court, no umbrellas but, better, the shade of the trees, the scent of the flowers. Coffee-shop, certainly; but in place of the air-conditioned soda-bar of Singapore or Manila, green coconuts and hamburgers, *alfresco*, under the jacaranda. If nothing else, I can say that I introduced the burger to Danu. They certainly hit the right spot. I flatter myself that I contributed to the easing of congestion in the Praça. Of tourists, however, no immediate sign.

As if to make up for this, I started to pick up an entourage. They weren't just employees in a Western sense. This was very much an Asian thing. I fed them, I housed them, I clothed them in my livery; they even got a little pocket-money. But, you know, it wasn't a question of callous cash nexus. This I was at pains to point out to Rosa. 'You couldn't call me a bourgeois,' I argued. 'I am a feudal despot here.' She would laugh heartily, exposing the scarlet horror of her mouth. She was quite unembarrassed by my flunkeys waiting on her hand and foot. What distinguished them from staff in the occidental sense was that their jobs were not limited by specific hours – no question of clock on at nine, clock off at five at the Hotel O. T. X-Ray, thank you very much – and that a sharp division of labour did not exist.

Cleaners would be required to bring drinks, cooks could become messengers. What united them was the need to pay court to yours truly. By chance if I saw them in town, they would be expected to carry home any purchases I might be bearing.

'Feudal, Hitler?' said Rosa after I'd been relieved of a bunch of purple bananas and some stationery. 'This is slave society you're living in.' Nevertheless, Rosa allowed my grinning boys to take her powdered milk to the crèche for her, which saved her a hot and boring walk.

It was as if I'd acquired an instant family, with yours truly – naturally – in the role of paterfamilias. From that moment I led a public life; privacy, that fetish of the West, was gone. It was actually one of the few aspects of the advanced cultures that I had never set much store by. I held my audiences out of a wicker-throne on the large, quarry-tiled verandah of the hotel. There were a few rocking-chairs for guests of honour who might drop in, stools and up-ended boxes for minions. With a snap of the fingers I could have red tea and fried sweetmeats brought, feed Chico for the pleasure of watching his skill at peeling fruit with his pink fingers. My peons were young people, apart from old Carvalho the gardener, that brittle stick whom I suspected of being part of the vegetable kingdom himself. Most were still in their late teens, both boys and girls. There were separate dormitories at the back of the main building, plank lean-tos. They seemed perfectly happy in them. A lucky one might share my bed for part of the night. From dawn to dusk there was never an hour when people were not about me. Childish laughter echoed among the trees, whether their leafy branches were transfixed with white shafts of sunlight or bathed crimson by fairy lights. It was open house on that verandah. You could see people on the coast road a mile before they arrived, raising the dust if, often as not, they were driving or cycling. (It was a journey of unmitigated tedium, straight out for three miles – though unfortunately just about conceivable on foot, which was why I got the little Yamaha). I'd step off the verandah, a monarch in rubber thongs and shorts, hand extended, to greet my chalky and perspiring visitors.

The first paying guests were actually locals, government officials who took rooms just for the weekend. They might as easily have driven the seven kilometres home to their suburb of Colonia, but chose to book rooms for the night. It was pure snobbery, but as the habit became fashionable who was I to complain? In the sense of natural facilities I have to confess that we were not blessed. The water off the beach was shallow and infested with dead coral which was exposed at low tide. The beautiful crescent beach of Areia Branca, so popular with Danuese at weekends, was another three kilometres away. In other words, on the far side of the moon in equatorial temperatures. In Danu energy was quickly dissipated. But the functionaries seemed pleased enough to walk on the sand and loll in hammocks under the trees. And after a while I won the weekday custom of authentic lodgers, genuine strays – businessmen and technicians from what I liked to call the mainland, Australia. An entire TAA aircrew of pilot, co-pilot, and two stewardesses from a Fokker Friendship once had to stay. I didn't hear them whingeing, to use their own expression, and I have to confess to eavesdropping.

All paid my audacious Chinese prices without demur. I knew they would. It was only company money. I remembered that much. Amongst the Chinese traders, it was allowed that I possessed some acumen after all. My stock rose.

FIVE

CAN I SAY, THOUGH, that I was not a 'blind' Chinaman with his eyes in the trough along with his snout? The first light airs of what was to become the wind of change had already reached Danu, and I felt them on my cheek even before people like Raoul or Rosa. Perhaps my cheeks were wetter. As I have had cause to animadvert in passing, the Governor and his police ruled with no very heavy hand, their laxness

'˙ of a mixture of financial bankruptcy, tropical
˙he weakness of opposition, and some shreds of
˙ie humanitarianism – in that order.

But change was occurring elsewhere.

The Empire had been falling apart under its own internal strains. Now this slow dissolution was accelerated by a collapse at the centre. The Dictator died. He'd been a contemporary of Hitler, Mussolini, Franco, a relic surviving in a new world, a political pterodactyl. When he went, there was a sudden vacuum in the metropolitan country. Communists, socialists, Church, conservatives, army, all joined in the scramble. There were some unlikely alliances forged. In the end – as ever – the army held the winning cards. But it was an army with a difference. They weren't neo-fascists in the Latin American mould. They were revolutionary ideologues. A caucus of majors and colonels was the driving force – their impetus swung the whole indifferent mass behind them and the generals had to follow. The Armed Forces Movement embarked on a series of radical reforms: confiscation and nationalisation at home and giving away the colonies abroad. They sent out a new governor to Danu, tasked with getting rid of himself. In his suite were what I would, in the old days, have called a group of secret policemen. They described themselves as Observers. I suppose that what they were was commissars. Never mind about their names. There were seven of them. As they were all men of short stature (perhaps why they had gone into this line of work) they were promptly dubbed the Dwarves. Two in particular stood out, Major Grumpy and Captain Happy (their leader was Colonel Dopey to us).

Within hours of their arrival it was a case of hey-ho and off to work we go for the commissars. I don't mean snatching Danuese off the street for a bit of third degree. These guys were on our side. The Armed Forces Movement had constructed a rough timetable for decolonisation. They wanted to get it over with. No specific deadline for Danu was mentioned but they had, I guess, about two years in mind for the transition period.

Differences now started to arise amongst our Danuese autonomists. Up till then they'd been united in opposition – if you could call their stance anything as strong as that. Now they were forced to redefine their positions. Some looked into their hearts and found that, after all, they didn't want to sever the umbilical cord which bound them to the Mother Country. Not entirely. Two or three others wanted to go the whole hog, turn Danu into a mini-Cuba. Later, when it suited them, they tried to deny it. But that's what they wanted, believe me. However, believe me also, they were the extreme wing of FAKOUM and untypical. Overnight, groups and parties sprang up. They smelled power, they smelled money. We Chinese were always accused of being unscrupulous bloodsuckers but we were the only ones who couldn't participate in this free-for-all. Politics were no longer abstruse, academic; it was about a division of the spoils. Not least, it was about doing down those you didn't like. In other words, nothing new.

The main parties were the Amalgamationists, the Independence Party, and the Federationists. The first, and I can't emphasise it enough, were not important for their numbers – tiny, never more than fifty or sixty – so much as for just existing, for the consequences of what manipulation by their masters over the border could result in. Media manipulation; they were a fig-leaf. Nobody took them seriously at the time – they were more despised than disliked. The IP – which was the matrix for what was later to become FAKOUM – was the major party. They were a ragbag. All kinds were in that. You had raving reds like Rosa; Christian radicals like Martinho; liberals – good old boys like the coffee-planter at the Literary Society who wanted to show (and I believe not just because to do so was expedient) that they belonged to Danu as much as everyone else. Even His Grace the Bishop of Danu, so one gathered from stray statements, looked kindly on the IP, though you couldn't actually call him a fully paid-up member.

The Federationists comprised maybe twice as many as the Amalgamationists. They wanted to stay with the Mother

Country, pure and simple. And they weren't all Fascists. Many of them were Communists, banished from Home in the 1930's, who'd stayed and married local women, had *mestizo* sons, much like Raoul's father had done. But they remained patriots – blood was stronger than doctrine. To be fair, they knew how backward we were. They feared we might stay that way. And being Commie veterans, they had no faith in the younger generation. Not a cheap gibe, I hope. They were joined in this party by their former enemies – those who hankered after the days of the dead Dictator. And they got on much better than the rival elements of the IP did with each other! After all, they were old-timers together.

One day, in the thick of this, there came a knock on the door of my hotel 'office'. It was Raoul. Straightaway I saw that he had been drinking. His eyes were bloodshot and his cheekbones pinkening. They say that Malays and other Orientals lack an enzyme in the liver to metabolise the alcohol and I, for one, believe them.

'Sit down before you fall down, Raoul,' I said, more genially than I felt. I resented the interruption. I'd been working on the accounts and they'd given me a headache. He fell heavily into the wicker. I took the up-ended glass off the top of my water-jug to pour him a copious draught. Didn't want him getting dehydrated with the alcohol and the heat; he *was* my friend, irritating though he could be. I hoped he hadn't written a political poem. But that wasn't why he had come. *Real* feelings he couldn't express by writing about them. He needed to talk to get them off his chest; he needed a listener; he needed me. His father had thrown a pan of boiling oil at him. Fortunately, it had missed, but it was the intention which had counted. Raoul was shaken. The peppery old Stalinist had taken exception to some of his son's remarks about the Mother Country and, specifically, the responsibility of the older generation for the condition to which the nation had passed.

'I didn't even mean the Communists, Adolph,' he said, his eyes, already bloodshot, brimming with tears. 'I mean they were heroes, goddamned heroes; it wasn't their fault the

Fascists won. What the hell, he's been here forty years. It's the perfect alibi.' Raoul's speech had taken on a distinctly American intonation and it was slurred with alcohol. Like many people who don't care to process emotion directly, he was playing a part: it looked like a mediocre Hollywood derivative. My heart grew cold. I didn't actually despise him, but his responses had become predictable, conventional. I suppose they weren't the less deeply felt for that – it was merely the mould he'd cast them in – but I couldn't become a participant. Without warmth I said, then: 'He'll get over it, Raoul. It's not the young who're unfair mostly but the old.' And as I uttered these words, I congratulated myself on the accuracy and originality of this reflection. I felt kinder towards Raoul, who had provoked this insight. But it went straight over his head and seemed no consolation, for he continued lugubriously: 'I don't know what's happening to us all, Adolph. Why are we at each other's throats? We're all Danuese.'

I refrained from saying that I was not, that I was a Chinese, and treated as such, that I didn't have a piece of the action. Now he actually gave a half-sob, took off his spectacles to wipe the lenses. I felt detached from him again. I wanted to get rid of him, but there would have been emotion and that was something I could do without. The accounts waited. 'Look, Raoul,' I said reasonably, 'people are what they are. If they can't agree at a debating society, do you think they can agree over real things?'

'We do debate real things,' he said with some surprise. I shrugged my shoulders. Plainly, he was beyond counselling in his state that night. One of my boys now came in and, to my irritation, offered Raoul a drink. As he accepted, I gritted my teeth. Jesus! – the boy only brought him the whole bottle. With the extra alcohol Raoul started to become seriously maudlin. 'We're not fit for self-rule,' he said, blowing his nose. 'How can they throw a bone like that to a pack of starving dogs?' I thought it one of his better metaphors and marked it down for re-use, but the rest was just a torrent of self-pity. Had it been one of our group arguments in the

Praça – it would have had to be something of no direct personal concern – the pack would have been merciless. He'd have been torn apart. After a while, I realised that the accounts were going to have to wait. I joined Raoul in the *aguardente* but left him to do the talking. We got half-way through the bottle, after which I had to let him stay in Room 18. I couldn't let him head back to town in his condition.

He thanked me by being sick on the bed.

SIX

IT WAS A SHOCK, THEN, TO MEET OSVALDO OLIVEIRA. He would have stood out anywhere. In Danu he was extraordinary. I saw him for the first time in the morning, after Raoul had gone, pale-faced and, thank God, silent at last. I performed the duty of a friend, sending him on his way with two aspirins.

It could be cool early on, with the sun rising out of the waves, dyeing the sand pink. Really very pretty. I'd gone by the water for a breath of fresh air while my peons cleaned after Raoul. I took deep breaths, inflating a puny chest. I decided I'd have to do some weight-lifting, like the boys in my magazines. From the direction of town came an ant-figure along the beach. It grew with unusual clarity and speed. Within a surprisingly short time it developed into a man, running. I say man – that might have been an unjustified assumption in the West; here, it was to bank on a certainty.

Well, it was Osvaldo. (You didn't think it would be anyone else, did you?) Stripped to the waist, he was wearing baggy khaki shorts, woollen socks, and army boots. He didn't move like a jogger. It wasn't a case of the heavy boots. You could see he was in good shape from his sinewy body, from the regularity of his breathing, but you could also see he wasn't much of a runner. I guess there must have been some element of recreation about the exercise, but it was purposeful. A man doing something to do him good and maybe getting to like the taste of the medicine, but still an act of the will. I think he must have been using me as a mark – that first morning of his return to his homeland, before things as trivial but important as how far he'd run in the mornings had crystallised in his routine – and he turned as soon as he came level. He didn't return my greeting, though he wasn't short of breath.

I saw him again soon enough that very evening at the party Martinho threw for him. There was no mistaking the energy in that wiry figure, but I felt I had an advantage over the others; had seen him at active contemplation, in his form of prayers. Ridiculous, I shall be the first to admit, but I felt there was a bond between us, however tenuous.

He did recognise me and I saw for the first of many times (not quite a thousand, as Raoul would have said, though) the natural sombreness of expression subverted by his boy's smile. And, in case you are wondering, no, I was not sexually attracted to him; although I was subject to his magnetism as much as anyone else. He didn't resemble his older brother at all. Where Martinho was inclined to stoutness, emphasised by a certain orotundity of manner of a high clerical nature, Osvaldo seemed to have consumed all that was comfortable about his own body, and then have discarded it with contempt. For a Danuese, even a *mestizo* with the infusion of the genes of Europe, he was exceptionally tall. 'I am the only FAKOUM CC member who can look the white man in the eye,' he'd say later, straight-faced. His hair had received the electric charge all *mestizos* got when they were born, but it was cropped short to look no more than ordinarily curly, and in those days he was clean-shaven. Not just without the frizzy beard – I mean razored smooth like a baby's ass twice a day. It was the eyes which were the man. They could be very calm. He had the steadiest gaze of anyone I ever saw. I never knew him to panic or lose his temper – but once. He could be in a hall full of shouting, excited Danuese, the spouters vying with each other for the mike, or at the centre of a real emergency, beside a wounded man, and be the only one who'd never lost his head. Or the eyes could burn, go black and hard, the worse for his not having lost control. In his moments of poetic excess Raoul might have compared it to the two faces of the Pacific Ocean, in storm and at rest, but I hope that I don't sound like some swoony girl. Needless to say, Osvaldo was a model of abstemiousness who drank alcohol only in extreme moderation and, rather more remarkably, was a non-smoker who also scorned the stimulation of betel. In a place where sloth, negligence, and fecklessness were a way of life (except, of course, among the cut-throat Chinamen) his meticulousness, his inner strength, and his self-discipline set him literally and figuratively head and shoulders above his contemporaries. Like so many natural or born leaders, it was his control over himself which allowed him to command others.

I think if I had to reduce Osvaldo to a single quality, one postulate from which everything else – the charisma, the flair, the courage, especially the courage – could follow, it would be this: *he had a strong, a perfect, sense of who he was.* He probably didn't even realise the source of his strength. Of course not: to be unaware was by definition part of it. To be self-confident is to take a lot for granted about oneself. He wasn't a thug, or stupid, or insensitive (though observation shows me that bullies are not always cowards, despite the cliché to the contrary: bullies can be extremely courageous). Even if you missed Osvaldo's intelligence in conversation, the article by 'Nicolau' in Martinho's seminarian's journal was enough to reveal not only an alert and incisive but also a subtle mind. His wasn't the poisoned gift of dumbfool cocksureness but the serenity that came through a lack of self-indulgence, of introspection. The mind played on the world, not himself, and the paradox was that it gave him total self-possession.

Enough – I can see Oliveira's scornful smile. But I'm wrong again: there was no scorn in the man.

He'd come back at precisely the right moment. There'd been all the confusion, all that talk. They were all sick of one another, disillusioned and distrustful. He came on centre stage at the beginning of Act Two, maybe like a Messiah for some (we had plenty of palms). In Africa they had never really trusted the Danuese – not in a colonial war. And they were right, I guess. Danuese got rear jobs, but Osvaldo had been unusual: he'd been in a lot of fighting. I asked him later, had he kept his head down, aimed to miss? After all, the Africans had been fighting for Independence, their freedom, just like the Danuese. Or, in actuality, *not* like the Danuese. And Osvaldo laughed. He didn't say anything, he just laughed. No, it wasn't in any sarcastic or superior way, just an expression of merriment. I suppose the thought of deliberately shooting to miss in some furious firefight, when the blacks were rushing in to chop off their balls, tickled his fancy. No, I didn't see Osvaldo doing that, on reflection. There was nothing half-hearted about him. If he found himself in a compromising situation he'd extricate himself as soon as possible. Until then he'd do his duty to the best of his ability. I think there is the cause and there are the men, and you have to distinguish; his first loyalty was to the members of the squad he led, not his own beliefs. Funnily enough, the blacks had no hard feelings about it. They backed Danu after they'd won their own colonial war and were unswerving and unstinting in their support at the UN after the *malai* invasion. They had several of the FAKOUM top brass, guys who'd actually fought them, over as guests during the brief period of the FAKOUM administration, and they seemed to like them more than those of us whose hands were clean of involvement. There you are.

Osvaldo had only been a non-commissioned officer, equivalent to First Sergeant. It didn't rankle with him. It wasn't that his abilities had gone unrecognised. It was precisely because they had, I should say. There were one or two Danuese officers, very junior, lieutenants or a rank even lower than that, which the Home Army had up its sleeve for them. Osvaldo's younger cousin had been one such. You didn't get the promotion for nothing, for being an ass-licker or collaborator; you had to be pretty darn good. Even these guys looked to Osvaldo for guidance; they looked up to him. He had to salute the uniform, call them sir, take orders.

Which he did with the most natural grace in the world. But outside normalcy, militarily speaking, when they were off-duty or, at the other extreme, when the shit and bullets were flying, they deferred to Osvaldo; they listened to him then. It was he who led, even if it was done at a remove. These guys had returned shortly before Osvaldo. They were waiting for him. Now in name as well as substance he became leader of the pack.

The top dog has his choice of bitch, too. What Osvaldo's sexual arrangements had been before he left for Africa I didn't know, and if anyone remembered they were not letting on. He wasn't a person you gossiped lightly about; he didn't figure in those wicked analyses of the Praça. Who knows, he might have gone to war a virgin, for he'd been a seminarian into his late teens; maybe he got his baptism in an army bordello. But shortly after his return it became known he was seeing Sonia Ferreira, an extremely handsome widow of twenty-eight with two children by her late husband, an engineer from the Home Country, who had died in a landslide two rainy seasons before. She was a good-looking girl, strong-willed and mature for her age, and well-connected – as I said, N.J. Pereira was her sister's husband. At this stage, with all the political alliances still in embryo, it didn't seem so odd to find Osvaldo's arm round her as they sat over coffee in the big square.

As the Danuese political parties began to emerge, so the Literary Society declined. With the passing of censorship, there was no further need for subterfuge or speaking in parables. Our attendances dropped, and in the end I put the brass-bound minutes away. Such was the public frenzy that even Raoul barely missed his declaiming opportunities.

I think the first Independence Party meeting I attended was also Osvaldo's inauguration into the domestic fray. I'd tagged along with Rosa to the open-air meeting. It was at the 'race-course', a small sand circuit where they bet on flea-bitten ponies and cockfights. Arsenio Remedios, lately back from Africa, still in lieutenant's uniform but soon to get promoted all the way to brigadier by FAKOUM, was haranguing the faithful through a battery-operated megaphone. It kept emitting terrible wails and whistles, and finally he discarded it. They had this habit of playing music – pop mostly, rock 'n' roll, country and western, some crazy, inappropriate stuff *over* the speaker's amplified voice. This wasn't *opponents* doing their best to drown your speech; it was your own people trying to serenade your message into the public consciousness. Well, after a while Arsenio had had enough and ripped the needle off the record. Even his parade-ground lungs couldn't compete unaided against Glen Campbell. They'd been playing 'Rhinestone Cowboy' and 'Galveston'. I was sorry. I liked the songs and you could transfer the emotion to anywhere you wanted: the redneck balladeer could have been singing in his homesick way about Toronto or Danu itself instead of Texas. I caught Rosa's eye and pouted but she ignored me, mere bourgeois flippancy on my part. She was tediously serious these days. But I think I got a glimmer, believe it or not, out of the corner of Osvaldo's eye as he turned round from where he was standing with Martinho at the front of the crowd. I think the turn, in the sudden cessation of noise, was probably a military reflex, some in-born twitch of command, but if he could recover himself and laugh it did him credit. Possibly, it was all in my imagination. But the reason for him being at the front of the crowd was concrete enough. Shortly afterwards, Arsenio made an announcement to the effect that the party was strengthened by the arrival of a new comrade. 'And, son of a bitch, those of us who were in Africa all know him for what he is, the mean son of a bitch.'

There was laughter in the crowd, in which Martinho joined. 'If he doesn't frighten all our enemies, then I'm a son of a bitch,' Arsenio continued, now without the loudhailer. This was the way they all talked to each other in that grim brotherhood when it wasn't about superstructures, internal contradictions, and objective and subjective. And as Osvaldo mounted the platform we all heard Arsenio say 'son of a bitch' again to his old comrade-in-arms, just in case any of us had missed this colourful address before, punching

Osvaldo on the arm as he did so. Osvaldo looked relaxed. There were a lot of people but it was quite informal, almost light-hearted, despite the bloodthirstiness of some of the previous speeches. There was a half-smile on his face but he grew serious as he went on. I'd have said he was the only real politician on that platform on that day, the best soldier, along with Arsenio, but the only one with a sense of a lobby. The others spoke for effect, self-aggrandisement, or just to get feelings off their chests. Osvaldo, in his very first speech, was making a play for a power base. He was making a pitch for the betel-chewing constituency, the mountain folk whose colourful feathered headgear and brilliant blankets signalled their presence among the drabber hues of the urban crowd. He was quite shameless really but contrived somehow to brown-nose with dignity. He spoke in an exaggeratedly rustic dialect, told some jokes coarse even by the standards of the enlisted men's mess, and filled his speech with metaphors of cockfighting (Danu: the pit; the parties: the bantams; the country-folk: the spurs, etc.). He also alluded to The Mountain, although he didn't use its name (it was kind of taboo), invoking everything that sacred place meant to the country people. He was skilled at playing on emotion, I'll give him that; the variety and rhythm of his speech were masterly. One moment he'd have them laughing as he spoke of them collectively under a single character, the common man's name of Mau Bere, as if to talk about Rastus, or to tell an Irish crowd about Paddy. From anyone else the knockabout routine and wisecracks at their expense could have come as an insult, but Osvaldo had them wetting themselves as they rocked in their market-day finery. The next, he'd pull them up short with The Mountain and their Ancestors, bring tears to their simple eyes. A few moments' solemnity, and then he'd have them cracking up once more. I was only surprised it wasn't punctuated with bright red spurts of betel juice, but Osvaldo had his scruples where polluting his own body was concerned, rather than other people's minds. During this performance I stole a glance at Rosa, my educated, emancipated companion. Her cheek bulged with her wad of leaf and she was guffawing with the others. She joined in the explosion of applause for Osvaldo at the end – it was actually led by the townspeople, with a lot of the older mountain-folk smacking their palms together with a blankly happy look, much like Chico the monkey, as if it was so unfamiliar an action it might have been something they'd never done before. Which for some was probably so.

And, I'll tell you, there were a few strange expressions worn on the platform even before Osvaldo jumped into the crowd rather than take the chair that was being unfolded for him.

That was how Osvaldo Oliveira found his way into the mainstream of Danuese politics. The mainstream! You just had to attend a meeting to be guaranteed a chance, at some stage, to get to your feet and spout. It was around about the level of the second year students at Toronto. There was a lot of cigarette smoke in small rooms, a lot of clapping, much self-consciousness.

The real horse-trading got done well away from this.

Osvaldo, Arsenio, and their other African comrades – the men who were to be the core of the future FAKOUM, though at this point they were still in the Independence Party, knew what mattered. They wooed the army. It wasn't difficult, not with rank and your chest glittering with medals. The garrison comprised three battalions of infantry, with an engineer company; some two thousand men. They were local recruits with the exception of the officers, some senior NCOs, and technicians. Not as totally reliable for the Governor as European troops but a lot cheaper, which was what mattered most at Home in those last days. Arsenio and Osvaldo used to stroll through the barrack-gates in their sandals, getting the recognition from the sentries they no longer had the right to receive. They held 'education sessions' in the mess hall. The Colonel did nothing to stop them. I don't think he liked it. Their proselytising was certainly prejudicial to good order, if not military discipline.

But he preferred these ex-soldiers, with their pedigree of valour, to the other local politicos: such as Teixeira or da Gama, the IP bigwigs.

'Comrades,' Osvaldo would begin his pep talks, which was nicely ambiguous: he could be referring to them both as fellow soldiers or as revolutionary zealots. He'd lay it on shamelessly, as he had the first time with the mountain-folk. Many of the troops were village boys come down from the hills. That was only logical – they needed work and it was the hill tribes who had that raiding, head-hunting tradition. Then Arsenio – it was about now that he took to wearing those reflective sunglasses all the time – would give them the spiel: they were defenders of their nation, the disciplined cadres in the sea of chaos, the crew of the ship of state, the corn in the chaff (he wasn't worried about mixing his metaphors, Arsenio). All this delivered as he stood on a table in the mess hall, hand on hip. There was no need for these histrionics – they'd already put chairs out for the African heroes, but Arsenio's picture of the ideal corresponded to fairly primitive notions of socialist realist art prevalent in the Soviet Union in the 1930's. You know the kind of jutting-jaw Lenins I mean. I got all this from Martinho, who accompanied his younger brother and Arsenio on many of their forays. His contacts from the days of the news-sheet were useful – most of the intense young seminarians he'd known had become NCOs by now. Within two months of Osvaldo's return the army was solidly with him.

It was now that FAKOUM was born, when it was safe to secede out of the IP. Whether they'd planned this from Day One we'll never know. I know what Teixeira and da Gama thought: that the FAKOUM commies had been plotting since the days of the Dictator; every move had been foreseen; every contingency anticipated. Teixeira told Martinho as much later on. Funnily enough, it was what FAKOUM would say about the CIA and the *malais*. It's the loser who believes in conspiracies, who finds a pattern and a history, who looks for an explanation outside his own weakness. I guess the winner just responds without thinking.

Arsenio, Martinho, and Osvaldo convoked an extraordinary meeting of IP members. It wasn't *just* a question of age, but their supporters were, on the whole, younger and – I think it's fair to say – more ardent. Sure, FAKOUM had the guns, the army; but that wasn't the only reason why they would prevail. They had idealism on their side as well. Many, though not all, of the remaining IP people were vested interests. You don't gather adherents around the banner of a 12 per cent profit on turnover; you don't even, consciously, motivate yourself that way. You start to talk about Motherland, Historic Ties, Blood, Honour, Tradition. That's what the IP did. But they were mainly the big estate-owners, or village chiefs who'd come to live in the town, or absentee rent-gatherers and their hangers-on.

Where did Arsenio and Osvaldo, the FAKOUM Alpha and Omega, choose to hold their inaugural meeting?

Where else?

I ask you.

After all, the Hotel Oscar Tango X-Ray was one of the few places immune to power-cuts, while the foreman of the generating-plant was an IP stalwart who wouldn't have thought twice about sabotaging the conference by tripping a few circuits. I decanted an extra litre of two-stroke into the little red Kawasaki, stuck six crates of Coca-Cola into the refrigerator, and put out spittoons for the betel-chewers.

Considering they were soldiers, Arsenio and Osvaldo managed beautifully. The key to it was directing things without appearing to do so, the façade of democracy concealing an autocratic leadership. There was a barbecue first, during which the future FAKOUM generals circulated, putting 'majority' proposals into people's heads and charred spareribs into their hands. There was no majority consensus on anything. But by the time the pair had done their rounds, it existed. 'The broad masses are what we appeal to,' I actually heard Arsenio saying, while the three ex-Lisbon students around him nodded their frizzy heads sagely. Their broad backsides! Arsenio and Osvaldo were far too acute themselves ever to think in the simplistic terms of the slogan:

they realised power was a mosaic, made up of all kinds of small groups, probably with little in common with one another. 'What this is about is to get the broad principles down,' Osvaldo said to the little group around him and, such was the force of his personality, drawing more and more people into his orbit until a hush descended over the whole gathering. Which was how official business began, without formally seeming to. Nobody wanted the fatigue of seeing to administrative details; they just wanted to *feel* useful, to be energised by the bursts coming off Osvaldo. They voted on setting up 'steering committees' (whatever the hell they were), a formulating committee to draft a party constitution, and an executive committee. It was the last which was important. The rank and file got to vote on the first two kinds of body but somehow not the third and last, which was the only one that mattered. This ended up packed with cronies, including Rosa, who got responsibility for the Organisation of Working Danuese Women. Then, almost as an oversight, they gave themselves a name. This the executive let the rank and file decide without undue interference. It took three hours and they wound up with the acronym FAKOUM, of which the first word was *Frente* (Front) and the last *Mundo* (World). It had a fine, business-like, aggressive sound – plenty of hard consonants and a nice build-up with the 'F', though to my ears it sounded a little like 'Fuck you' (which might have pleased Osvaldo, if it had occurred to him).

But the stroke of genius was this: who they elected President of FAKOUM. It was Arsenio's aunt, a betel-chewing mountain woman from the family's ancestral village near the sacred mountain.

Of course, they were 'encouraged' in this apparently eccentric selection by Arsenio and Osvaldo. 'Guided Democracy' was the title of the pre-military regime of our neighbour, which was a superb euphemism that could have applied equally as well to the internal machinations of FAKOUM. It wasn't as crude as Osvaldo looking suitably bashful and suddenly saying, 'Hmm, no, not me, but what about... Comrade Remedios's auntie?' but there was a germ of the actual in that, as to how they contrived it. To choose her as titular head was to kill several birds with one stone. It made them look less like military adventurers, frizzy-haired Napoleons – and this, for them, with their penchant for historical parallels, was a problem of self-image, identity; it would have disturbed Arsenio profoundly to have seen himself as the potential devourer of their revolution's children. His aunt was an appeal to traditional montagnard Danu, those people who might feel they had little in common with the ardent young NCOs and returned students of the town. Just by being older, she appeared a stabilising influence. She could pull in conservative and rural support and swell the FAKOUM numbers with dissidents from the IP centre who would have run a mile from weapon-toting Trots like Arsenio and Osvaldo. Martinho also had his uses as moderator. He, too, though merely an *éminence grise* (or more accurately an *éminence* in olive-green) conferred respectability and steadiness upon the party by his association. He'd never lost the clerical manner – do I harp on it? – that priestly dignity, and in his person Marx and Christ seemed reconciled. Even His Grace granted him an interview. What passed between the two old adversaries remained private, though I don't doubt Martinho kissed the ring before the 'full and frank' exchange of views. That there had been a meeting at all was what counted – as His Grace was well aware – with the result that the wily old ecclesiastical politician succeeded in hedging his bets and ensured representation with the Commies without ever formally countenancing them. He'd been on amicable terms with the Fascists (no surprise, I trust, without wishing to appear cynical), had co-operated with the Independence Democrats, and was prepared to liaise with the godless devotees of Engels. And the Church, if not the venerable Bishop in person, was still around long after all these others had gone to the dustbin of history.

Of course, the IP didn't just roll up its eyes collectively and take a back seat. You couldn't do that in a little place like ours – it's never been possible in those places, the Caribbean, the Pacific, the Indian Ocean, it's all the same. Graceful surrender, abandonment to the democratic process, are luxuries of the advanced societies where, among other things, all the faces are not known to you. We operated the politics of the grudge. Behind the sloganising, the grand statements of principle, not far behind it all, were self-interest and survival. There's a law: the more tinpot the banana republic the more flamboyant the flag: eagles grasping cobras, that kind of thing. And the more sonorous the party programme, the pettier and more virulent its sectionalism: Motherland and the death squad.

The IP couldn't back off from Osvaldo, Arsenio, Martinho and their supporters. It was all or nothing. There would be no elegant retirements in Danu. It was power or prison.

Not everyone knew this. Teixeira, da Gama and their pals at the head of the I P did. They knew, too, that Oliveira and Remedios in FAKOUM knew that they knew this. That was the 'subjective' factor in the descent into Civil War. It was what put the vicious kink into that spiral.

Now the two sides had to go through the motions: the canvassing, the rallies, the distributions of food and drink, the planning for a plebiscite where, to overcome illiteracy, people would vote by placing stones in different baskets. I do believe, firmly, that had there been an election FAKOUM would have got in by a substantial majority, not the landslide Martinho was publicly predicting with the same confidence he felt in private but, nevertheless, a firm mandate from the mountain and at least seventy-five per cent of the town. We assume, do we not, that the polling would have been both fair and free.

The IP knew this. To take my earlier reflection further: they knew that FAKOUM knew that they knew that FAKOUM knew they knew this. The rest – are you still with me? – followed quite logically and inexorably.

This, by the way, was a great time for the cafe proprietors of the Praça. If you were just a casual visitor you couldn't get a table there for love or money. The motorcyclists and scooter drivers gave up trying to beep and thread their way through the gelatinous crowds and it became a *de facto* pedestrian precinct. The roar of conversation – or to be more accurate, monologue – would have drowned the buzz of the bikes. Certain tables were reserved for the big-shot politicos, the owners at those cafes nailing their colours to the masts of the differing barques they fancied. Lacking a senate, a parliament, we turned to the Praça as our *Duma*.

At about this time Raoul changed tables. That is to say, he made a political choice and lost his friends. Before the IP – FAKOUM split he still sat with Rosa, Martinho, and the rest of them. I'd noticed he was a little quieter, but attached no importance to it. I was rather glad of it, diagnosing acute withdrawal symptoms from the lectern. But it was a silence of pent-up rage, with the poison of guilt and uncertainty in it as well; it was an angry sty on his mind's eye. It all came to the surface and burst, not on the Praça but at Rosa's crèche. That was where the Organisation of Working Danuese Women hung out, if you hadn't already guessed. Arsenio was doing the rounds with Rosa, Dr Maria, Raoul, and myself in his wake. It won't surprise you that, to use his own expression, that mean son of a bitch paid a great deal of lip-service to the idea of the emancipation of women. Osvaldo didn't – lip-service, I mean. So, we trailed after Arsenio's jungle-booted, green-uniformed figure, festooned with hand-grenades, as he tramped round the cots and made the children cry. In addition to wearing the shades, he was smoking a big cigar. As the tension rose, all the FAKOUM leaders had started to look like Fidel; you didn't see them in civilian dress anymore. Rosa had laid out tea and cookies for us in the shade of a tree. For this, Arsenio removed his harness and grenades. Talk got round to secession, and Arsenio made a few disparaging remarks about the Home Country. Raoul burst out: 'And you're so good, you FAKOUM people, you couldn't even arrange your own mothers' funerals.'

Arsenio looked at him hard and said slowly: 'We'll see how you cope with yours.'

81

An uncomfortable silence followed; it was more, it was ugly. What was really bad was that Arsenio hadn't been at all taken aback by Raoul's heartfelt interjection. Attack from this unexpected quarter should have dismayed or at least startled him. But he had taken it without surprise. The atmosphere of double-dealing and plotting was such that betrayal from one's nearest and dearest did not seem to be exceptional. Maybe Arsenio and Osvaldo worried about each other, happy team though they appeared. We'd become fouled with cynicism. And Arsenio's rapid rejoinder, which I still believe was no more than a reflex knee-jerk of parallelism, the easiest thing being to turn Raoul's remark against himself (Arsenio being a man of deeds rather than words), nevertheless sounded like a threat. It wasn't even meant to be ambiguous, but it came out like a promise of death for Raoul's family. And it struck silence in the group. If Martinho, even Osvaldo, had been there, I'm sure Raoul's future would have been quite different. I could see Rosa longed to say something; but couldn't find the words. Something sharp but funny would have released the pressure. Dr Maria wasn't sufficiently in with FAKOUM to be the person to say it meaningfully, though I saw her open her mouth and then purse those bee-stung lips. Martinho would have put Raoul down, to start with, as effectively but much more kindly. That was why he was so valued by the military hotheads. But instead we were left with Arsenio's angry retort, and a cold finger down the spine. On such small things can a destiny turn. Discussion resumed in the end; Arsenio might even have offered Raoul the plate of cookies or the sugar-bowl; but the damage had been done.

SEVEN

WE WERE NO LONGER ALONE. Vultures had been attracted to the feast. Or, to put it more flatteringly, the eyes of the world were upon us. Half an eye, in any case, for the duration of a blink. The press had come. Not the elite, I have to admit, but some interest was a lot better than no interest. They were mainly Aussies and Kiwis but there were also two Americans, a Canadian, and, for no good reason I can think of, a Pole. They were the lowest of the low: 'freelancers', though some were quite influential in that they were 'stringers', if that is the correct term, for large international agencies. A violent yank on the string in Danu could now certainly produce a faint ting in the great metropolises of the world.

FAKOUM cultivated these strays with an assiduity that amounted to brown-nosing.

On the strength of his brief career as mimeographing seditionist Martinho fancied himself to have been a newspaper editor, while Joaquim Lobato, one day to be the FAKOUM Minister for External Relations and Information and then survivor and representative at the UN, had been a journalist during a punitive exile to Africa. Arsenio Remedios also fancied himself as a media expert. Probably because he read newspapers. Well, I'll give them their due – they appreciated their McLuhan, the FAKOUM boys and girls.

The correspondents hung out at the Lusitano, 'downtown'. Nobody ever stayed with me, though they'd motor out for a drink once in a while. They wanted to stay close to where things might happen. There was always that feeling in the last days. Jean Carmichael and Bill Mabbeley were the best of the bunch and, coincidentally, and I really do believe it a coincidence, the most sympathetic to FAKOUM. There's no reason why left-wing journos should have a monopoly of talent or conscientiousness. Carmichael, a tall, horsey-faced girl with hairy legs, was the Canadian. She had a phenomenal capacity for hard liquor, without any of the competitiveness of the male imbibers at the Lusitano's blue-lit, indoor bar whom she'd frequently drink off their stools. 'Cripes, I'm fucking pissed,' was a frequently overheard remark at the Lusitano, or the more plaintive, 'Just a minute, fellers, I'm feeling a bit crook.' For each of their lagers Carmichael would put back a very large highball and only seem to become more focussed as the evenings wore on, her brown eyes glittering while her ideas grew more rather than less inflexibly 'correct' doctrinally. Arsenio was screwing her. I don't doubt he performed this task with the same address and vigour which hitherto had distinguished his military and political careers. He ministered to the interior in more than one sense. Maybe he was also under orders on this occasion, though it was where his inclination lay anyhow. There'd been competition, from amongst the Aussie hacks as well, for the only white chick in town. Chick, that scraggy hen! For her part – I never dared breathe this – there was some element of exploitation, of inverted racism, or at the very least of profit from a situation, in Carmichael's choice. She'd never have got a stud as handsome or virile as Arsenio anywhere else.

Martinho wasn't above standing his round at the Lusitano, either. All things to all men, the priestly manner wasn't much in evidence there, though the tipsy Queenslander who called him 'a po-faced cunt' received a look icy enough to have come from His Grace himself and surely sufficient to put extra beads on his glass of Foster's. No, the FAKOUM mentor was a democrat only in the sense that he'd condescend entirely on his own terms. But he bought Dicko Brown another beer, as was politic, and only flinched slightly at the 'Good on you,' and slap on the back which followed. The owner of the Lusitano had had shipped in from the Northern Territory a juke-box in pretty good working order (and I kicked myself for not having got one myself earlier). Nice, catchy tunes. 'Twenty-four Hours from Tulsa', 'Everybody's Doing the Locomotion', 'Young Girl Get Out of My Life', 'It's My Party and I'll Cry if I Want To'.

Increasingly I deserted the O. T. X-Ray for the congenial company and music of town. I'd sing along to those lachrymose tunes with the rest of the drunks. Bill Mabbeley would collar me with his great hairy bunch of fives as we perched on our stools. 'Rudolph, it is Rudolph, isn't it, mate?' I'd nod, seeing no need to be pedantic and withhold assent. 'You're wasting your time here, mate. This is the arse-hole of the world and we're half-way up it. You want to go to Sydney. Great city – they'd love you there. Wouldn't they Dicko?' And Dicko would nod too. 'We'll pull the strings.' And I'd blush at his huge, warm, conspiratorial wink. Next night: 'I'm proud to know you FAKOUM people and I hope you're proud, too. Proud of what you're doing, boy. You've rolled back a hundred years of backwardness in one hundred days.' (He was rather proud of that headline.) 'Right, Dicko? You're building a nation in front of our very eyes.' He was sincere, too. Both times. At those specific moments he was. I'd never knock Mabbeley, not now.

The IP people weren't in so close with the foreign correspondents. Most of them didn't speak English that well, though many had a perfect command of the metropolitan tongue. (It didn't sound like a Western European language at all; it was slurred, more like the tongues of Eastern Europe.) Whether language was cause or effect of the two different political stances I'm not sure: IP people turning in towards the Mother Country and FAKOUM looking out towards the English-speaking world. In the end it didn't matter, of course. But, at the time, it meant FAKOUM got favourable coverage. To read the papers you'd never think the authors of those precise, those impersonal paragraphs had spent the previous evening carousing with the officers and 'spokespersons' of their reports. (Or being fucked by them, for that matter.)

Rosa and Carmichael were instant allies. Sisters beneath the skin, so to speak. Rosa admired Arsenio and approved of the match. Carmichael, in turn, got Rosa's crèche photographed and wrote up the OWDW. ('Soares, 28, a plump, smiling dynamo of a woman, who believes female liberation from the traditional social and tribal constraints is a precondition of a general emancipation of Danuese society...') I'm not sure how much Rosa liked 'plump', but her crèche got more attention than any other institution in Danu, so she could be satisfied. Earlier sneerers, including yours truly, were thus discomfited. Rosa's journeys of mercy to the children of the mountain villages were also allotted a paragraph, although you would have searched in vain for the name of Dr Maria Nolasco da Silva. In the early evenings Rosa drank Coca-Colas with Jean at the Lusitano. She would have coped better with Carmichael's highballs than Jean could have with the headspinning packages of betel. Rosa kept her friend company until Arsenio rolled in for his Australian lager quite late in his role of off-duty revolutionary. He had been sufficiently obliging to lend his girl-friend his personal jeep, with Rosa as chauffeuse. He wasn't just being gallant, of course. I often think of the different people who rode in that fatal chariot, their separate fates and entwined destinies. It was the one which appeared at the dock just before they killed Mabbeley. Major Rebus commandeered it after that. Mrs Goreng used it. And, of course, Arsenio died in it.

But I get ahead of myself.

EIGHT

THE IP GOT THEIR BLOW IN FIRST, as they had to. At the hotel we missed any direct involvement. All we heard was the gunfire and, after that woke us up, the spectacle of a few flashes. The guests walked around in their night-clothes, whispering, God knows why.

'Ha, ha, just a few drunken soldiers,' I lied. I didn't think I sounded very convincing, but they grabbed at the reassurance, the men repeating it to the women, as if every time it was said it became more likely. We sold some brandies, I tell you.

In the morning, from the O.T. X-Ray, the town looked no different. There hadn't been fires. I was fairly certain as to what had happened – I just hoped that FAKOUM had won, that's all. I wasn't actually a party member – the bastards had an unofficial Chinese exclusion policy – but I was a little too friendly with them. You'd better choose your friends carefully in places like Danu.

In town it was a different story. There'd been fighting around the arsenal and barracks. You could read the story in

86

the pock-marks and gouges in the brickwork and concrete and the rubble and splinters in the street. The big iron-and-wood gateway to the stores compound had been blown off its hinges, and there was a burnt-out lorry only fifty metres beyond. As the vehicle was pointing in, with the wheels slewed right, I imagined it was part of the IP assault group rather than FAKOUM. Which surmise proved correct. An officer unaffiliated to any of the Danuese political parties had come running out with a 66 mm Light Anti-Tank Weapon – the green disposable tube still lay there – and done FAKOUM a favour by putting the rocket straight between the vehicle's blazing headlamps. That broke the momentum of the surprise attack ('an act of deepest turpitude,' Martinho proclaimed to the party faithful), thus preventing the IP from seizing any great quantity of weapons. Not that it would have had a great effect on the eventual outcome. The IP withdrew, fighting through the streets to the back of town, leaving a rearguard while most of the rank and file, and all the leaders, escaped into the hills. This covering party kept up a fusillade until dawn broke, about two hours later. Then they surrendered. It had been bad. I think they had reasonably expected to get away with their lives. The FAKOUM troops shot four out of hand and beat the others with rifle butts before Arsenio and Osvaldo could get there. For their own protection, as much as to neutralise them, Osvaldo put them in the town jail. He had to release the inmates, a handful of petty criminals and drunks, who then ran through the bullet-scarred streets, whooping, hardly believing their luck.

But for one of them fortune took an unfavourable turn. He'd grabbed a package of cigarettes out of a broken store-window, in all senses dying for a smoke after the deprivations of incarceration, and was promptly shot through the head as a looter by a FAKOUM corporal. This sword-wielding angel was an ex-seminarian.

That sobered me up. I was on the other side of the alley when it happened, also holding a package of (my own) cigarettes. It was a nasty moment. The corporal looked across at me. Smiling weakly, I wondered if I was going to be blown away on false premises. Funnily enough, I couldn't stop myself fumbling for a cigarette and putting it in my mouth when I should have crushed the whole pack for concealment in my palm. But he looked straight through me. I guess the immediate assumption was that Chinese didn't steal – not in the sense of petty larceny or looting, anyhow, and the patrol moved off.

In Danu town that was the extent of it. But in the mountains and the smaller towns along the coast it was much worse. We had many killings there, Danuese murdering Danuese. Really, it had nothing to do with any modern notion of ideological conflict; still less with the issue of Independence. The village chiefs had ruled their communities as they pleased before the big uprising against the colonial government in 1912 and part of the price of pacification then had been a continuing hands-off policy. The IP-FAKOUM struggle was just a mask for the expression of feuds and grudges already old when Marx was in girl's clothes. Those ancient enmities burned long, and it took blood to extinguish them. Up in the mountains there wasn't a lot of shooting. They settled their scores with traditional weapons, knives, spears, parangs. Messy, but effective and also – I guess – more satisfying. There was a kind of economy to the killing. It was only a few hundred bumped off, but probably they got more of a personal kick out of it. When the *malais* did their killings on their home island ten years before, they used the kris, and they butchered almost a million with that magic, wavy blade. In Danu we were more abstemious. Even on a percentile basis.

Where we did have shooting was at Bacalhau, the country's second town. This was where I'd landed with the Aussie hippies and geologists on my return from Toronto. A man called Leitao, one of the IP minor leaguers with ideas above his station, had coffee estates in the hills. The IP were victorious here, for a while. Leitao had been stockpiling weapons for some time. He had a good variety, too much of a variety, ranging from NATO standard calibre, to sporting arms, to antiques. With these he armed his estate workers (little more than a private army) and descended on the town of Bacalhau. They shot the place up, as if they were in a Western, rampaging through the old covered market, firing into the air and breaking into the Chinese shops. All I can say is that they didn't become drunk. Heavily outnumbered, the FAKOUM supporters in this town were taken by surprise and, unable to hightail it to the hills, barricaded themselves into a bar which in reality was nothing more than a military brothel. Didn't I say FAKOUM had a lot of army support? A siege began. Unfortunately the FAKOUM people in the bordello had no way of communicating with Danu – the telephone wires were cut (God knows who did that, one or other of the sides) – and they didn't have a radio. In fact, they were unaware there'd been a coup attempt in the capital and as to whether they'd been singled out for destruction or whether it was part of a general attack on FAKOUM throughout the territory. Employing a megaphone, and from behind cover, Leitao told them that Arsenio Remedios and the Oliveira brothers had been captured and that they should surrender at once, but all he got for his pains was a volley of shots. They had guts, the FAKOUM boys. In this building, as ill luck would have it, were two members of Martinho and Osvaldo Oliveira's immediate kin: their youngest brother (eleven children in that good Catholic family) and their father, the schoolteacher's, older brother. The boy, Eduardo, was seventeen. They'd come up to try to cut the ground beneath Leitao's feet, only to get trapped themselves.

Who else should also be in Bacalhau but Raoul. By then he'd dropped out of impolite circles in Danu. He'd done this not at once, straight after his exchange of verbal gun-fire with Arsenio, but little by little, showing his blade at a few meetings, drinking with his friends on the Praça, but at greater intervals. Every day became every other day, then twice a week, then once in a week, a fortnight passing before they saw him again, and finally his departure went unremarked. Why it was like this – though in retrospect it seems the natural way – I'm not quite sure. What passed through the little man's head? Was it sorrow at losing friends, was he trying to live on dying memory, to spin out the thread that bound him to his past – a fruitless attempt to postpone the moment of final severance. Or was it just sensible to do it like this, a lot less dangerous?

I'm not just being whimsical. 'You have a cold heart, Adolph,' Rosa said to me once, meaning I didn't seem to possess normal human feelings, warmth. But it's not that. It's bafflement at the mystery of others. Are they much better than me? Or much worse? When you're weak, when you're looking for quarter or understanding then, somehow, it's easier to hope that others are more magnanimous than you.

As to Raoul I'm in the dark. I don't know whether it was love of his friends or of his own skin which led him to plan his escape in the way he did.

After a while the FAKOUM people began to run short of ammo. They'd blazed away promiscuously, more to keep their spirits up than anything else. That's what came of the advantageous military connection which had accustomed them to ready supplies. Leitao's people were more sparing. As the FAKOUM fire slackened, he sent up an incendiary party with bundles of dry cane. Two or three got hit, but the remainder were able to set the building blazing. The FAKOUM people stood it a while; the odd shot would ring out from the inferno. Raoul could see people running around inside, roaring, with their hair and clothes on fire. Finally, a bunch of them dashed out, shooting aimlessly, to be cut down by a burst from the pride and joy of the IP armoury, a Japanese light machine-gun of Pacific War vintage. Ones and twos spilled out for a little longer, all cut down by the line of guns outside. They were probably enjoying the turkey-shoot but you could say it had its humanitarian aspect, putting the shrivelling creatures out of their agony. At last there was just the rush of the flames and the crackle of wood.

They'd sorted out the bodies and were on the point of leaving when the three who actually were soldiers, from the non-FAKOUM minority in the army, who'd gone to clear the back of the building, shouted exultantly.

They'd found seventeen-year-old Eduardo Oliveira. Under cover of smoke the kid had climbed out of a back window and hidden himself in a drainage ditch. He was, said Raoul, dirty and very frightened, but otherwise unhurt. They dragged him along the ground by his collar, booting him once or twice but not inflicting any serious harm and finally flung him in the back of Leitao's car. Now comes the bad piece.

Leitao knew Raoul's past, of course, who his friends had been. At ten o'clock that night, after a celebratory dinner at which they all had too much to drink, Leitao arranged for the company to be taken to the bean warehouse where they were holding young Oliveira. This was a rickety, thatched construction in the middle of the estate. Just as they were finishing their Luzon cigars, a note came for Leitao. As he read it, his face became grave. With his heavy silver signet ring, he rang for silence on a brandy balloon. He told them a black act, a cowardly atrocity had been committed, something which spat in the face of IP restraint and magnanimity in victory. He handed the note to Raoul. It said his father, the old Stalinist, Joaquim Garcia, had been shot – executed in cold blood by FAKOUM the day previous. With his low threshold of tolerance for alcohol Raoul was not in the best state to receive such news. He claimed the shock didn't sober him, but I imagine his eyes went even redder. Of course they gathered round him, gave him sympathy and support. That made his eyes wet. He sat next to Leitao on the drive out to the warehouse. Leitao made sure of that. The seat of honour, the Siege Perilous. They flung open the doors of the warehouse, parking the vehicles in a semi-circle and leaving the headlamps on, as if they were floodlights and the interior a stage or set. Leitao walked with his arm round Raoul's thin shoulders. Eduardo Oliveira lay with his back against some sacks of coffee, his hands and feet tied. He hadn't been hurt, Raoul said. There wasn't a mark on him.

'This bastard,' Leitao said. He kicked the sole of the boy's boot, but no more than that. 'It was this imp's brother,' Leitao said to Raoul. Raoul looked at the boy. In his face there was nothing of Osvaldo or Martinho, but then those two didn't resemble each other either. He thought Osvaldo would have looked defiant, Martinho – he did hope – would have possessed some serenity, but this kid looked plain terrified.

'You had some nice friends,' Leitao said, and in this Raoul discerned a hint, the merest, of a threat, gone as soon as it was uttered. It wasn't as fierce as Arsenio's retort, but where I believe Arsenio had meant nothing at all, Leitao meant to convey everything. At the very least, Raoul was being invited to prove himself before his new friends.

'I think,' said Leitao gently, 'that your father was made to suffer. But this bastard will get a clean death.' Raoul looked at Leitao quickly, who closed his eyes momentarily and nodded, as if he knew details but refused, absolutely, ever to divulge them. For the first time, Raoul said, the shock wore off and he felt angry. Someone, he never saw who, passed a revolver into his hands. Not a semi-automatic pistol, a wheel gun. Leitao then took it from him, cocked the hammer and gave it back. He stepped away, as did the others, leaving Raoul in front of an audience. All eyes were on him. He had their attention, totally. It must have been a moment of purest intoxication for him. There was no need for words. He stepped up to young Oliveira. The boy had closed his eyes. His lips were moving. Just as he had touched his breast with his hand in the final movement of that arcane gesture of extremity, Raoul shot him in the temple.

And they applauded.

Raoul said he saw sparks shoot out of the rusty chamber of the antique six-shooter. Eduardo fell back and a little sideways. There was mess, but no need for a second shot. By luck, rather than judgement, it was clean in that sense. Still clapping, Leitao came up quickly and repossessed the piece. Knowing Raoul better, I'd say with his sense of dramatic effect he was more likely to turn it on himself than upon anyone there. They drove back, Raoul the centre of attention. He got so shitface drunk he couldn't remember the rest.

Well, the IP's little success didn't endure. Two FAKOUM regular companies came up and knocked three kinds of shit out of their ears. It was professionals against amateurs. FAKOUM had recoil-less rifles and some 81mm mortars, as well as small-arms. Osvaldo and Arsenio were away commanding separate battalions. Arsenio had worked out a manoeuvre to flush and trap the bulk of the IP forces under their No.1 man, Teixeira, who'd withdrawn from town after their failed coup attempt. But the seminarian NCOs sent to Bacalhau knew their trade. They pinned the IP down under heavy calibre machine gun fire from the flank, then proceeded to cream them with the mortars. After a while a white flag went up. The FAKOUM boys lobbed over a few more bombs, then ceased fire, under control of their leaders. Many IP were killed and wounded but the surrender was accepted in an orderly way here. Raoul stressed that to me. Leitao and a couple of others got away in a four-wheel drive vehicle, early on, but were never seen again.

I guess they were hit by either FAKOUM, their own people in error, the *malais,* or simply drove over someone's mine.

This was a small affair. The main fighting took place more than a hundred kilometres away, near the border with the *malai* half of the island. Arsenio was the architect of the swift and decisive FAKOUM victory. At that level he was better than Osvaldo, the 'Trotsky of our revolution', as Rosa called him, clapping her hands together in a strangely girlish fit of enthusiasm. I thought it an unfortunate analogy but you can't blame Rosa. Those were heady days, the time of the FAKOUM victory and reforms. The town literally buzzed, people on motor-bikes going around carrying the pollen of gossip. Once again what was surprising was how reliable, how accurate rumour was. I've never despised word of mouth since then. If not exact, it was rarely completely false and could be a presage of things to come. At the very least, it was truer than newspapers.

Word of FAKOUM's military successes piled on, each account augmenting the effect of the last. They danced, yes, they did, in the streets. And the Chinese stayed in their shops.

Osvaldo and Arsenio returned at the head of their battalions. There was a mixture of olive military and garishly painted civilian transport, the latter commandeered in the main from my reluctant countrymen. Osvaldo and Arsenio rode in one of these trucks, bedecked with flowers. A choir greeted them with a specially composed tune. The FAKOUM troops, a dissolute-looking crew by Western military standards, with their beards and unkempt hair and their casually toted arms, preserved the most perfect order. There was not a single *feu de joie* or negligent discharge. And, of course, there was no looting.

They didn't tell Osvaldo about his brother for twenty-four hours. Martinho was in Bacalhau trying to find out as much as he could about Eduardo's last moments. They told Arsenio first. Osvaldo was too high up to hear the rumours and whispers that everyone else did. He moved in a vacuum. They didn't want to sour the celebrations, for themselves or for him; they didn't want to impair his concentration; and they were frightened of him. For these reasons they kept quiet. Now Osvaldo did pick up on these 'vibes' in the end. Leaders do have antennae for that. At length Achilles told Ajax the score: Arsenio took Osvaldo aside. The underlings made themselves scarce. That afternoon Osvaldo held a conference for his lieutenants at which he laid out plans for mopping up remaining IP resistance, policing the towns, and patrolling the Border. He spoke in a level voice, but didn't make any of his usual jokes. He was always a good speaker, with a sense of when the audience needed a break. But that day they didn't get one.

Martinho returned with the prisoners the next evening. This was a good deal more discreet than the victory parade. They slid them in at dusk in a convoy of three lorries. Hardly anyone actually saw it but by daybreak everyone in Danu knew. The prison searchlights were on all night. I expect the townspeople were waiting with bated breath for those fusillades against the grey walls – which never came.

Raoul was one of these prisoners.

What I relate next I learned from Dr Maria Nolasco da

Silva, who, at Arsenio's request, was in attendance at the jail. Martinho wasn't there. He hadn't actually begun a retreat, but he was literally and figuratively above all this, on top of the hill, on his knees, up at the seminary, praying like a good one. Praying for his enemies and for the power of forgiveness, as he might be forgiven.

The jail was filthy. Maria was appalled. At the best of times it was hardly salubrious. After ten days of gross overcrowding, with many of the occupants suffering from wounds, and the application of systematic neglect (in Danu we specialised in that particular paradox), the prison was a mess of bloody cloth, faeces, pus, and piss. The stink got to the back of your mouth as soon as you went in.

But they were holding Raoul in a cell to himself in the basement, a luxury he would no doubt have been happy to forego. Dr Maria arrived somewhat later than the two FAKOUM commanders. She came down a corridor lit by two kerosene lamps. There were now so many power-cuts, having electricity in town was what was abnormal. At first she didn't see Raoul. He was sitting on a wood platform that swung out of the wall on chains – his bed in other words. The tall figures of Osvaldo and Arsenio blocked him with their backs, casting long shadows into the corners. There was a third man, much shorter than the two soldiers whose face was overcast in shadow. As she came in, Osvaldo was speaking in a voice too low for her to hear. She launched straight into an attack on them for the conditions – that was Dr Maria for you. But they just ignored her. That is to say, such was their absorption they remained unaware of her. Osvaldo brought the third man into the light, held the lamp by his face.

'You see,' he said, 'there is no mistake. It is him. I want you to see it is him.'

Maria saw by the swinging light what Raoul saw. It was old Joaquim Garcia, his father. Alive, well, but extremely ill at ease. Not a trace of argumentativeness now about the old Stalinist. Osvaldo pushed him back, gently, into the circle of darkness. I'd imagine he was pleased enough to get back into the obscurity. Osvaldo was still holding the lantern, but Arsenio cursed (it wasn't 'Son of a bitch'), and he kicked the planks between Raoul's legs hard. It didn't hurt Raoul, just lifted him with the impact. Arsenio drew his fist back, but Osvaldo got his shoulder in the way, blocked him off from Raoul. 'No,' he said. He handed the lamp to Arsenio, and it swung crazily, but enough for Maria to see it wasn't Raoul on the bed, and then that it wasn't the Raoul she knew. His face was very swollen, one eye like the slit of a coin-box, an ear mutilated, the mouth bad too. And, she said, the strangest thing was the look on his face, hard to categorise, of dogged obstinacy, resentment, but not directed at his captors, in some way at himself. Osvaldo touched him very carefully on his contused cheek-bone, tenderly, hardly a brush. He held his face between the finger-tips of both hands. And he said, 'Why, Raoul?'

I think Raoul was more frightened than he appeared to Maria in that bad light and with his puffy face. I think he was in mortal terror. I think I knew Raoul better than she did, for she was a noble creature, too. At any rate, she now smelt a bad smell, a new and fresh stench to add to the old stinks in that hell-hole. Osvaldo touched him again for the last time, with that great gentleness. That must have been when Raoul knew he wasn't going to die after all, for he began to weep. And Osvaldo said, 'It is not as bad as you think.'

That was the greatness of Osvaldo Oliveira.

Maria caught them in the corridor. She said: 'This man has been badly beaten. *Raoul* has been badly beaten. He must be taken to hospital.'

Without turning, Osvaldo said, 'Take him.'

Old Garcia said, 'Colonel Oliveira, can I go?'

Maria said the old bully's voice shook.

Osvaldo said, 'Go, take your son.'

And he and Arsenio clattered up the stairs.

Altogether maybe two thousand people died in the Civil War. In the sense that everyone knew personally at least two or three and maybe even ten of those killed, it was bad. Compared to many civil wars it was small; compared to what would happen it was nothing. Arsenio as much as Osvaldo did his best to ensure there were no reprisal killings of the disarmed and defenceless, particularly in the mountains. I have to record that Osvaldo was going to have six or seven people liquidated, but Arsenio and Martinho wouldn't have it. Osvaldo wasn't Jesus. Don't let the little tableau with Raoul in the dungeon make you think that. He wasn't even Martinho, let alone the Lamb of God. He saw things clearly and he reckoned it would be easier and would save life in the long run if he bumped off a handful of key trouble-makers. Maybe he was right. He was ruthless, Osvaldo; never spiteful, never small-minded, and a worse enemy for that. But Arsenio wouldn't let him have his way. Perhaps the army had been right after all to promote him lieutenant and leave Osvaldo a sergeant. This latter shrugged. He thought he was right; knew he was right, but surrendered to the Quixotic notions of his two peers. Teixeira, Soares and the other IP bigshots scuttled over the border, into the arms of the *malais*. Strangely enough, the Amalgamationists, the ones who wished to be taken over by the *malais*, stayed put in Danu. I guess they knew they were taken so lightly, enjoyed such small support, that they'd be left alone. They might also have been under instructions from their paymasters to remain.

Theoretically, we were still a colony under the control of the Mother Country through the Governor, but FAKOUM now had a clear field. They wanted to bring us into the twentieth century. There were mass indoctrinations ('political education', as Martinho preferred to call it) with flag-wagging (black and red was the FAKOUM emblem) and a specially composed anthem. It was actually a darn good, catchy tune, as you might have expected from the Danuese: 'O, Mighty Mountain!' Despite all, you found yourself moved to hear a thousand people singing it in the Praça. I was moved, standing next to Rosa and Maria.

The good doctor now had three jeeps at her disposal and

was quite in her element. Health and Education – these were the two prongs of the FAKOUM fork. They were going for the young. Osvaldo told Maria not to give drugs or inoculations to anyone over thirty, preferably only to children. As for literacy, the unlettered adults would have been unable to cope anyway. That required fresh, pliant young brains.

Martinho then stung the Chinese a ten per cent tax on imports and set up toll posts on the roads to take a levy on trucks. As the Chinese monopolised transport, this was also an impost which hit them hardest.

But they paid. You didn't fuck with Osvaldo's boys, not with the stubby barrel of a G3 held to your head.

They also nationalised Teixeira's, Soares', and the missing late Leitao's coffee-estates. Now that was a prize. As luck would have it, a harvest was due which would put a decent sum in the FAKOUM coffers. This was the time when the world and his brother were going long on the bean. Six months later, shortly before the invasion, a lighter full of coffee left Danu. By the time it reached the world, FAKOUM had taken to the hills.

Carmichael, Mabbeley and Co were cock-a-hoop. They behaved as if it was they who had fought the Civil War and won it for their friends. From this time Bill started to wear a cast-off pair of Arsenio's boots. The correspondents, who were a little cleverer and much wittier than a casual perusal of their 'copy' might suggest, gave him a predictable baiting: too big for his boots, dwarf in giant's clothes, and (from Carmichael) stepping into dead men's shoes. That should have sent cold shivers down spines, but didn't.

They gave FAKOUM the decent press, then, which by and large the party deserved.

Then the sabotage started. Trucks lurching along the mountain roads never came back. They'd be found lying on their sides by a blackened hole. Mines, of course. Crops would start blazing in the night. Then, after a few weeks of this, people would start to disappear in the day. Their bodies were never found, that is if the general supposition that they'd been kidnapped and killed was correct. FAKOUM sent troops up on guard and patrol duties but they never came across the culprits. It was the *malais,* of course, arming the IP refugees and putting them across the loosely defined border. After they'd done their mischief they'd re-cross to sanctuaries in *malai* territory. It had a disruptive and psychological effect out of all proportion to the actual physical damage they were able to do in the short time they dared to stay. It was difficult catching them; they knew the ground.

All the while Radio Malai bombarded us with their nonsense. Ninety-nine per cent was lies, but there was a tiny seed of truth. A distortion or an exaggeration is always more effective than a fabrication. FAKOUM were making the women of the villages infertile; planning to remove children from their parents and take them to the town. Osvaldo had personally tortured three IP prisoners in the jail; Arsenio and Martinho had fallen out and come to blows. A curfew was coming into force. (Not so ludicrous when I looked at the blackness across the bay.) One day the *malais* simply stated that they had begun an invasion. Total panic in Danu. Arsenio had to drive round town with his loudhailer to put that one to rest.

A little later they did start shelling over the border, four or five dropping at a time, from proper artillery pieces, not mortars. FAKOUM drove the journos up to have a look at the craters. By the time they got up there, they were just water-logged pits. Never one to be held at a disadvantage for long, Arsenio had the puddles sprayed with larvae-destructive oil. They bumped back singing, the foreign press corps joining in a chorus of 'O, Mighty Mountain!'

They weren't bad days by any means. The fear which overhung everybody made what we had seem all the sweeter. While it lasted, anyhow.

One day it happened. A *malai* raiding party came over the border to burn down a village. They wore uniforms and they left the villagers alive, so that the incursion would not go unreported. Otherwise they would have been happy to massacre the lot. That night Radio Malai said they'd been in hot pursuit of a FAKOUM 'gang of provocateurs' who'd crossed into their territory. Exquisite irony! Done straight-faced, or should I say straight-voiced, by their announcer, a man we never saw but whose threatening, insinuating, mincing tones were as familiar to us as our next-door neighbour's. He had a slight metropolitan accent but we couldn't work out who he was or what he had been. Night after night the *malai* anthem could be heard – yes, we were all unpatriotically tuned in: do you expect anything else? – the martial music interspersed with threats of retribution and justice.

Osvaldo paraded the troops through town, took them yet again to the jungles and border. He was as much a victim of the situation as the simplest villager. If he had a weakness, it was an inability to get beyond responding to what was below his nose. He always did that magnificently, but he didn't see further. It was the obverse of his strengths, the price of the things he did do better than anybody. Arsenio was smarter, as smart as a waggon-load of Chicos. He knew we had to get into the frame of that bigger world, that empyrean from which I'd been hurled flaming, headlong. That's how I saw it, romantically: far from the prosaic reality of droning back in the cramped plane, dreading each change in the engine pitch. Arsenio knew he had an ally in me here, or at least an informal adviser. At the bar of the Lusitano he'd pump me, fondling Carmichael's left boob as he did so. And I'm half-inclined to believe that was done as a cover of casualness, calculated petting, or at least utilitarian caressing. He called me the 'man of the world'. Me! I was proud, but it was pitiful. I basked in the attentions of the FAKOUM warrior – much like Carmichael, I guess – but afterwards, maybe shaving in the morning, I'd catch my eye in the mirror and be ashamed. 'You must have been sorry to leave all your good friends behind,' he'd say. He was an oblique, wily bastard sometimes, that Arsenio. 'But then I expect you're a good letter-writer,' he'd continue.

'Most Chinamen are,' I'd counter, with a hint of maybe not resentment but sauciness. It was a sore point for the

Danuese that the Chinese would suck them dry, then send the money off the island in the shape of remittances to Taiwan, China, Macao, and Hong Kong.

'Pah,' said Arsenio, carefully keeping his face expressionless. He wasn't quite certain *how* much of a man of the world I was, to the extent of poking fun at my own people. Arsenio had learned long ago that you got further by under- rather than over-estimating others.

'They are probably important people by now.'

'Who, Arsenio?'

'Your fraternity.'

'That's American. We didn't have that in Toronto.'

He gestured impatiently with his free hand (the other being now around Carmichael's neck) before he recollected that he was doubly a suitor.

'Contacts,' Jean Carmichael suddenly said. 'Contacts. That's what it's all about. Never mind about the writing. Contacts are what makes a journalist.'

'I'm not a journalist.'

'You're better than that, Ng,' Arsenio said, eagerly seizing the main chance. 'You're a Danuese.'

I was generous enough to accept this as the compliment it was intended to be.

'You can give it the personal touch. Your friends will see it clearer because the face belongs to you. What do they call it, Jean? Human attraction?'

'Interest,' Carmichael corrected.

Yes, you're humanly interested, you bitch on heat, I thought. Aloud, I said: 'You flatter me. The people I knew won't have amounted to much.'

'We all have to start somewhere,' said Carmichael.

I said I'd heard that one of the Canadian members of the North and South Club was now working for UNESCO. Arsenio drove his fist into his palm. 'You see! That's just the kind of contact we need.'

Privately, I doubted this very much. However I allowed myself to be cajoled. My God! I didn't want to argue with Arsenio Remedios. But once we got off the embarrassing subject of me, he started to talk a lot of sense. 'We need to send delegations abroad,' he said. 'Canberra, Wellington, New York, Washington, Jakarta, KL, Lisbon, Manila. Maybe Brazil.' He lined up the empty glasses on the bar to represent each pivotal point of world influence thus listed. 'They've got to be good people. Some of our best.'

'The best you can spare, Arsenio,' Carmichael interrupted. 'You can't go yourself, or Osvaldo.'

'No,' Arsenio admitted. 'The soldiers are needed here. But look, they have to be good English speakers. No good sending anyone who can't talk to people on their own terms. Brazil and Mozambique would be OK, though.'

Carmichael looked at me. 'What about Mr Ng? He speaks beautiful English.'

For a moment Arsenio looked at a loss. Then, 'Sure, sure,' he said, 'he'd be just great.' He smoothed over the awkwardness well. We looked at each other for a moment, Carmichael the outsider who'd never know she'd blundered: of course it was impossible for a Chinese to represent FAKOUM, even if he'd wanted to. Danu for the Danuese.

I gave Arsenio a few tips, however. He'd never been to the North American continent, although Hollywood had given him a pretty good idea. In the end the evening spread itself out – as all the evenings of that period did – in a welter of heat and alcohol.

Nevertheless, if Arsenio had been evasive about my own role, he was perfectly serious about wanting to get down to some international lobbying. FAKOUM passed the motion, i.e. Arsenio chewed the fat with Osvaldo over a couple of beers; they informed Auntie, who presented the idea to the 'Central Committee' (those big titles with the glamour of history and the greater world still upon them!) – when after some flourishes and posturing, and climbing to one's feet in his olive uniform, something got done according to O. and A.'s original notion. They didn't send delegations. They didn't have the people, good-looking, charming, sinuous, ruthless people with a perfect command of the languages. More to the point, they didn't have the money for the air-fares. So they sent a one-man band. They had to rely on him to play the proper tunes loudly enough outside the correct doors. In the right key. It was Joaquim Lobato, with whom one day I'd share a Kona and blueberry pie. He wasn't a bad choice, suave even by standards wider than the limited ones of Danu, not leftish enough to scare any foreigners but a trusty FAKOUM man.

What a schedule the poor guy had. In Canberra he called on the Brazilian, Portuguese, Chinese, Canadian, Dutch, Russian, British, German, and Swedish ambassadors – this ardent twenty-five-year-old. What they made of him, and Danu, of us, can be imagined. In his absence FAKOUM appointed him Minister for External Relations and Information. They could have called him the King of Danu – he'd still have got the royal brush-off. At best he received a polite hearing. He was too innocent then of the ways of diplomacy to realise the true futility of his mission, doomed before it even began. Australian friends and sympathisers – private individuals, good people – helped him the best they could. Up in the Northern Territory he heard something on the radio to make him come home – our impending unilateral declaration of independence. He was duly sworn in to the cabinet. Six days later, on Osvaldo's insistence, he flew back to Darwin again. Even then I think Osvaldo knew what lay in store: I think he'd had his little walk in Gethsemane, though he had to look optimistic for the benefit of his fellow countrymen. Three days later the *malais* were blowing Joaquim's friends off the jetty.

I think in the light of Lobato's later career as FAKOUM torchbearer and thorn in the *malai* side where it mattered – abroad – they'd have traded each and every life they took on the water-front for his alone.

But weeks before that the *malais* had already shown they meant serious business. Shown the world, I mean: the eyes of the world. Thrown dust in the world's eyes. They'd decided to come over the border in strength.

At the time of this attack we had a couple of TV crews with us. Arsenio and Lobato's international PR drive had done that much. It's worth repeating: *if it doesn't get on to TV in the West, it hasn't happened.* Well, behind the bare chests and tubes of Swan lager in the hand this ragged troupe of Brits, Kiwis, and Aussies were pros. They had an impressive-looking camera, sound-recording apparatus on it, clapper-boards, God knows how many tin drums of film, but I don't mean that. As much as Arsenio and Osvaldo they were veterans of war and plague. In fact, their sound-recordist and director strongly reminded me of the FAKOUM Alpha and Omega. The same will and energy, identical young faces of resolution. White faces, of course. Carmichael, the horny cow, I caught eyeing the cameraman in his khaki shorts and shirt-sleeves. She had the grace to flush.

Arsenio gave them a Toyota land-cruiser to get up to the border. This was a few days before the *malai* made their push. And, no, he wasn't getting a rival out of the way. They got up to Balibo, a sleepy settlement close to the frontier and made their base there. Their director's notes record an illusory calm. 'Sleep beautifully, Balibo,' that young man wrote.

When the *malai* attack came the crew were still in Balibo.

Let me be as logical and open-minded about this as I can. Let me be as fair and unprejudiced as the Australian government was, even in the case of its own nationals. After all, we don't want to make any assumptions, do we?

What I can safely say is this. The TV crew were alive when the *malais* entered the village. By the time the *malais* left they were dead.

I am adumbrating a temporal sequence, not implying a causal connection. If you think Pascal, Descartes, and Mr Burnett have turned my brain, you might just be right.

We have two last images of these young men, the first in the film of a crew from the metropolitan country who left the village earlier, showing convivial young faces sitting over beers. The second is their own – the last can of film they managed to get away. From that final testimony we know that Greg, the director, had taken the trouble to paint in bold capital letters 'AUSTRALIA' on the wall of the house they were staying in.

FAKOUM didn't surrender the place without a fight. First there was heavy shelling from the invaders. Then an exchange of mortar and recoil-less rifle-fire across the hillside, with FAKOUM machine-gun teams firing and manoeuvring as they covered each other's retreat through the settlement. The TV crew had refused to leave the previous day. They'd said their job was to cover the fighting. Which it was.

For some of us, what occurred in those few hours has been quite clear from the day it happened. To other interested parties, it has been equally evident, though the accounts differ radically.

Here's what the *malais* say happened. The TV people were hit by FAKOUM shell-fire and/or stray and misdirected bullets from the same source. Or FAKOUM soldiers dressed as *malais* were responsible for the atrocity!

Here's what FAKOUM, 99 per cent of the Australian press and most of the Australian public think happened. The *malais* lined the white men up against the wall and shot them like dogs. Apart from one, who was blown away while he tried to escape along a path.

Take your pick.

I saw Arsenio when he got the news in the Lusitano. For a moment, for just one shameful moment, a split-second after he'd assimilated the report, he looked pleased. Then, regaining control of his face, he looked convincingly sombre. Like many others in Danu, he thought it would swing public opinion in the Antipodes behind us; force the Australian government to back us.

But it didn't.

At the time of the killings it was a Labor government in Canberra. It could have been either of the parties, it would have been the same. They had this bee buzzing in their bonnets. It was quite a sane and reasonable bee, if you looked at it in logical terms. They had this huge nation of one hundred and fifty million people as their nearest neighbours to the north and they wanted to be on cordial diplomatic and profitable trading terms with them. Ergo we, the Danuese, 700,000 of us, were a goddamned nuisance and they'd do everything they could to expedite the *malai* solution. The Labor government fell in a constitutional crisis in early November, and a caretaker Liberal administration took over until elections scheduled for 13 December. Liberal, Labor, they could have been Fascist for all the difference it made to their attitude to us. In fact, the Liberals won the election.

There was a fuss in Oz – the journos' unions, among decent, concerned people. The government behaved like a government.

Weeks later, the *malais* produced some human ashes. Oddly enough, the personal documents of the dead men were only slightly charred. And, for practical purposes, that was the end of that. Five brave young men turned to dogmeat.

But that's just a personal opinion. Don't let me influence you for one moment.

Two things then happened in Danu. Number One, most of the journos fucked off. Number Two, some while later, we had our Independence Day fiesta.

Carmichael wanted to stay. She was a girl who didn't lack pluck. Maybe she liked Arsenio more than she knew. They argued in the Lusitano. Arsenio got so vehement, maybe *he* liked her more than he knew. They were at the bar. The other journos, looking a little sheepish – but no one in their right minds could blame them for going – were talking in subdued voices at two tables near the door. Occasionally you could hear Carmichael's voice, rising as she interrupted lover-boy. Rosa was nodding at everything her friend said, glaring at the recalcitrant Remedios, with Osvaldo smiling to himself, nursing the orange juice Bill Mabbeley had bought him. Osvaldo was deriving innocent enjoyment from the predicament of his only peer. Arsenio decided to put his shades on, in the gloom of the Bluebird bar, but with a stained finger Rosa flicked them off. Despite his irritation Arsenio laughed.

'If it's so damned dangerous, everyone ought to get out,' Carmichael argued. We all smiled at the notion of the FAKOUM general fleeing on the next TAA flight.

'It's my country, Jean,' Arsenio said. Really, he was being very gentle and very honest with her. 'I have to stay. It's not your country, you don't have to stay.'

'But I love Danu,' Carmichael wailed.

Arsenio smiled, because he knew he'd won. Jean Carmichael would not have brought emotion into it unless she'd surrendered. 'We know you do, Jean,' Arsenio said.

'And we *appreciate* it,' said Osvaldo, taking pity on his comrade at last.

'Look, Miss Carmichael, you'll help them *more* by being in the big world,' I butted in.

Arsenio looked gratefully at me, and I proceeded to rehearse, with some enjoyment, all the arguments Carmichael had used on me when we'd been dealing with the question of my mythical North American 'contacts'. Finally it was settled. Carmichael agreed to go, but only after the Independence Day celebrations.

Celebrations! If you can call a wake a celebration. This was after the killings at Balibo. But, as you'd expect from Martinho, Osvaldo, and Co, there was a very good reason for it. Since the Civil War, FAKOUM had been running the place but they hadn't bothered to legitimise their regime. It suited them to have a link with the Home Country, maybe get a few escudos, have some kind of European connection to make the *malais* think twice. But now they had to make a formal declaration of autonomy, proclaim sovereignty purely so that the invading *malais* could be seen to have violated it. It was a pragmatic, not a flamboyant, act.

They held it on the Praça. Considering the original motive for the ceremony, considering the in-born Danuese talent for making a shambles of anything, for manic disorganisation, it turned out to be not only a moving but also a disciplined spectacle. We had a makeshift podium for Martinho, Osvaldo, and Arsenio. It was just a desk from a government office with three swivelling chairs behind it, and the

FAKOUM/Danuese flag, a remarkably restrained creation by a mountain textile weaver (again, smart constituency work by Osvaldo). They were on the same level as everyone else, not above the crowd, I mean. Arsenio still wore his lieutenant's uniform. Why he kept doing that, I don't know. To wear the colonial colours at this celebration of secession was not a little strange. Maybe Osvaldo told him to do it – to make a gesture to the old followers of Teixeira and da Gama, who hankered after a tie with the Mother Country. What spoiled the effect was that he had two days' growth to go with the reflective shades. Behind them stood the leading FAKOUM people, everybody except Martinho fully armed. Two or three of the women found their pistols and grenades a little heavy and put them on the table. During the rendition of 'O, Mighty Mountain!' what with all the stamping and swaying the grenades started to move. Not the oval fragmentation grenades but the canisters, the ones like green beer tins with yellow instructions on them. I was standing next to Bill Mabbeley, towards the front by courtesy of Rosa, and I watched in fascination as the grenades first started to tremble, then rock, and finally roll this way and that. I really wasn't sure what to do. I mean, really, I figured it was better to be blown up than interrupt 'O, Mighty Mountain!' Osvaldo caught my eye, threw his head back, shot out his chest and joined in the chorus with gusto. I also made my mouth move, not wanting to be a suspect Chinaman (there were few enough of us attending in all conscience). But I couldn't help allowing my eyes to stray downwards. Those rolling bombs, they mesmerised. Always quick, Osvaldo realised what I was thinking and, still singing lustily, flicked a grenade off the table with his fingernail. *Jesus Cristo!* It was the end of the chorus, so I clearly heard the clunk of the grenade as it hit the cobbles. See it I didn't because I'd shut my eyes. In all honesty I couldn't say I'd ever found that Osvaldo had the greatest sense of humour but he had me that time. What a time and place, too. Son of a bitch.

Later (it was much later, in the mountains), he told me it had been quite safe – the fuse assembly hadn't been inserted.

They issued the two parts separately to each soldier. Should give them to two *different* soldiers, I thought. 'It was a smoke grenade, was it?' I asked, knowing somewhat more about these things by then than I had done. He smiled. 'It was White Phosphorus, Ng.' I'm still not sure.

Bill Mabbeley had heard the words of the anthem often enough to know them and was bellowing away, like a bull moose in shorts, way out of tune and audible over the birdy melody of the Danuese.

And at the end he gave the FAKOUM clenched fist salute. Ridiculous, brave old bastard. Arsenio had been prepared to let *him* stay on afterwards, but not Carmichael. She didn't reproach him with sexism. A roar went up from the crowd at the end. And having enjoyed it, they gave themselves an encore: sang their anthem not twice but three times in the end, shaking their flags and banners in a flurry of colour. There were middle-class people from the town, beggar-kids, montagnards, soldiers, children in school uniform and Carmichael crying her eyes out. I think she really did like the Danuese. If I've ever spoken slightingly of her, or of Martinho, or of Raoul, or of Rosa, I don't mean to. You must make allowances for me, my acerbity. Jean was a fine, brave, generous girl. Speeches followed, surprisingly short, terse deliveries. Martinho wasn't permitting any self-indulgence: these were joyful and proud celebrations but held under a terrible shadow. They'd soon come out of that dark valley if they followed their leaders, etc.

I don't think any of us there, whatever happened to us afterwards, wherever we ended up, ever forgot that day.

Nothing the *malai* did could blot out that memory. It was worth doing. You need a focus for emotion, even hardened cadres like Osvaldo or the ostensibly cynical like Dr Maria. You think you are immune at such spectacles. But you aren't.

There wasn't a lot of drinking or noise afterwards. By midnight the streets were empty.

One thing stands out in my memory. Arsenio walking round with a kid on his shoulders, the boy's legs wrapped around his neck. He'd given the urchin his lieutenant's cap and shades to wear. The boy was nothing more than a barefoot street-arab. And he was followed like some piper, khaki rather than pied, by a tail of beggar-kids, imploring him for a shining bullet or a chance to touch his pistol.

That was the second to last time I ever saw Arsenio Remedios.

PART TWO

PART TWO

NINE

MAJOR 'JOHNNY' REBUS DID NOT LOOK like the fiend incarnate. Those people seldom do. But we called him the Devil. He was somewhat dark. In common with other Asian races, the *malais* frowned on too deep a colouring as indicative of humble origins. It was felt it was a trait which could be transmitted from previous generations of labourers in the field to those made good. Their president, the former General, had come from a poor family, but he was pale-complexioned. In other words, he'd found his right level. I don't know whether this was what had soured Rebus from the start, the cruel mockery of children. There could be no doubt he was as black as a Negro but shinier, blue if you know what I mean. He had wavy hair, always sleek, whether with brilliantine or natural oils, it was difficult to tell. The flesh under his fingernails was a deep purple, with the half-moons a glowing contrast. He was slim, trim, about 50, but without a single grey hair. The *malais* could actually produce quite large men, for Asians, but without being tiny Rebus was not one of these. His staff and bodyguards were all well-built guys, 160-pounders to the man, kind of an honor guard, and I suspect they were chosen for their physical attributes as well as loyalty and brains, in that order. Being in charge of these brutish specimens somehow gave Rebus an extra authority. We were all scared shitless of him and them. More of them than him to start with, since they looked fierce, had hair sticking out of their snouts, carried non-standard issue survival knives (which, somehow, you felt they were readier to stick you with), and moved with an uncouth violence. How wrong. Compared to Rebus, his bodyguards were a bunch of pussy-cats. He didn't soil his own hands with killing or torture – those stories of cannibalism, of eating the hearts and livers of the FAKOUM top cadres were precisely that, outrageous but effective fabrications (why shouldn't FAKOUM dispense a little propaganda of their own, when the *malais* had almost all the American press sewn-up?).

But Rebus attended those terrible sessions in basements. His was the mind which first contemplated, then ordered, the destruction of whole villages, his the hand which didn't shake when he pointed at the photographs of those who were to disappear. He knew every detail of what his men did. There are those at the top who put to the back of their conscious mind that knowledge of their subordinates' misdeeds of which they would rather not be cognisant. Innate shrewdness prevents them from believing their own pronouncements, but they wilfully close their eyes. And there are those who live with that knowledge. Rebus was one of the latter, minority category. He was a ruthless, implacable killer. I won't say he was a sadist in the Japanese way, that he enjoyed death and the infliction of pain, that he derived a quasi-sexual gratification from it in the way of Bushido. But he seemed to get a grim satisfaction from a job properly done. He believed in severe solutions; by temperament, he was a Draco. And if considered judicial sternness at the top got translated at the remove of four descending orders groups into a bloody frenzy, a welter of crazed killings and rape at the sharp end, it was a transformation he could tolerate. He knew and understood it. He thought he was immune but he sympathised with the affliction. That glee for blood, the joyous knowledge that all control was gone, that others had no claim and there was only the gibbering, dancing core of self with its lust to kill, all those things existed in a private part of the *malai* soul. Rebus's men didn't go amok in loin-cloths and waving knives; they did it in uniforms, firing M-16s. There'd follow some attempt at disciplining them; some words of reproof. Openly to condone men going beyond the control of their officers was not possible. It was an infraction of the military code. And Rebus lived by that.

He'd been to the US. Several times. As a captain, he'd also visited Peking in the days of the old *malai* president's flirtation with Communism. Flirtation is the right word. The former president had been a pock-marked old lecher. Rebus's most recent trip hadn't been to West Point or anywhere like that. It was to a discreeter kind of place. He was the only Asian; it had been full of Latin Americans. He often spoke of it, with nostalgia, particularly when weary. It was as if he wanted his batteries charged again. Perhaps that's an unfortunate expression. They were great believers in electric torture there. Not much could be actually demonstrated – it was the land of the free and the home of the brave, after all. Plus they didn't have the live subject exactly in abundance. But, to borrow a phrase, the sons of bitches weren't above giving each other a nip with the electrodes. Without the application of water and not on a sensitive part of the male anatomy, but they all learned what it felt like. It gave them an insight. 'Hurt bad,' Rebus would say, 'but leave no mark.' And then he'd rub his arm thoughtfully. Although he was of relatively junior rank and had certainly never received staff training, he disposed of a general's influence. He belonged to some shadowy organisation in military intelligence, with undefined and therefore untrammelled power. Certainly officers of a theoretically senior rank were extremely careful in their dealings with him.

I had his retinue at the Hotel Oscar Tango X-Ray. For a short time I had the honor of the Great Man himself. It was not an honor any sane man would seek. It was like being at the court of some ancient despot. In fact, I'd say the *malai* military were the lineal descendants of the piratical rajahs and sultans in their island nests. You trod carefully. Their moods were arbitrary. Certainly it would have been perilous to have been the bringer of unwelcome tidings. They didn't make the logical distinction between intelligence and bearer. To them it was all part of the same context. Of course, one of their own men would have been able to make an accurate situation report without dread; yet heaven help a Danuese coming with news of a FAKOUM action near his village.

The *malais* were foolish here. They cut off sources of information. Which Rebus soon realised – although he himself had been responsible for a few cases of brutal pique beforehand. In the early days it was dangerous to be a collaborator, not just because of the possibility of FAKOUM

115

revenge but as a result of *malai* thoughtlessness. And they never really made up for those early errors.

I actually received payment for accommodating the little major and his thugs. This was unusual. The *malais* were great thieves. They were one of the corruptest nations in Asia. Believe me, that is to say something. They stole everything in Danu, including what was nailed down. Refrigerators, cars, air-conditioners, all got loaded up in front of the amazed eyes of the Danuese and shipped back to the *malai* capital. These were the perquisites of senior officers. The men had to be content with wrist-watches and cameras.

No, Rebus didn't pay me because he was scrupulous. He did it because it made him look big. Mind you, he set the rate himself and it was something like a quarter of the usual tariff. He went through the farce of having his aide count out the money in front of an appreciative audience. We were still using escudos then, which had become ever more inflated. In the end it turned out that Rebus was only paying himself. He must have liked what he saw at the O. T. X-Ray because he cut himself in on the action. After breakfast – and the major preferred the eggs and toast of his American sojourn to the fried rice and prawn crackers of his suite – Rebus had me summoned to the cane throne he'd usurped. 'You need capital,' he said. The *malais* were actually an excessively polite race, when the blood-lust was not upon them. Even the most belligerent hinted, rather than demanded. You had to pick up the cues. They were subtle people. Of course, if you didn't pick up Rebus's cues he stopped being so subtle.

'*Tuan?*' I said.

Rebus smiled. He could see I was puzzled, but knew I was smart enough to grasp the point eventually.

'Time,' he said, 'you took on a partner.'

I think my face betrayed my feelings. Who said the Chinaman is inscrutable? Whoever it was, he was wrong, very wrong. To be frank, it hurt me as much as the invasion. I don't say that like some Chinese I'd have died rather than surrender my property – like the storekeepers the Japs

116

bayoneted in 1942 – but I was pretty darn sick. He was taking what I had made out of nothing, my creation, my little kingdom. What mattered was that it was *all* mine. The reality from now was that Rebus owned it lock, stock, and barrel. I was no partner. I was a salaried employee, a manager at best. If he could have gotten someone else to run it profitably he would have done. But he was no fool. Every *malai* general had a Chinese behind him. They didn't have the head for business. They had to have someone administer the fortune they'd made out of squeeze and corruption, make it grow, or just ensure they didn't lose it. Swiss bank accounts, Wall Street, CD'S, bearer bonds, foreign currencies, portfolio reviews – this was where the wily Chinaman came in.

So when I swallowed, tried to bring a smile to flaccid cheek muscles, Rebus had seen it all before. His grin broadened. 'You make more money, Chinaman,' he said. The irony was insupportable. He wasn't lying, you know, to wheeler-deal. He knew I knew. In me he was punishing every Chinaman who'd ever screwed a *malai*. He was provoking me. If I'd gone for him, he probably wouldn't have had me shot. I'd have provided testimony of a success. Of course, I didn't have the guts or the stupidity. Instead I went away, with tears pricking my eyes, to sit on one of my precious flush toilets. *His* goddamned flush toilets.

You're probably appalled by me. Who's he to whine about losing toilets. People were killed. OK. Agreed. But let's see how you'd feel. I loved those toilets, knew every crack and every stain I hadn't been able to bleach away. Now they were the major's.

Others had been less fortunate. The malais hadn't only taken things from them. They'd given them something. This was our women. They'd given them babies. I trust you take my meaning. They'd raped them, gang-raped them in many instances. This hadn't stopped them from shooting or stabbing some of the women afterwards. I'll give them credit where credit is due. Rape and killing chiefly took place on the first day. After that, it tended to be just plain rape. Ten soldiers round a female, waiting their turn. They didn't need anyone to hold them down; the women knew better than to resist. Not that many of those violated survived the first day. They weren't very selective, the malai. They fucked anyone female between the ages of puberty and 70 that they could. After that they became more choosy. They started to pick pretty girls, girls who caught the eye from a passing truck, someone glimpsed about their chores through a window. Women weren't safe doing their washing in a stream. If they liked the look of their calves, the malais would screech to a halt and have no compunctions about molesting them. It was quite an epidemic.

Among the number of these unhappy women was Rosa. How she'd survived that first day, I don't know. As well as the purely random killings, that crazed butchery, there had been targetings, purposeful assassinations. Their elite cherry berets had been assigned top cadres and administrators to hit and then, after that, some secondary targets, lower-grade people. They already knew where they lived. In the event, about half the big people had gone before they got there, and they had to be content with killing underlings. Rosa was an underling but had a high profile. They must have had a photo of her. Anyhow, she looked the archetypal Commie. Other people's wives and daughters had been gang-banged in front of them (a favourite *malai* infliction, this) and then, often enough, the couple shot. But Rosa, like me, like Dr Maria, made it through the day without becoming a lump of meat.

They caught Rosa at the crèche at the Organisation of Working Danuese Women, which might have been what saved her. She was there seeking shelter with Dr Maria Nolasco da Silva. This must have occurred at about the time they were shooting people off the jetty in front of us, making us count as the bodies hit the water.

Two ten-ton lorries full of troops, escorted by an armoured personnel carrier, came pounding down the road to the crèche. Maria told me she watched the vehicles coming more than a mile off, with a sick feeling in her stomach. It was plain they were coming pell-mell for them, but she didn't want to believe it. The *malais* were roaring along as fast as they could, in a great cloud of dust, and you could hear the drivers working through the gears. But they weren't chasing a retreating enemy, they weren't attacking under fire; there was no need for the breakneck speed. In a terrible way, Maria found it funny; it was absurd. Finally, they doubled the bend before the main drive and drove straight over the flower-beds the women had troubled to plant in the middle of the roundabout. As the troops piled over the tailboards and sides the 'big gun' on the APC stitched a burst of shells across the plaster over the main entrance, sending everyone scurrying for cover. They rushed in, weapons at the ready, but were still sufficiently disciplined not to shoot everybody as they stood. There'd been a FAKOUM Observation Post and radio on the hillside behind but they'd cleared out long before. After a while of rooting beneath beds, kicking cupboards open, and jumping through windows, the *malais* came to realise there was nothing there in the sense of a military threat. But they had not acted out their notion of themselves. There was still that potential for action, undischarged, in them. As well, not actually contradictory, there existed a sense of relief. Who wants to die?

They began to look at the women.

The officer was outside. He had a cigarette. With that he had to be content. To that extent I have to say the *malais* observed discipline and good military conduct. Being a sergeant was best. That give you privilege without the responsibilities of the officer. They got to choose the youngest and best-looking women. I say that, but Rosa didn't escape; Rosa, my friend, the swarthiest, hairiest, least desirable of women. It was a gross violation of what she was. She did struggle; there was that much of FAKOUM in her. And it amused rather than angered them. It was a little sport, the combat they'd missed. She cursed them until they punched her and pushed a scarf into her mouth. They laughed as they turned her over, at her quivering buttocks, her short, plump thighs, her hairiness. When they'd finished, they left her on the floor. I guess you could say she was luckier than Sonia Ferreira.

Dr Nolasco da Silva was the only woman in the place to escape the ordeal. The white coat, the air of authority, they struck a chord in the *malai* military somewhere.

When the officer came in, she made a straight line for him. She had the guts, the presence of mind to complain to him. Maria expected something of the world, you see. She wasn't fouled with cynicism. The victims expected nothing but the worst, and the *malais* lived down to their expectations. Not that I seek to lay blame for the transgressor's crimes at the door of the victim. But they weren't capable of indignation, of the genuine outrage which gripped Maria. The officer pretended not to understand, even when she spoke her excellent English.

'But she was mad,' Rosa herself said afterwards, in wonder. 'I've never seen anyone so angry.'

She threatened him with his commanding officer – so what! – told him his men were animals, a disgrace to their uniform. This last would have had some effect; possibly saved her from a back-handed blow, with worse to follow once her invulnerability had been compromised. They did think of themselves as real soldiers. The officer barked a couple of commands to the corporals, pushed Maria away, and they went off, collecting the men from their various hidey-holes. It would have been a great time for a FAKOUM counter-attack, the US cavalry catching the Apaches with their pants down. But, you know, we were the Apaches.

During that first week we kept our heads down. In the first 48 hours you hardly dared breathe. There was a curfew. Redundant regulation! No one wanted to be about after sundown. But no one! The Danuese scampered indoors, like Transylvanians in a Dracula movie. At 8 p.m., midnight, and 4 a.m. *malai* patrols would move through the town, kicking store doors (long since looted) and smashing with their rifle-butts any windows through which the merest chink of light might show. Food, fuel, and news were in short supply. Of work – unpaid – there was no scarcity. All the fires, except the one at the oil tanks, had gone out, but rubble and splinters infested the roads and town, worse than the time of the IP coup. On the third day there was an explosion in the park near the Marconi Centre. Idiots that we were, we all came rushing out, having learned nothing from experience. Curiosity was stronger than fear. The *malais* came rushing, too. It was an unexploded shell which one of the labourers had hit with a pick. Fortunately, no soldiers were killed, only two Danuese. They'd have put a few of us against the wall, otherwise.

Rebus had confiscated all radios, including transistors. Penalty for possession was their only sanction at that time: death. I'd hidden my short-wave receiver as soon as the *malais* released us from our body-disposal detail. I don't claim to be particularly audacious. After they'd promulgated the death penalty I was just too scared to hand it in. And I was frightened to turn it on, what with Rebus being in the building. But I couldn't resist the temptation. Despite myself, I'd get it out – it wasn't a small thing, you know – from its cubby-hole under the floorboards and watch, with trepidation, as my hand stole out to press the button. It sounded too damn loud always. I expect I had it on at a whisper. Once, even I, with my sensitive, straining ears, couldn't hear it and I rotated the volume wheel. My anxiety made me clumsy, and the six o'clock news from Darwin boomed out through the loudspeaker. I'd always liked the superior bass quality of that set, till then. My God, I cringed. Waited for the sudden silence in the building, the shout, the stamping footsteps, the door being kicked off its hinges. But there was just quiet. Did it stop my trembling fingers from reaching out again? No, it didn't.

The world certainly knew of the invasion. The crackling, adenoidal tones of Darwin confirmed that. Judging by their resumé it appeared to have gotten into all the major newspapers of the world. The slant seemed extremely favourable to us. The deaths of the television crew had achieved that much. There was an eerie moment, a feeling of dizziness, heightened in my already nervous state, when I heard them play the words of Pedro Ribeiro which they had taped as they received them, Ribeiro's mayday, the plea I'd heard at the Marconi Centre, clear as crystal, within a metre of the man, as it was uttered, now become an item from the archives, dramatic, fuzzy with static and the crump of distant explosions I'd failed consciously to register at the time as I sat by Bill Mabbeley. It seemed a million years ago and was just four weeks.

TEN

IN THE END NORMALCY RESUMED. It's not, in fact, normalcy. Not under our kind of circumstances. But the psyche can only take so much abnormality. It rebels in the end, fails to register, refuses to endure. In the unusual it discerns only the usual. It habituates itself to the grossest of existences. From an unplanned string of horrors it extracts a timetable of the banal. Just as I'd seen my tourists gradually blind themselves to the existence of the filthy beggars in Danu where in the first days of their sojourn they'd squander their loose change and even notes on useless philanthropy, so we closed our eyes to what the *malai* had devised for us. Thirst, boredom, lust, curiosity, the desires for companionship and laughter – these remained. They were human constants, but they insidiously prepared our acceptance for what we were becoming. They were the fifth columnists of our own minds. We didn't even notice our surrender; defeat had become a matter of perception. And curiously enough in that total powerlessness and abnegation you could find a kind of relief.

We were correct to think that we had no control over our destinies: to consider that resistance was futile and bravery superfluous. From the start, our fate was determined not by ourselves, not locally or by the invader even, but abroad, in Canberra and Washington. That was why the *malais* had tried to destabilise the FAKOUM regime, to disseminate a campaign of lies. In purely military terms a straightforward

122

surprise attack would have been the most efficient strategy, entailing the least loss of life and material for them. I think such had been the desire of most of the Colonels and many of the Generals. A former divisional commander himself, their President had to listen to his officers, as the head of any military dictatorship prudently does, but in this instance he had to allow the suaver diplomats to have their way. International opinion had to be assuaged, the Americans cultivated. In fact, I am sure they had the benefit of US advice, for public (meaning civilian) opinion was not something the Generals knew much about. The distortions of the press campaign provided so many pretexts which, however intrinsically flimsy, could be used to veil the issue, obfuscate. The disinformation – a word which had been much relished by Martinho who only heard it for the first time then – was as vital to the success of the invasion as the strafing and the barrage. Just going in without warning would have been too blatant, too startling to the Australian and US public. It was a matter of lodging a sense of mission or even of resentment in the consciousness of that great American television audience who comprise the Circus of our day: thumbs up or thumbs down.

The American executive could not keep the invasion totally secret, otherwise they would have opted for the covert; so it had to be clever PR, followed by a blackout on news emanating from Danu. They smeared FAKOUM with the Commie brush. What FAKOUM did do in its short life, surely what it ought to be judged by, has never been relevant, so much as what the Americans and the *malais* said FAKOUM *would* have done.

And the question of legitimacy, that spurious, sterile, legalistic argument paraded up and down the international debating halls ever since, has come to assume proportions no sane person could have imagined at the time. The Danuese had the right to self-determination, and the government they chose was FAKOUM. To say they wanted the *malais* or the *malais'* puppet was fantastical! The assertion bore no relation to what was happening in the real world. But on paper, at third hand, it seemed as cogent as the reality ever could. I refer to the outrageous plebiscite, taken at gunpoint, when even the *malai* military didn't dare allow a mass referendum but 'consulted' a few hundred chiefs 'mandated' to express the 'wishes of their people'. They were bribed, cowed, hand-picked for their malleability. And the result was as predictable and foregone as that of a firing squad.

Only their own silence can damn the guilty.

It doesn't matter how cynical a pretext may be, how gratuitous the act, how cruel in its execution, so long as mouths move, words are said, statements issued, then anything can be justified. A weak argument, stated confidently, becomes a strong argument. 'Spokesmen' say something, anything, any nonsense, the words might as well have no meaning or the special meanings attached to doublespeak, and then there appears to be a case made, a position established. Say anything – it's only words and they have the same valency as those of the victim. The world doesn't see what actually happened. It merely hears a 'balanced' account, both sides getting the same amount of air-time (if the victim is lucky), and that device equals things out to the culprit's advantage.

The reality is separate from the words.

The reality for the Danuese was a state of starvation in the town and utter famine in the countryside. The fighting and the forced relocations of people away from areas where they might aid FAKOUM distorted what had been an economy operating at slightly above subsistence level. Now people could actually starve to death.

Will you be pleased to hear that I personally had as much to eat as I wanted? Rebus, no doubt, feared thin Chinamen. With others it was a different matter but I think they forgot what it was like not to be hungry. That played its part in eroding the will, too.

One of my jobs was selling food for the *malais*. At first it was stuff they had confiscated, oil, rice, and flour from the Toko-ru warehouse. Later, it was the powdered milk and soya flour of the international relief agencies. They figured that it would be easier to let hunger do the work of getting money from people, rather than go to the effort of beating it out of them. I said the *malais* were a lazy race. But they were right. It was amazing what people had, the poorest-looking ones. You'd never suspect it. The *malais* preferred chattels to cash. Gold, chiefly, was what interested them, though silver and even semi-precious stones, in the end, held allure. A wedding-ring or a tooth could get you a two-pound sack of rice or a tin of bully-beef. The *malais* being the subtle, indirect people they were, didn't like to perform this trade face to face, so it got delegated. I didn't mind being useful here as well as on the hotel front. Figured it would enhance my chances. Mostly, I did it for Rebus's bodyguards. The Danuese disliked me no more for this than they had done before. All round, Chinamen were a necessary evil.

I did get the chance to do a little good: sop to conscience. I have a strong conscience. For one thing, I was able to be kind to my friends. The *malais* expected me to take my perquisite. Nothing was said – subtlety, indirection, etc. – but I was paid no money and never punished for pilfering, say, one tin or sack in ten. Some went for my own stomach. I gave the rest away, and hope you believe me, because no one else except maybe Maria did. I was a *stupid* Chinaman, and knew it as I dispensed my largesse.

Things got a lot worse for the Danuese as time went on, but the level of my stores remained constant, being independent of what happened on the island to an extent.

'Business good, Chinaman?' Rebus would enquire when he saw me. And he'd chuckle, the murderer. Those were the only times I saw Rebus laugh. He had a frightening face, mostly. I'd play the fool, to kind of nullify the danger of my brains; to make him think I was good with money but had no wits otherwise. I don't know if the gambit was successful. If you give credit to Rebus for minimal intelligence – and you have to – it wouldn't have done, would it? I always had the impression he was mind-reading me or laughing at the open folly he could see. Now, away from him and the stifling, scary immediacy of his presence, I don't think he had any particular insight into me, although at the time it felt like he was staring down a skylight in my skull. He was like a powerful computer which hadn't been fed a particular programme – the programme being me, a quirky guy with an odd history. It just wouldn't have been possible for Rebus to comprehend me. It was pure bluff. I think he knew that just by laughing at someone you'd give them the shivers; that if you wore a smirking, knowing look they'd think you really did know what they were up to. In other words let *them* do your hard work. Plant the seed and watch it grow. It was much like getting squeeze from the people through the food programme. What Rebus knew was that if you got people into thinking you knew more about them than you actually did, they'd get so jumpy in the end that they'd finish by incriminating themselves.

Maria thought I was crazy, told me I was drinking too much coffee. That was a joke, with not a cup to be had, Rebus's superiors having sent every bean home. Maria led a charmed existence. She went where she willed, got things out of thin air. She had a different way of coping than I. I tried to wrap myself around the situation, think myself into the *malai* mentality. For me, safety lay in camouflage and integration. Maria's approach was simpler: the refusal to believe problems existed. She developed a severe case of tunnel vision. But, amazingly, it seemed to work. For a while.

One evening she came round with Rosa. I hadn't really seen Rosa since before that terrible day of the invasion. Once or twice I'd glimpsed her in the street but you didn't hang about gossiping in those days, not with a cherry beret on every corner, with a sub-machine gun strapped to his shoulder. Just for talking too long or with too many people you could have got yourself hauled away and never seen again. I'm not kidding. Conspiracy, you see. We aimed to shuffle about our affairs with our eyes down, even me. Anyway, I was ashamed. Degraded by what had happened to Rosa. I didn't feel she'd been degraded. I had. I felt embarrassment. Strange how these polite notions survive at points of extremity when you'd think they'd be irrelevant. I wanted to spare her my presence.

But it was the same Rosa. Being with Maria helped her. You got a charge off the good doctor. She wouldn't let you slump.

'Hello, Hitler,' Rosa greeted me, and for once I didn't resent the peculiar address. I was going to ask her how she was in the conventional way, but the query stayed in my mouth. I think she saw it in my eyes, but she didn't look away. I couldn't face her smile, but it was still there when I met her gaze again.

'Adolph has landed on his feet,' Maria said. Knowing her, I believed it was a statement rather than an accusation. 'He has largesse to bestow.'

I did my best to look quizzical. To be honest, I wasn't sure what that famously sarcastic tongue had in store.

'Oh, those poor children. You are a saint, Hitler!'

Now I began to have some idea.

Rosa was really quite effusive, for her. 'It's knowing it'll come regularly, that's the thing!'

'Now, girls, listen, it's not...'

But Maria would brook none of my feebleness. 'We'll send the people up to you. . . no, I'll do it myself. I don't trust any Danuese.'

Danuese Rosa nodded vigorously; she knew just what Maria meant. I was quaking in my boots just thinking about it. *Seriously* stealing from Rebus and his bodyguards. I mean over and above my understood allowance. Jesus! They'd cut my balls off and stuff them up my ass. I didn't say this to Maria. I could only too well imagine the scornful retort of: 'You should be so lucky.' Instead I said, and to my shame my voice trembled, 'I won't give you more than a kilo a week. They'll notice otherwise.'

'Five kilos a week,' Maria said firmly.

'Three.'

'Four.'

'OK,' I said weakly, with panic fear gripping my bowels already. I was amazed at myself, how shame could make you do things you didn't want to. Peer pressure. It's a good expression, but the words aren't as strong as the thing.

It was for the crèche, of course. That was still going, with Dr Maria in attendance. She'd never had more than the scantiest pharmacopoeia. Now it was nothing. Not even aspirin. But there was the force of her personality, which was not to be discounted even where adults were concerned, let alone poor, impressionable kids. She more or less willed them well, those who didn't die along the way.

So it was settled. I became an unwilling philanthropist. Those damn brats. And there wasn't the hint of thanks from Maria. She neither expected it for herself nor doled it out to others. She might have got more done in her life if she had realised not everyone was as pure or as self-sufficient as she was. But then that, I guess, was also part and parcel of being Maria.

ELEVEN

THE MALAIS WERE NOT, OF COURSE, having it entirely their own way. I can give us credit for that. Down in the town we weren't in the full picture. The malais fed us selected palpable untruths. A meagre diet, though not quite the starvation rations of our real meals. If you were to believe them, they'd nailed most of the FAKOUM high command on invasion day, which we all knew was a lie. We'd seen the bodies. The corpses we'd disposed of were nearly all ordinary people, except for Sonia Ferreira and Pedro Ribeiro (whose body no one had actually seen). That excluded the many dead Chinese – who in South-East Asia never qualify as ordinary people. There were, they claimed, a few 'bandits' in the mountains but they were mopping up even these.

So what had all the dead and groaning *malais* we saw daily evacuated to the dock been doing?

(And that wasn't a good time or place to be caught hanging around.)

It became plain after a while that the *malais* had not spread into the country much. Their grip on us, in the town, was total. Which had led us townspeople to assume that they also controlled the mountains. In reality they hadn't moved more than four miles beyond Danu. Their last outpost was a roadblock in the hills, at exactly the point where in the days of our mobile clinic I used to look down on the town and become depressed, and Rosa and Maria, on the other hand, would become gay and sing. Down in town we couldn't hear any gunfire. Such fighting as was occurring was taking place miles beyond. It wasn't heavy stuff, like invasion day. The *malais* were confining themselves to probing patrols. They were consolidating. There were several reasons for this. In the first place they'd won *de facto* political control and some international recognition just by taking town. Secondly, there was some dispute going on in the *malai* capital between hawk generals and dove generals, with the President doing the mediating, balancing act on which his power depended (a subtle and sensitive people, etc., who preferred to arrive at a consensus rather than a diktat). Then, finally, as the Japs had found thirty years before them, outside Danu it was difficult terrain for an occupying force – perfect guerrilla country. So they were just keeping the pot boiling by sending out small detachments. It was a few men against a few men, but their losses were disproportionately heavy. I'm not being partisan. Osvaldo and his boys were better at it, more hardened, resourceful soldiers than the *malais*. This wasn't immediately apparent, but you deduced it with the passage of time. The *malais* took it out on us civilians. We could tell from the increased brutality of the *malais* whenever FAKOUM had enjoyed a success up in the mountains.

Did we think that FAKOUM would swoop down from the mountain and liberate us at a stroke? Never. The *malais* had hit us on that first day with such overwhelming force and ruthlessness that it had stunned everyone, knocked the spunk for a fight right out of us. Most of us.

And the *malais* had so much equipment, so many big grey ships floating in the harbour, so many planes overhead that it seemed impossible to resist.

While certain things became clearer in the way that furniture in a strange room assumes a proper shape as the

129

light greys, others remained in a profound night. What had happened to Martinho? Even more enigmatical was the fate or whereabouts of Raoul. The reasonable assumption was that Martinho was in the hills with his brother but taking a back seat, or busy elsewhere, or trying to join him, or sick, or dead. But Raoul wasn't a bigshot. He had no reason to flee the town – more than the rest of us, I mean, after that first day of atrociousness. Certainly, he had every reason not to throw his lot in with Osvaldo and Co. As much as me, he was no hero. He was not cut out to be one of life's guerrillas in anybody's cause, let FAKOUM's alone.

Yet I hadn't heard of him since the day of the Fiery Pillar and the dropping manna. After Osvaldo had made his great gesture, for once showed himself more magnanimous, more conciliatory than Arsenio, Raoul had gone to ground with his father. His old friends now shunned him. He'd been glimpsed in their garden, watering the lilies. And then that was that. Because of this banishment, I'd lost track of him. As time went by and he failed to appear at the periodic flushings-out the *malais* would order, I came to realise he wasn't in Danu.

Maria came to the conclusion at the same time.

We were at the crèche. The two women didn't like going out to the Oscar Tango X-Ray – that exposed walk, and, worse, the journey back under the eyes of Rebus and his brigand-like minions. It had required courage to come to me about food for the children. Maria said: 'Do you suppose Raoul is OK? I wonder if he is still around. We should make the effort, don't you think?' From the formality of her phrasing, the stilted words, I knew she thought he was dead, or had flown.

Rosa grunted unamiably. 'That bastard. Good riddance to him.'

'Now, Rosa, he is your friend, our friend, the friend of all of us.'

'Was, you mean,' retorted Rosa. I noted her suffering had not made her a more compassionate person.

'Wherever he is, he's not here,' I said. Maria nodded.

She'd been thinking about it for some time. Apart from her being who and what she was, she had, I think, a feeling of special responsibility for Raoul. That night she'd gone to the prison and borne witness to his condition, when she'd demanded medical treatment for him of Arsenio and Osvaldo – the memory of that had made her feel a bond with him. In the way it is with people, her own altruism and courage had stimulated her to give yet more; generosity and selflessness piled upon each other. Spite and meanness reproduce only themselves. That's the way it is. You get all or nothing from people.

'I'll ask the *malais*,' she said.

I was aghast. 'You will do no such thing, Dr Nolasco da Silva,' I said. I could just imagine Rebus's incredulous reaction. She'd have been shot for that. Probably a quick and clean death, but they'd have bumped her off. The effrontery of it. They really didn't like you enquiring after any one who'd disappeared, even if it wasn't someone they'd eliminated themselves. It was kind of an accusation by implication and association. 'He has gone to study abroad,' they'd say of the disappeared, even notorious illiterates. And pretty soon the questioner would also be furthering his or her studies, two metres underground.

Maria would have done it, if I hadn't pulled her up. Fortunately, she wasn't by nature a reckless or stupid woman. There was no need for argument with her. My genuine consternation sufficed.

Rosa mumbled something, too, like 'Don't do it, Maria, it's trouble,' which reminded us both, Maria and myself, if we needed it, what the *malais* were capable of.

'Well, I don't think he's dead,' Maria said, to break the pause, awkward because of Rosa, her stubbornness persisting only on this point, the fact of her friend's survival. I, too, had a feeling that Raoul was one of life's survivors, that he was around somewhere, maybe in Bacalhau; so, not just to placate Maria, found myself agreeing. We left it at that.

This was about five or six weeks after the invasion, when you had time to take stock of more than yourself, when you were taking your head out of the sand for the first time. Those of us who weren't Maria.

Strangely enough, Raoul would have done better than most in the new Danu. The *malais* needed to win friends and influence people. Don't laugh. This was the directive from their President. Having been a soldier himself, he wasn't ignorant of what was happening on the ground, the potential of his troops for mayhem. But he knew terror and a cowed population weren't enough. He badly needed collaborators to legitimise the regime in the international forum. It would also make their task easier within Danu. In short, he needed a puppet. That was an indigenous *malai* concept, by the way: puppetry was a national art form, both the solid puppets and the silhouette puppets of their shadow theatre. One of the chief touristic glories of the picturesque land of this subtle and sensitive people. There was one such to hand: Abdullah, the leader of the Amalgamationists. In turn, to strengthen his gubernatorial platform, he picked a Vice and two Assistants, the former being superior to the latter. No. 1 was a crony from the Amalgamationists, No.2 was a man called Joaquim Soares.

We'd see Soares about the ravaged town, walking with the *malai* officers, those of Rebus's rank or superior. There was going to be regular, rapid rotation of both commanders and men, but that we didn't know then. Soares was doing his patent best to ingratiate, to get on a personal, pally relationship with them of favours performed and returned. Talk about body language! He was perpetually bent over, nodding his head vigorously or cocking it to one side to give the speaker his instant, undivided attention. These high-ranking *malais*, they didn't give a flying fuck for him – not as a civilian alien, and it showed in the way they'd wave him silent or walk away while he was talking, or close the group to exclude him. He'd stand kicking his heels while they conferred, trying to save his dignity by making notes on a pad, or consulting his watch for the benefit of the Danuese. He didn't let the generals see him doing this. He didn't want them to think he was chivvying them, after all. The Danuese were careful with Soares, though. They didn't allow themselves to be caught looking too long. They weren't sure how long or how bitter his memories were, but presumed to endow him with their own worst instincts. As a Bacalhau man, he didn't like the people of the bigger town much, anyway. But I'll give him credit. He only selected two or three of his worst enemies for retribution and he tried to moderate the early excesses of the *malai* military. Because of their President's directives they couldn't ignore him totally. He had a jeep initially but then they reckoned it was too good for him; so, without leaving their stooge wheel-less, they reappropriated their vehicle to give him something with less than four tyres. It was a motor-bike.

A Yamaha.

I'll swear to God it was mine. The number plate had been removed so I couldn't be totally sure but I was near as damn it certain. Who took it on invasion day, I'll never know. Probably someone fleeing for their life or – I like to think – maybe a FAKOUM trooper commandeering it to get up to the mountains to fight another day. I don't begrudge anyone a joy-ride even. But to watch the *malais'* errand boy buzzing about his chores on my toy was to know the deepest chagrin.

Yesterday my ball-cocks and cisterns. Today my transport. Tomorrow ... my body? My life?

One day it got too much for me. Soares had parked the Yamaha outside the crèche. He'd visit once a week. Just because he'd been IP and was now a collaborator didn't mean he was all bad, although it was impossible for me to see that then. He probably really did want to help Dr Maria's kids, many of whom were now foundlings and orphans, but I guess he was still a politician as well. He thought patting a few bottoms wouldn't hurt. Rosa wouldn't even see him. That former FAKOUM stalwart hated him. But Dr Maria was on terms of cold civility with Soares. She'd never been an ideologue, even if her friends had been 100 per cent FAKOUM-ites, and that decent woman's ordinary comportment was one of a sarcasm and disdain so impartially meted out that to include Soares in it made him no exception. He could be grateful for the put-downs which came his way from her.

He was in the building when I arrived. I arrived on foot and hot and dusty and perspiring and mad. The sight of the bike was the last straw. I determined to confirm my suspicions once for all. I marched over to the machine. Since I'd last seen it, if it was it, and now I wasn't so sure, the bike had got a little beaten up. The front mud-guard was bent and the wires to the lamp hadn't been showing, but then you'd expect that from the treatment it had probably received over the last several weeks. Look for what was there before. I knew the brake-squeeze on the right handle-bar was always a little stiff, slower than the left; so I tried it. They were *both* stiff as hell. Frustratingly inconclusive because it was perfectly possible for the left handle-bar to have seized up as well. I unscrewed the cap on the gas-tank. What I was expecting to find, I don't know. I hadn't actually scratched my name on the inside. He had half a tank slopping about inside there. Busy guy.

At that moment a violent hand seized me by the shoulder. I just about puked up my heart. As I turned, I cringed, expecting a rifle-butt in the face. But my hands were also across my gut, against the eventuality of some bayonet's shrewd thrust. They liked to pork you to blood the magic kris. But it was a Danuese. As yet Soares had no *malai* soldiers attached to him; his bodyguards were old IP heavies, now bereft of firearms. This goon had the dagger on a shoulder lanyard, which Rebus allowed them. The three-ply golden cord made it more official, I guess, when they stuck you.

Being a *mestizo* with the vices of two races he'd been chewing betel and also smelt of garlic, like the old colonial administrators after a productive siesta, but there was nothing of imperial benevolence about this thug even though he spoke the metropolitan tongue. 'Son of a whore,' he said, pressing his hairy face close to my smooth, startled one. 'What fuck's business are you about?' Of course, I now began to regret my stupidity, but at the same time I felt relief that it wasn't a *malai* who'd caught me. I was careful not to show this; the situation could be awkward but manageable.

I thought so.

But I'd not banked on what I carried being brought into the balance.

'What shit is this, you pansy Chinaman?' I didn't take it personally. I was obviously just a specimen, so far as race was concerned, and if he was accurate on both counts, the last accusation was just a fluke. Not so much even that – the metropolitan culture, while basically Atlantic rather than Mediterranean, still partook of that Latin uncertainty of gender which expressed itself in exaggerated displays of virility. 'Queer' or 'pansy' were standard terms of abuse. How right you are, my friend, I thought.

But I was in deep trouble. I had three packets of sugar with me.

I'd already braced myself for a scolding from Maria. She didn't like me bringing that particular commodity. She wouldn't dignify it by calling it a foodstuff – 'empty calories' was the expression she used, which I immediately appreciated as a description though, personally, as Adolph Ng, I was somewhat dismayed by this reception for my daring generosity. She preferred KLIM, flour, soya, rice. However, as I pointed out, beggars were not in a position to be choosers, and what there was in abundance at the officers' mess was sugar. They had a shocking sweet tooth, the *malai*: syrupy purple or turquoise drinks with shaved ice and red beans, lethal sago puddings, even the satay and chili sauces were sweetened with a liberal hand.

Well, the pansy Chinaman had sugar with him. And Soares' goon leaped to but one conclusion when he saw me with the gas cap in one hand and a bag of sugar in the other. When he had time to think about it, his face lit up. He started to look cheerful at the thought of what would happen to me and what his own alertness had forestalled.

'You're a saboteur, Chinaman,' he said.

Now, what *sang-froid* I'd mustered on seeing I was dealing with a Danuese and not a *malai* dissolved. When I saw the low, crafty expression on his face, the pathetic self-congratulation, I didn't know whether to laugh or cry.

'Sabotage' was a bad word. Saboteurs figured frequently in Rebus's threatening edicts. He actually believed in them.

'No, you're wrong,' I said. I was trying not to show panic.

His face clouded over, as if I was personally inconveniencing him by not being what he knew I was. I think I was spoiling a beautiful dream about his own prospects. He extended two fingers and cocked his thumb, levelling it at my head. 'Pow!' he said. He hadn't bothered to unsheath his dagger. We both knew it was the *malais* who counted; like a dumb giant, they loomed over our little encounter. He wasn't in the position of bully so much as tell-tale, though I'm sure this fink had made his bones in the Civil War. By executing helpless prisoners, I reckoned. How this would have ended, I don't know. I wasn't sure whether the best course of action was to hit him over the head and throw the sugar in his face before hightailing it, or to offer to suck his cock. Those hairy types could be surprisingly amenable sometimes, and, after what he'd called me, it should hardly faze him. Fortunately, I had to adopt neither of these courses of utter extremity, for, like the ministering angel she wasn't, Dr Nolasco da Silva appeared with great appositeness from the crèche in the company of Soares himself. Now that girl was one of the quickest thinkers on her size-three feet that you could hope to meet. Generally, I'd had cause to lament this sharp-wittedness, but this time Maria did me proud. Without betraying by the smallest change of expression or faltering in manner her instant appreciation of whatever mess I'd gotten myself into, she snapped: 'What's kept you, Ng? You should have been here an hour since.' She'd had no idea I was going to turn up.

The goon saw his leader and smirked. But before he had time to disclose his nut-blackened teeth and tittle-tattle on me, Maria was relieving me of my white packages. 'You must tell Major Rebus what a great man he is,' she said smoothly. 'Senhor Soares, would you be so kind?' And she had the sublime effrontery to load him with the sugar.

'We have many diabetic children, you know.'

With good grace, Soares undertook the peon's task of

carrying in the deliveries. 'Look, everyone, I'm not too proud to stoop to help my fellow Danuese,' his whole manner proclaimed. Thus we left the goon with his stained mouth open and Maria had made Soares himself the agent of my deliverance. Inside, we were exchanging civilities – the smell of piss pretty bad – when I felt the gas-cap still in my hand. Unconsciously, I'd been clenching it, like some talisman or prayer-necklace, but I had the presence of mind not to drop it as the hot chestnut it had undoubtedly become.

'Is anything the matter?' asked Soares with an assumed concern. 'It's the heat,' Dr Maria said crisply. 'The man has got heat-stroke at midday to help our children.' She went to soak a cloth.

Soares was starting to fidget. He wanted to get on and, really, the kids had made the place smell terrible.

I said, 'O, Senhor, I forget. This was on the ground as I came by. Could it be from your motor-bike?'

'*Ai, bom!* It must be from the gasoline reservoir. A thousand thanks.'

'The pleasure is entirely mine, Senhor.'

Soares blew on it. To lose something like that in Danu, even before these times, was a headache. Such dedicated little items were irreplaceable, as I had cause to know. Spare parts didn't exist. You never threw anything away.

When Maria returned she led me to a chair and Soares made his excuses. I had to overcome the desire to run away out of the back door, which would have been to heap folly upon my earlier idiocy. They spoke outside for quite a while, and I was glad as hell to hear him kick-start the bike and go.

When Maria heard what I'd done she cursed me for a fool. It made me feel better, in a strange way. Like many prudent people, I liked to be thought reckless from time to time. She smiled when some scrap of information occurred to me as I was leaving: 'Isn't diabetes a disease of later life?'

And it was a sour smile I got: 'They say a great shock can provoke it, Adolph. Be careful. A little knowledge is always a dangerous thing.'

When I got home, I realised I hadn't thanked her.

TWELVE

I CAN ACCOMMODATE MYSELF TO ANYTHING. By now I'm sure I don't need to tell you that. But I've never been destined to stay on the same course for long. I don't think I am guilty of glamorising myself.

For a few weeks the *malais* had found it quiet in the hills. That had been the reasonable assumption from the small number of wounded taken to the dock. We'd learned why we'd stopped seeing any of their dead there. The injured got taken to a hospital-ship for transport the odd 100 miles down the coast to the big town on the *malai* half of the island. The dead were flown in green body bags back to the capital on their main island, a thousand miles away. They landed at a remote Air Force base. All this was to keep the extent of their casualties secret. Someone had seen the lines of bags at the airstrip outside Danu. For the same reason, their wounded didn't get to fly home. They wanted to keep it quiet. If they could have, they would have kept them stabilised on the hospital ship without landing at all, but that would have been bad for the morale of the others. The *malais* weren't that stupid. They didn't have a snooping, out of control press. It did what the government told it.

Our conclusion was that either FAKOUM were up against the wall or the *malais* were avoiding contact. I thought it was the former.

Great minds think alike. It was what Osvaldo thought we were thinking.

We weren't to be allowed to think that.

When he came, I was tucked up in my bed at the Oscar Tango X-Ray. You'd have thought I would have been safe enough in there. After all, I'd slept through a Civil War in my bedroom, the night the IP went for the FAKOUM arsenal. But this time the bastards came right out for me.

I took it personal, as they say.

In fact, they were after Rebus, but the old fox wasn't there.

I wasn't sleeping well. I was under some strain – you'll believe me, won't you – and my belly rumbled nights from hunger as well. So I was lying on my back, playing with myself, when I heard Chico's chain rattle. Now that was unusual, for the monkey changed character after dark. All the mischief left him to be replaced by antique terrors: prowling leopards, pythons. He'd climb the tree to his little house, whimper, and shrink. Where by day he'd spitefully defend the territory defined by the radius of his chain, he'd flee at night. Through the sliding mosquito screen on my window I could hear pretty well. His misery concerned me. Bouncing and stiff, I went to the window to see if there was a dog on the loose. Chico would make a nice meal in these straitened times. But there was nothing.

I returned to my amusing pastime, about the only consolation I had left these days when I came to think about it. And I did, often. About thirty yanks on the bell-rope later, the fairy lights we left on in the courtyard went out. Locked into a generating rhythm of my own, I was aware the dependable red Kawasaki was still thumping. The fuses were going to get blown in quick succession in that case. My toes were just curling backwards when my door opened. I was momentarily hopeful, though somewhat rueful as to the timing.

But it was armed men in FAKOUM uniforms, which even in the dim light showed deterioration from the parade crispness of Independence Day. I threw the sheet over myself in a hurry, I'll tell you. At once a parang flashed. 'No, God, I'm not a *malai*,' I babbled.

'Shut up, Chinaman,' hissed the first one of the three, 'or you'll get it.' I sat up, knees to my chest, for a whole variety of reasons.

'Where's their chief?' the one with the parang asked. I could make out corporal's stripes. 'He's not here anymore,' I answered, unsatisfactorily, for he put a knee on the bed and took me by the hair. The parang glinted, just below my chin, but I was more worried about the tearing in my scalp. 'I'm telling you the truth,' I enunciated as clearly and as calmly as I could through the mistreatment. He gave the hair one last wrench before releasing me. I wiped tears from my eyes. As frightened as I was, I patted my head to check if he'd left me bald. It felt thinner on the crown. The bastard.

'Where is he now?'

'He's in town at the Customs House. He shares it with the Air Force Commander.'

'You take us there.'

Oh, shit. 'Don't you know the way? You're a Danuese, too.' Panic fear made me speak with an audacity I regretted as soon as the words had left my mouth, but I didn't get porked for it. In fact the guy got the chance to make what he obviously thought was some kind of grim joke. 'We're tourists, Chinaman,' he said. 'Get dressed.'

This I did with as great a slowness as I dared. We were going through the door – they made me carry my rubber thongs – when I thought I had better mention this: 'Some of his bodyguards are still quartered here.' I was motivated less by patriotism (in fact, as you may surmise, not at all) or even by the desire for revenge, than simple self-preservation. I didn't want my rescuers/kidnappers – whatever they turned out to be eventually – to be caught with their pants down by Rebus's boys. Figuratively, I mean, not literally like yours truly. To say the least, it would have been a compromising situation if I survived the encounter, let alone, as most likely, got cut down in the cross-fire.

This piece of intelligence had a bristling effect on them. I was tense, but they'd stopped being nervous when they'd found they had just me to deal with, instead of Rebus. Now they started to sweat again. I got better treatment as soon as they became more respectful of the exigencies of the situation.

'Where are they?'

'Second and first floors, west wing.'

'How many in a room?'

'They have a room each.' And so does everyone who wants to at the O. T. X-Ray, I restrained myself from commenting.

We went down the washerwomen's stairs, then across the courtyard and up again by the service stairs of the west wing, instead of going directly across the long corridor. There was no cover in its inordinate length and the floor-boards could go off like a starter's pistol. Amazing how thoughtful fear can make you. In the courtyard were more than a dozen others. FAKOUM had never been the greatest spit and polish outfit but these guys looked like scarecrows. Their G3s, though, were clean and had the look of perfect maintenance about them. I didn't recognise any of the men.

Rebus's thugs slept the sound sleep of the unjust. They were masters of the town; they'd never encountered the slightest resistance. They hadn't had to go out into the hills on those unpopular patrols. Although they knew an enemy existed out in the boondocks, they hadn't actually been shot at, felt their bowels melt as the rounds cracked overhead. And that made all the difference. One thing to know a fact, quite another to feel it. They'd gone careless, and soft, I think, they'd been a long while.

It was brutal but quick.

They hit all five rooms simultaneously, three men to a room, while I lurked nervously in the corridor. Except for what was going on in the rooms, it could have been normal; me hovering politely outside, maybe discreetly insinuating that it was time a check was honoured, respectful of privacy, while the guests vacated. The difference was that there was less noise than with an ordinary departure. From rooms 10 and 16 there wasn't so much as a squeak, with those teams out in seconds. A sleeper's babble came from 14, then silence followed by a little creaking. But the occupant of 18 – who was their master-sergeant – called out, angrily, without fear, before they got to him, and he woke up the man next door in 19, who did cry in surprise. I think the sergeant believed he was being inconvenienced by a servant and died in ignorance, but before they despatched the last *malai* there was a scuffle and stifled shouts, a big thump, as of a body hitting the floor, and smaller, quicker raps as of feet kicking. It didn't take much longer than ten seconds. I expected them

141

to look serious. They didn't. When they emerged, some were grinning. Not the corporal. I wondered if he'd been a seminarian in the old days.

Rebus's bodyguards had a truck, which we piled into. I wasn't happy, felt we were compounding our misdeeds. Crazy! As if we could do worse to the *malai!* I guess I possess an over-healthy regard for property. It was a lot safer than walking along that road into town, cut down the time. We were actually less conspicuous roaring along than as a silent file of armed men. We had already passed through the outskirts, perhaps two kilometres away from Rebus's new HQ, when things went awry. From the docks there came an explosion, not as loud as the *malais'* aerial bombs, but it was followed by another bang, and then all the windows of the buildings came out, the net drapes billowing after them, and the road was showered with spears and triangles of glass. Immediately afterwards, over the cheerful carillon in the road, was the roar of a greater explosion, which we actually seemed to feel through the wheels of the truck. The corporal cursed in his native dialect, while the others held on to their hats. I actually started to feel better, though. By one of those strange tricks of association, it reminded me of an idyllic Canadian December when I'd gone on a sleigh-ride with Annie Laval, the bells jingling, and snow crackling much like the shards of glass were now crunching under the tyres of our truck. It was all in the open. There wasn't the dread of discovery; we'd been found out. Or rather FAKOUM had shown their hand too early. One thing about Osvaldo and Arsenio was their punctuality. You could bet on it. It was what had made them superior in Danu, and they had insisted on it in matters civil and military. Now the charges set by the demolition party had gone off at the naval magazines bang on cue. But they hadn't taken into account the fact that the hit team had been unable to get to Rebus yet. As well as the destructive effect, the charges had been intended as a diversion to cover the retreat of the would-be assassins. It was the one time a little procrastination and delay would have helped, that Danuese inefficiency would have proved benign. Instead the game was blown wide open.

On we thundered. The shortest route out to the hills lay through town. The driver trod on the gas pedal with more than usual Danuese recklessness, throwing us from side to side as we hurtled across the Praça, weapons, men, and equipment flying everywhere. I hoped the safety catches were on. As we got to the die-straight roads of the newer parts of Danu, the men lined the sides, propping their G3s on the slats. A roadblock appeared in the headlights' beam. Men were running everywhere, like crazed moths: some spilling out of a guard-house, pulling up their pants and buckling webbing, others diving into weapons-pits. Our guys opened up simultaneously without a word of command, banging away freely with their G3s, blinding us all, despite the flash-suppressors. Cartridge cases clinked on the metal floor, one sending a sharp surge of fear through me as it hit my leg. I tell you, I was shit-scared. I couldn't stop watching, though, my fingers gripping the slats and an eye pressed to the gap. Our guys were missing an awful lot. I wasn't seeing any *malais* go down, but then nothing seemed to have hit us either.

'Hold tight,' the corporal shouted but his men kept blazing away and the heavy truck had generated sufficient momentum to sweep away the road-barrier with ease. Then we were rushing along an empty road with only the odd angry shot coming after us. We'd got round a bend before they could open up with the machine-gun, its vain chatter receding all the while behind. We were starting to climb, the driver changing down with an execrable grinding, going slower and slower until in the end, slugging doggedly up the increasing gradient, we seemed hardly to be moving, proceeding with deafening toilsomeness at less than walking pace. I had a brainwave. 'Let me out, I'll walk – lessen the load,' I yelled into the corporal's ear. He looked at me evilly, showing the blade of his parang. 'No, you don't, Chinaman.' I could barely hear him, and we were all choking now in the thick fumes of the exhaust. The headlamps showed nothing but a void on either side and a golden column of insects attracted by the light. I was torn between anxiety about the glare and noise betraying our whereabouts to pursuers and fear for what might happen if the driver had nothing to see his way by. We were starting to go downhill, along the edges of those fearful precipices Rosa used to skirt with such insouciance, and the engine lost its note of agony. I looked at my watch: 4.30 a.m. In a moment my fears were confirmed – out of the frying-pan into the fire – as the corporal leaned over into the cab to tell the driver to turn off the engine and lights. We began to coast downhill, soundlessly except for the wind and the faint whine of the tyres. But there was a good reason for this. They knew of the post out here, commanding the first pass into the mountains.

These *malais* were in a state of readiness, having seen and heard the shooting and explosions in the coastal plain below, but they weren't expecting a vehicle and one, moreover, in the colours of their military police. FAKOUM had cut the wires coming up here and it was notoriously a radio dead spot. Well, thank God, because we still took a good burst on the approach, which knocked out the radiator without hurting the driver and then some rounds in the back as we turned on the engine and gunned up the road. Some of the FAKOUM guys were hit. I heard them cry out, and the others rushed to the tail-board, returning heavy fire. Then there was a great whoosh and sizzling 80 metres behind among the *malai,* night turning into white and purple day back there, sparks and clean, steamy smoke shooting up and sideways like a chief's feathered head-dress. We heard screams, short, raucous, and then two figures, alight, rolling in the road. The Corporal had dropped a couple of white phosphorus grenades from the lorry as we passed. The FAKOUM boys interrupted their fusillade to cheer and with a spattering of last shots, we were gone.

There wasn't much life left in the truck but we pressed on some few kilometres more. They were always going to ditch the vehicle anyway. We were bound for mountain paths which even ponies found difficult. At first light we abandoned the vehicle by the roadside, first throwing a torch of lighted straw into the tank. It went up impressively. During the drive a man had died and another had become unconscious. Another groaned quietly to himself. I think he was trying not to be a nuisance. They were good troops, the regular FAKINTIL, which was to say the military wing of FAKOUM. I wasn't so pleased when I drew the detail of helping to carry the wounded guy. I wasn't getting any more reconciled to this chore, whether for *malais* or FAKOUM. In fact, the corpse I'd carried at the jetty had been a lot easier; it had been dead weight (forgive me) but you didn't have to be solicitous. Every time I slipped now or bumped their comrade on rocks or thorns, I drew black looks from the rest of the party. As if I was doing it deliberately.

To add to my woes, the sun was getting up. Poor, burdened, sweating Chinaman. This was not my role in island life. I wiped the salt drops from my forehead. They stung the eyes. I didn't know if I was crying. I asked for a swig from someone's canteen and was refused. Now tears did come, at the unfairness.

At midday we stopped in the shade of rocks. They'd cached water here on the down-trip, and I finally got a warm, plastic-redolent drink. I only got it because they didn't want me collapsing and I was useful.

In the afternoon my man died. He'd never complained much, superb stoicism which shamed me. He was a mountain man, not a town Danuese. I never knew exactly when he had gone. He didn't go cold or stiff in that time, but, man, he was gray. I think he bled to death internally. As for me, my arms felt they were floating up in the air, as if I could no longer control their blissful lightness, when, in actuality, they were hanging at my sides. The relief was joyous.

If I'd thought we'd get to our destination in a day I was wrong. The night was worse than the day. Instead of thirst, cold. More painful than the rays of the sun – the bugs. My eyes were so swollen in the morning I had to squint to see. We kept climbing, out of the savannah, way up to the edge of the tree-line, over paths it was impossible to recognise as such, along dried-up river beds, through gullies, skirting cliffs, over vast, rotting tree-trunks. And on day five we arrived.

It was in the forest. We'd descended again (more treacherous than the ascent) from the razor-back peaks of the centre to the other side of the island. The huts, the fires, the drying-posts, the racks of weapons, the platforms, the pits, the tunnel entrances – these I registered superficially and instantly. What I had eyes for was the man perched on an up-turned wooden bucket in the middle of the clearing. It was Osvaldo.

Standing talking to him, with her back to me, was a woman. As she turned, I saw her face. It was Dr Maria.

THIRTEEN

MY POSITION WITH THE GUERRILLAS rapidly lost its ambiguity. This was thanks to my previous acquaintance with the FAKOUM leaders. I'd been carried off half as prisoner, half as guide, maybe something of a hostage. They didn't have the leisure or the opportunity to beat me up on the way but I felt tainted by the unspoken accusation of collaborator. What was I doing with half a dozen of the worst *malais* in Danu under my hospitable roof?

Osvaldo set me at my ease. I got full rations and a good hut and the men took me at their general's estimation. The women, as women do, liked me for what I was. I'm nobody's threat. I'd sit and watch from the bank of the stream as they did their washing, slapping the clothes on flat rocks. They'd make saucy remarks, with their skirts drawn up over their strong brown thighs, apparently under the impression that I didn't know the mountain dialect. I'd call back, more rudely than them. Once, following some badinage, when they'd offered to throw me in after I'd ordered them to do my laundry, I stood up and stripped to my shorts, hurling each article of clothing down amidst the shrieks and splashing. It was difficult to imagine there was anything out of the ordinary happening in Danu, that we were outlaws hiding in the hills and there were tortures and killings going on down below.

'He'll be useful to us,' I overheard Osvaldo saying once, as I was summoned to the command hut. That was over-kind. I was a useless extra mouth to feed, if the truth was known. Maybe Osvaldo thought he would put me on the shelf, like a strange tool, against the day when some task would turn up for which I was uniquely fitted. More likely, he was justifying himself to his followers without appearing to do so. That cat had nothing to learn about the wiles of leadership.

Dr Maria had lobbied in my favour, I daresay. Now *she* was useful.

When we compared notes I discovered they'd targeted her for abduction, liberation – call it what you will. Unlike me, she hadn't been accidentally swept up in the course of events. They needed a doctor up there, badly. It wasn't so much with health and hygiene, though she was to contribute there as well, but with wounds. Osvaldo had seen a lot of his men perish, he thought unnecessarily, because they had only the most rudimentary first aid. In many instances limb wounds had terminated fatally. It was terrible for morale. Dr Maria was able to save the two surviving casualties in my group. That was her first job – she'd come in just eight hours before us. They'd allowed her to snatch a few personal effects in the way of clothes and toiletry, which was more than they'd let yours truly do, and they'd raided *malai* military stores for bandages and a few drugs, mostly chloroquine, aspirin, and basic antiseptics, as well as suturing thread and needles. That was it – a meagre pharmacopoeia, but it was who administered it that counted. What Maria could do, and this was most important, was extract bullets and shrapnel. She had the skill and nerve to cut, probe, and excise the offending objects, if the men had the fortitude to endure the operation. They didn't, of course. It could be horrible. I was detailed to be her orderly and I fainted during an arm

147

amputation. Fortunately, nobody else could stand watching it either and I recovered fairly quickly to see Dr Maria Nolasco da Silva imperturbably stitching the flaps while two ex-seminarians held the groaning man down.

She'd done a theoretical course in gunshot wounds with the military surgeon three years previously but the only case she'd seen, a negligent discharge on the range, had simply blown off the conscript's toe.

'The problem with these high-velocity bullets is the destruction of the tissue,' she told me, while I poured antiseptic over those shapely Chinese fingers. 'It's not like the old bullets. When these things hit they do terrible damage. The round has got such tremendous energy to dissipate it sets up hydraulic shock in the cells, one passing on to the other, and everything is destroyed. The man yesterday...' – I remembered him, poor bastard – '...had a cavity in his forearm you could put batteries in.'

'Like dum dum bullets?'

'No, worse. Much worse. If these hit a bone in the arm the whole limb comes off.'

'Thanks for telling me.'

'Wound production, my friend,' said an amiable voice. It was Osvaldo coming up on us unnoticed. He smiled. For all his force of personality, he didn't set out to intimidate. 'Some good brains have devoted their lives to it. Our tool is the Heckler and Koch G3.'

'That I do know.'

'Well, it's a German gun and it fires standard NATO 7.62 mm ball which is a heavier, slower round than the Americans now use in the M-16. We can expect to see that in *malai* hands one day soon. It actually fires 5.56mm, so they can carry twice as many rounds as our men for the same weight. And the lighter round can still inflict terrible wounds, especially if the bullet has been made to tumble, say, on a leaf or twig during its trajectory. Easy enough in the jungle, doctor.'

Maria's face was blank of emotion, of participation in Osvaldo's easy smile as he shared his sorry science. I wasn't

148

sure whether it was professional *sang-froid*, disapproval, or a registering of her resentment for being abducted. So many times you couldn't work Maria out. She was a closed book, even to Rosa and me.

Osvaldo said, 'They'll live with you to look after them, some that we would have lost.'

'Pass my gloves.'

'Of course, the 7.62 mm bullet guarantees a better one hit kill ratio. It's a much more powerful round, especially the German manufactured one, which is the next best thing to an explosive bullet. But then which makes better military sense? To eliminate one man by killing him or to take out three? I mean the one you have hit and the two men to carry him away. It's more troublesome to look after a living casualty than to walk away from a corpse.'

'You sound like an accountant or a time and motion consultant,' I said.

'We could do with more of both in Danu. The small things can be the most cost-effective, you know. Look at this.'

It was a green metal sphere, about the size of a hen's egg. The round wire loop through the release lever showed what it was. 'It looks far too small to be a grenade, though,' I said.

'That's exactly what it is,' Osvaldo replied. 'It's tiny, but it'll prove just as effective as the big ones if you know how and when to use it.'

'Looks like a bird laid it,' I said.

'Put some grease on it and try,' Osvaldo laughed. 'In fact, that would be a good place to hide it. What is your professional opinion, doctor?'

'Get out of the way, you're in my light.'

Osvaldo sauntered off. He didn't seem to mind Maria speaking to him in this way. She was always a law unto herself. First the *malais,* now him.

The rainy season was just getting under way. That put an end to campaigning, for both sides. Despite the modern equipment the *malais* could call on, the planes, choppers, four-wheel drive, it was impossible to progress over the terrain in that weather. Even tracked vehicles had to admit defeat. Ordinarily, it was difficult. When the skies opened, you could forget it for three months. This was rain that seemed to usurp the medium of air. It wasn't drops coming down, however heavily, but the sea collapsing on your head. You wondered if you could breathe. And it persisted, day in, day out, from sunset to dawn. It washed out the paths and tracks. The metalled roads couldn't take it either. Landslides blocked the way every 100 metres. Sometimes the road just vanished. Pebbly paths where insects buzzed in the brutal sunshine underwent a character transformation, revealed as the ferocious, boulder-rolling torrents they truly were. Bridges would be there one day, gone the next, without even a girder or plank to mark their position. The accumulation of days did the damage. After six weeks of incessant downpour everywhere was isolated. And it still went on!

Osvaldo's timing had been perfect. The raid was the last word in an argument that could not be renewed until the next calendar year. It left the town with a reminder which could not be obliterated and the *malais* unable to counter.

On the mountain we sat in our huts, oiled the guns, planned and waited.

Food was easily the biggest concern. Not guns or bullets. One thing FAKOUM didn't need was weapons. Osvaldo disposed of a prodigious arsenal of small arms. These were expertly preserved and cached.

I'd noticed gardens all round the camp, each with its rows of beans, gourds, tomatoes, tubers, or maize. Osvaldo had concentrated on making his people self-sufficient. There'd been discontent, I learned, among the battle-hardened Africa veterans, who thought of themselves as warriors, not 'pansy' gardeners (that word again). Osvaldo had been forced to set the example himself, painstakingly cultivating his patch with digging-stick and seed bag. It had worked. They'd stored enough to get through the season, just. What lay ahead after that was another matter, but then it always had been for the mountain Danuese with their precarious lives.

It was a time of rest and of repair, traditionally. Also of recreation in those care-worn existences. The men sat in the huts, smoked, told stories. The children played. But now it wasn't with leaf whistles, spinning-tops and whipcord, or bamboo flutes, but mock shoot-outs and ambushes with carved guns. They lurked under trees, took cover in dark corners of huts, sprang out from under slithery rocks, rushed from caves, shouted from behind tangles of roots. Pow! Pow! Bang, you're dead! And then ran away, glistening with the rain, laughing, frolicking. Osvaldo encouraged them. He didn't have the same rapport with kids that Arsenio had enjoyed, but they responded to him. They didn't see the dark side of the adult, just the tall, smiling man who was also the leader. He believed it was never too soon to start training a soldier. Or a priest. That was the influence of the Jesuits on him. The only one I could discern, as a matter of fact. He thought of a war that would last for generations. I could already see that, though it was something he wanted to keep to himself, not wanting to discourage anyone else. The troops hadn't wanted civilians about them, not kids for sure. Women, yes. Sex they craved. Combat sharpened that need: the dread of death inspired a lust for the sensation of life. After battle, in the relief of delivery, the hormones rushing round the system had to be used. It's a common thing. Osvaldo knew it from Africa. He didn't want his own men raping. And the price of the women for the troops was their acquiescence in the children.

I'd see the kids in a ring around Osvaldo as he lectured them. He and the children were the only ones who didn't seem to mind getting wet. Even in the few weeks after my arrival I had noticed a greater sophistication about the games. You'd get bushwhacked and be unable to get away for intent-faced boys shouting: *'Dukka, dukka!'* There'd be a little stop group to prevent your escape, two killing groups laying down enfilading fire, trip-wires that pitched you face-down in the mud (these were meant to represent boobytrap wires). He'd divided the kids into proper-sized fire-teams, squads, and platoons as well, giving them unit designations.

Basic fire and manoeuvre, flanking assaults, the immediate counter-attack into an ambush, were the least sophisticated of the tactics I saw 10-year-olds putting into practice.

Osvaldo didn't miss my observation – I wouldn't call it interest. I was pressed into service. I daren't object, not if I didn't want my full daily ration sticking in my gullet. Thus I learned the craft of war at the same time as the children of Danu.

One morning they went too far. For the first time in weeks, the rain had stopped for a few hours. The sun had come out, but steam rose off the jungle. Visibility was only marginally better than when it had been pelting. On the edge of the vegetation the kids had formed a line. The vapour made it difficult to see. I thought they had their hands up. A smaller number of kids paraded in front of them. They levelled their wooden replicas. I heard the familiar incantation. And as they swung and worked their tongues staccato, the line fell like dominoes, one after the other, rolling, then lying perfectly still. I ran out. Before I reached them they had jumped up, laughing, and run off into the jungle, into the green dankness and swirling mist. There were three of the youngest, six- or seven-years old, whom I hadn't remarked. They stood on the edge of shallow pits, freshly dug, by themselves I should imagine, the spoil around the lip, and on the cue of Pah! from a trio of gun-wielding older boys, fell backwards on to the soft wet earth of their graves. I grabbed the oldest, a 12-year-old, and began to lecture him severely, but he broke free and led their escape, shouting exultantly, 'Osvaldo! Osvaldo!'

I don't know why I found it so sick. I'd seen the real thing and this was just play-acting. But it was excruciating to watch in company. I might have left them to it, if I'd been spying on them alone. When I came back Maria had on her most sardonic look. Her distinctive lips were really made for that expression. She said, 'I heard your type made the best scoutmaster.' I could have strangled her.

There was a history to piece together before I could participate in the group. Their recent past, the experiences they had shared, the trials they had undergone, were closed to me. Nobody was volunteering anything, either. My hints went ignored. When I asked straight out, faces closed. They behaved just like Chinese.

Maria shrugged when I mentioned it to her. She didn't care. That was the science background for you; it reminded me of people I'd known in Toronto. They were content in the moment; its significance was sufficient. I had to know, ascertain my spot in the continuum, if I was to be at ease with myself and confident of behaving correctly.

They certainly pumped me. The hours I spent repeating myself to Osvaldo! My excited monologues, my chatter of the early debriefings became filled with pauses, longer and longer, in which I listened to the raindrops rattling off the thatch. Osvaldo was as grave and attentive the 33rd time as he had been the first. He liked to keep notes but had the grace not to refer openly to them in my presence. Once or twice he'd pick me up on inconsistencies or contradictions and I'd explain why they weren't such. He was very clear-cut in his way of looking at things: matters were a certain way or they weren't. There was no room for ambiguity. And certainly something couldn't be two things at the same time. I don't think like that. By way of refuting a single point I'd try to lay bare the limitations of his whole way of thinking, but he'd steer me clear of the context and back to the particular issue. Like Maria, he thought things could be understood in isolation. Courteous as he was, he'd often leave me rueful.

So he learned of the shootings on the jetty, of Pereira's valiant good deed on that day, of Rosa's rape, of the warships in the harbour, the scarcities, the new *malai* units, and the length of their rotations. He didn't ask about Sonia Ferreira. He already knew her fate and he cut me short with a savage movement when I alluded to it. He seemed more interested in my account of Arsenio's last moments. All he had known for certain was that his comrade was dead. Arsenio's bodyguards must have been killed themselves shortly afterwards, for they'd never been seen again. The *malais* must have captured the jeep, rather than discovered it abandoned.

And what did I get in return? I learned Martinho was still alive. This pleased me. He had been at the seminary when the first landings occurred. Since his reconciliation with the Bishop, he'd taken to frequenting his old alumnus and, later, with the connivance of one of his ex-mentors – a true Jesuit cynic – established his office there. The FAKOUM CC member housed on Church premises! Castro in the Cathedral! 'He was on his knees when he saw the parachutes,' Osvaldo remarked with grim amusement. 'He must have thought they were angels.'

'Or manna,' I said. But the appositeness of my analogy, at least I thought so, for it had struck me instantly at the time, was lost on Osvaldo. He felt he was the only one who could speak of Martinho with less than reverence. I'm sure, as a product of the establishment on the hill himself, he must have known what manna was.

Well, Martinho had evidently stopped praying with some abruptness, run down towards town, thought better of it – even before he heard the first bombs – and hurried up the hill with the first cracks of small-arms fire spattering up from below like festival firecrackers. He was older and not as fit as Osvaldo, so he must have been panting by the time he got up to the seminary gardens again. He could sweat like a pig, too. I'd seen him do it. He stopped looking so goddamned holy then. He had the presence of mind to go back into his office – the courage, too, I suppose – and bring out an untidy sheaf of files which he dumped in the centre of the lawn before running back for more, picking up the ones he had dropped on the first trip. His old praeceptor came to his aid, wheezing, tripping over his black skirts, paper flying everywhere as the two middle-aged men crossed like industrious dung-beetles. They were lucky, as I remember, that it was a breezeless day. Neither of them smoked and it was quite difficult to find matches in the seminary but finally the priest came back with a spill from the kitchens to set off the contents of the first file. They were able to destroy the most important records, the register of members notably, and the details of the coffee account abroad, tending and building the blaze like a pair of Old Testament prophets. From the seminary you got a grandstand view of town: on that day of circling jets, explosions, duststorms. Finally, as the oil-tanks went up in that great orange ball, Martinho's nerve broke. Not waiting to see if their weight would extinguish the fire, he threw the remaining files on and fled to the hills with his saintly accomplice. Half a mile up the steep path they ran into armed men. Jumping into saw-edged grasses, Martinho ripped his hands but it was a FAKOUM group Osvaldo had sent to escort his brother to safety. And that was the only harm he'd come to on that terrible day.

I'd just missed him. A fortnight before Maria and I arrived he'd left camp to organise at the extreme eastern end of the island. He'd had to begin his journey before the rains made the tracks impassable. They'd heard nothing since but trusted his guides had got him there. Despite the close-lipped silence on their early days, I got the impression that Martinho wasn't missed.

The best hut in the camp, the thickest thatched, the driest – waterproof even after two and a half months of downpour – and the most closely guarded, was not Osvaldo's. It was the radio hut. This was their line to the world, via the Australian Northern Territory distress network, meant for the Flying Doctor. They could get word to the world through this – until the Australian government did the *malais* a favour and cut the line. After that, FAKOUM messages became more a matter of hit and miss. Typically, no one had told me about its existence. But there was no mistaking it the first time I heard the hisses and feline yowlings. They had to change frequencies very often. We were high but there were still other peaks intervening and, of course, at this time of year the atmospherics were atrocious. It sounded like a whole orchestra of lovelorn cats. Well, curiosity was what killed the cat and I'm nothing if not curious. A coward, but incorrigibly nosey. Taking courage in my hands, I directly approached the construction and just walked between the sentries. They weren't standing in the *malai* mode but sitting on their cans, resting the butts of the G3s against their balls. Betel, from the areca palms that grew so readily on the island, was a commodity that was never in short supply and their jaws worked monotonously. The spurt that shot across my path was no interdiction but simple uncouthness. I had such anomalous status. Everything seemed permitted me but nobody gave me respect. And even if I could get away with something at the time, I was never quite sure if I was inviolate from retribution. I'd call the condition, freedom. Its price was uncertainty.

There were two surprises for me when my eyes had adjusted to the interior. One, how small the set was for a transmitter. Two, the operator was the Danuese I'd last seen at the Marconi Centre on the day of the manna and Fiery Pillar. I didn't recognise him; it was for him to greet me. And the thumbs-up sign and grin were the same he'd given when I had walked in on Mabbeley and Ribeiro. He now had a frizzy beard and hair to his shoulders and the moccasins and smartly creased pale slacks of his Marconi days had become tattered shorts and sandals. The air of authority and calmness were the same, though. He was quite exemplary for a Danuese, this guy. They'd rigged up a generator powered by a bicycle, which sufficed for his purposes. A kid pedalled on his direction. I pretended to whip him. He had a somewhat cheeky rump. No one laughed. I guess they felt, howsoever small, no one's contribution should be mocked. I decided to restrain my various penchants, including the one for facetiousness. Suppose they cut my food dole for a good joke?

Just then Osvaldo entered the hut. I'm not sure if it was coincidence or if he had been alerted along the camp's effective grapevine. There undoubtedly existed a network of informants feeding in to the leader. It would have been excessive to call them spies on one another, but there was mutual surveillance. It was a real community, morale was high then, they had to pull together against the common threat – which was all the more why privacy was a dangerous notion. It was an Asian thing. You couldn't call it tale-bearing.

Osvaldo was tall enough to block the light. He was carrying his G3 on a sling over his shoulder, with tape over the barrel to stop rain getting down it.

'Making a phone call, Adolph?' he enquired.

I had to smile. 'Trunk or local?' I replied.

'International is what we prefer,' he said. Then: 'It's only the collect local calls which we discourage our guests from making.' Subtle bastard. He was playing Arsenio's old game of oblique remarks. I decided we could get on to dangerous ground if we were not careful. Dangerous for me. 'Osvaldo, I'm 100 per cent for FAKOUM and 101 per cent for you. You know that.'

'What I know is that political power grows out of the barrel of a gun.' Then he laughed. 'I've always liked you, Ng. It's good to have you with us. Come and talk with Maria.' He threw his arm round my shoulders and I accompanied him, somewhat sheepishly. But, out in the rain again, he appeared to remember something, waved me on, and turned back. When I looked round he was talking to the sentries and this time they were standing.

FOURTEEN

THE DOWNPOUR CEASED TO BE CONTINUOUS a fortnight later. You'd see the sun more than twice a week. The pattern became one of a fine morning, followed by a two-hour rain in the afternoon. Then the p.m. event became less reliable. Finally, it stopped happening. But travel was still difficult.

At the end of the month a group of guerrillas arrived in the camp. It was Martinho and his escort, with some of the FAKOUM scatterings they had succeeded in locating.

Osvaldo walked down the clearing with his arms spread. A little theatrical for my taste, but I saw Maria smiling without a hint of mockery. That surprised. The two brothers, physically so ill-assorted, the big, bony, bearded soldier and the little cleric, still rounded-looking even after the months of hardship, met and embraced. After they'd kissed each other on both cheeks, and Martinho was disentangling himself, Osvaldo, not to be denied, put his elder brother in a bear-hug and kissed him again. Probably wants to eat him, I thought gloomily. Belts had been tightened, as traditional, at the end of the rainy season. I actually wanted to pump Martinho by the hand – not kiss him, please – for his presence was a ray of light to me. Someone else in the camp who wasn't a man of blood, someone else from the Praça. Maria, of course, was in every sense the reverse of a man of blood, but there was no comfort in her brusque and unsentimental efficiency. Dear Martinho, with his hauteur and self-righteousness, as well as his undoubted kindness and probity, was in his small person a bridge – I hoped – of memory to a past of normalcy and safety, no matter that at the moment he was indistinguishable from the others in his camouflage pants and army smock, plastered with drying orange mud. 'Here I am, Martinho!' I wanted to shout. 'Look, it's me, Adolph Ng! The man of the world, the Honorary Secretary of the Literary Society of Danu, your friend!' But I didn't. I guess I knew better already. He passed by and his eyes ran over my expectant face, along with the others. He didn't miss who I was, he recognised me OK. But there was no double-take, surprise absent. Well, I couldn't help being hurt. Then I put myself in his shoes: he was returning after a long absence; many changes had occurred; he couldn't see the uniqueness or the recentness of my presence. I was just one of the many differences he found in the camp – all lumped together as one fact of existence, a simultaneous event, not separate sagas. After all, his whole life for four months had been just that of finding waifs and strays. One more was hardly remarkable.

Yet something had been lost, which even the unsimulated friendship and warmth of his later greeting couldn't make up. In his smile and handshake existed the trace of apology. All's well again, our eyes tried to say in reassurance to the other. But it wasn't.

Martinho had had a tough time of it. All through the wet, they'd had to keep moving. They'd never sheltered for longer than a week anywhere. As well as being physically taxing, it had been exposed, dangerous work. They'd had to enter strange villages as a matter of course to announce their presence in the area and to enquire as to the whereabouts of other FAKOUM parties. They had to advertise themselves. And even with patriotic Danuese and in the close season, it was risky to do that. Those months had taken their toll on Martinho's nerves. He'd acquired a tic below the right eye and there was a big patch of baldness in back of the frizz. Maybe the effect of a tonsure wasn't altogether displeasing to him. The method had been to send three men in to a settlement first, never more, never less. This was after they had surveyed the place covertly for a couple of days for signs of *malais* or hostile sympathies on the part of the villagers. How the hell they were meant to discern the last, I don't know. The way they walked, the songs the women sang? Most IP people in the villages had fled long ago and the *malais* had started to make that old difference look very small.

But sometimes Martinho didn't like the smell of a place. The guy he had as his second-in-command – an old acquaintance of mine, by the way – was less cautious and he'd argue. But Martinho carried the day. Naturally, Osvaldo's sixth sense would never have been questioned. Yet once Martinho and his deputy both agreed a place looked suspicious. And on the way home, making a detour to give it a second chance, they'd seen a *malai* cherry beret come out of a hut and yawn. Even in the friendly places Martinho never showed his full hand, hinting there was an army of his men in the jungle. It was shoddy bluff – the amount of food they requisitioned couldn't be disguised. Nor would they stay longer than five days. This was as much to leave the villagers with food as to avoid getting caught by the *malais*. They had strict orders not to antagonise the local populations.

Having set out with eight men, he'd come back with more than thirty. These were old followers of Arsenio or Osvaldo who wished to rejoin their comrades. Martinho had left the remainder in the bands in which they found themselves, but with a line of communication established, relays to designated villages, secret signs. All agreed on the need for a coordinated strategy – they were good soldiers, I've had reason to say in other contexts, and all pledged themselves to Osvaldo's leadership. The peacetime central committee members of FAKOUM now took a back seat. Osvaldo led them directly, not through nominees or influence. It was, at last, the day of the warrior. Party control over the army had always been an article of faith for the likes of Arsenio and Osvaldo. They'd had the two separate organisations, in the manner of NLF and Viet Cong: FAKOUM and FAKINTIL. The distinction had always been slightly blurred, mainly because of the smallness of Danu and the interconnectedness of the elite, with people serving on both bodies. There hadn't been so much talent around that you could afford to waste it on pedantic distinctions. Now people began to talk more of FAKINTIL than FAKOUM.

Martinho's Number Two on his tour of the jungle had been none other than my old friend Xavier Ray Xaneros, the builder of the Hotel Oscar Tango X-Ray. He wasn't wearing his yellow protective helmet any more but an Aussie bush hat, with the brim jauntily pinned to one side. Nevertheless, I recognised him at once. He, however, took a while to place me, which was sobering. Had I changed so much? But when he did, he was (for him) effusive.

He called me Senhor Ng, which made a nice change from Comrade or Chinaman.

'Is the hotel still standing?' he asked, and was comically relieved to hear it was.

'In fact, it was the HQ of a *malai* intelligence chief.'

'Then we must blow it up!'

We chuckled. He was a fairly basic guy, when you got behind the taciturnity. He seemed to have made the switch from builder to soldier with facility. He'd always been used to giving orders and keeping his betel-chewing work-force on target. It had been an occupation of man-control and overseeing physical tasks, so the similarities were great. He had earned his men's respect. I suppose he was natural officer material. He was bright and practical and made up for lack of experience with a meticulousness foreign to the Danuese nature. He wasn't in the mould of, say, Arsenio Remedios, not as many-sided as that great man of Danu, but he was a valuable asset to FAKINTIL nonetheless. By all accounts, he killed with total lack of compunction. That had always been just beneath the peacetime surface. He handled his G3 as if he'd been doing it all his life.

I told him I was sorry about his policeman brother, Danny. I didn't say I'd seen him shot, not after Osvaldo's violent reaction about Sonia. But X. Ray didn't even bother to acknowledge my condolence. He didn't want anyone's sentiment. He remembered his brother every time he pulled a trigger.

That dry season was one of unrelieved FAKINTIL successes. Osvaldo took the initiative and never let it slip. Sabotage, ambush, assassination – the *malais* never knew where they'd be hit next. Raid followed daring raid. Once, they lured out a *malai* punitive column, attacked in greater numbers than usual, and left it a smoking wreck. FAKINTIL were easily outnumbered but because Osvaldo chose the time and place he could bring superior force to bear in any given encounter. If he didn't like the odds he refused the engagement. FAKINTIL just melted away to reappear at a moment and locale of their choice, leaving the *malais* pissing into empty bushes. I could now see that the strategy of Rebus and his superiors was purely reactive. But like a lion having his tail tweaked, they didn't know where to turn next.

I have to admit I was surprised. How could something so obvious work so well? I mean, it was fairly blatant what Osvaldo was trying to do but that didn't seem to stop him achieving it.

I put this to him. He laughed; it was something many of my naive questions made him do, going back to the time I'd asked him if he'd aimed to miss in Angola. He didn't seem to mind the light relief. 'There's a big difference between knowing what the enemy is doing and knowing how to prevent him from doing it. It doesn't matter if our plan is obvious – they can't do anything about it. We don't just have a military plan – our movement is founded on objective social criteria, too.'

'The people the ocean, and the guerrillas the fish?' I said, remembering a Toronto debate.

'Well, exactly.'

'What's to stop the *malais* reading Mao Tse-tung, too?'

'Nothing, but it really won't do them any good.'

'I thought surprise was the essence of military success.'

'That's tactics, Adolph. We're talking strategy. Look, they can win in the short term, make things go on longer. In the medium term it might get harder for us. But nothing can stop the march of a people seeking their freedom. Nothing and no one.'

He was patently sincere, and the smile had left his face. I judged it better not to argue and did my best to look convinced. I'm not certain I made a very good job of it. The Cynical Chinaman, there was no room for him in the camp, that was for sure.

Weapons and ammunition continued to be in abundant supply. A lot of the gardens had been washed out in the wet months. Still, Osvaldo's foresight literally bore fruit. We were nearly self-sufficient.

The *malais* had control of the skies, of course. There was nothing we could do about that. We'd see the vapour trails high in the cloudless blue heaven of the dry season, quite often single trails, sometimes criss-crossed, the scrawl of the *malais*' signature on our skies. I couldn't work it out. What were they doing, soaring silently up there? It seemed so remote from earthly concerns. They couldn't hurt us from there. At first, I'd thought it was going to be high-level bombing, like the B-52s we knew the Yanks had used in Vietnam. But the *malais* didn't have planes like that. Maybe they were mapping the terrain, taking fancy aerial photographs. Osvaldo had ordered that we should take cover when they passed overhead. Common prudence indicated that. People had dived face-down for the dirt the first time it happened. Osvaldo had said that one face looking skywards was a beacon for bombs. Other than scratches from thorns there were no casualties. People started to get blasé. It became enough to get into the huts and put out the cooking-fires. Finally, we just put out the fires. Unflummoxed, Dr Maria had continued to give her open-air surgeries throughout these episodes. I'd felt foolish, lying on my belly, looking at her neat ankles while she was upright, all 40 kilos of her. You almost wanted a bomb to drop somewhere in the jungle to save your face.

For that, I didn't have long to wait. The occasional high-level flights became aggressive mid- and low-level sorties. You could actually see the planes, not just detect them from the white exhaust wakes. We did jump to it then. Osvaldo had us change the camouflage every other day – browning vegetation in the netting was as good an indication as a fire. Here was a useful chore for the brats.

We saw them bombing in a valley 10 miles away, three planes circling, taking it in turns to make fast passes. Long after the clouds of smoke and debris had risen, you got the 'crump' of the bombs. They circled some more, then rocketed the ground. I recognised the big flashes I'd seen previously on invasion day, at an uncomfortably closer range. We watched from our height, the planes sometimes below us.

'Are they bombing a group you located?' I asked X. Ray. Privately, I thought: well, that's the end of them. Bet *they* wished they'd joined Osvaldo. But X. Ray shook his head. He looked sad. 'It's a village,' he said, 'an ordinary place.'

Of course, guerrillas would hide themselves. But a village … it had to exist, as it had always done.

Osvaldo was watching through field-glasses. I hoped he knew what he was doing – the betraying flash was all we needed. He was talking to a sombre Martinho. Of them all, Osvaldo looked the least troubled. In fact, he seemed tastelessly cheerful. I could see why. It would drive people to FAKOUM as their last resort: the surviving men would join

FAKINTIL. It strengthened his hand, without weakening what he had already. Son of a bitch.

Nevertheless, he knew when to temper daring with discretion. Three weeks later we shifted base. There'd been a little too much over-flying for his liking. For mine as well. The planes moved too fast for them to spot much detail in the rugged country, but it was unnerving. There was no sense tempting fate. We moved down the spine of the island by some 30 kilometres, away from Danu and the *malai* half. I say 30 kilometres; it took nearly three days, which gives a better indication. We left a small group to tend the gardens, a few fighters but mainly women and children. Osvaldo was truly smart. He wanted to diversify his resources, his areas of production. He'd realised long ago that food, not bullets, was the crux. Even while the new shelters were erecting, under X. Ray's supervision, he had parties clearing the undergrowth and turning over the soil. What was unavoidable was leaving signs of our activity. The plots were at a little distance from the camp itself but they were far more extensive than the old ones. I don't think he had a choice. We had to live by the consequences of that necessity.

Reports of minor successes continued to come in. Osvaldo allowed his local commanders a considerable latitude. He didn't want to stifle initiative – that was the key to keeping the *malais,* as Mr Burnett would say, on the hop. As a junior leader himself in Africa he knew better than to dictate from the rear. He let them sneak in to blow up bridges by night or snipe by day. The bigger engagements of a couple of hundred men at a time he had to co-ordinate himself to ensure FAKINTIL applied maximum force to the weakest *malai* link.

I think these months were the greatest moment of his life. I think he'd found the role, that notion of himself, which suited him best. It was ludicrous to say it, after the destruction, the killing of his friends, the enslavement – and it was little better than that in Danu: prize slaves would certainly have been better fed than the average citizen of our town – but Osvaldo had found a certain accommodation within and without himself. He was too busy to know it – that was part and parcel of the condition – but he was happy.

Something else happened. It was predictable, but I was slow to notice. In fact, I must have been one of the last. My antennae were never good for that kind of thing. Those who've had the sickness will recognise the symptoms more speedily in others. The immune are the more obtuse for not having experienced the malady.

I'd thought Maria was also one of the clear-sighted unafflicted, someone who saw people as they were, without illusion. But I was wrong. Even in disappointing she had the capacity to disconcert. She'd always dealt sharply with Osvaldo. She was someone who, whatever the circumstances were in an objective sense, never considered himself or herself to be in a plight. She didn't truckle to Osvaldo because she discovered herself in his power. He was amused and intrigued by that. It went back beyond camp, to the night in the prison when she'd stood up to him and Arsenio over Raoul.

I'd see them strolling by the vegetable patches, Osvaldo awkward, shortening his long stride while Maria proceeded with the unhurried detachment of a general making an inspection. You could understand why Osvaldo had taken to gardening with such zeal when you saw the serried ranks of cabbages, the regimented upright canes of beans and tomatoes. It actually wasn't the place for a romantic or contemplative wander, stinking as it did of the encampment's shit. But then what they wanted was some solitude, individual breathing space. Through the mouth. Stertorously. I tell you so. I can smell that awful whiff as I write. I saw him hold her hand as she jumped a drainage ditch, and he kept hold of it. Even then I didn't realise. After all, it was the way all of us men – not just those like me – had walked with each other in the days of the Praça. It was pure friendliness, in all senses. But I still should have known.

Sometimes I couldn't find her at all. When I left the shaky lean-to that served us as the dry-season sick-bay I searched in vain. I asked my friends the washerwomen, and drew giggles more hysterical than the fact of my mere personal ludicrousness warranted. Well, I was put out somewhat, more by being mystified than laughed at; so I exposed myself to them. Screams of laughter, an old woman falling backwards into the shallow water. One of them threatened to come up with her parang and chop it off. Thrusting out my hips, I rolled the whites of my eyes, tongue curling from the side of my mouth. Innocent japes. Dead on time, as usual, Maria was at the sick-bay for her afternoon round. One of the washerwomen was on hand to collect the disgusting bandages. Eyes down, she was on best behaviour, blank-faced; they did hold Maria in some serious awe since the days she'd gone into the mountains with her clinic to work miraculous cures on the children, human though they now had the advantage of knowing her to be. I raised my eyebrows at the mountain-woman, pursed my lips. That was enough to crack her up. She fled, hand over her mouth but not troubling to suppress her titters once Maria was out of sight. Still grinning, I turned to Maria, saying, 'And where were we this afternoon?' in that inoffensive, light-hearted way of mine that the ladies like so much from the harmless faggot, so I was startled, even from Dr Maria, when she snapped, 'Mind your own business.' I gave her my coldest smile, which had no effect whatsoever; she was a pastmaster at getting the upper hand in senseless little confrontations like these. Her whole life was made up of it, when she wasn't playing Dr Schweitzer.

Then, some nights later, I observed her going into Osvaldo's hut after we'd eaten. I didn't think much about it, but when I saw her emerge from it in the morning I sure as hell did. So I put two and two together and came up with the correct total of five.

In hindsight it was predictable to the point of banality. These were two exceptional people and what they did was a cliché. It was a mix of the familiar, of the history of men and women together, and the unknown, the different thoughts and needs of women as against men, and vice versa. Knowing Maria, I trusted that there would be none of that false sentiment which appears (to an outsider at least) to confuse the relationship of the genders when physical sex is brought into it.

With Osvaldo and Maria what would never have happened in town and in peacetime took on inevitability in those mountains and in that war.

At length it became common knowledge – I doubt if there were many as slow on the uptake as yours truly – and finally just another part of camp life. It was happening throughout the group. Some of the washerwomen were starting to look very round indeed. There'd been regular to-ing and fro-ing between huts, like the kids' game of musical chairs, as people sorted out their various mistakes and predilections. One in the front door and another out the back. I speak figuratively, you understand, although in actuality Osvaldo had insisted that X. Ray should build shelters with more than one exit. There weren't any fights – among the men – I'll give them credit for that.

Now here was where brother Martinho got in on the act. He was not at all pleased with this kind of thing. Sometimes he could be a goddamned hypocrite, that Martinho. Worse than if he'd actually had the courage to take the cloth. He might have been more tolerant then. Martinho liked to be different. He would have been a worldly priest. As one of the laity, he strove to project the image of a super-sacerdotal purity. He did his best to discourage casual liaisons between the men and women (and, no, he never concerned himself in the least about what I did). The men had to put up with the imposition of the fatherly word, mainly because he was Osvaldo's brother, but they didn't like it much. Who exactly did the son of a bitch think he was?

So Martinho thought the Leader was setting an example to be deplored. Profoundly so. He went to work on him. It wasn't the claims of the flesh itself he reprehended. No, it was the irregularity of the union. He went on and on about it, Maria told me; didn't let go. Osvaldo never once walked off or told him to shut up. Amazing. Fr Molloy, Martinho's old mentor from the seminary, was recruited to the cause. I don't think this old boy gave a damn himself. He was more of an academic than a pastor. What concerned him was not so much the flesh as the intellect, finer points of theology, intellectual transgressions, and I think Osvaldo's all-consuming sin would have been that of pride. But he went into action, with Martinho working his strings behind him. Arsenio wouldn't have put up with it; he'd been intolerant of priestly interferences in all areas. The seminary had put him off religion for life, left him a militant atheist. But Osvaldo was more ambiguous on the subject. Strange to say, he was a little superstitious. He did have a gold crucifix on a chain around his neck to go with the dog-tags, which was probably worn for more than decoration. Who am I to poke fun? After all, Arsenio was dead and Osvaldo was still alive. I'd say Molloy and Martinho got a little more than Osvaldo's usual courteous hearing. But he resisted. There was the part of him which didn't like being told what to do, didn't like it at all. Martinho knew his brother, and that if he pushed too hard or too persistently it would end with Osvaldo determining to go his own way; so he worked a circumspect campaign. God was a soft sell.

How it would have gone is anybody's guess. I'm not so sure Osvaldo wouldn't have run out of patience and told them both to get lost, Martinho retreating to his hut with heavy tread more in sorrow than anger. It was Maria herself who averted what might have been an unhappy chapter. Apart from her being who she was and the relation in which she stood to him, her arguments cut that much more ice with Osvaldo anyway. As could be expected, her rationale was both sound and unsentimental.

She chewed it over with me first. I was flattered to be her confidant. In her scathing way she was rueful. Incredulous at what she was about to suggest, go through with. She thought Martinho's was a good idea. I was aghast at what seemed such feebleness, genuflection to conventional church morality, the more craven for coming from such an unexpected quarter. But when she explained herself it was clear she was right. Already there had been some mild amusement over Martinho's zeal to reclaim his brother from what one might technically term a condition of sin. Maria, morbidly sensitive in some ways, excessively impervious in others, had picked up on this ripple. And she'd seen it would, given time, extend to Osvaldo himself. It might weaken his leadership. 'That's dangerous,' she said, 'We can't afford that.' I nodded. Privately, I thought: 'You think it'll be dangerous for everybody. It's much more dangerous for *me*.' I could see what might lie in store for the Useless Chinaman if anything happened to my protector. Of course, Maria was just concerned about a degeneration into Danuese chaos. She saw things big, that girl; she had the ability to step outside her skin. There was also the positive side to her analysis of the situation. 'We need a party,' she said, and left it at that, with a smile that contained no hint of mockery. And I saw at once what she was thinking.

The camp needed a focus; it needed a landmark in time. They had to set some event between themselves and the invasion, so that they could distance themselves from the trauma of that defeat. They must no longer think of themselves as vanquished, as the impotent. They were at least holding their own, getting the better of the many small-scale conflicts going on, and stopping the *malais* from winning any more territory. And to celebrate that and just to snap the tension, forget our hardships for a few hours, we needed, as Maria put it, a little party. It would be a symbol of more than one pair's union.

Osvaldo didn't wait for his brother to come to him again but strode straight to his hut to tell him of his agreement. That made it look more like his own choice.

Well, it was some affair. Food was what we thought a lot about and while Osvaldo couldn't wave a magic wand over the crops, or cast a spell on the beasts of the forest such as would entice them into our snares, he could certainly release a portion of the stores. There existed a few jealously guarded tins of bully beef and stew as well as what we had grown ourselves. In normal times, the *pièce de résistance* of a big man's wedding would have been a slaughtered buffalo. That didn't even occur to any of us; it was outside the possibilities of the shrunken world we inhabited. So imagine our incredulity when a pair of grinning perimeter guards escorted in three mountain men (actually two boys and an old man) and ... stately, snorting, recalcitrant, one of the mighty animals. It stood in the clearing, steam mushrooming out of its great nostrils in the cooler air of the heights. People turned out of the huts, the kids came running back from their games in the forest, the women hurried up from the stream, and, I'm sorry to say, eventually all the non-seminarian sentries. There we were crowded round the thing, its flanks still muddy, eyes starting to roll. The press parted for Osvaldo, with Martinho and Maria close behind him. He let the village headman, for it was none other, make his little address. You could see straightaway the old boy was a bad actor; he wasn't very happy. His words rang hollowly, about how they wanted to contribute to the happy occasion, what a great man Osvaldo was, how honoured they would be. And, as I looked at him, and then at the grinning soldiers, their casually borne weapons, the slings drooping from the muzzles, I realised what the score was.

So did Osvaldo, for I saw his face darken. He shook his head and handed back the halter to the headman. The grins vanished from the faces of the guerrillas; they'd no doubt taken a long time applying persuasion to the village elders. It was a grave disappointment, almost a slap in the face by way of thanks for their efforts at a surprise. Martinho's beam broadened, which was how I could tell he was suffering from terminal embarrassment. The headman stood there, nonplussed, as well he might.

Osvaldo did like to make the big gesture, usually at his own expense, but when you do it at other people's expense additional complications enter into the picture. This was also the one time, though, when it would have been expedient for us to be noble. Osvaldo knew he had to keep the local population on good terms with his fighters; it was vital to our long-term survival. But there was also the morale of his own men to consider. At that moment it wasn't a consideration, though; it wouldn't have stopped him sending the forced gift back. And then he couldn't have gone back himself; it would have been too late; he'd have lost face.

Once again, Maria intervened to protect her lover's position. She whispered in his ear – she had to stand on tip-toe to do it – and personally accepted the rope from the bewildered old montagnard. He was shaking his head as he left. It must have seemed townsfolk didn't know their own minds, even when they were robbing you.

That buffalo was the monarch of the clearing for three days; visited, admired, patted, fed handfuls of grass and the tenderest bamboo roots. I couldn't understand why the Danuese tribesmen venerated the dumb beast so. A pig would have sensed its fate; sent out truculent squeals when approached. The king just lowered his marmoreal horns to chomp placidly at what was offered.

The women had themselves a field day with Maria's outfit. Weaving was an art form in rural Danu. It was quite something and fully matched their singing – red, blue, and yellow natural dyes, repeating motifs of dogs, monkeys, moonmen (I called them, with their huge, alien heads) and – in this twentieth century of ours – airplanes. They put together a really beautiful outfit for her. I'd never seen her so well-dressed in the peaceful, affluent past. Yes, I was in the hut with the women while they dressed her. They'd made her leave Osvaldo's cabin, quit his bed, as soon as the prospective union had been announced, so that she could go from her bridal home to ... her in-laws? To Martinho anyway. They did her hair with forest oils and orchids. I couldn't believe it was Maria. She seemed to enjoy it. It seemed she was liberating a part of her nature she'd always denied. Or maybe she was a better actress than I gave her credit for. As they worked on her coiffure the women sang. I didn't know whether they were specific songs appropriate to that part of the preparations, or if they were just clearing their throats for the serious stuff later. I got to put a flower in my friend's hair, but one of the washerwomen stuck a pin in me. Probably deliberately. Well, that was good for another laugh and, after a second, I joined in, too. Sucking at the red dot on my thumb as I retreated outside, I saw the buffalo being led uncomplainingly away. They'd butcher it away from camp, not from any feelings of delicacy but to avoid attracting the flies – one advantage of the rainy season gone being the absence of insects for long periods. I looked back at the scene of flowers, the chorus of song in my ears, and I went out to the place of slaughter. The kids danced attendance on their elders. I was in time to see the first blow of the traditional parang, brought down with the full force of Osvaldo's sinewy arm. He hit the buffalo well back into its neck, where there were at least 40 centimetres of bone and muscle and, do you know, he must have got half-way through. My surprise kept me watching as he raised his arm for the second blow – the beast on its knees – with the massive head hanging by the merest thread. The final chop I didn't watch, which was stupid as I'd already seen the worst. The FAKINTIL corporal who'd brought me to the camp caught my weakness. He grinned unpleasantly – I'd never quite got reconciled to this guy – and he said: 'Only once for the head of a man.' I had a feeling he wasn't talking emptily but from experience. I made no retort but moved away; still he followed me and, clutching my arm, said: 'If he was your friend. Twice, if he was your enemy.' I shoved him away, more roughly than was prudent and mixed myself up with the kids. Some seminarian he must have been.

By now the great head was lying on its side in a lake of gore. Osvaldo had relinquished the parang to one of three minions who commenced butchering the carcass. It got too much for me when they started on dragging out the guts, and I retreated to the hut.

Witnessing the carnage did not, however, spoil my appetite. None of us had tasted a scrap of meat, beyond a fragment of pigeon or morsel of rodent, for at least half a year. Oh, the aroma! There wasn't a corner of the camp it didn't penetrate. My mouth filled at once with saliva. I do not jest. I do not exaggerate. Like a dog I slavered. It kept coming, too. I had to swallow, and gulp again, and again. I was amazed at myself. Nor were others more dignified. Martinho was in the same animal condition as myself. And the kids round the fire, where the ribs and flanks turned slowly on a bamboo spit, blue, black, and pink, fat and juices spitting and flaming on the grey embers, the poor kids just stood and drooled, not troubling to wipe away what trickled from the corners of their mouths. Still the women sang – that must have dried the mouth.

It was in the late afternoon that Fr Molloy performed the spiritual ceremony of union, all in that powerful aroma of carnality. He stood before a crude trestle of an altar while Martinho, in contravention of all known rules of God or Man, assisted him in the performance of his office. Once, as Fr Molloy hesitated, Martinho prompted the older man's Latinity in a voice as strong and unfaltering as his younger brother's. It must have been more satisfying to him than the day he was elected editor of the seminary news-sheet. The choir of female voices, Osvaldo in his regular army uniform, Maria in her loaned ethnic finery, the children throwing flowers in their path, it was like something from a dream. The meat in the mouth wasn't, though. That was real enough. I tore at it with my incisors, ripped chunks off, swallowed them with the merest apology of mastication. I burned my nose on some fat but didn't let it distract me. The savour was indescribable. And yet, after a while, as my stomach bloated, I began to crave salt. How people's expectations rise, how they always want more. There was palm wine, sticky, cloudy-white stuff, like an ejaculation in water. It was a dirty-looking brew, but that I had as well. After a while I became light-headed. I started to join in the singing. The women had interrupted their feasting to perform a kind of clapping dance, swaying from side to side in time with their music. I joined them, lurched and fell over, which was probably a very good thing. A little later I began to feel sick. The nausea built up, as it does, with the sudden awareness that one's body has been unhappy for some time without the mind listening to it, then the successive waves of giddiness and unease as the flesh takes its revenge. The throwing up itself was nothing. And, like the apocryphal ancients of Rome, I returned a new and empty man to the festive fray. To judge by the shadowy figures leaving the firelight to bend over on the edge of darkness I wasn't alone in my predicament. And did I think I saw a round, dignified figure, not at all unlike Martinho, walk with strange purposiveness into the night to bow at the extreme verge of vision not to God but in thrall to the base exigencies of his own body? Done, no doubt, if truly it was him, with utmost poise and condescension. On and on it went. If the fire flaring into the jet of night and mountain worried Osvaldo he didn't show it. There were still men posted around the environs, according to the dispositions learned to be best in Africa, but the details sent out to relieve them half-way through departed in a sorry state. That night we were defenceless. Our leader might have gambled on one night's wholesale dereliction acting as a purge for Danuese fecklessness, strengthening the sense of duty in the long run. Certainly it would have been unlike him to have lost all foresight simply because it happened to be his wedding day.

They looked a good couple, against what might have been my expectations of only a year previous. He towered over her while Fr Molloy and Martinho conducted their ersatz ceremony, but it didn't make you laugh. The Danuese costume she was wearing had a lot to do with that. It was singularly graceful on anybody and it suited her, down to the ground. It was that it forced her to move elegantly, the fit of it, I mean, and keeping it on; so that her usually chopping and impatient little stride had to be smoothed and slowed, in the same way that a woman carrying a jar of water on her head would be forced to proceed with care and poise. And this made her look more lissom, taller. She'd justified the whole thing to herself in terms of expediency, but she was a woman as well (sometimes it was difficult to remember that) and as she danced she forgot she had a front to maintain. In the uneven firelight, her face flushed with exertion and heat, she looked as happy as I'd ever seen her.

FIFTEEN

IF YOU COULD HAVE PORTRAYED IT as three ascending lines plotted on a graph – the aspirations of a trio of basically incompatible human beings thinking convergent thoughts for an all too brief span – then Martinho, Maria, and Osvaldo's expectations of the Movement and each other intersected the day of the marriage. After that it was never the same again. Maria and Osvaldo stayed together. Martinho moved down and away, quite in the opposite direction. To reveal this, it took bad luck and reverses. When things went well, you could cover it up.

Morale remained sky-high for a few months more, soaring up into the blue, dry-season heavens with only the dispersing clouds of the occasional jet-wake to presage a less cheerful future.

I went on one of the successful raids of that time. It wasn't so much induction as initiation. Osvaldo was moving into Phase Two, he thought, of his ten- or (who knows) hundred-year plan, planting his seed corn. Don't think of me as the macho killer. I went out with the kids on their first attack, all virgins together in a manner of speaking. Osvaldo wanted to blood them, the FAKINTIL initiation rite, their passage into full service to the movement. As their scoutmaster, I got drawn in. Anyone could have told you I'd be a liability on a FAKINTIL mission, more a threat to my own people with a rifle in my hands than the enemy. But I got a weapon, sixty rounds of 7.62 mm NATO ball, and a week's instruction from my bête noire, the kidnapping Corporal. A week's victimisation, I should say. 'I never met a Chinaman who wasn't good with his hands,' the introductory comment after my first attempts to field-strip the G3, had become, by day five, 'You're the only stupid Chinaman I know, Ng.' Still, I had fired a passable group, zeroed the sights for my personal use, and was able to estimate ranges. It was re-assembling the weapon after I'd stripped it which defied my best efforts.

I was actually no worse at doing it with a blindfold on than sighted. The rag over our eyes was to simulate doing it in the total darkness of a jungle night. I can always run away in the blackness, I consoled myself. The meagre issue of ammo was a quirk of Osvaldo's. We had more than enough, but he looked to the future. He didn't want the kids to take it for granted. Deep down, despite the lucky or good run, despite his gift of courage (or, to put it another way, his lack of imagination) Osvaldo was always a pessimist. It was deep in his nature; after all, he was a religious man.

We set off at – if I may put it that way without sounding ludicrous, speaking as a man who'd used leaves rather than paper for nearly half a year (but never water and his fingers) – at a civilised hour. Somehow I'd imagined us departing in the middle of the night or at dawn, but there was no cause for Osvaldo to tire us from the start: every reason not to, in fact. There were no *malais* nearby for us to conceal our movements from. I must have been thinking of the kind of time for attack.

Osvaldo himself did take charge. He was the mother leading her ducklings. I felt a lot better for having him there – someone who knew what he was doing better than anybody else. Foolish me, I thought he was invulnerable. Well, he got a curt goodbye from his new wife, and we were off. X. Ray and Martinho remained in charge at camp. It was three or four days to where we were going, on the edge of *malai*-controlled territory. We took it easy, though the kids, beside themselves with excitement, had to be made to go slower than they wanted. Apart from the guns, it was like the junior woodchucks. With me in the role of Unca Donald. That the Corporal and six of his sidekicks went along as insurance didn't detract from this impression – they were the gruff, biped, Disney dogs, maybe with sheriff's stars on their chests. I'd discovered by now that the Corporal hadn't been a seminarian but a policeman – very possibly the one who had given the Australian hippies such a hard time at Bacalhau airport all those years ago on my return from the big world. He had indeed been based there and certainly possessed the meanness of spirit.

The third night saw us post sentries in earnest. Osvaldo had toured the perimeter on the first night and found a boy asleep at his post. There'd been no punishment, just a few words of disappointment, which had the child in tears. The morning saw us on a ridge over the Bacalhau-Danu main highway. I was on my belly with the rest. By now, we all knew not to crest the sky-line. Osvaldo had his Africa bins out. With the naked eye or 'eyeball mark one' as the Corporal called it (oh, the surprising wit of the rude and licentious soldiery), you could see there was nothing moving for miles around. Still, I liked Osvaldo's action. We didn't stir for 20 minutes. Then he sent a group of five scuttling down the slope to the road. These junior sappers were under the Corporal's direction. Four fire-teams Osvaldo placed: one on each side of the road in both the Bacalhau and Danu directions. This was to protect those laying mines in the road. He also sent out scout parties to give us plenty of warning if the *malais* should come along. I'd have thought he would have done better to send the scouts out first, but who was I to tell him his trade? I had the extreme good fortune to remain safely lying down with Osvaldo's own little section. At least I had just congratulated myself on my lot when Osvaldo – could he read minds? – said, without moving the binoculars from his eyes, 'Go down and watch the kids, Adolph.' The fact that he called me by my first name rather than, 'Ng', made me uneasy. Was this a mission from which I was unlikely to return? Disguising my reluctance as best I could, I stood upright and started to pick my way downhill. It felt horribly exposed.

'You will need your gun, I think.'

How had he seen? I thought I saw a smile around his lips, though his eyes were hidden.

It was not the most relaxing walk. The kids were already halfway through excavating small holes in the dirt. It was an interesting pattern, much like the five on a die. They were going to put two mines in each rut, about ten yards apart and one in the centre between the wheel marks. It was a case of gamekeeper turned poacher, as Osvaldo had seen this prove one of the most effective patterns employed by his erstwhile foes, the 'terrorists' in Africa. He said it was surprising how often vehicles simply drove in the ruts formed by their predecessors even when there was a known danger of mining. The kids clustered round the Corporal as he armed a green plastic mine about the size of a dinner plate. At this stage we still possessed a stock of standard military mines. He let the kids cover it. These were anti-vehicle mines which needed a lot of pressure, maybe 80 kilos, to initiate the detonator, then the booster, followed, hopefully, by the main charge. I looked back up the hill. Couldn't see a darn thing. But I knew Osvaldo had us under surveillance. Again, it wasn't the most comfortable feeling in the world.

'Hey, Chinaman! Wake up!' My friend the Corporal was throwing a mine at me. I did jump, though I knew the device was as yet harmless. The kids used their hands to scoop earth over the plates, then disguised them further with pebbles and the odd branch. After sweeping our footprints with a leafy switch, we moved on 50 metres to repeat the process. This time the Corporal took the opportunity to pee on top of a buried mine, but the puddle vanished into the thirsty earth, leaving a rime which soon disappeared also. It was as well, since it was the dry season. But the kids loved it. Soon they all had their little dicks out, a line of them pouring from their tiny spigots. I don't know what Osvaldo made of it through his lenses. Altogether we mined some half a kilometre of road. After that we sowed a single field of three mines in an arrowhead formation about an hour's walk down the highway. The *malais* would just have picked up speed again and started to relax. And they'd spend the best part of an hour looking for devices that weren't there. It had a great beauty to it. It amused me.

We spent eight days without incident, touring the centre of the island without ever retracing our steps, planting mines, cutting wires, felling trees, breaking a bridge or two (for that we didn't use explosive). It was pretty well a kid's dream come true: elder-led delinquency. At no time did we mount an ambush over our mines. Osvaldo was bringing the kids on slowly.

'It's like gardening, isn't it?' I observed to our leader on the last day of our operation as we watched the kids, who no longer needed supervision, arming and putting down the mines. Osvaldo looked surprised; I don't think this extremely trite analogy – don't they talk of sowing mines? – had struck him. He had a powerful but very straight-ahead intelligence. *'Ai, bom,'* he said, regarding me with interest. 'I hadn't thought of it that way.' After a while, he added, 'But we won't be here to enjoy the results.' I didn't reply.

I didn't want him leaving me behind to report back to him on any consequences. My big mouth.

The expedition ended without incident. I don't know what happened to our devices, whether they ever got a result. Odds were that, if the triggers worked, something would go over them by the end of the season. I just hoped it wouldn't be a Danuese driving.

Missions Two and Three were different. Pardon me for referring to these forays in this way – it was how I thought of them at the time, without a hint of irony. You know, when it's your own skin, it's not ironic anymore. They weren't kids' outings. Unfortunately, by going out with the junior woodchucks, carrying a rifle, and somehow contriving not to perpetrate a negligent discharge, I'd got myself on the list of possibles for any fighting. Stupid me. I didn't want to be on the team! My arguments, which elaborately avoided any hint of self-interest, went disregarded. 'I'm pleased you think that highly of me,' was the gist of my stammering prevarications, 'but don't you think I'd be more valuable helping Dr Maria?' Osvaldo's grave face betrayed no trace of sarcasm, but the Corporal didn't trouble to hide his contempt. Betrayal came from an unexpected quarter. 'I can make do without you, Adolph,' said the good doctor herself. 'No one is indispensable, you know.' Bitch. Did she really want me to get killed? Her only friend in the place? She couldn't call Osvaldo a friend – he was both more and less than that. I controlled my expression best as I could, but it must have been a treat for the Corporal. The Inscrutable Chinaman, indeed.

Well, off I trudged to draw my G3 and 60 rounds.

There were 16 of us on this one. Fourteen hardened FAKINTIL regulars, including African vets, and an idiot hotelier with a self-loading rifle.

X.Ray led.

Six days out of camp we discovered ourselves on the edge of the highway. Same road, but 50 kilometres nearer Danu. Take the play behind the enemy's front line – he won't expect it there – had been the rationale of Osvaldo. To me it felt like putting one's head in an especially hungry lion's mouth. Every day, every step, on the out-trip was a pace into peril. It was the voluntariness of it all which got to me. Look, we're safe now; we don't have to do this, you guys: you could read the frantic thoughts in a bubble over my head. But, no, we marched blithely on into danger when with every step we could have been putting distance between our persons and it. When we got there, as far as X. Ray wanted to take us, it was a relief, almost. We'd bottomed out. Now our effort when we would travel – and it *was* effort, with my hands blistered from the machete – would somehow be constructive.

On my belly again, watching the trucks and half-tracks rumbling along, my thoughts were not positive.

We had to go down after dark this time. No mad scramble down the slope in broad day; it was too busy here. I got chosen for this. Naturally. I had a sack of six mines, an entrenching tool, and a knife. I could always cut my own throat. My G3 I had to leave behind. There were three of us, slithering like snakes in the moonlight. I was so tense I lost my fear of the mines. The scrape of the little folding spade was unbearable on the stones. When I stopped, god damn it, I could hear the noise of the others. 'Not so loud, you sons of bitches,' I hissed. I expected a reprimand for breaking silence – not that I cared – but whether I was making sense or if it was a case of the colourful military vocabulary, the clinks and crunches became more subdued. I thought they merely sounded furtive, more suspicious, but I grubbed with the rest of them. I was first to finish and half-way up the hill before the next was done.

'You were damn quick, Chinaman,' the Corporal growled.

'Uh-huh,' I said, retrieving my G3. I never thought I'd be so pleased to get my hands on it. I'd felt naked. I guess at the back of my mind was the thought that I'd rather get killed cleanly than be brought in to Rebus. That didn't bear thinking about.

X. Ray was going to set up an ambush around our mines, which were situated just after a bend in the road. That way we'd bunch up the *malais* for the killing group, leaving escapers for our stop groups at the beginning and end of the ambush. We didn't have any command-controlled devices, so it depended on a vehicle actually running over one of the things. There was a high degree of certainty in X. Ray's mind that one would. I held on to the hope that it wouldn't. We had one machine-gun with us, fitted with dial sights and fixed on a sustained fire mount, so that in darkness or smoke we could just click up the likely spots on known bearings.

X. Ray conferred with the Corporal and they set the gun up to interlock with the arcs of the other weapons. I knew enough by now that it should be positioned to give flanking fire, i.e. not shoot directly head-on when the bullets only had one target but rake sideways through the enemy in depth. Miss one, hit another. As it happened, head-on was best with the motorised column now. The zone the gun could beat was very wide indeed – if you used it properly. I was starting to like the deadly science, the logic, the frugality, the economy of effect. It was Chinese. After all, hadn't Sun Tzu written the first military classic, long before those Germans? These reflections I kept to myself. They might have amused Osvaldo, not X. Ray. We were given a dead tree as a landmark to direct our fire and X. Ray put two twigs in the ground by me to delimit my arc should anything happen in darkness. I drew encouragement from his presence.

It was a quiet night. Not much happened in the morning, either. About two p.m. a convoy came from Danu in the usual storm of white dust. It looked like it was split into three parts, with four or five vehicles moving very fast at the front, leaving their own dust behind, while a slower-moving and bigger cloud obscured the main body of trucks in the centre. At the rear one vehicle moved slowly enough not to raise much in the way of cover. Under the frequent FAKINTIL attacks the *malais* had evolved the best arrangement of defence they could contrive. X. Ray and the Corporal were familiar with it: a light tank or armoured personnel carrier in the van, supported by a couple of jeeps armed with .50 calibre machine guns and a truck full of infantry, then another armed jeep at the rear. I was surprised by how unapprehensive I was, in a funny way looking forward to it. X. Ray had given instructions that no one was to fire until he did: *not* to fire when there was an explosion, but only on his cue. The armed jeeps – no APC this time – were just a few hundred metres away. I brought the G3 to my shoulder and sighted on the second jeep. Unapprehensive was I? The rifle shook so much that the foresight blade in its ring bucked like a mast on the sea. The four jeeps went past – no explosions. I wasn't too happy about this but X. Ray seemed unperturbed. Then a lorry went up in the air, the two front tyres off the ground, rearing like a circus elephant, earth and dirty smoke fountaining like some giant's fart before *woomf!* – the explosion reached us and the wounded beast fell on its side. I could see the wheels were still spinning – crazy. Silence. A whistle blew further down the road. *Malai* shouts. Everything is happening very slowly. Their infantry spill like angry ants out of the truck. The jeeps begin blazing away at the vegetation on the far side of the highway which conceals our other fire groups and at the slope we, the platoon HQ, are on. This isn't an instance of typical *malai* indiscipline but sound tactics – the aggressive, instant response so desired of ourselves by Osvaldo. The distinctive bellow of the heavy machine-gun assails our ears, rock splinters and ricochets whine everywhere. Why hasn't X. Ray fired back? Has he lost his nerve? But I keep my head well down and don't look. The shooting stops. More whistles and shouting. I look up. Shit! The *malais* have sent out a scouting party. They are less than 100 metres from us. But our men are veterans; they stay cool; they don't shoot. The *malais,* only five of them, kick at rocks, confer. They turn round. Later, our men will say the *malais* lost *their* nerve, but I don't think so. I think they are a brave race. But lazy. Very lazy.

I watch them move downhill. I admit they do appear more eager to rejoin their comrades than they were to probe the hill, but of course it's a lot easier and quicker to go down an incline. They help lever the dead monster off the road. Even with the jeeps towing, it's plainly hard work. Out come planks for the rest of the convoy to skirt the natural potholes beside the crater our device made. The *malais* seem well practised at all this. The rest of the convoy moves on. I wait for another explosion. Nothing happens. The trucks keep moving. X. Ray grimaces. I see him mouth a few swear words. But he doesn't open fire. The others look at him. He ignores them. The last three trucks, followed closely, too closely I learn later at our debriefing, by the rear jeep, trundle past. The jeep's antenna flicks like a fishing-rod as it goes over the ruts. I realise this is why X. Ray has waited. He wants to wipe out their communications at the same time that he announces his presence. The boom of his rifle takes me by surprise and I jump. Right on top of his report the others open up. It's not frightening; it's a wonderful, reassuring, virile sound, better than any music I ever heard. Best of all, I'm flat on my face, out of harm's way for the time being, inflicting damage on those I hate. Eager to add my contribution to the glorious chorus, I pull the trigger. Nothing happens. What the fuck? I pull again. The *malai* cherry tops on the jeep remain immune from me. I feel frustrated, impotent, but still not scared. I check the breech. No. God damn it. The selector is in the high safety position. I push it down hard and say 'Son of a bitch' for the sake of saying it. I pull the trigger, forgetting about squeezing and first and second pressures, and am rewarded with a tremendous burst of five or six shots, the weapon bucking uncontrollably, and the muzzle climbing to the heavens. Shit again. I pushed it down all the way to full auto. I select semi-automatic fire, but not before the Corporal calls me something unmentionable. We're not supposed to use the G3 like a machine-gun, too inaccurate and wasteful besides burning out the barrel. As I sight on the *malais* again, they're picked up in the air and slung backwards off their Browning as our own HK21 general purpose machine-gun, lashes their vehicle with a long, chattering burst. Formidable! What power! It fires the same bullets as the G3 but, as the loathsome Corporal says, the combined effect of a hail of bullets is much more than you'd expect merely from aggregating the single capabilities of each round. Well, he was right! But the surviving vehicle has got us, the gunner has walked his rounds up to the hill-crest and is moving slowly along the line of our flashes. I'm mesmerised. I'd like to run, but that would be worse. How can it all be so slow? In five or six seconds the earth will be flying around *me*. Rapid volleys from our enfilading squad. The big Browning falls silent – they've hit the gunner in the back. Now we start to shoot at the trucks. The GPMG works them over but can't get any to burn.

X. Ray and the Corporal are now frantically trying to control our rate of fire, after the permitted intense shooting to take full advantage of the ambush's opening seconds of surprise. We are too distant to be really effective with the G3 rifles at such a heavy volume. They try to get us down to rapid, a shot every three seconds, but the men are excited. They'll run themselves dry soon, if this goes on.

X. Ray shouts 'Grenade!' This doesn't mean what it seems; it's the pre-arranged signal to withdraw. I am in the first part of our squad to go, while the others continue to lay down fire. We join the flank protection team, grab our packs and those of the others and start to move. At the rendezvous we wait for the other squads, then really motor. We don't stop till pitch-dark.

Well, to yours truly it seemed like a successful raid, the ideal action, in fact. We'd hurt the enemy at no cost to ourselves. Coming up from the cowed, vanquished town, as I had, it was something for Danuese even to be retaliating. But X. Ray was mad as hell at us. Madder than the

Corporal. This last was shooting black looks even before we'd stopped doubling along. X. Ray didn't turn or swear; it wasn't his style. Back at camp, all the guerrillas, not just us, got a pep talk from Osvaldo.

Someone had omitted to arm their mines. The Corporal looked meaningfully at me but my innocent indignation was not assumed.

For once I hadn't screwed up. I'd set my stuff up nicely. It was my devices which had gone off. X. Ray admitted as much when he told the Corporal to lay off me.

Osvaldo went on and on about carelessness. Didn't he realise he wasn't in the regular army anymore? He was laying down the law, and there he was with a beard and a head of frizz down to his shoulders. I resolved to mention this to Maria, who might pass the idea on. He should try seeing himself through the eyes of others. Martinho was nodding away behind his brother. For once Osvaldo was saying things he liked. FAKINTIL, heroes of the resistance, were nothing more than a bunch of cut-throats to him, the FAKOUM CC member, who still presented a clean-shaven appearance to the world. The men listened cheerfully; they weren't taking the smallest notice. Sullenness would have indicated the sermon was getting home.

Osvaldo might as well have saved his breath. Things kept going on the way they were. Hit or miss – literally and figuratively, though we roamed and attacked more or less as we pleased. Stocks of ammunition and weaponry were holding up well: plenty of NATO cartridges for the G3s, still some shells for the recoil-less rifles and a few bombs for the 81mm mortars. But we'd run out of mines. I regretted the devices we'd sown, it now seemed so promiscuously. More, I brooded on it. It seemed our most effective way of harassing the *malai*, the most cost-effective, too, in terms of the casualties on our own side. Yes, I liked the idea of not being around when the *malais* got hit. And I found something peculiarly appealing about it on an intellectual level.

What was it I liked so much?

I liked the spite. Spite is for the weak and I knew myself to be weak. It was clever, and I was cleverer than the enemy. By far. In the most dramatic way it was a reminder to them of my existence. And I was in danger of forgetting who I was. It was a craft – mining, booby-trapping – that was peculiarly Chinese. I mean in its ingenuity, in its low small-mindedness, its attention to detail, its pettifogging neatness. At that kind of handiwork the Chinese traditionally excelled. There was also the consideration of putting one's capital out for the most effective return; it was the entrepreneurial venture so beloved of my countrymen, with additional and attractive overtones of gambling. The mental one-upmanship, the game of bluff and deception, answered to another quirk of the race, the effort to read the other fellow's mind: much like the traditional game of hand signs – stone, paper, scissors – begun instead of spinning a coin in the Occidental manner when rival choices were to be made, when closed fist (stone) shattered two fingers (scissors) but open hand (paper) could wrap stone but be cut by scissors. And what could be more Chinese than gunpowder pyrotechnics? Or be more like Chinese checkers than planting those round mines in the most efficacious pattern on the board? Oh, it was me OK, the Chinese Sapper.

I had a word with Osvaldo. I wished to volunteer. I wished to be useful to FAKINTIL. I broached my schemes. Well, I got more than the usual grave and courteous hearing from our leader. Courtesy and gravity were going out of the window these days, for all except Martinho. I hadn't mentioned that mining was a method of warfare which was relatively safe for the practitioner, but Osvaldo pointed it out straightaway. He was unembarrassed about self-preservation; mark of the truly brave, I thought. We got on to the question of our dwindling stock of mines. (They were Italian-designed, but made under franchise in the Home Country.) He grimaced. 'The one thing we're short of, if you forget anti-aircraft missiles.' We couldn't help smiling at the thought of us possessing some shoulder-launched missiles for shooting up Mr *Malai's* ass as he flew past – it was like wishing for an ice-cream. Quite out of the range of our possibilities.

'Well, I've a few ideas,' I said, and proceeded to tell him.

Osvaldo's experience had all been counter-insurgency. It required a big effort of mind for him to think himself into the guerrilla role: the raggedy black fellow in the African bush. He'd done it – we had the results before us – but he was no improviser. That was the real thing. In his soul Osvaldo would always be a regular. For me the make-shift, the third-hand, the modified, the refurbished were already second nature. Not just as a Chinese, more as the creator of the Oscar Tango X-Ray. I actually relished the challenge.

I began in a small way with booby-traps. Osvaldo had been on the receiving end of these in Africa. No need to tell him how vexatious they could be. They had, he said, an effect on morale out of all proportion to the actual damage they inflicted. I liked the way he put it. Every soldier dreaded losing his balls, or his eyesight, or just his foot. Even when there were no traps it slowed up their advance. He told me of stakes, of trip-wire triggers, of pits.

And I went away and added malice all of my own devising. My God, I might have been born for it. I'd discovered my true métier, which was to be a hotelier in hell, dispensing my own brand of warped hospitality. The Vietnamese punji stick of bamboo was just the beginning. Sharpened to a needle-point, it would pierce the sole of a combat boot with the ease of a Q-tip going into Vaseline. Bedaubed with shit, simple old shit, it guaranteed the wound would fester. To tell the truth, these were as effective as the more sophisticated devices and certainly took less time and effort both in their manufacture and deployment. But they lacked charisma. I wanted to hijack the *malais'* imaginations. I wanted to make their own mental processes work against them. And that demanded something more ingenious on my part. Well, I thought about our own patrols and how I'd arrived in the camp, exhausted from the burden of the dead man. I decided that the victim himself was only a small part of the equation, of the chain of inconvenience, fear, and disruption that could be caused. Osvaldo had half-glimpsed this earlier when he'd lectured Maria and me on the technology of wound production. The victim ought to be a nuisance to his whole outfit, preferably a noisy one. I wanted them to hang around, sweating, having to work hard to get the guy out of his predicament, dreading a burst of fire at any moment. I wanted the *malai* to scream a lot while they got him out of whatever I could devise. So I thought of a concealed pit with the stakes in the side, half pointing downwards, half pointing upwards. The latter would lacerate him as he fell, the former act as barbs, making extrication painful and difficult. I could just imagine them getting sick of their comrade's cries and expostulations and finally wrenching him out with the brutality normally reserved for Danuese. When we learned the *malais* were being issued with steel-plated combat boots I went further: the two pivoting plates armed with nails that fell apart as the victim trod on them. As he fell into my little hole he'd be jabbed through the calves on both sides above the boot. I worked out ways of sending retribution from above, logs that would fall and crush a man but leave him alive and pleading. I devised a travelling mace, a ball of wood on a rope, armed with spikes, that would be released on a trip-wire and swung across a path on a rope at face height. I hoped for a file of blinded *malais,* proceeding with hands on one another's shoulders. I invented a bow that sent an arrow up into the groin. Now that was a terror weapon. I don't believe I ever got anyone with that one, at least I never had the evidence in the form of blood-drops on the ground or leaves, but there must have been a couple of near-misses. I believe just its existence in the enemy's mind was sufficient. I know it won its deviser, anonymous, God be thanked, no small measure of notoriety. Osvaldo had mentioned a device encountered in Africa which they'd called the Bouncing Betty. It was a little Eastern bloc mine which, when activated, was thrown to waist-height before exploding. My device was the low technology Bouncing Betty.

But, as ever, the best was the simplest. One thing, as I've

said, that we possessed in abundance was ball ammunition. I pondered how to make use of it. Extracting the bullet for the sake of the powder in the cartridge and making a bomb from it was rather long-winded for an ineffective result. But how about this: I glued a tack to a wood base. Over the tack was six centimetres of metal tube, just wide enough to take a 7.62 mm round with difficulty. The percussion cap was a couple of millimetres above the tack. Peeping over the top of this lid-less box was the tip of the bullet. You buried the contraption with the earth smeared round showing fractionally over ground level. A soldier trod on it and boom! smoke curling from the path and someone minus half a foot. It was a far more selective weapon than anything else: the bare foot of a Danuese villager couldn't set it off. I called it Jack-in-the-box. Like it? We planted them liberally. In defence, they were placed across the trails that led to the camp. I kept a careful record of where they were. The Danuese were actually about to deploy them without bothering. Can you imagine? It was on the same basic level of organisation as field latrine hygiene: you didn't want to tread on your own turds too much, either – yet they'd have neglected it. I handed the master plan to Osvaldo with some pride, and was pleased when he recommended an additional system of field signals as well: knotted grasses, sticks pointing towards the hazard. Unless they were very unobtrusive, there was the danger of an alert enemy interpreting them as well but that was better than scoring own goals (X. Ray's phrase). In offence, I placed them around our obstructions. You could actually predict where the *malais* would have to alight from their vehicles and channel them towards the traps. I also employed them to protect our home-made anti-vehicle mines.

It proved a logical progression from the little Jack-in-the-boxes to these. If you had the imagination, you could make something from anything. It was all upstairs, in the head. You could get materials that would produce an effect; it was just a question of the ingenuity to put them together. Here was the inherited wiliness and economy again, the abomination of waste. With every passing day I reverted more to type! Whether it was the incompetence of their armourers or soft jungle soil that was to blame, the *malais'* bombs and shells frequently failed to explode. Their uninitiated ordnance seeded the hillsides of Danu. So of explosives there was no shortage to hand. First problem eliminated. Packaging and detonating were the big things. It came down to handiness and concealment. Well, this needed a lot of thought. In fact, I almost admitted defeat. But I had help. X. Ray sent someone round to my hut. It was João, his peacetime electrician, the guy who'd rewired the hotel and set up the Kawasaki. He'd had a hard hat, as a mark of his skilled status. I can't say I recognised him. Frankly, he looked like the wild man of Borneo. Yet he knew what he was at. It was strange to watch this caveman, with his broken, black nails and skein of hair at the waist, performing the delicate, complex tasks of the twentieth century.

'Can we make a bomb explode with electricity, João?' I asked, knowing we could and not ashamed to put it as simply as I could. (He'd then understand exactly what I wanted and it would give him confidence to feel superior to anyone who could ask such foolish questions – Oh, I understand how to manage workmen.)

'*Sim*, Senhor Ng,' he said, restraining a broad smile. That was OK by me. Let him laugh. We could actually get a grenade to initiate a bang that would set something bigger off, say a 105mm HE shell or 250 or 500 lb bomb. The eggs were designed so that you could detonate them electrically. João started talking and getting complicated. I had to make him halt and resume, at different points, three times, not the beginning on every occasion (I'm not *that* stupid). I learned. I'd always thought, kind of, in the way of a spark leaping one-way down the wires but covered by plastic, which was a somewhat inaccurate way of visualising it. João spoke of 'completing the circuit'. That was a great expression! You linked the whole system together at the moment of initiation, you, target, munitions. Pow! I liked it – bringing retribution home. We stripped the wrecks of lorries for any wire we could get. We had two of the women, who were *ikat* weavers, regularising and splicing the copper strands for us. Which they did with a dexterity wondrous to behold.

At this time I had a few other ideas. To give a non-command activated device a better probability of being initiated, I simply put a larger pressure plate over the detonator. In fact, I did it even with those of our own mines that we had been able to dig up again. You had to strike a balance between a plate so large it dissipated the weight, to the extent of not striking the trigger hard enough, or a plate too small in area to catch any prey. It worked like a dream for big aerial bombs. You just dug them in and put the metal plate on top. The small area of the nose of the bomb would otherwise never have been contacted except by a fluke. We could also fill a pot or coconut with explosive and bury it with a grenade. The safety pin of this would be wired to a stake buried under a tarpaulin. When a vehicle drove over the cover it pulled the wire, and bingo!

Then with a truck battery and wires connected on the one side to an unfilled sandwich of two pressure plates just under the earth and on the other to the munitions, you could have the circuit completed by an unwary enemy pressing the plates together a long distance away from the charge itself. So the *malai* on point could blow up the rest of his squad 50 metres distant. When it was vehicles, with our plates situated in a straight line with the charge but 200 metres ahead up the road, we could get their scouting party to put something off under the main group of the convoy. You could space the blasts like a daisy-chain. That was where Chinese checkers came in. Stone, paper, scissors was when we faked signs of mining, but there were no mines! And sometimes I'd put down a few Jack-in-the-boxes next to what looked like a poorly camouflaged anti-vehicle mine. The *malais* would be so bound up with the big bomb they'd forget the little device. You know, it was so simple I wondered how no one else had addressed themselves to it. But then it had been the same with business. Taking money from the Danuese had always been like stealing candy from a baby.

Rehabilitating the unexploded *malai* ordnance wasn't as big a deal as you would have thought, either. As I say, this offered a limitless supply of explosives, a cornucopia lowered from the heavens. I often thought if we required more we should simply light fires where we weren't and wait for the offering. More fiery pillars and manna. I kept the notion to myself. The scheme smacked too much of treachery and betrayal. My position was still not so secure that I could afford to jest like that. João and I went out grubbing for shells and bombs. We'd made ourselves little wooden probes, somewhat safer than metal. The big aerial bombs could be lost for ever, way deep down in the earth. It took us a long time at first, before we learned not to look in the big craters. We acquired an instinct in the end, like pigs that root out truffles. I can tell you about the fuse of a 500-pound bomb, but as to what a truffle looks like, frankly, I've no conception. Sometimes we had to go down in excess of five metres. Deeper than a grave, I said. You know, it didn't faze me. I'd get the kids digging, then when the heavy spade-work was done João and I would jump in to proceed, admittedly, with greater circumspection. There were two kinds of fuse: impact and barometric. The first kind wasn't yet armed on the bomb-rack of the plane. Too goddam dangerous. A little propeller on the nose, the size of a model airplane's, wound as it dropped. After a certain number of revolutions it armed the bomb. Trouble was, the *malai* pilots weren't dropping them from the right height or the artificers had calibrated too many turns. Phut! Into the mulch they went. The barometric fuses were designed to give an air-burst with a greater radius of devastation. If it worked, it was stupendous. Often it didn't. Perhaps they didn't realise how high we were in the mountains. Or maybe the fuses were too advanced for their armourers or came from faulty batches dumped on a third-world client state. We used the HE anyway. The White Phos I didn't want to know.

Doing anything a lot gives you confidence. I'd whistle away as I poked and prised. It all depended on you and the nimbleness of your fingers. It was quite peaceful, and I figured you'd never know if you made a mistake. It wasn't like the horror and confusion of a firefight, your ass-hole twitching as the rounds cracked overhead. I had quite a little team around me, at my beck and call. It was like the hotel again. Do this, don't do that. I strode around like... like Osvaldo, I guess. I was in the pit, tying the rope around the greasy fins of a 250-pound bomb when there came the unmistakable sound of clockwork fizzing inside the cone. Shit, that hole emptied before you could say long live the glorious FAKINTIL. João jumped in and got the assembly off. After a few seconds I followed him down. It seemed the natural thing to do. All you had to do was topple. Gravity did the rest. He handed me the fuse and we grinned at each other. After a while the Corporal's face appeared on the edge. 'Here, catch,' I said. I think my face must have looked like that when Osvaldo pulled his stunt with the rolling grenade during the singing of 'O, Mighty Mountain!' on Independence Day. I could see the Corporal pondering whether to butt-stroke me in the face with his rifle, but then he just said, 'You've got balls, haven't you, Chinaman?'

Me? That was a joke. But as we came up the path to camp, hours later, with the black bomb swinging on two poles like a slaughtered boar, the kids running in front to announce our triumph, I thought, yes, I think I understand a little what it's like to be Osvaldo, or Arsenio, or Maria. It's easy for them to be who they are, in a sense. Responsibility is a kind of anaesthesia, or better, it had been the bamboo-cane to the sickly tomato plant of my courage. I'd behaved according to the notions and expectations of others, rather than my own. Just being in charge had forced me to behave more ambitiously and, in fact, had actually blunted my perception of the very real dangers. It was a tonic, leadership, but it had better be imbibed with caution for its intoxication was fatal. Later, I was to see that very clearly.

SIXTEEN

THE RETURNING WET SEASON brought an end to all campaigning. I was glad by that time for a rest. I had no complaints about my dripping roof, which put trickles down the back of my neck. It was fair exchange for rounds overhead. I amused myself with some new inventions, the Leonardo of guerrilla warfare – I'd insufficiently appreciated the uses to which the tensile properties of strips of truck tyres could be applied – and found some dignity in my post of quartermaster-general. As it was me who drew the most ammunition nowadays for my Jack-in-the-boxes, it had been decided I was the right person to oversee its distribution. I didn't see the Danuese logic, but I took the job; I was a glorified shop-keeper.

By now, we were having difficulty with food – the full-time gardeners left behind at the previous camp had not been as productive as hoped – but morale remained high. We were winning, we thought. No one looked beyond the result of the last skirmish.

That rainy season Martinho cultivated me with his utmost assiduity, with all the grace and suavity of the ecclesiastical politician he should have been. I could see through the snow-job, but I was deeply flattered. He'd come over in the mid-afternoon, with two boys protecting him with banana-leaves. He made a point of keeping his acolytes on, in the dampest corner I'm afraid, while we talked. It was clever of him, and what we said and how we put it was way over their infant heads, bless them.

'No one could have led us like Osvaldo,' he'd pronounce.

'That's true,' I'd say. So what? was my unspoken thought.

'I don't think Napoleon could have done a better job this last year.'

'Napoleon was a *malai* – he was against the Spanish guerrillas.' I forebore from mentioning that it was where the word had originated.

'Ha, ha,' laughed Martinho, with the most blatant lack of sincerity.

'Of course,' I said, 'Napoleon didn't know when enough was enough. He should never have tried to attack Moscow in the winter. Come to think of it, Hitler overreached himself, too.'

Martinho nodded sagely. 'He should have listened to his civilian advisers, they say.' Then he remarked, 'Of course we don't have winter and summer here at the equator.'

'Just the dry and rainy seasons,' I said.

He smiled, in an unfocussed, absent sort of way, his eyes fixed on some spot on the wall above and behind me, but I wasn't deceived. We left it there and a little later Maria joined us.

I don't give Martinho, particularly, any marks for prescience. Our little chats, or the parts of them that stuck in the mind later, would have seemed without significance if things had gone on the way they had been. I don't think he had the first idea of strategy or campaigning: he was sick of the life and its hardships, yet at the same time, driven by his ego, wanted to play a bigger part in that life. He was conciliatory by temperament and, unlike his younger brother, thought beyond the present. He wasn't by any means a spiteful or treacherous person. To make a U-turn often needs more guts as well as imagination than to persevere in the same old rut. I thought a lot about Martinho's mental state later, tried hard to assess his motivations because they threw light on mine as well. He was indubitably a better man than I, and I so much wanted to come up to his level, rather than bring him down to mine, even if it was only in my own mental wanderings. You'll see what I mean.

That dry season – the third since the invasion, my second with FAKINTIL – began as it would end. And it was the beginning of the end, too. The big difference, to put it very simply, was that the *malais* came for *us* this time. They took the initiative and they didn't let it go. It was concerted. After it had been going on a while we learned it had a name:

Operation Anthill. I don't think I'm making egregious assumptions if I say we were the ants. Soldier ants. Well, they certainly stomped on us. After a good smoking-out. It was thought out and it used all their resources, for a change. A *malai* brigade moved in from the west, another from the north. That effectively encircled us by pushing our backs right against the wall of those barren mountains and the sea. They cut us off from our food supplies. They bombed the gardens with defoliants and poisons; they drove the villagers away from their settlements. There were no massacres of civilians, which was not the *malai* style at all. Not until we had all those hungry mouths flocking to us for protection did I realise why.

They also started to play us at our own game – and beat us at it more than once. They took up aggressive patrolling: small recon groups and then slightly larger fighting patrols. We took a while to realise it. One day a FAKINTIL squad went out and never returned. I thought they'd run away, deserted, or just gone AWOL for a week, to see their relatives. It seemed more likely than that they'd been hit by the *malais*.

But they'd been wiped out.

A few days later the *malais* ambushed another group. Probably the same *malais*. This time two men got back with the story. They'd been moving along a path – probably taking no care, though they couldn't admit it to Osvaldo, of course – when all hell had broken loose. The squad leader and the No.2 had been cut down straight away, not by gunfire but by claymore mines – curved devices like miniature radar dishes which threw ball-bearings in a deadly arc like a hundred shot-guns. As the others dove for the cover of a tree-trunk and a ditch they'd tripped a daisy-chain of grenades and those who weren't hit by the splinters had been channelled into a zone the *malais* had pre-targeted with their automatic weapons. Of the two survivors, who came back separately, one had been far behind the others and another, in blind panic, had run straight at the *malais*, overrun them, and gone on, which had saved him. It was what Osvaldo had taught the kids, but I think the guy had just bolted. He'd lost his weapon, certainly, which was the most heinous offence in the military and especially FAKINTIL canon: you can be stark naked but with a rifle you are still a soldier. Without it, fully equipped in every other respect, you're nothing. He got no sympathy from Osvaldo. He was locked up for three days.

There were no more contacts in the jungle, for a while, but the *malais* had made their point – it was no longer our element, our sanctuary. It had destroyed our sense of ease, our proprietorship.

And there was another unwelcome shock – the OV-10 Bronco. If there was one weapon the *malai* possessed which gave them superiority, which terrorised FAKOUM, this was it. Quite suddenly it appeared in the sky above us and after that it was perpetual menace, a sword of Damocles as we ate, slept, worked. It vastly extended the duration of the enemy presence. To look at, it was nothing. A dinky, little twin-engined *propeller* plane, with a vulnerable-looking bubble-blister of a canopy enclosing two heads that seemed to be just asking for damage to be done to it, maybe by heaving a brick through. Its stubby fuselage, so short as to appear deformed, hung from the hunched wing and rack-like tail-boom. The twin-tail appeared a quaint rather than a technological detail. In general it resembled nothing so much as a modern witch's conveyance, a halloween bubble-car. It buzzed leisurely through the sky at about eight hundred metres, like something clockwork. Leisurely was the operative word, the key to its effectiveness. The capacity of the OV-10 to dawdle was its most dangerous feature – truly a plane for Danu! The hugely more expensive and higher performance jet fighters the *malais* had been using were not well-suited to the kind of war they'd been having in Danu. The jet-engines were more efficient at high altitude, the pilots could spend only a small amount of time over the target, and they swept over far too fast. They were expensive playthings for their airforce generals, the macho jewellery of the third world, maybe useful in their confrontation with their Malay cousins but air superiority (which the machines were designed to win) was not at all contested in Danu. They had the skies without a contest. We weren't exactly sending anyone up to have dogfights with them. The Bronco did its job perfectly. The fact that it was so slow didn't make it vulnerable – not with the weapons FAKINTIL had. We learned that the hard way. At first they didn't need to search too hard for us. The slow-moving, low-flying toy was just too much to resist for the itchy-fingered warriors of FAKINTIL. The guns went up, like a line of sportsmen, and away they blazed. Poor ignoramuses! They paid dearly for the lapse. Temptingly vulnerable though the Bronco looked, it might as well have been moving in a magic dimension for all the effect the FAKINTIL guns could have. It was untouchable. The effect of gravity was such that the bullets would expend their energy, fall impotently to earth way before they reached the aircraft. Six hundred metres was a feasible range for the G3s in the horizontal trajectory. Vertically, we might as well have been shooting at the moon. I think the Bronco pilots flew deliberately low, low enough to be hit, then climbed a little before plastering the gun-flashes. It was bad, real bad. The little planes could carry a lot of weaponry: they had rockets, machine-guns, napalm, white phosphorus, and HE all ready for us in the one visit. The first group to be caught were actually near Bacalhau, roaming near the highway. They came back with a lot of wounded, having been bombed and rocketed out in the open. But the real beauty of it for the *malai* was that they could come visiting *chez nous*. Half an hour's flying from Bacalhau airstrip, and then they'd loiter above us for two hours or more. It was the insolence as much as anything else which drew the FAKINTIL fire, until we learned fear. We objected to them doing what they wanted over our heads. It made nonsense of time and distance, of the terrain which put days of travel before the *malai* troops, even if the distances were relatively small as the crow flies. Now the crow flew with a vengeance. On the second occasion – it happened before the first group to be strafed had returned, so it seemed like the first – a big party in the forest (the numbers had given confidence against the little toy in the sky) had opened up on two Broncos. Osvaldo couldn't discover who'd been first to breach the strict fire-discipline he'd done his best to inculcate. The company leader swore he hadn't given the order to fire, which I was inclined to believe. The culprit was too wise to own up – that, or he was dead. In any case, the whole party had gleefully followed his lead, not a few blasting away on full auto.

They paid.

Only 15 out of 70 were uninjured. The Broncos made slow, deliberate passes in pairs. That was the first time we had fire-weapons used against us. They dropped napalm right on top of the group, then put in rockets and on the third, fourth, fifth, and sixth passes machine-gun fire. It went on and on. That was what had got to them, the survivors told Osvaldo, the persistence of it, rather than the breathless terror of the searing, air-destroying fire. The spite, I guess. Our sentries in the trees and observation posts on high ground saw the broiling orange pillar, that black-topped column of wrath, expand over the forest some 20 kilometres away, though the flying insects that had created it remained both soundless and invisible. Including the harassing passes as our men tried to withdraw, not caring whether they revealed themselves or not, the ordeal lasted more than 45 minutes before the Broncos headed for base. Osvaldo went out with his best men and ran into the surviving group half-way. They had some terrible burns among them. It was the first time I'd ever seen Maria taken aback, in her professional capacity. The dead ones were just charcoal, they didn't trouble to bring them. I saw them later with X. Ray's retrieval group – like burnt chicken, legs curled and shrivelled. The ones who were still living looked kind of pink, where they weren't black. It didn't get better with time but worse. You see, the napalm – which was evil stuff, jellied petroleum: corrosive white goo (which I saw later) – kept on burning in and on the skin. You couldn't put it out, not with water which was all we had. Maria and I had to be careful when we attended to the burns. There wasn't a lot we could do except give them a drink, for they were desperately thirsty. Given the state they were in, they seemed oddly glad of that. Maria knew she was looking at 99 per cent dead men. I didn't then. There was no morphine but we did our best. They seemed lucid. I mentioned this with some hope and surprise to our doctor but she shook her head. Shook it angrily. Many of the casualties were sitting up, smoking, chewing betel a couple of days later. Within a week all of them were dead, of hypothermia and pneumonia. Hypothermia? In Danu? The irony was insupportable.

After that, there wasn't too much of shooting at the Broncos, I can tell you.

The planes were from the Americans, by the way, and about as good a gift as ever was given. They swung the whole balance the *malai* way. Even a .50 calibre machine-gun would have given FAKINTIL the chance to bring one of these budget gunships down, at least spoiled the pilots' field-day – its rounds reached that much higher. But we didn't have heavy machine-guns. The *malais* made their own helicopters at home, under licence, but as useful as they were they didn't have the impact of the OV-10. Frankly, a nuclear weapon would have been less efficient against us than one of these little planes.

We had to become nomads and foragers. The cosy days of being able to stay put in one camp for long periods were gone. Left to themselves, the men might have remained out of default, sheer inertia. They were nearly as bad as the *malais*. X. Ray was a man who liked to live solidly, in the same place; he wouldn't have stirred till the camp had been flattened around his ears. But Osvaldo had us moving in 24 hours. Howsoever mean a place, however makeshift the life, its expedients and subterfuges, it is impossible not to become in some way affectionate about a habitation. Even familiar terrain inspires the knowledge of ownership. Osvaldo didn't wait for the burns to die, so that we could bury them in a place they knew. He had them stretchered away, still conscious, still apparently recovering. Maria didn't object. She knew what was going to happen. Observing the decencies would make no difference to them, those men under sentence of death, talking and smoking on borrowed time. She was as hard-headed as Osvaldo.

Well, in a day or so they were all dead, shivering and gasping their last, while we sweated as we watched them in the dank forest. From now on, we never stayed anywhere longer than three weeks. The kids adjusted the best. I don't think they knew any better, had forgotten what ordinary life was like. Besides, three weeks is a long time to a kid, as long as three months for an adult. I remembered those interminable school semesters with the Brothers in Macao; 12 weeks had been for ever. While Osvaldo could keep control of his own people – he could have organised two men on an upturned canoe – the constant moving placed terrible strains on the links with the other FAKINTIL groups who acknowledged him as their commander. It just wasn't possible to impart news of one's whereabouts that was up to date. Messengers would arrive to find sites long deserted, with just a few blackened logs and browning shelters resisting the jungle's stealthy reclamation. These scouts couldn't be totally sure the *malais* hadn't bushwhacked the entire group. It was an enigma, a tricky and dangerous one sometimes, for in the early days we took to booby-trapping the old camps.

Well, the rains were kind of a moment of truth this time round. It was true that we could stay where we were – we didn't have to be marching from place to place. Yet we faced an even more terrible threat than the OV-10. It was starvation.

To be honest, the food situation had been deteriorating even before the appearance of the toy planes and the *malai* ambushes. That hadn't been, directly, the *malais'* doing. There was something wrong with the forest soil. Danu was an infertile island in the case of food cultivation at the best of times, if not where the rampant growth of the jungle was concerned. Nor were the hill people clever farmers in the way of the Chinese or even the *malai* central islanders. Although famine was not a recurrent feature of island life, like India or Africa, abundance was a stranger to us. To try to turn soldiers into farmers in conditions as unpropitious as these was to ask for a miracle. It became apparent we'd managed to eat too much of the grain, not left enough for seed. Damp and mildew had spoiled some of what we'd managed to conserve, while rats and smaller critters had made their inroads.

The last straw had been the enforced running around. For lack of water, gardens had withered and died; no doubt for lack of shit as well.

As the heavens opened, and we stood bare-headed, the drops falling disregarded into our eyes as we looked at the empty little rice-barns and maize bins, the extent of the catastrophe came home to us. It came slowly. Osvaldo and Martinho must have realised before the rest of us. City boys like X. Ray were slower. You see, the piles of vegetables looked quite substantial at first, if you just thought of what one person's requirements were. I mean, there were enough of these to feed one person for years. When you divided it by more than 100 mouths it was incredible to see how the horn of plenty shrivelled into a peanut-shell. Or alternatively, how you had to multiply one person's requirement into a mountain to provide for all. You go and try to feed the multitude on five loaves and five fishes, I thought bitterly as I looked at Martinho's empty face; you just try it.

That was the start of the Bad Time. Osvaldo had us on half rations at once – i.e., half of what was already a meagre sustenance. It wouldn't have been enough to preserve your life if you had it every day for five years; it was enough to stop you dying quite so soon as nothing. It was a quarter of an ear of corn per day mixed with a handful of rice, alternated on different days by a piece of sweet potato slightly smaller than a hand grenade, or some chips of yam. You picked off the yellow beads of corn and mixed them with the rice and then you gnawed and ate the hard cob. The tubers were the most filling but Maria said the corn and rice did most to keep you living. Big deal. It seemed hardship at the time but was nothing to what followed only a little later. I mean it was really quite civilised – it was only that your stomach cramped, or got bloated with air, and you did rabbit pellets when you shit, but what you did get to eat – insufficient as it was – could be recognised as food. It was wholesome, it delivered protein and vitamin. Hell, it even tasted good.

We were free to supplement the group ration with what we could individually forage – a good old military tradition, of course, being just licensed theft from civilians. In our case, there were none handy to dispossess. Oh, that day of carnage! How it lived gloriously in the mind! I don't mean the successful ambush. I mean the feast of buffalo meat on Osvaldo and Maria's wedding-day. I thought a lot about that, even dreamed of it a few times. Also of the good dinners with the District Administrator at Boa Vista in the days of Dr Maria's mobile clinics, the fried pigeon and his home-made wine. Strangely enough, I didn't dwell too much on the T-bones and hamburgers of my Canadian days – just the ice-cream sundaes I'd enjoyed in Annie Laval's company.

Where we found ourselves there wasn't much wildlife. It was more a question of searching for fruits, wild vegetables, and berries. Bamboo root was good, I'll say that. Sure, I'd eat it again.

I used to look at my quartermaster's stores: the green boxes of ammo, the bright, brassy disintegrating-link belts of bullets for the HK21, the little black machine-pistols with their long magazines, the stacks of light anti-tank rockets in their cases, sufficient for taking on a *malai* division. And I'd think: 'Yes, all that gear, and we'd trade half of it for ten tins of bully beef.' I'd remember the days when I was the *malais'* frontman for blackmarket food, and all those tins of KLIM I'd given away to Maria's kids. Why hadn't I kept just one, had the foresight to keep it with me at all times and brought it up here? In all seriousness I taxed myself with the ridiculous accusation.

By the week, we became feebler and more emaciated. At some stage, I can no longer clearly remember when, I stopped shaving. I wasn't so weakened that I couldn't – it was not so bad as that – but the starvation sabotaged the resolve in some strange way. You didn't care any more. For me, it was a great abrogation. I didn't mind being hairy like a bear. Correction, I wouldn't have minded being hairy like a bear. But what I grew, with my genes, were those grotesque, thin, billy-goat tufts. I hated it – the archetypal Chinaman, though my nails were not his talons but grimy scabs worn down to the quick with grubbing in the soil for the booty of inedible tubers and larvae. You never thought of yourself as a walking skeleton, like the others you saw. I dismissed the fact that my uniform hung on me like a pup-tent. It was some weird accident, the reverse of shrinkage in the wash.

Osvaldo now performed one of the few discreditable actions I ever knew him to do. He was, and always had been, capable of ruthlessness, but this was mean-minded and an exploitation of the defenceless. He cut the juvenile ration to half of the adult. That was, they got about a quarter of what they had been receiving in the previous dry season. I could, I am glad to say, look beyond my own narrow self-interest as an adult, on this point. He did it on grounds of rationality – oh, his reasoning was impeccable. Maria was the Nazi doctor to his camp commandant: the children expended fewer calories than the active combatants. They didn't have to travel long distances, carrying weapons, fight and run. That was bullshit. He did it to consolidate his hold over the men. It was the politician in him, coming out against the grain of his magnanimity. He reckoned, correctly, that so long as people can see someone worse off than themselves, they will endure their own condition the better. That's what you might call the psychological aspect of it. The other was simpler. It made Osvaldo popular with the troops. The kids had no vote, no lobby; they were not a constituency.

Did I take it up with Osvaldo? Did I hell. I didn't want to find myself on four centimetres of corn cob as well. He was a practical guy, Osvaldo, and sneaky with it; he didn't believe in the academic opinion, abstractly held. Osvaldo believed in putting your ideas into practice. I'd have had my words to eat. Nonetheless, I mentioned it to Maria. She reacted badly, sure sign – I thought – of an uneasy conscience. I thought:

'You have come a long way, my darling, since the clinic.' What would Rosa have said to her? What would Jean Carmichael have said to Osvaldo? Or Arsenio? It was shameful.

'You think you know it all, don't you?' Maria attacked me – the more fiercely because she was defending her brave like any good squaw. 'You're a sentimental fool. You set yourself on a height, looking down on those who are better than you.'

This was a novel experience, being called sentimental, me, the man usually upbraided by his female friends for having no discernible emotions. I said, 'My dear Maria, you mustn't misunderstand me,' crapping myself now that she'd bear tales to the terrible Osvaldo (though in hindsight I know she never would have descended to that). 'It's just that, well...' I didn't bother to finish; it would have got me into deeper and yet more dangerous waters. What I was going to say was that Osvaldo was conceding a victory to the *malai*. He'd always thought of those kids as his seed-corn; yet here he was throwing them on to the fire, on to stony ground, wasting them, abandoning them to survive as they might. And in doing this, he was being dictated to by the *malais*. He was giving up part of his long-term game-plan for short-term expediency.

I thought a lot less of him for it, I have to say.

The kids took it well enough. Their love and admiration for Osvaldo weren't affected. How can I put it? There was dismay, expostulations, some tears, but – which was important – no sulking.

Resentment was absent. In their place I'd have felt it, though not shown it. But the kids hadn't got to the stage where you knew how to hide deep feelings like that.

In the end, things weren't as bad for them as you might have thought. They had time and the keen eyes to go grubbing for what the forest had to offer. And quite a few of the adults – not me – gave them some of their own hand-out. Including, so I was told, X. Ray (which didn't surprise me) and the Corporal (which did, greatly).

205

SEVENTEEN

AT ABOUT THIS TIME, I BECAME VERY ILL. This was distinct from the chills and gut-aches that were an ordinary part of the FAKINTIL life. As the dry weather came, Osvaldo decided to double-bluff the malais and take us low rather than high, at least for the start of the campaigning season. In fact, with the OV-10s, we were no longer safer on the mountain-tops, so we didn't have a great deal to lose. It was a ruse to buy us maybe a few weeks' concealment. Unfortunately, dropping below 1500 metres exposed us to the female of the Anopheles species. Mosquitoes is what I'm talking.

Within three weeks of descending I started to feel unwell: fever, aching limbs, hot and cold turns. This was nothing new for the group but whereas the others were able to recover from relatively mild bouts after a day or two, with no semi-immunity I was in trouble. I'd taken the precautions, covered up after dark, burnt a few witch-doctor's twigs in the corner; however, you could run but you couldn't hide. I was trembling in the 'sick-bay' amongst those I was supposed to be tending – four or five splinter cases who were doing nicely after the weeks of recuperation – when Maria removed the bowl of herbal compresses from me and said, without evident concern or sympathy: 'You're sick.' I denied it. Not being brave (who me?) but knowing there was no false sentiment in the camp. Maybe Osvaldo would cut the allowance for the sick next. By the following evening I was raving. God knows what I was shouting. I hope it was in English. When a Danuese got sick, he'd receive half a chloroquine tablet. Those pills were like diamonds to us. Usually, that would get them over the attack. But not with one guy. He started to piss black – the parasite breaking down his blood, Maria said – and within a day or two he was gone. All for want of a white pill.

She kept me alive. I don't know how many of the priceless little things she squandered on my useless life, but at the end of a week I don't care to relive even in the mind, weak, damp, and exhausted, I was still with them. The kind of weakness I had was a good weakness; you could feel yourself getting better; you could luxuriate in that kind of temporary feebleness.

Martinho came calling. He said he'd come to my side with Fr Molloy many a time in the course of my fever but I hadn't recognised him. Thank Christ, I thought. I would have imagined they were administering the Last Rites.

He still had boys with banana leaves covering his progress, this time to shield him from sun rather than rain. While the acolytes fanned him slowly, we spoke of this and that. Like the rest of us, he was starving, but that hadn't stopped him from securing for himself such creature comforts, such dignities as he might. He had no material possessions; but he still disposed of authority. Really, there was a creditable side to it. You could say he hadn't lost his sense of what he was worth. So far, that had been proof against tribulation.

The boys put their backs against the trees and chewed the areca nut. Martinho prated of inconsequentialities. Napoleon didn't come up. I was waiting all the time for some of his double-talk, but he avoided anything meaningful. I think he could feel me waiting, sense my expectation and, being the awkward son of a bitch he was, decided he'd not broach the issue.

Before I was 100 per cent again – more accurately, 60 per cent, if you measured it against the state of my peacetime health – we were on the run again. A reconnaissance plane, a propeller contraption but not one of the deadly little Broncos, spotted us and buzzed around for ten minutes. Our radio operator found the frequency and we heard the pilot get on to base. He sounded extremely excited. These little aircraft were unarmed except for some white phosphorus rockets employed as markers for the jets or artillery. He didn't put any down but we still struck camp within minutes. I was stretchered out. I'd stood up, to be immediately assailed by a dizzy fit, but had valiantly overcome it and was packing my haversack when Maria caught my arm. She made the splinter cases walk. The junior woodchucks carried me and mine in relays: six boys, four on and two resting. One thing FAKINTIL had was efficient stretchers, I'll give us that. The traditional skills were there, the material all round us in abundance, and above all the need. What more prerequisites are needed for even the greatest invention? The contraptions were springy but robust. For my part I had sufficient energy to keep a watch out for myself. From my own experience of arriving *chez* FAKINTIL with a mortally wounded man on my back, I realised it was better to be querulous and bad-tempered than an uncomplaining lump of meat. They'd get pretty quickly negligent if you didn't remind them of your existence, that you still set store by yourself, that you'd resent being dropped, or dragged through thorns. In fact, I armed myself with a good switch, which I didn't scruple to apply to errant hindquarters or legs. Thus, like the old man of the sea, I directed my invalid progress. I'd rather be a tyrant than a martyr.

We had to move six times in the month that I was recovering, and on the last occasion we were slow enough to get hammered for our tardiness. It was three Broncos hunting in a pack. The only reason we survived this was because they must have dropped all their main ordnance on another target beforehand. It was unusual to see more than one or two, so they must have responded to some jubilant fix from one or other of their number. It was just machine-gun fire. I don't suppose they ever knew they'd wasted their napalm and rockets earlier. This was the boss man they had squirming underfoot down there. We'd been forced right back on high, ascending each time we broke camp and the forest here was well broken up with rock and creeper. It meant there were caves and crevices you could squeeze yourself into for shelter but also that the bullets ricocheted, throwing up thousands of splinters. It was a hellish noise. I found myself sharing the space under three rocks, you could hardly call it a cave, with Maria. It took me a while to realise; at first, from the size of her, I'd thought it was one of the kids. She had her fingers in her ears and her eyes closed! Despite the danger and the fear, I couldn't help grinning. Maria as useless and scared as anyone else – that was worth seeing. There wasn't much time for chit-chat, with the Broncos coming in fast in shallow dives and banking steeply for position afterwards. It was virtually non-stop. But I had time to say, 'You'll feel much better when you've got something to do, Maria.'

She kicked me backwards in the face hard enough to make me think my nose was bleeding. For all her qualities she was sometimes simply a bitch. I forgot about the center of my face – the supernova I could feel expanding out of its very middle – as yet another Bronco made its pass. This was like queueing to kick someone in the head on a city pavement, I thought. Those clever little machines, the highly trained young men who were their pilots – but when all was said and done, it came down to that. It was just done at a government level, that was all. On this run the strafing – the last pass, as it turned out – was uncannily, horribly accurate. When I looked over my cover I could see the four lines of dirt and pulverised rock and lichen kicking up towards me. They advanced quite slowly, the bullets streaking down, of course, but the storm approaching me only at the rate at which the pilot altered the angle of his nose. This he did a degree at a time, with skilled deliberation. A few seconds later the burst was rattling around our ears in our little hide, like the twittering of a thousand metal sparrows, the debris flying every which way. I was trying to burrow under Maria but ended on top of her, as if I was screwing her from behind and was trying to kiss her mouth. (No chance, darling Maria.) I heard the change in pitch as the OV-10 climbed away but it wasn't replaced by the whine of the next diving at us. The drone of their departure faded into nothing, to be replaced by the scream of forest birds and monkeys. Maria gasped something to me, with pain and difficulty.

'Darling, what is it? You're hurt?' (Surely not? I'd have been hit first. I congratulated myself, shamelessly, on not having succeeded in getting underneath her.)

'Get off me, you fool. I can hardly breathe.'

For good measure she punched me on the chest after I rolled off. But there *was* blood from somewhere. No, I checked it wasn't the kick to the nose. Nor was it a serious wound to the body but a nick to the top of my right ear, probably from a flying rock-chip. You couldn't say it did more than sting but there was really a surprising amount of red liquid around. Typical of even a non-serious head wound, of course, what with the generous supply of small blood vessels at the surface. Now that was a piece of acquired knowledge that was reassuring. So often it was knowing something that made it spookier.

Maria had recovered her composure – if she'd ever really lost it. She was running round, checking the bodies. From their various hidey-holes the guerrillas emerged; we were snakes. Very many of us as thin as serpents. I let myself bleed; no point staining my shirt sleeve as well as my collar, while leaves or grass would only infect it. It would soon coagulate. Besides, thought I, it would do no harm, no harm at all, for my comrades to see the Chinaman bleeding in the Cause.

We had this system for sorting out casualties, devised by Osvaldo from African experience but colluded in with great willingness by Maria because, I suspect, it answered to a similar exaltation of the efficient and the ruthless in her personality: there were those so badly hurt that they'd die no matter what you did, so you did nothing for them; there were those who were likely to recover from light wounds, so they could wait for your attention; and there were those badly hurt, but not so they were hopeless cases, who needed your immediate attention, and got it. This was a system which should have been based on heli-evacuations and good field surgery, neither of which we had, but it was a logical if cold-blooded method which worked better than no organisation. My task was to classify the wounds (easy enough, depending mostly on where they'd been hit; anything in the chest or abdomen for us and it was *finito),* and to check how many wounds they had. It was no good dressing a foot when the man had a hole the size of your fist in the small of his back.

I started to go about my work with what I thought conspicuous gallantry, the blood caking in the sun around my neck and cheek. We had three killed outright, one who died 20 minutes later, two badly wounded, and five or six with minor injuries like mine, including a washerwoman who'd turned her ankle on a root. Strapping an ankle was easy and satisfying – it also worked; stopped swelling, the cells bursting. Gut wounds, as I say, were nearly always a death sentence. It was two boys aged 13 and 16 who'd caught it this time. One was screaming. I don't think he was playing for sympathy and attention. Our kids were no longer like that. I think it hurt like hell. The screams came very regularly, interspersed with crying. The other just lay there against a tree, with the yellowest face I ever saw. He was clearly on the way out. Any sympathy I felt for the kid screaming – he'd been one of my bearers, our roles now reversed – got used up pretty fast. I wished he'd stop screaming. Maria had nothing to give him. Morphine – don't make me laugh, don't make me cry. We all stood round him, the kid dying quietly was left alone. This one stopped screaming long enough to signal for water. They gave it him. There was nothing to lose. Then he threw it down without taking more than a mouthful. The screaming started again. He began to cry for his mother, sobbing as I'm sure even X. Ray or the Corporal would have done in his position. Osvaldo spoke to Maria who shook her head. He unfastened the flap of his pistol holster, moving behind the boy as he did so. No one said anything. I think there existed a silent consensus on this subject. All, apart from Fr Molloy – the most useless mouth in the camp, more even than the Chinaman. He jumped forward with uncharacteristic promptness, waving his hands in horror at the mortal sin Osvaldo was about to commit. The stupid old fart, I think, regarded it as worse than an ordinary killing because it was merciful. Martinho followed him. I wasn't sure whether he was going to assist the priest or pull him back. Then I saw

211

that Martinho didn't know either. Osvaldo saw them coming out of the corner of his eye – he'd been giving all his concentration to the boy – and holstered his Browning. I could tell he hadn't forsaken his course of action, though that was how Molloy interpreted it; his face was suffused with self-important indignation. Osvaldo didn't have the 2,000 years of Church history behind him which impelled Molloy. On the other hand he was the steadiest guy you could want, steadier than St Peter if you're using the Bible as collateral. He had put his pistol away so that it would be safe; he didn't want an accident and he wasn't threatening anyone either. This became clear as, like a young shepherd defending his flock from a giant crow, he fended Molloy off with his left forearm. Unfortunately, in losing his balance the old priest took Martinho sprawling with him. Osvaldo grabbed one of Molloy's arms to help him to his feet. Molloy was spluttering about his cloth, which seemed both excessive and unfair to me; it made all his reactions appear those of a hysterical man. X. Ray and Martinho, both, supported him.

All this time the boy had been crying and groaning. Osvaldo gave him the water canteen again. He took it, reflexively I think, with both hands. Then Osvaldo stepped behind him, brought the Browning out, slipped the safety, pulled back the slide, released it, and shot him downwards in the nape of the neck. He then picked up the ejected cartridge and put it in his shirt pocket.

That was it. After the enormous, the simply enormous, report the silence was amazing.

The other boy died of his wound a short time after, just before we left. The bodies were put in a crevice and covered with rocks.

For the next few weeks it was run, run, run. We dodged this way and that, circled, doubled back, climbed, descended. It was no good. The *malai* airforce had us squirming on a pin. We needed to throw them off for a week, at least. That would have considerably widened the area they had to search, but when they just had 20 or 30 square miles to cover they could always find us if they looked hard

212

enough, even if they'd overflown on their previous two or three missions. I also think they got a lot better at reading the terrain and us.

They had learned to use their airpower and their troops in conjunction. We had a very scary experience a little later when we were strafed *and* ambushed in quick succession. It was one thing to be bombed, rocketed, and cannonaded. That had an end when they flew off. It was terrifying, but impersonally so. One way or other, your woes were finite. The day they heli-dropped troops and then used the planes to drive us towards the carefully laid ambush was the blackest in the FAKINTIL annals. The *malais* on the ground couldn't match the devastating firepower of the planes, but the engagement wasn't self-enclosing; it went on. It was a different kind of strain, which could bring a weakling like me closer to breaking-point, though it was the planes which – funnily enough – disturbed the hardened African vets the most. The Broncos had sent us scuttling down from the heights to where the forest was thicker. We always moved fast after the planes had gone, not troubling too much about the noise we made. They'd hardly hear it up there.

I was at the back with Maria and the kids when I heard the crack of the claymores, followed by the long, luxurious bursts of automatic fire the *malais* would allow themselves. Our men shot straight back. It had become instinct. Hunger, faintness had – I think – made them like animals. Within two seconds a furious firefight was in progress. I heard a whistle go, probably X. Ray's. There were four or five reports, and from the corner of my eye I saw the flames of the back blast from the 66mm AT rockets our men had volleyed at the *malai* muzzle flashes. This brought about an immediate but short-lived slackening of fire from our ambushers. Unfortunately, one of the women had been caught in the face by the hot exhaust gases of our own weapons and was writhing and screaming woefully on the ground. I considered, briefly, following the god-like example of our leader but the impulse vanished. It wasn't me, was it. However, I fired back at the hidden enemy. I didn't shoot

213

with any method; I didn't aim to hit and hurt. I was thinking more of laying down a curtain of lead, as if it might shield me. The loud reports, for once, were a comforting reassurance. I heard the Corporal's voice, urgent, angry, barely audible in the din of gunfire: 'Smoke! Smoke!' Immediately the *malai* fire seemed to concentrate on him. But three or four green beer cans sailed overhead, one hitting a branch and dropping perilously near the Corporal. 'Shit!' Without a thought for the rounds now freely coming his way, he jumped up, ran ten yards, and dove behind a tree-trunk. The guy led a charmed life. Bullets kicked up the dirt around his boot-heels but nothing hit him. Just as he reached cover the white phosphorus grenades thumped off with their unholy white and red glare, showering the smouldering debris everywhere. But they did give instant smoke, which was exactly what the doctor ordered, believe me. The *malais* were still banging away at us but blind, and though it was scary you were much less likely to get hit if you stood up and ran. I heard a voice call, 'Left flanking, go!'

Osvaldo had the anti-ambush drill to perfection. In fact, I think the kids were best at it. While a small party with automatic weapons laid down heavy covering fire, the main FAKINTIL body withdrew. I was always one of life's withdrawers; there was no point pretending otherwise, and Osvaldo always knew it. However, what I always had, too, was a truly lousy sense of direction. It's all in the ears: the ordered to do the listening with and the leader to have the organs of balance to lead. A leader is exactly that: he shows the way to go. It was he who took them across the primitive savannah on those hunting forays of early man, and back to the cave again. Or, later, navigated the haunted seas. He knew where he was, as well as who. And in that smoke, amidst the confusion and noise, yours truly went the wrong way. Within a little while I was alone. Worse, the smoke was starting to dissipate. I could see the *malai* gun-flashes better and their indistinct forms moving weirdly in the mist. Fortunately I'd been going to the side rather than straightforwards. It was a very bad moment, worse than that first day of the invasion when I'd hidden under a newspaper in the Marconi Gardens, for here I was with a rifle, a fully fledged enemy. The jungle offered a lot better cover than the radio company's lawn but of the two predicaments I'd now gladly have exchanged my present fate for the earlier lot.

The shooting from our side was getting feebler as one half of each fireteam made their getaway and the *malais* started to push forward, eager not to let their prey escape.

I was too timid. When I should have made a break for it, through the thinning smoke, I remained on the dirt. By the time I'd nerved myself to bolt it would have been suicide. I pushed my face more into the ground but there was no disguising my presence. Oh, Jesus God. I decided I would have to play dead. I wished I didn't have the G3 or at least that I wasn't holding it. The *malais* came forward. Someone called, something to the effect of, 'There's one here,' and I knew I was dead – whether I surrendered or let them fire checking shots into me.

At that very instant, as if he were the Archangel Michael, Osvaldo Oliveira and five of his vets, the Corporal included, floated through the dying clouds of phosphorus, their guns ablaze like burning fiery swords, sweeping aside the *malais* as if they were dried grass. They came – God bless Osvaldo for the supreme warrior he was – in the classic flanking counter-attack, firing across the line of their enemy's revealing flashes. That first charge, with its steady shooting and wild shouting, accounted for a whole squad of *malais*, the leading group, the ones who'd made me their business. As my saviours ran past, I leaped to my feet to follow them to safety, relative safety, which turned out to be a perilous assumption for my comrades were almost my undoing. The Corporal bringing up the rear heard me crack a branch underfoot, whirled and fired. He favoured a sub-machine gun, not the prized German or Israeli weapons thankfully, and it jammed on the third round of the burst. Nevertheless, I felt a heavy blow on my thigh and staggered one or two steps before finding myself on the forest floor. My thigh was wet and it burned. The Corporal ran on, trying to clear his gun on the move. I don't think he saw who he'd shot at all. And in my extremity, my fear and pain, I called, 'Don't leave me, for Christ's sake, don't leave me behind, Osvaldo!' I could hear the *malais* calling to each other a short distance away. Just to postpone the final moment of my reckoning, not in anger or as my duty, I put the G3 to auto and loosed off a whole magazine into the undergrowth. That desperate action, thoughtless as it was, had a result that skill and planning could never have achieved, for I heard two separate screams and then the sounds of the *malais* going to ground. As I was fumbling with a new magazine someone arrived from the direction the Corporal had gone. It was Osvaldo. He didn't waste a moment, threw me over his shoulder, took my rifle in his spare hand, and ran. I clung to his neck with the love and tenacity of a child borne piggy-back by his doting father. It wasn't the securest ride – I could feel Osvaldo stagger every now and then under my weight as he found a root or uneven ground, the force of his footfalls transmitted from the soles of his boots up his pelvis and back and into my. thighs and ass – but I trusted him neither to fall nor to drop me. Burdened as he was, he never thought of jettisoning my gun. Behind us, the *malais* recovering from the surprise of my lucky burst, were advancing, no doubt with somewhat more attention. Osvaldo gasped – he was quite severely out of breath, more than I'd have expected – 'My belt order, there's a smoke grenade, third pouch on the right hand side. Pull the pin and drop it.' Well, I complied with some alacrity, leaving the can fuming slowly in our wake. Now Osvaldo started to jink from side to side, breathing really fast and hard now, and the sideways lurching made me whimper in pain. But it was a timely piece of evasion for the *malais* were firing after us. Then we were with Osvaldo's elite squad in a little clearing. The Corporal had been setting grenades on a pull-wire, which he now made taut. Osvaldo put me on the ground, shouldered his own pack, and had the only other guy in the squad without an HK21 take me up. They carried the guy's pack between them. I saw the Corporal slinking into heavy cover on our left, while we others fled. Two minutes later I knew why as the booby-traps exploded, followed by a long burst of flanking fire. A monstrous, fallen tree trunk blocked our path. The packs, and me, were flung unceremoniously over the top, yours truly last, though, so it was a soft landing. I was able to take it on the hands and not the leg. They switched burdens, Osvaldo and my bearer staying, while the others staggered on with Chinaman and equipment. And so the chase continued in relays, until the firing grew irregular and more and more distant, and at last ceased, with only the noise of Osvaldo and the Corporal rushing through the undergrowth to rejoin us for the final time.

It could have been the finish for FAKINTIL. None of us was in any doubt about that. The jaws of the trap had sprung that close, caught our tail in its teeth. What had made the difference was Osvaldo, the quality of his leadership and the preparations he'd made long ago against such a contingency. But this was just the first time. We'd been lucky, but we'd have to go on being lucky. Permanently. And that was a statistical impossibility.

My own wound – a real one this time – wasn't serious. I mean to me it was *damn* serious. That bitch Maria pooh-poohed it. 'It's missed the bone, luckily for you, and gone through a fold of flesh and exited,' she said crisply. 'It only has to be dressed and guarded against infection. There will be fragments of cloth and what-not inside, but you'll walk again. It's not serious.' I can't begin to tell you how much I resented this cavalier approach. OK, there were terrible cases lying all round me and I did get into group one of the triage – immediate attention – but she didn't show a friend's concern. I thought I'd been too brave; should have come in screaming. She didn't even ask me of the circumstances in which I'd taken the round; other than to say I'd been lucky to be hit by a pistol bullet. 'Sub-machine gun,' I corrected her indignantly, though of course it was the same 9mm round. She shrugged. 'It's not material.' As I lay there I was mighty pissed off with her, I can tell you. It was starting to throb like hell, uncomplicated flesh wound or not. About three a.m. I got the same bark and berry decoction I'd been doling out to others as a pain-reliever. My initial scepticism turned to pleasant surprise as it started to work. Left you groggy and was about as powerful as aspirin, but who was complaining? I had a limp for a month – which I maintained for another four weeks (whenever I could remember to do so) if anyone was looking and then, apart from a small scar, no worse than a vaccination mark, I was a whole man.

Well, thank Christ for the rain. I thought of it now, gratefully, not so much as the season of non-communication as of non-molestation. For a while we were safe. Instead of coping with the cherry berets and hunger all we had to endure was the growl of our own stomachs. It was dire enough. The raids and disturbances of the dry months had prevented the FAKINTIL gardeners from doing much of their work. We had even less food than before. It was now that we had our first deaths directly attributable to privation rather than the bullet or the bomb. Some infants had already died. I don't count those. They were the product of the liaisons between the fighters and the washerwomen. Only their mothers mourned them. We didn't notice or, to be honest, care. They'd never been people, except perhaps as a theological point.

It was when some of my woodchucks went that I cared. There were two boys in particular, street arabs from the town who'd adjusted well to life in the mountains and who had grown as familiar with the forest as their contemporaries from the hill-tribes. For a while they'd supplemented their half-rations by expert foraging and some quite effective snaring, of birds mostly rather than floor-dwellers. But the jungle had become jealous of its resources; the food had never come freely; now the supply closed up altogether. Whether it was simply the fighting – the noise, the destruction of cover – or, as the more paranoiac camp gossip, always repeated out of earshot of Osvaldo, had it, a sinister new pesticide or obnoxious agent employed by the *malais* and dropped from the Broncos – one could not tell. Personally, I thought it was neither but simply the creatures getting wiser. Whatever, the difficulty of supplementing their diet hit the children hard. To this was added a sudden epidemic of dysentery followed in short order by what we reckoned was influenza, rather than malaria or tropical fever. In our weakened states it hit us hard. With their smaller history of exposure to similar viruses it hit the juveniles the hardest. For dysentery we could administer herb tea or ground bones and charcoal. For this we could do nothing – in that sense it was worse than malaria, for which, at least in theory, chloroquine or Fansidar existed. I had found some ease and amusement with the two boys I've mentioned. In return for favours I'd give them a scrap or two of my own adult ration. I'm not so sure – though they denied it with wide eyes and scandalised expressions, the little hypocrites – that they hadn't already earned pennies for this in Danu. Don't think I'm excusing myself. More hemlock, Socrates? Atillio, who was the oldest, had been tall enough to act as one of my bearers when I was sick, though he was only 14. Luis was my favourite – a dark boy with curly hair, thin feet, and very purple mucous membrane. Funnily enough, after my previous misfortunes with the fever and the wound, I wasn't at all affected by the mystery bug. I think it was being the 'man of the world' who had encountered all the germs of North America. I was immune, whereas the island-dwellers were innocents. Certainly the African vets and those who'd sojourned as students in the Home Country were also less badly affected.

I nursed Luis, who was first stricken, with especial assiduity, then; gave him hot water to drink, sweated him, held the bowl while he puked. One thing I didn't give him was more of my own food – thankfully, I wasn't put in the intolerable position of having to deny him since the influenza destroyed the appetite of its victims. After 48 hours Atillio, the big boy, who'd watched his friend solemnly with those liquid eyes of his, began to ail. In addition to the physical misery of the symptoms he was also assailed by panic. He'd already seen two of his friends go into holes in the ground. He kept asking me as I brought him steaming water in the

219

half-coconut, 'Senhor Ng, I'm not going to die, am I, Senhor Ng?'

'No, Atillio, I promise you you're not,' I said, not liking to catch Maria's eye. I was frightened she'd tell him the truth; by then, she was equal to anything. It was actually Atillio who died first, though he was the bigger and stronger boy. I think, though he'd succumbed to the illness first, Luis wanted to live more; maybe because he was younger (and knew no better).

It depressed the hell out of me, I'll tell you. More than ordinarily because no one else in the camp seemed to give two damns, not even Osvaldo. Grief was too strong a word for what I felt, but I felt it alone which always magnifies the sensation.

As if to prove the wrongness of my theory of immunity, the only adult to die was Fr Molloy, for he was both old and from the larger world and should on both counts have escaped. He didn't die well. He'd become a grumbler, that was from being a parasite and a pedant in the first instance. Then, since the time Osvaldo had put the wounded youth out of his misery, Molloy had taken badly against him. This antipathy had taken hold to such an extent that it had become an unreasoning bitterness which blamed Osvaldo for everything that was unendurable. That was from the dotard who'd never given one piece that I could see (and I kept a look-out once the thought had occurred to me) of his full ration to the younger and less fortunate. It was part of my duty to tend him, or rather to watch the old fellow die, as there was nothing we could do for the stricken.

He was full of bile, in the figurative sense, I mean. There was nothing gracious about him; he didn't try to live up to the cloth whose privileges he'd been so quick to annexe. He was pettish and vindictive to the last. In his weakness he was still virulent. Those spiteful meanderings of the old man! He would have been a harmless old buffer in normal times at the seminary, benevolent even. Out here he had become a menace to unity and morale. How he cursed Osvaldo, for a murdering atheistical Communist! For all the world he sounded like Radio Malai, except for the occasional interjections of 'God will not be mocked' and such like. He didn't even have the excuse of delirium for his rantings; he was weak but he knew who and where he was. At first, when he wasn't so sick, I tried to reason, coax him out of his intransigence as one might a difficult child, but this was to cast petrol on the flames. He got even more furious in his denunciations, having at that time sufficient energy. I took to waiting on him in silence, hoping this might act as a rebuke. It didn't. The stupid old fool didn't even moderate his comments in front of Maria. I was surprised to find she treated him no more roughly than she did, say, Adolph Ng. Only when Osvaldo came by the men's beds (beds!) did he shut up. 'And how are we today, Father Molloy?' the leader would ask with scrupulous politeness, Molloy not actually replying verbally but moving his head or making some inarticulate grunt which could be interpreted any way you pleased. He wasn't quite lost to all sense of shame: didn't want to be caught out in inconsistency in front of his captive audience, saying one thing behind big O.'s back and another to his face, yet lacking the guts to show his true colours before the FAKINTIL commander. Osvaldo knew anyway but didn't betray that knowledge by expression or action, gentle and imperturbable as he was in his personal dealings. I say that, but I wouldn't have liked to be Molloy.

Martinho, of course, was a regular attender at his mentor's sick-bed. Molloy turned up the volume when the older Oliveira was around, really laid about the movement and its leader. And Martinho just sat there, head bowed, and took it shamelessly. Listened hour after hour to this vitriol, the sick old man's nonsense, without a word of remonstrance. I'd pass him about my rounds and I'd think, 'How can you, Martinho? How *can* you?', sending mental arrows into his hunched back till he must have bristled like Sebastian. He was able to look me in the eye without self-consciousness or awkwardness.

It was I who felt embarrassed.

EIGHTEEN

ONE WAY OR ANOTHER, whether they were casualties of the fighting, of disease, or simple malnutrition, by the end of the wet months the FAKINTIL complement was about 60 per cent of what it had been at the start of the resistance. Osvaldo had always tried to make it a community, spanning ages and sexes, rather than a pure military force; that way, it would have been to an extent self-regenerating. But the rate of attrition was too high, like a forest unable to regulate itself against the depredations of man. If you didn't think his way, see things big, it didn't look so bad. Someone like the Corporal or even X. Ray would be less worried than the best brains. That was one excuse for Martinho, I guess.

We began the new campaigning season early – set out through mud and a heavy downpour, in fact. Osvaldo wanted to get the initiative before the *malais* took it from him. He wouldn't admit it was *malai* equipment which was beating him; the fault had to lie with himself somehow. To admit the former would have been to confess the situation was beyond his control and he'd court-martial himself rather than do that.

We couldn't find any goddamned *malais*. The highways were deserted. The odd chopper thumped overhead, forcing the men to scuttle for cover, but even then the Broncos weren't aloft. At first we thought it was our earliness and the congenital laziness of the *malais* but as the days passed that explanation failed to satisfy. It was the damnedest thing. Not a soul to be seen. The FAKINTIL squads extended their patrol ranges, gingerly stuck their noses out of the hills and forests, then roamed into the coastal plain. Still nothing. It was as if the *malais* had surrendered and withdrawn under cover of the rains. Ridiculous though that supposition was, as we all knew it to be deep-down, I found myself with others of a like mind (we didn't dare even breathe the notion), listening with a fresh avidity to Australian radio. *And now the foreign news. In a startling development...*

222

Some hope.

We'd leave the radio hut without comment. We were far from the stupidest in the camp either. To realise there existed a world beyond the *malai* military, that there was a political sphere which enclosed the armed struggle, took a massive adjustment of vision; required the thinker to get out of his or her itchy skin, beyond hunger, illness, fear, to that objective realm where destinies were determined in the mass. Not everyone could do it.

After a while the probes came across depopulated villages. There were no animals, crops, or food stores but the houses hadn't been damaged. I can tell you there were no booby-traps either because to yours truly fell the creepy task of checking out the huts. They were eerie, those places, at the best of times if you were a city person. Ju-ju, witchcraft, you know. You expected to find shrunken heads on the walls.

At length Osvaldo decided to push towards Danu. This simple determination sparked off a furore. For Osvaldo, from the very first speech he had made on his return from Africa, the political sphere had always enclosed the military struggle. Blinkered in some respects, this was something he'd always perceived. That was why he had felt it necessary to take the terrible risk of descending from the mountains to the town the first time. It was imperative for his role not just to be a bandit skulking in the hills but to appear as the focus of a national resistance. The townspeople were as much his constituency and audience as those of us under arms. To him the concept of a descent wasn't an audacious gamble but an on-going strategic necessity. For different reasons X. Ray and Martinho were totally opposed. X. Ray's natural caution came out. Martinho was panic-stricken. 'It's a trap,' he proclaimed in open forum. 'They want to flush us into the open and finish us.' Xavier Ray nodded in his enigmatic way; that was what he thought too, but he was content to let others voice his thoughts. No. 1, because he didn't like to speak out at the best of times, No. 2 because – no doubt for good and bad, creditable and discreditable reasons – he didn't want to contradict Osvaldo in front of the rest of us.

Others had their chances, got their parts, I should say, in some cases: that old FAKOUM love of spouting hadn't been impaired by our hardships: danger and hunger actually seemed tongue-looseners for many. After a while around the fire – we didn't need it, I think Osvaldo had it for morale – it became clear that a majority were behind the leader. Now Martinho became desperate; he became offensive. 'Can't you see?' (And his cravenness made his sonorous voice quiver.) 'You fools, don't you see?' Like many people who preserve an artificial dignity, one that is neither unconscious nor instinctive, once he'd let go of the rope he found it surprisingly easy to go over the edge. He gave the impression of hearing his own voice ringing strangely in his ears – unaccustomed notes – but also of finding a strange joy in letting it continue unchecked. 'We'll be doing exactly what they want. There'll be no escape from them then.' His eyes darted round his audience, beseeching support. It was a sorry spectacle. I looked at my knees the whole time I could. He wasn't a very gracious loser. After a while he started seriously to insult his listeners. In his position Osvaldo wouldn't have done that; not only did he have more class than his semi-sacerdotal sibling, he was too astute. There'd be another day and another issue. You don't call the electorate names after it has rejected you – that's its privilege. Besides, you need its good will again. Have you ever seen a politician do it? Martinho started to run out of invective (don't forget it had to be decent – he couldn't cuss and swear like a trooper, after all). He faltered. And then he sat down. It was this which inclined me to think he was plain frightened. He had no arguments as such or he wouldn't have dried up. Panic was what he was all about. All his little tantrum did was make it impossible for a sensible guy like X. Ray to have his say and maybe convince everyone on pragmatic grounds.

Osvaldo was quiet a while, then he said: 'Go for the simple explanation. Maybe it *is* a trick, Martinho, but you go for the simple explanation first. You'll be wrong less often that way. We *have* to go to the towns. We will always have to, even if it means our destruction in the end. If we don't, we will be nothing anyhow. We also need to change our tactics. We've tried to attack them at their weakest spots – now we surprise them by hitting them where they're strong. We get the initiative back that way. Those were Alexander's tactics.'

'You are not Alexander the Great.'

Osvaldo roared with laughter. After a while the vets and X. Ray joined him. It was infectious. The bearded men guffawed and slapped their knees in the firelight.

Martinho's expression was that of a saint being reviled before his death by pagans.

It took longer than you'd think for a raggedy-ass bunch of nomads like FAKINTIL had become to get moving. Osvaldo wouldn't go unless he had a secure line of communications set up and, above all, ordnance dumps strewn about the jungle. He always had this thing about ammo. We still had plenty of it – no protein worth speaking of but plenty of lead. I've heard it said that every general has his own pet mania, a particular bee buzzing in his bonnet. One believes in the undervalued strategic importance of dental hygiene: the men must have new tooth-brushes every month; another is obsessed by boots: his soldiers cannot deploy to achieve his master-plan unless they are well shod. Osvaldo's was ammo. Perhaps not surprisingly as all his battle experience, varied and intense though it was, had been at a junior level. He was always going on about it, how even a well-disciplined soldier (which the average FAKINTIL fighter wasn't) could get through all his magazines and clips in ten minutes of fighting through a well-defended position. Fire control was what all the FAKINTIL junior leaders had drummed into them. Their job was to husband their men's bullets. So he secreted piles of cases behind our jumping-off point into the plain, with relays of men to bring more up. He thought more like a regular, I always thought; was a gamekeeper at heart and not a poacher.

The plan was this: a very small group under the Corporal would make a series of reconnaissance patrols by night, returning to the forest by dawn. On the fourth excursion they'd stay out – hole up by day and gather more information for the next two nights. They'd return and, if all looked well, they'd lead the way out for Group A, headed by Osvaldo. Group B, led by Xavier Ray, would follow 36 hours behind. Of course, each group would be further subdivided and separated in itself, so as to avoid us being caught with our pants completely round our ankles. No, I don't think Martinho's resistance had made Osvaldo more cautious; he was smart enough to have proceeded like this anyway. To my mind he was more or less a perfect commander; his resolution was tempered by sense. Circumstances conspired against him. I'd never blame him for any of our ill-luck.

I was in Group B, the rear party. The night before we were due to set out Fr Molloy took a turn for the worse and lapsed into unconsciousness. It was pretty clear he was on the way to meeting his Maker; the natural history of the disease was overly familiar to me now after watching Luis and Attilio go. But Martinho couldn't admit the inevitability of it to himself. I'd like to say he didn't leave Molloy's side but that would be an untruth. He did. At food time. You didn't trust anyone to bring your plate of boiled roots to you. Otherwise he was there. I spied him on his knees with increasing frequency, that goddamned rosary in his hands. Molloy had enjoyed an influence over many of the women, an unwholesome ascendancy I reckoned (no, not impropriety of any kind), and now many of these females were gathered round him and Martinho, washerwomen with the overtones of cleansing, baptism, and winding-cloths. I was repelled. Vanity and fraud on the one side, superstition and vacuity on the other. Molloy was out of it, of course, except as the main property in this pious little tableau. Soon, the drone of prayers became audible. They weren't singing, that would come later. I could hear Martinho leading the weaker female voices, weaker until they burst into song, but not yet. I found X. Ray by the fire where he was cleaning his new acquisition, an M-16 taken from a dead *malai*. He smiled and made room. I was always Senhor Ng, the client, to him, whatever my status in the camp was among the others. He'd just accepted without demur the fact that he was going to embark on a mission he personally thought misguided. To Osvaldo's proposition, once accepted by the others, he'd uttered a hearty *'credo!'*, whatever his private doubts and fears. He didn't want to infect anybody else with them; it would just make things worse. He was the very opposite of the self-indulgent spouters who'd brought both FAKOUM and the IP to the state they were now in.

'This gun was very dirty,' he observed, looking me gravely in the eye.

'Uh-huh.'

There existed a whole world of implication behind the remark, the incompetence of the *malais,* their state of morale, the inappropriateness of the advanced equipment the Americans sold their Third World friends so readily, the quality of the NCOs and officers, the silver lining there might be in the present FAKINTIL cloud. Watching him give the little black rifle its field-strip, I decided it would be no bad idea to see to my own weapon. I got it from the rack and sat cross-legged by my old builder and present superior, a little closer than I'd been before; then had to jump up with an exclamation as I'd sat on a thorn. One of those minor perils of the outdoor life. The cleaning-kit had gone from its little home in the butt, but X. Ray passed me his without comment. He clicked his tongue as I applied the bottle. 'No, Senhor Ng, no. So much oil! Your gun will smoke like a chimney.' I wiped off the excess with alacrity; I didn't want every *malai* gun in the jungle fixing on yours truly. Just as I was putting the rag down came this terrible wailing and lamentation from the sick-bay. Well, I had a good idea what that was about.

When I got there Martinho was up to some mumbo-jumbo with Molloy. I strongly suspect he'd been administering the Last Rites which he, as a layman, had no right to do. The women were crying and carrying on in an excessive way, considering all the deaths we'd seen and the

227

fact that the good Father had been a complete non-contributor. Martinho was full of himself, of the majesty of the situation, of the part he played in it. In his eyes I could see an anger that was perfectly genuine but also that he rejoiced in feeling, for it gave him – a weak man, it's fair to say – strength and a high that freed him from the privations and ignominies of the moment and place in which he found himself. He was luxuriating in this heaven-sent wrath. And in some weird way I believe he blamed Osvaldo for Molloy's death.

At this moment Molloy farted and sat up. Oh, Jesus! I had a fit. Martinho didn't hear it. He was so bent on who he was and what he felt that everything peripheral was excluded. He didn't even hear my explosively suppressed snigger. And I'm afraid some of the washerwomen became implicated in my low mirth, the shock of it being too much for their self-control. Others just looked stunned. Poor Molloy looked round himself and said, his accent very strong and reverting in his daze to that of much earlier years, 'Some tay would be nice, to be sure.' Now Martinho could no longer close his mind to the inconvenient tenacity with which his saintly mentor was holding on to the scene of this earthly existence. I'll swear he actually looked dismayed for a moment. Then he said, 'Ah, Father, it's a miracle!'

I can't tell you how disappointed I was in Martinho. The vulgarity, the crudity of it! He'd come down to the level of the washerwomen, for the remark was at once seized upon by them and, in the blinking of an eye, the gigglers had solemn faces and from being a breaker of wind Molloy had become Lazarus. I left them to it.

X.Ray had correctly guessed what the commotion was about in the first place, but when I informed him of the latest developments he was unphlegmatic enough to swear. We had orders to follow Group A a day and a half after they'd set out, no more, no less. Molloy had been a worry to X. Ray. Osvaldo had stipulated that his brother was to accompany X. Ray, the leader of this FAKINTIL group, as kind of an overseeing civilian commissar. X. Ray was too good a subordinate to resent this – as many would, natural leaders being the overweening 'sons of bitches' they are – but he wasn't prepared to compromise himself and jeopardise everyone by hanging around, waiting for Molloy to die and Martinho to leave his side. This had been a problem Osvaldo should have foreseen. I could now see X. Ray had been brooding about it – the kind of thing obvious to the man in charge but to no one else. Cleaning the M-16 might have been his version of knitting, of occupational therapy.

There was nothing for it. X. Ray went to the bower and told Martinho to get his gear ready to go in an hour. Martinho refused.

X. Ray argued. Martinho dug in his heels. X. Ray ordered him. Martinho told him it was he, the FAKOUM senior surviving CC member, who gave orders. I could see X. Ray deliberating. He was seriously considering having Martinho brought along by force. I don't know whether it was political considerations (Martinho being Osvaldo's older brother when all was said and done) or practical – the nuisance and absurdity of physically compelling him to accompany us – which won in the end, but X. Ray turned on his heel and strode off. Martinho went quiet after that; the showdown took something out of him. I wouldn't be surprised if we weren't all a little bit crazy by then, the starvation, the fevers, the strange roots we'd eat without a moment's hesitation, all combining to produce, if not hallucinations, at least delusions (of grandeur in Martinho's case) and something akin to religious frenzy. It's the small, closely-knit group besieged on all sides which is the most prone to such manifestations. So my readings in Toronto taught me, at any rate.

I made an obscene gesture in the direction of the washerwomen before rejoining X. Ray. He was slotting rounds into his M-16 magazines from the stripper clips. For a moment I wondered if he was planning to shoot Martinho. What a notion! I wasn't so sure I'd have stopped him. His cheek flicked where he was gritting his molars. X. Ray wasn't the excitable type but he was mighty pissed off.

Neither on the building-sites of peacetime nor in the camp was he used to being disregarded by no matter whom. The gun, bucking and snapping in his competent hands as he reassembled it, seemed to possess a life of its own. He didn't speak but I left him in no doubt as to where I stood.

The next morning, dead on time, we left. The file of grim, thin, bearded men was silent, in contrast to the usual FAKINTIL departure which was an oddly cheerful affair considering the risks they all had to take. Martinho moved from Molloy's side to watch us go, his arms folded across his chest. The benignity had left his face. Strain had changed some people, but left others the same. In the last category were people like X. Ray, Osvaldo, the Corporal even. Martinho was one of those who'd altered. Danger and privation were like solvents or strippers which peeled away what was cosmetic or superficial on top of a man's character and showed the warped or contrary grain beneath. If what one did and how he showed himself to the world were consonant with what he really was, then there was no contradiction between the selves. He, or she, only became more what they were. Yet the slightest hypocrisy or inconsistency became glaringly apparent. The truth was, Martinho was not as good a man as we younger ones thought. As he'd allowed us to think. I don't believe he was ever guilty of the sin of pride but he'd been happy to go along with a version of himself that was, to say the least, a corruption of the original text.

I waved to him.

To my surprise he returned the friendly gesture.

Osvaldo had left reception parties for us along his route. Oh, how thoughtful of him, might be your first reaction. Well, it was, of course. But, looking back, there was a military police element about it, too. I mean, he wanted to be damn sure there *was* someone covering his ass. For some things he had a sixth sense. Outwardly serene, aloof, he was anything but remote from what was going on underneath him. The good thing about arriving at these staging-posts was that the work of bivouacking had already been done for us. I suppose we should have camped elsewhere to minimise the risk of aerial detection, but that was Danu for you. In hindsight again, I guess Osvaldo wouldn't have been too sorry had the *malais* exposed their hand early and hit his rearguard while he was sited near the protection of the forest. We were out to discover what the hell was going on, in any case.

No sooner had we put out our sentries and commenced preparing food (this level of the forest not having been so thoroughly scavenged as the higher and yielding a somewhat better provision) than the noise of men moving carelessly through the undergrowth impressed itself upon our heightened senses. No prizes for guessing: it was Martinho and his merry men. Those few who'd remained with him were the worst soldiers in the camp; they really were god-awful apologies of combatants, worse than yours truly, who could be credited with possessing some intelligence even if he was a true coward: in fact, cowardice enhanced the workings of the brain. If there'd been any *malais* nearby, the crashings, the crackings, and – Jesus Christ – the loud conversation, would have alerted them to our presence long ago. It was so outrageously inept that I couldn't forebear from snickering. But X. Ray was mad as you could want. So should I have been – they'd endangered us all. Martinho wasn't a stupid man; I can only presume he had a strong death-wish. They strolled into the camp as if they were boy-scouts on a weekend excursion. A positive way of looking at it was that if they'd come in stealthily, like the African professionals, they might well have got themselves shot to pieces, for so angry had X. Ray been, so pompous Martinho at the time of the original departure that there'd been no times fixed or passwords agreed.

Martinho blinked in the light of the little clearing. He appeared quite unflustered, absolutely unembarrassed. As X. Ray bore down on them, he nodded coldly. His whole demeanour was one of injured magnanimity. When X. Ray got within about ten feet of him, he stuck out the flat of his hand and said: 'Father Molloy died three hours after you

231

left.' It wasn't as bad as it might have been. I guess he could have put it worse: e.g., 'Father Molloy has passed away,' 'Father Molloy has gone to his reward.' X. Ray, I know, would have liked to say, 'Fuck Father Molloy,' but he had sufficient self-control. Martinho managed to make what he had said partake of the nature of an accusation rather than a statement. But if it had been three minutes instead of three hours I doubt if X. Ray would have experienced the smallest twinge of conscience. Me neither. Martinho said, 'He was a great man.' I was interested he didn't say 'saint'. Well, some of us begged to differ, even on that point. However, X. Ray was politician enough to incline his head slightly, ambiguous movement which could have conveyed agreement or merely respect for an opinion he didn't share. Food was found for the new arrivals – which they'd done nothing to deserve – and, such were our material circumstances, the prospect of a half-full stomach did more to make things up than the humblest or most honeyed of speeches. Martinho deigned to eat what was in his tin with the condescension of royalty in exile.

That night, you might be surprised to hear, I slept the soundest of sleeps. The middle of the next afternoon found us poised on the edge of the forest, peering down on to the coastal plain. Not a soul in sight. It was creepy quiet, not placid. I didn't like it one bit. The only thing that gave me the guts to go down after the others was this: all the times in the past one had dreaded the worst, with a sinking, sick feeling in the pit of the stomach, only to find that it had been imaginary and one had got away scot-free. And I don't just mean the Danu war but lonely streets and potential muggers in Canada, dark parks one risked for sex. You thought – I've been as jittery as this before and nothing happened; maybe it'll turn out the same again. Yet you put one foot in front of the other in a continuing delirium of terror. It was like you were floating outside yourself; you'd abandoned all responsibility to yourself. I don't think guys like Osvaldo or the Corporal ever felt like that – they didn't dissociate from the present, they belonged to the moment. That was their strength.

Our orders were to move out from the tree-line after dark. We got our equipment together in the day – taped together any loose items that might clink together on the move, loaded mags, filled water-bottles, cleaned the trusty G3. It was really surprising how X. Ray's final check could pick up potential glitches of the most elementary kind. You'd stare in amazement and contempt at the ass-hole who'd left his cutlery loose in his cooking canteen, or had an uncovered aluminium water bottle glinting on his webbing (with some indignation, too, for he would have endangered you as well as himself) only to find – in my case – that my Seiko would have beeped hourly. X. Ray seemed to have an eye for everything; I loved that silent man for his meticulousness.

Night-fighting and its associated skills were not FAKINTIL specialties, though the African veterans had it in their repertoire. Within ten minutes of leaving the start-line all was confusion, our line breaking and falling into disorder, small panicky groups of men lost in the blackness, bumping into and challenging each other. The real soldiers, Osvaldo's Africa cadres, just detached themselves from the chaos. I couldn't say they abandoned us, but they sure as hell didn't take too much trouble keeping us with them.

Worse was to come. About three in the morning, to the left of the ruins of a dispersed column formation (or maybe it was just me being way to the right of where I should have been) came a single report. This was followed by another shot, then hard on the heels of that a whole fusillade of single and automatic. In the middle of this a whistle blew insistently. That was our signal to cease firing. Even though I wasn't shooting it took me longer than it should have done to interpret it as such. Slowly, the gunfire spattered out. Seconds after the most trigger-happy had concluded and all seemed over came the thump of a hand-grenade in centre line. As if that wasn't enough, it was white phosphorus, the intense red-hot glare and snowy sparks visible probably for ten miles around. To be fair, the dumb fuck had actually thrown the bomb five seconds before. It was a false alarm, of course, someone – we never found out who: the culprits in

233

these situations seem to lead charmed lives – hearing a noise and losing control of themselves, their ill-directed shots initiating a free-for-all. And the more shooting there was, the more likely it seemed that you were under fire from the enemy, culminating in those earnest, deluded firefights between our own FAKINTIL units. We managed to kill five of our own men and wound ten in that idiot's exchange. X. Ray's feelings can be imagined. It wasn't just the unnecessary casualties, the waste – and we felt it, Danuese or not – or the fact that we'd blown our whereabouts to all interested parties – but that X. Ray felt he'd betrayed Osvaldo. Let him down in a terrible way. That might seem ridiculous: it wasn't the ever-steady Xaneros who'd lost control of his nerves and loosed a shot off into the dark against imaginary foes. But X. Ray knew the price of leadership was responsibility for everything: whether taking the can for his bricklayer's carelessness in better days, or as now. He was in a mean mood the next day.

That morning found us several miles short of where we should have been. Some people had to go out to get the bodies in – no way of locating them in the dark. The men wanted to bring in their comrades but, less sentimentally, X. Ray wanted the weapons retrieved and to conceal what could still be concealed.

Martinho put himself in charge of this detail. It was amazing how friendship and the regard of years could melt in the heat of crisis. At that juncture in our joint histories he was an odious smug bastard. No one blamed X. Ray for the accident except himself. Certainly Martinho had done nothing to forestall it; by arriving so late he might be said to have contributed towards it, as a distraction. He was no Cassandra. But his whole demeanour said: 'Look what you've gone and done now!' He was like a goddamned vulture. The Corporal did the hard work of bringing them safely back just before dark. The bodies were pitiable. We all stood in a circle round them. They were full of bullet holes, really badly chewed up. Most had been in a group clear of the rest, taking the brunt of everyone's fire. The fact that it was our bullets in them made you think. The tragic waste of it. You remembered what you had carried in your ammo pouch, thought of the bright cartridges you'd so carefully loaded into your mags, and wondered if they'd ended up in your comrades. Martinho wanted to speak over the bodies, but X. Ray wouldn't let him. That was a good decision. He made a short, dignified address himself, surprising me with his ability. When he wanted, he could do it. That was X. Ray for you.

The next day we rendezvoused with Osvaldo. He'd seen the pyrotechnics going on behind him but had, of course, kept his cool and not turned tail for the forest again. I think it had been in a way a relief for him to see the shooting, what he thought was fighting and an enemy revealed, for he was inordinately disappointed to discover it had been a false alarm. This disappointment of his, that preoccupation with his own bafflement in a military sense, was itself a source of dismay to me. It appeared to eclipse any sorrow he felt for the pointless deaths of his own men. That coldness frightened me. Surgeons, they say, also possess that chilly detachment and generals, which Osvaldo was despite his years, have it in abundance. To say we were expendable to him would have been an untruth – there weren't enough of us: part of his strategy had to be to husband his resources – but sometimes I got the feeling we were just counters. I told myself that was the only way he could operate, that we were safer with a man who could think like that, but I could only believe my own propaganda in the shallowest way. Only Martinho treated his brother coldly. No one else seemed to be as sensitive as us, but then that was the least surprising thing of all.

What we did next could be described as recklessness or gross carelessness on the part of Osvaldo. I think it would be better to call it clinical daring. He wanted a result. He wanted the *malai* to show their hand – the earlier he could tempt them, the easier it would be for us to extricate ourselves eventually.

We combined our two groups and went across the plain in daylight.

It wasn't quite as bad as I made it sound – we were still sub-divided and strung out – but pretty well all the eggs were in one basket.

We pushed to within 30 kilometres of Bacalhau. I was in the front group this time – one's luck couldn't hold out indefinitely – when I heard a faint throb. It was so far away it was more of a tiny vibration in the temples than a distinct sound. But the Africa vets knew what it was straightaway and reacted with urgency. I believe I actually heard the choppers before they did but I didn't appreciate the situation or what to do about it. *They'd* been used to riding in on the airborne charabancs against the guerrillas in Africa, so they had a good idea what to expect from the hunter's point of view. All round me they were going to ground. The throb had become a steady *whunk-whunk-whunk* and was just converting to a giant chirruping. The Corporal was struggling to mount a machine-gun on an AA mount. Behind him some African vets were lining up to try to coordinate a cone of concentrated G3 fire. They might as well have had pea-shooters. 'Chinaman, get down!' the Corporal shouted. He didn't add, as he well might, 'you fucking fool', and I was quite touched. I think he wanted to preserve my precious life. I ran for some grass, where I found João the electrician and X. Ray. They had a machine-gun but no mount. From Bacalhau six or seven green bugs appeared out of the sun. They seemed much punier than the noise they made. Two started to circle, flashes appearing from the side-doors, while the others descended. Our men were firing heavily themselves. I didn't shoot but kept watching the dropping helicopters. Unfortunately I lost sight of them some way from the ground. As I focussed on the two machines strafing us X. Ray had definitely the most glorious moment of his life. The choppers had been concentrating on the Corporal's gun and one had come too low, about 600 metres away from us. X. Ray opened with a huge burst – he was no gunner – and the tracer extended under the chopper before he corrected and hosed rounds over the cockpit and into the door. I could see bits flying off the machine. It was about as lucky as being attacked by a rabid dog and hitting it on the snout first time with a volleyed rock. A cheer went up. The machine came down in jerky circles, smoke pouring out of it, but the pilot was able to land and it didn't explode. The crew of the other helicopter tried to give their comrades cover – two men came out of the wrecked machine – but they had to come too close to do it, and they soon flew off. Probably under standing orders.

Osvaldo was first to get his face out of the dirt, with his squad close behind. The helicopter crew, not surprisingly after the impact, weren't making a very good job of their escape. Some crazy, indisciplined fool behind Osvaldo fired at them, and was lucky he didn't succeed in assassinating the leader of FAKINTIL. Osvaldo shouted that he wanted them alive. X. Ray organised us others to follow behind. Soon after, three mortar bombs dropped where we had been taking cover. That speeded us on our way.

We could see the chase ahead, as if it had been devised for us as an entertainment. Osvaldo and two others had ditched their packs and were reeling in their quarry all the time. The rearmost of the *malai* chopper crew drew a pistol, turned, and fired on the run, then lost no time in resuming his flight. You could tell he didn't want to hit anyone, just hold them back a bit. It didn't slow Osvaldo down at all, in fact he speeded up, but his shadow – one of the toughest African vets – shouted a warning, then disobeyed orders, and fired, hitting the *malai* in the leg. He went a step and a half and fell. The other *malai* kept going but Osvaldo almost had him now. The guy was zigzagging to throw people's aim off but it only meant Osvaldo gained faster and a flying football tackle brought him down. God knows where Osvaldo learned that – it was basketball at the seminary. He disarmed the *malai* and then just sat on him. As we others came up I could see Osvaldo was laughing, as merrily as if it had been a game. The *malai* who'd been shot lay on his back with that white, shocked expression. Osvaldo brought over the one he'd caught and we stood round them, about 50 of us. The uninjured one looked shit-scared, the other was well out of things. So I thought. But when the Corporal trod on his leg he screamed. A couple of guys started to boot Osvaldo's *malai* in the body while someone else made to butt-stroke him in the face, then jabbed him with the barrel. I looked to Osvaldo, expecting him to put a stop to this, but he didn't. If nothing else, the *malai* was his property. There were times when Osvaldo asserted himself and there were times when he didn't but his choice of moment always surprised me. Mistreating the *malais* was a luxury, though, as another three mortar bombs landed between us and the last point of impact, showering the area with their nasty fragments. We got moving, pronto.

After a while, the Corporal and ten vets fell back to cover our flight – standard FAKINTIL tactics. The more I thought about the Corporal the more it became apparent he had his virtues and uses. He never whined; he took the ugly, dangerous jobs without even having to be told; in short, he was putting his precious ass on the line for us. No wonder he was always so pissed off.

The *malais* didn't seem too eager to catch us, for we never heard gunfire from the Corporal's group behind us.

Osvaldo was taking us back to the forest and mountain, that was apparent. He didn't like the look of the plain any more. We kept moving fast for a couple of hours; then he halted to speak. We were an unwieldy group, far larger than the normal FAKINTIL operational unit. Men, women, boys. Maria was patching up the wounded *malai* while her lover spoke. I didn't find a whole lot of point in her doing this. My educated guess was that the two *malais'* troubles were far from over. Why repair the guy when odds were he was going to get busted up all over again? It was futile work, like painting a hotel during the rains. However, Osvaldo made no attempt to stop her, though I saw him having a word with the uninjured *malai* who turned out to be the crew chief; the pilot was the wounded one.

Our route took us north-east. All the time I was waiting for the Broncos to hit us, imagining the drone of the deadly little machines. But nothing.

238

Then around two in the afternoon a big plane appeared unusually low some three miles ahead of us. It wasn't a jet. Even from the ground we could tell it was a vintage machine; its propeller engines sounded awful. It kept going across our path, not at us. It banked, came round again the way it had come, and then from the tail an object slid backwards, soon revealed as the chute fully opened. A whole stream came after that. You could see it was men and not equipment or containers. They hung there, suspended in the air, not seeming to be falling at first. There wasn't any wind at all. It felt completely different looking at them this time. I didn't think of manna, so much as spores.

Osvaldo, though, looked very worried, as near to panic as he could ever get. He shouted something I couldn't catch but he was plainly pointing north-west, away from the para-drop. I certainly didn't need to be told to get out of the way of it and switched direction instantly. Five minutes later I turned round and found myself on my own, though not out of sight. My heart-rate still sped up. Nevertheless I had sufficient self-possession to wait to see if the others were coming after me rather than maybe waste energy by doubling back. They came, and my relief was great. Osvaldo was first up. 'Don't run off again, Adolph,' he said, with forgivable curtness. 'We all stick together or we're lost.' They had the unhurt *malai* with them, the crew chief. They'd taken his helmet away. I could see he was an older guy; the calm, reliable type. By which I mean he wasn't the berserk type of *malai*. He was more the technician. Air forces are generally better than their ground counterparts. Osvaldo began to speak to him in *bahasa*. Thirty months in the camp and this was the first time I'd had an inkling of this particular accomplishment. Who knows, maybe he'd only learnt it recently. Osvaldo's personal ruffians stood behind the *malai*, looking as if they'd like to cut his head off and play football with it. There was nothing particularly threatening about Osvaldo's own manner, but the *malai* was talking pretty freely. He knew how things stood. We found ourselves on slightly raised ground. Moments later a salvo of mortar bombs, probably from the helidropped teams who'd been harrying us along into the para-drop, burst all around us. We were on rocky ground, which made it a lot worse, with the bombs failing to penetrate and us getting the full force of the blast, let alone the goddamned splinters which whined everywhere some time after the shock-waves had passed. Thankfully, the *malais* hadn't quite got the range right – a breeze had sprung up from nowhere – and the rest of our people were still some way off, so they didn't catch it in our stead. But when we picked ourselves off the floor, we were all bleeding and one of Osvaldo's guys was seriously wounded. It was blood on Osvaldo which really freaked me out. Osvaldo wounded? I didn't believe the guy could bleed.

The *malai* crew-chief looked the most shocked, more so than the badly wounded FAKINTIL vet, even though his cuts, like mine, were superficial. I guess it wasn't so much being hit by his own people's rounds as being totally unused to getting caught by anyone's rounds at all. I found myself hoping that he'd get to learn what strafing felt like, on the receiving end, until I realised that it would entail me being on the receiving end, too.

As everyone else came up, I saw the other *malai*, the pilot, had been getting attention from his custodians. They'd got him well away from Dr Maria. (And I also think the little bitch was turning a diplomatic blind eye to what they were doing to him.) He was moaning and groaning, yelling every now and then as one of his bearers contrived to bump his thigh. The bandages were soaked through with blood: a goddamned waste of time and a complete farce. Going straight over to him, without further preliminary, Osvaldo drove the butt of his G3 into the wound. Well, the *malai* was weakened with loss of blood but he still had the energy to get half-way to his feet with the agony of that. He was crying, I mean weeping, I think with the exasperation and humiliation of the torment as much as the pain. You know, one moment he'd been invulnerable, aloft, punishing the insects with the stern aloofness of a member of an elite corps, the next he was having his violated body rubbed in the dirt by said insects.

Osvaldo lifted his gun again, and I turned away, not feeling sorry for a fellow human being, just lacking the guts to look at what was being done in my own interests. But I heard no shout of pain. When I opened my eyes they'd picked the *malai* up again and were hurrying off. Osvaldo hadn't hit him. As I followed the others three mortar rounds came down, way off to the left. I don't think it was this which had caused Osvaldo to stop working on the *malai*. He probably reckoned that at the stage the poor guy had reached anticipation was as effective as sensation.

When we stopped again he didn't have to resort to brutality. The *malai* was gabbling. I could catch a few words here and there. 'Operation' was *Operasi,* and he kept going on about his legs. That and 'barriers'. It seemed to mean something to Osvaldo, though it was pretty much nonsense to yours truly. I think it was corroborating what the uninjured *malai* had already told him. That was all the torture had been about – just a check. Osvaldo had got the essential intelligence already, freely volunteered in a civilised debrief with the crew-chief. 'Foot barriers', or 'leg barriers' the pilot also seemed to be gasping through his pain. I imagined he was saying he'd like to walk but couldn't, which rather appeared to be stating the obvious.

Osvaldo doubled our speed up yet again; we were coming very close to an uncontrolled flight, except that he was keeping everyone together, making sure none of the injured or the young people fell too far behind. And we were taking it in relays to carry the *malai* pilot – I'd just got detailed for this increasingly unpopular task.

It was starting to get towards dusk now – the transition between light and dark always very short-lived in these latitudes, one moment brutal sunlight, the next sombre isolation. I never timed a Danu twilight – time wasn't ever that significant there and it would have been as useful as weighing a butterfly – but I'd put it now at under ten minutes. Osvaldo got all the groups together in a little over that time. When he'd finished it was totally black. Notwithstanding the experience of X. Ray's night march and

241

our self-inflicted casualties, Osvaldo was determined to keep us moving through the hours of darkness, with only a small squad scouting in front. I agreed, for what it's worth. Not that my opinion carried any weight in the councils of war but it made the trip a whole lot easier for me, in my mind. Fear made the *malai,* my pack, and my rifle seem all the lighter. Dawn was shortly before five a.m. The blackness got diluted, you saw the ghost of your own hand, then the face nearest you. It was a cheerless, dull light that time of day but I welcomed it, even if it meant danger again. I was beat – not out of breath or legs buckling but a deep fatigue of the will. Lack of sleep made you careless, too; your resistance, your desire to live faltered. There were no *malais* around, so I didn't have the chance to test the genuineness of that abandonment.

Towards mid-morning the edge of the forest appeared on the horizon, with the ground rising steadily behind that shimmering ribbon into the foothills of the central mountains. Every pace forward now was a step nearer safety. Why had we ever left our mountain sanctuary? Even with the Broncos, the ambushes, it seemed a whole lot securer than this nude plain.

We'd got to within three miles of the trees when it happened. These insects came out of the jungle. There was no attempt at surprise: no concealment until the last moment, no particular speed of movement. The formation was not, according to my limited understanding, military. A long line of people merely walked out of the undergrowth towards us. They didn't appear to be armed either, though without the binoculars X. Ray and Osvaldo held to their eyes, X. Ray with absorption, Osvaldo somehow very relaxed in his neatly rolled sleeves despite all, it was hard to be sure. We were waiting for orders when we heard again the drone of aircraft engines. It wasn't the sound of an OV-10. I correctly recognised the signature of the Dakota from the day before but this time there were four, lumbering from the direction of Danu itself. They seemed to fill the whole sky with parachutes, oddly some of these pink or yellow. I found myself wondering if the *malais* were running short of the dark green ones. I was starting to get the disembodied, distant feeling of my non-combatant days, and I recognised it as a very dangerous sign. I watched Osvaldo for instructions. I expected him to wave a magic wand to make those parachutes disappear and I don't think I was alone in this hope. As if all this wasn't enough, the thud of helicopter blades added itself to the score. The tiny bugs were arriving from the south which meant that we were now encircled, blocked in on all sides. Shit! There were not a few despondent faces looking to Osvaldo and, I saw, to Martinho. What was *he* meant to do? Strike the ground and open up a cavern for his Israelites? The choppers were landing troops, I'd estimate a couple of miles away. They'd learnt from their previous experience. When they'd finished this they came towards us, but remained high enough so we couldn't reach them. And there they just buzzed backwards and forwards, no doubt reporting all our movements to the commander on the ground.

We headed for the forest and the high ground behind it. Good. That was my natural instinct. We didn't split up but stayed as one group. That made me feel better. Wasn't it wiser to string out, make us less of a concentrated target? No. Osvaldo wanted to focus us on the *malai* line and break through in force. I took a tighter grip on the G3 – my hands were sweating profusely. I wished I was wearing a head-band. The salt drops from my forehead were blinding me. I'd always resisted wearing one – didn't care for the macho look and I figured I was more likely to be shot wearing it. Unjustified assumption, I know. The choppers came closer and fired a couple of bursts at our stragglers then, strangely, left it at that. I didn't understand why, when they had their noose round our necks, they didn't yank it taut. I'd have dropped the paras much closer, too. The *malai* line coming from the jungle was turning into a crescent as the wings advanced to enclose us. It now looked much more like a line in depth, or even three lines. I was in Osvaldo's own squad, rather than with Maria and the brats – no particular order from above but the vets had accepted me into the group. I heard Osvaldo swear as he put his binoculars down. He knifed his hand forwards – into the trees at all costs. We were jogging through knee-high grasses by now. I checked my fire-selector. You could make out individual *malai* soldiers coming towards you. Except they weren't *malai* soldiers.

It was Danuese! They were civilians and what was more they looked like townspeople.

A loud whine came from the trees, followed by static. In Danuese an amplified voice said: 'Put down your arms. Surrender. You will be well-treated.' I actually stopped. The complete unexpectedness of it, my fatigue, the fright, combined to produce a state in which it was beyond my capacities to simultaneously move and think. I received an unceremonious push in the back. It was the Corporal. God knows where he'd sprung from. He must have herniaed himself to catch us up. 'Forward, Chinaman.' I trotted on.

The loudspeakers – they must have had them in the tree-tops – crackled again. 'It is useless. Lay down your guns. Osvaldo has betrayed you.'

I'll tell you, I wasn't the only one who was stunned. The use of our leader's name was a masterly psychological stroke on the part of the *malai* director of this branch of warfare. (It was Rebus, I later discovered.) 'The people of Danu are here to receive you. Give them your weapons. You are surrounded. You have no hope. We will kill you all if you resist.'

The last two statements sounded more like the *malais* I knew and loved. I switched the G3 to full auto and fuck fire-control. I could see the faces of the Danuese now: nobody that I personally recognised. Then mixed up with the men and women I saw bad faces. Even in civilian clothes they couldn't disguise what they were. They were too fit, too well nourished, too young, too hard. They moved differently. Most of all, they were too mean. And when you looked closer they carried themselves with the furtive assurance of men who bore concealed weapons. They might as well have been wearing their cherry berets.

'This is your last chance. Throw down the guns. We will accept your surrender.' There seemed a tinge of disappointment in that otherwise inhuman voice.

Osvaldo was shouting orders and signalling to his vets, his wiry, emaciated figure full of an electric energy. He looked like a berserk marionette. He fixed the unconvincing modern bayonet to his G3, and without being told I imitated him. Our countrymen approached steadily, some hitting the grass with sticks but all looking scared. Osvaldo's squad fired over their heads and they wavered and stopped. The plainclothes *malais* urged them on. One drew a pistol on a recalcitrant Danu man. The Africa vets in my squad were in an arrow formation. Osvaldo had them jogging now and finally they charged in extended line, screaming like lunatics, Osvaldo as well. The *malais,* well mixed up in the civilian line, opened fire, many with carbines with folding butts. The clatter of their weapons simplified everything; it made what followed not too difficult. To defend ourselves we had to shoot through and into the Danuese whom the *malais* were using as a human shield. Osvaldo gave us the example. He was firing from the hip as he ran, without taking too much care selecting his target. That's what it seemed to me. I might be wrong. We others followed suit. I saw an old woman go backwards with the impact of the rounds – it looked as if they were Osvaldo's. The civilians were bunching up for protection, which was only natural but just about the worst thing they could have done. I could only watch as a whole group got mowed down by a long burst from one of our HK21s. The funny thing was, you got more careless with your shooting the more Danuese got hit; you just didn't give a damn any more; the damage had been done, the ice broken. Two young women, running, blocked a *malai* firing at us and caught his burst straight across the hips. As they went spinning down into the grass, hair flying everywhere, our machine-gunner almost cut the *malai* in half. He really caught it, that *malai*. I banged away at what I thought were a pair of *malais,* and missed. Fortunately, because as they

245

dove into the grass it became apparent they were unarmed Danuese boys. Fright had made me as trigger-happy as the worst *malai*. Out of the cover the two boys had found, a figure jumped up and I was overly reluctant to react. The *malai* got off at least four shots at me before I could fire back, and then I missed wildly, the muzzle of the G3 climbing uncontrollably skywards. Next moment, the top of the *malai's* head flew off, hair, scalp, bone. In the general din and confusion it was difficult to see whose shot it had been, but when I looked back João the electrician was closest and he gave me a thumbs-up sign. Putting my selector to single, I scanned the grass ahead and, sensing movement, fired into the waving vegetation. Don't know what it was or whether I hit them but it made me feel safer. We were moving pretty fast all this time, pressing the attack fiercely because it was also our retreat. I'd never fought so desperately or taken so many risks. In its way it was intoxicating; throwing yourself into it like that, you didn't have so much time to get cold feet. A great burst of concentrated firing broke out behind, the rounds passing close by me. Something told me to turn and I saw one of our men crumpled on the ground with his rifle flung aside. Three *malais* had waited for him to pass and shot him in the back. I put the G3 to my shoulder, sighted, and fired fast single shots, the brass pouring out of the ejection slot. I spun two of them – funnily enough, I wasn't a bad shot by now, but still poor on the maintenance – and as the third fired at me one of the vets, wounded earlier by the mortar splinters on the little knoll, shot him in the back. Now he was a real soldier, full marks to him. He didn't look at me but limped on, glaring from side to side under his bloodied bandana. Firing was slackening a little – God knows how many Danuese died in the heavy cross-fire – when a man popped up from a bush on my right with a semi-automatic pistol. He'd got two badly aimed shots away when the weapon jammed on him and I pinked him in the chest with great satisfaction. I'd taken him a little high, in the top of the lung, and he was conscious when I came up. Who should it be but my old friend Soares's goon, the one who'd given me a hard time outside Maria's clinic when I'd been inspecting his master's motor-bike with the purloined package of sugar in my hand. I felt my face go into a spasm, I was showing my teeth in some uncontrollable grin. He was frothing pink at the mouth but his eyes were quite aware. I said, 'Remember me?' I repeated the sentence in the metropolitan tongue for this mestizo's benefit. He didn't reply. I waved the rifle threateningly. He shook his head on the ground still. Of course he didn't recognise the filthy, mad, red-eyed creature above him. I said, 'I am the Chinese queer.' He still looked blank and his eyes were filming fast. I said, with a degree of licence, 'I am the Chinese faggot you saw putting sugar in Soares's motor-cycle,' and as I saw the spark in his eyes, I gave it him through the throat with the bayonet. I did that twice more and left him gurgling.

Some 30 metres of open ground lay between us and the first trees. As I came up to it I found Osvaldo and X. Ray lying prone. My own first instinct would have been to cross over into the shelter of the forest but for those two it had killing ground written all over it. They were right, too. There were *malais* dug in all over the fringes but, I'll give them credit, well camouflaged. Nevertheless, Osvaldo's expert eye had already spotted some posts. He was arranging cover, squad by squad. It was going to be tricky because many of the FAKINTIL people had run out of ammunition. Even I was getting low. In a short space of time Osvaldo and X. Ray had briefed the squad leaders, set up the MGs, and it was now or never. Smoke went down, the canisters fuming away on the earth. It took about half a minute to become effective. I now had time to fret. So many of these military things took time, longer than you'd want. You'd think: Christ! they must be getting ready for us. Even with the interval of the fuse on a fragmentation grenade, the interminable delay between throw and explosion was awkward. Even good soldiers like Osvaldo and the Corporal seemed slow and clumsy. But in their method was science.

Osvaldo blew his whistle. And, as arranged, no one went. Immediately, the *malais* put down this wall of lead. I mean, the roar was incredible; the rounds just whipped over two feet above my head. Shit, was I glad I was lying down. Through the smoke you could make out some of the closer muzzle flashes. We had some light and medium AT weapons left, which the squad leaders volleyed off at the flashes, the rockets flaring off into the cloud to burst with gratifying effect. Those Africa veterans were very accurate with them. It brought about a slackening in the *malai* fire and we set off at a brisk run, firing from the hip as we went. The gunners behind us were starting to lay down suppressive fire, supposedly in given arcs, though I wouldn't like to say what happened in practice as opposed to theory. Anyway, Osvaldo now departed from his plan and shouted: 'Everyone, now. Yes, gunners come now,' and they followed the rest of us through the blessed, saving clouds. A phosphorus grenade went off to the left, lighting everything up for a split-second, then giving us yet more cover. I ran over two dead *malais* at their machine-gun – it was a US M-60 – and was thankful for the work of Osvaldo's squad in front. Then, surprising myself as I did it, I turned back and retrieved three belts of ammo. Some figures flitted across my path and I knelt. I didn't want to shoot my friends and I didn't want to be seen if they turned out to be *malais*. After that, I kept going without stopping.

Soon the smoke swirled away. I crashed through the branches without caring; figured I'd put distance between myself and my pursuers before stopping and moving with quiet sneakiness. I'd thought I was alone but soon found myself in the middle of a fast-moving FAKINTIL group and my morale rose accordingly. We were able to re-group an hour later, pick up a few stragglers, and that was that.

Osvaldo had got away with it.

NINETEEN

'HE IS THE ROBESPIERRE OF OUR REVOLUTION. He is devouring its children.' Martinho was singing his old refrain, but more ardently. 'He has lost all sense of accountability to us or to God.' We were in my bower, looking at a bundle of roots bubbling above a sulky fire. Despite all, the hunger that never got assuaged, the fever which had returned with its sweating and its chills, the memory of that ill-fated incursion into the plain and the malai Operation Fence of Legs, I had to restrain a smile. Martinho's theology was getting as shaky as his history. I defended the leader. 'Under the circumstances he's done as well as anyone could have done. We've always been at a disadvantage.'

'That's it,' Martinho said. 'And it's getting worse all the time. He should know when to end it.'

I couldn't believe my ears. In fact, I refused to acknowledge the obvious meaning of Martinho's words. He'd never put it this openly. However low we got, no one in the camp ever spoke of defeat or surrender. It was so unthinkable there wasn't even a regulation against it. I said, very deliberately, 'I think, Martinho, that I misunderstood what you just said. I think you didn't mean what I just heard.' And I looked into his eyes and wouldn't turn my gaze away, but though I tried hard it was I who broke first.

'You are a fool, Adolph,' he said.

I said, 'I am a lot of things, but that I am not. Please don't underestimate me.'

Martinho put his hand up deprecatingly. He felt morally superior to me. On the other hand he didn't want to offend me, too much. He persisted. 'We murdered those poor, innocent people. Our own people. We shot them down as if they were dogs.'

'It was terrible, Martinho. But it wasn't our fault, still less was it Osvaldo's. We pulled the triggers but the *malais* put the people there in the first place. They were the real executioners.'

'We murdered them. No one else.'

'What are you saying? That we should have let the *malais* capture us? Or just stood there and been gunned down? That's not reasonable.'

'The Christian way was never the reasonable way.'

I was starting to get annoyed now. Gone the Toronto days of disinterested, academic argument without heat, when you could magnanimously and cheerfully admit your opponent was correct and you were wrong; when it was a pleasure to allow yourself to be ensnared by the other party's dialectic. This was for real.

'The trouble with you, Martinho, is you don't want to get your hands dirty but you're willing to live by what others have done for you, whilst you shudder and call them filthy savages.' If I'd been in his place I'd have been furious. I was almost sorry I'd said it. To me it seemed to go to the core of Martinho, the hypocrisy and inconsistency of his position. But it left him quite unmoved. Such is the mystery of another, the gap between their version of themselves and the image we have of them. There was a long pause in which the fire got stared at a lot by both of us. There was the sound of the kids shouting and playing in the background. No amount of hardship seemed to interfere with that. Martinho sighed. He said without evident pleasure or glee but probably only because he was a better actor than I gave him credit for at the time – he was now playing his trump card – 'There is something you should know.'

'Yeah?' (I am afraid this was the very Yankee-ism I used.)

'This is not the first time.'

I didn't say anything but waited for him to go on. But he was silent. I wondered whether he'd had second thoughts, regretted whatever indiscretion it was. Then I thought: 'Not the Martinho I know and love; he's just tantalising me.' I made a display of my uninterest; in fact I only exaggerated it a degree or two. Martinho had to continue, but this time he retaliated by dropping a bombshell from which I didn't recover. 'He murdered Raoul.'

'*What?*'

For the first time, Martinho started to look complacent. The funny thing was, that look of self-satisfaction – which hadn't been on his face for a long time that I remembered – actually improved him. It made him look like the tubby, kindly episcopal Martinho of old. Maybe we'd always mistaken him being pleased with himself for being pleased with us.

'Osvaldo killed your friend Raoul.'

'No, he didn't. I know he spared him. When he needn't and shouldn't have done. Raoul killed your little brother, but Osvaldo gave Raoul his life.'

Martinho smiled thinly. He said, 'That was the first time. I'm talking about up here, up in the forest.'

I think my face must have been a picture, of surprise, incredulity, horror, hurt pride; the desire not to show the revisions going on inside my head. You see, I didn't want to show there were things I didn't know. How pathetic our egotisms are. And this was my friend's fate we were discussing! I was quite transparent to Martinho, I who'd been sitting in judgement on him a few moments before. By way of punishment he made me wait.

'I don't understand. What are you saying, Martinho? How could Osvaldo kill Raoul here?'

'My dear Adolph, it is really very simple. You tell someone to pull the trigger. Or do it yourself if you have the stomach.'

I was trying to keep the conversation going while assessing the veracity of all that Martinho had told me. Whatever the latent faults that a life of hardship had brought out in him, the man was no liar. He wasn't a gay fantasist, by any means; never had been. If he was lying, then there was a purpose to it. Was he unscrupulous enough to do this? Yes! If he could convince himself there was a higher purpose which justified it. But in this instance I had the growing impression that he didn't need to. His whole manner told me he was speaking the truth; he was revelling in it too much to be telling lies. Our roles were reversed now; in a matter of less than a minute, it was me wooing Martinho for information and him playing hard to get.

'But why, Martinho? I don't understand – he'd spared him before, when he might have done it in the heat of the moment. And when are we talking about? Did you actually see it?' I no longer cared that I was his suitor. I just wanted to know. Bit by bit Martinho let me have the tale. He played me like a fish on a line. And by the end I was his, totally; gaffed, floundering, gasping, and out of my element and in a strange world where I was no longer sure I knew anything about anyone.

It was something he'd rather forget, Martinho said. Except he couldn't. Ever. It haunted him at nights.

That I wasn't so sure of – he'd kept it from me quite happily all this time, hadn't he? He just wanted to dramatise and simultaneously exculpate himself – eat his cake and have it: a balancing of contradictions which only Martinho could manage.

Raoul had been under house arrest at the time of the invasion. Not at his father's place but in the old metropolitan governor's house, vacated by His Excellency (who'd watched the incursion aboard his corvette at Toro island). Well, that was one mystery solved anyway. All the time Raoul had been a mere mile away! Martinho said he'd been confined there for his own safety. Raoul had been glad to get his face off the streets and sleep soundly at night with a FAKOUM sentry to protect him. I actually believe Martinho: he had no reason whatsoever to lie. At this stage Osvaldo had no intention of harming a hair on Raoul's head.

Shortly after the first *malai* planes had bombed the port, but before they'd got to the gasoline tanks, perhaps at about the time I was sputtering around the Square of the navigating Henry astride the Yamaha, Arsenio had sent orders that all the IP detainees, Raoul included, should be taken from their secure places and brought up to the hills with the main body of FAKINTIL forces that Osvaldo and Arsenio had decided not to waste in a forlorn battle to hold the town. Even by the standards of Danu confusion abounded. The troops were itching to fight, defend what was theirs. Don't forget, they'd only ever known victory there. They took some holding back; I believe a few actually disobeyed orders, snuck back into town, and sniped at the more careless or over-confident *malai* looters. No one, including I suspect Osvaldo, knew what to do with the IP people. They were no longer the enemy. Had it been Hollywood, and it had been John Wayne taking the baddies back for trial, he'd have unlocked their handcuffs, given them back their six-shooters, and they'd have held off the Sioux together. Then the chief badman would have shot the brave aiming his arrow at Wayne's back. You've seen the movie, I'm sure. But this was real life, and Osvaldo kept the IP people tied together and unarmed, anomalous though their position was. They kept climbing into the forest and mountains, with the smoke of the stricken town still at their backs. They didn't know exactly what had happened, the full scale of the *malai* atrocities in the ville. Twenty-four hours passed. Thirty-six. Then Martinho, Fr Molloy, and their escort came in, followed shortly by FAKINTIL stragglers and other refugees. They told the boss exactly what had transpired down there, on that crazed and bloody mid-morning and afternoon. Some details he missed and I later told him. But they got the basic picture. Arsenio's death hit Osvaldo hard – I think it left him very lonely. He was without an equal after that. The fact that Arsenio had been going to pick up IP people as well as Bill Mabbeley at the time of his death was, for Osvaldo, an unendurable irony. When he then heard of the shooting of his parents, of the death of his mistress, he just flipped his lid. I mean, I wouldn't say he lost control. He succumbed quietly to the worst that was in him. That was, he ordered the execution of the 80 or 90 IP hostages they had with them.

Martinho didn't want to be very precise about this. Although he was telling me all these tales to bring me round to his side and it would have been effective in proportion to the detail and colour of his relation, he was too squeamish to linger on the mechanics of the operation.

I made him linger.

He squirmed a little. Genuinely, I believe. Sure, it all added to the story, but Martinho also thought if he could push it to the back of his mind it would be as if it had never happened.

They couldn't shoot them all at the same time, not handily anyway. Martinho said the Corporal wanted to set up an HK21 on a tripod and work it down the line, but Osvaldo didn't want to squander ammo. Even then. So it was ten at a time by G3s. Jesus Christ.

'Did he make you shout the count?'

'What?'

I thought to myself: they would have had to dig their own graves. Of course. The banal logistics of termination.

'And Raoul? Which group was he in?'

'I don't understand.'

I meant, as you as well as Martinho perfectly well understood and understand, that I wanted to know when Raoul was shot. At the beginning, middle or end. By himself, or with others. Martinho said he didn't know. Couldn't remember. That's a good one. We always say that, don't we, for I don't want to remember. I kept pressing him. The old cant-monger began to weep. Crocodile tears. Perhaps that's not wholly fair. After a while his manner indicated that he was not unwilling to be pumped some more: Osvaldo hadn't done any personal trigger-pulling but delegated the business of killing. They'd put them on the lip of the trenches, knocking them in backwards. The Corporal had fired pistol shots into their heads afterwards. They'd all been bound but were standing. Some died defiantly, others begged. As for Raoul... he'd been in the middle somewhere. It had all taken about an hour, the digging included.

'How did Raoul go?' I asked.

Martinho shook his head. 'I didn't look when it was his turn. I couldn't bear to.'

'Didn't you try to save him?'

'There was nothing I could do. Osvaldo was a madman that day. He blamed everything on the IP.'

'Christ, and you all watched?'

Martinho blew his nose as he nodded.

'The kids, too?'

Again the affirmative. And that was something else explained at last, too, as well as the veil over FAKOUM history, the reluctance to tell me anything about the time before I'd come: the macabre game I'd seen my woodchucks playing on the edge of the steaming forest in that sudden break during the rainy season, the line of kids toppling like dominoes as the older ones sprayed them, dukka, dukka. Don't they always imitate their seniors? Then the bloodthirsty little delinquents had run away from me, shouting the name of their hero and exemplar, 'Osvaldo! Osvaldo!'

'Didn't any of them get away? Not one?'

Martinho shook his head.

No, I didn't think so. It figured. Osvaldo was efficient about anything he'd set his mind to. He was capable of clemency but – how can I put it? – like in 100 per cent doses. He wasn't a 50-50 liberal. For him the world was black and white, as I've had occasion to remark; it was part of his nobility and his baseness, too.

I asked Martinho where the graves were. (That pettifogging Chinese mentality – hard to shake off, even for the man of the world.) He shook his head; the jungle was the jungle to him: a trackless waste, like it was to me. It might have been the sea.

'Much lower down, nearer Danu than Bacalhau.' Well, I wasn't about to exhume them to confirm the accuracy of his relation anyhow. Then he said something which should have made me sceptical but instead heightened my interest considerably. 'They took the heads of the most important people.'

I said, 'What do you mean?' but I knew what he meant.

'They chopped their heads off with the parang. Adolph...' and his voice sank to a stage whisper, '... they dried them over a fire. They made *shrunken heads* from them.'

I burst out laughing. Martinho was prepared for almost any reaction from me. If I had puked on to the fire and put it out, he could have handled it. Or if I'd gone for his throat with my bare hands. But he hadn't expected to tickle me. He looked genuinely disgusted, not hypocritically. I said, 'I'm sorry, Martinho, don't take any notice of me.'

It wasn't that I disbelieved him, it wasn't that I found the death of my friend Raoul amusing, or those of the strangers who'd died with him. It was Martinho who was lugubrious.

I'm an ass-hole, I guess. Controlling myself, I asked him, 'Did you see them ... you know, doing it?' He shook his head. But he said he'd seen them start hacking at some of the corpses before he'd turned away. I knew they packed the heads with hot sand, probably pickled them with herbs as well, before smoking them in the special long-houses. I'd discussed it with Rosa one evening in the Praça. She'd heard it all at her mother's knee, long before the name Marx ever reached her ears.

I wondered if it was the same parangs which had butchered the buffalo that evening of the feast, light-years away. Sure to a certainty to have been. I don't think it would have spoiled my appetite even had I known then.

Martinho was staring into the fire, mumbling more to himself now than me. He'd miscalculated. He'd expected to horrify me, to bring me round to his way of thinking. But all he'd done was spook himself. He didn't eat his roots with me but left to proselytise elsewhere.

It was now or never. I'm sure that was the thinking behind Martinho's move. Better to negotiate with the *malai* while there was still something to put on the table in exchange, however small. As a prisoner of the *malai* there was nothing to negotiate about, or to hope for, except a speedy death. I have a feeling I've been unfair to my good friend Martinho. Of course, there was the strong element of self-preservation and advancement in all his actions – he would have been inhuman otherwise – but he wasn't necessarily taking the easiest way out. There were two ways of looking at it. You could say he and his supporters were too soft to hack it when the going got tough. But an alternative view might be that it took more courage, more imagination to make a clean break from things as they were. You didn't lightly contemplate handing yourself over to the *malais*. They might chop you down even in the act of surrender or, typical *malai* behaviour, give you a few weeks of freedom before hauling you in and terminating you with extreme prejudice. To stay up in the hills, in a sense, required less balls. You didn't know what your long-term future was but you were in command of your short-term destiny. Walking out to a *malai* post with your hands up, every second could be your last.

If I've been harsh on Martinho it is because he was a man whose best qualities were brought out by peace. Osvaldo, the 'man of blood', excelled in time of war, but Martinho would have eclipsed him in settled conditions. Martinho genuinely believed we'd never beat the *malais* and that the best course for Danu would be to make an accommodation with the invader. You could say pride prevented Osvaldo from adopting such a course; that Martinho possessed humility and courage both. If he was wrong in his thinking the fault lay not in him but in the *malai* military. I can see the justice and logic of his point of view now, of course, but I couldn't then.

I could feel the camp buzzing, like the alert bee-keeper can sense a change in his hive. Our narrow escape on the plain tended to reinforce existing views: those who loved Osvaldo began to think of him as endowed with supernatural powers – the hill people who had been his from day one, since his first public speech in Danu, gave him a special, quite untranslatable name, a spirit title – but for the malcontents, it was the last straw.

Who could Martinho draw on? Well, the washerwomen, the devout, the impressionable, but also some fighters. There'd been relatives and friends among those unfortunate Danuese caught in the crossfire between ourselves and the *malais*. Rebus was no one's fool. An Africa NCO, one of the cadres, a real hard case, thought he'd seen his kid sister go down in a blizzard of tracer. I think he was insinuating that X. Ray had shot her. Personally, I thought it very unlikely. How was he going to recognise his little sister after more than three years? Girls grew fast in Danu, matured early. She was probably pregnant by some goddamned *malai*. No, I didn't say that to him. Did I want a knife-fight? But that put thoughts into a few other minds. These guys weren't neurotics – they didn't have the brains for it – but after all that time in the forest it was easy and tempting to superimpose familiar features on to the panic-stricken faces that had run into the blond, bloody grass. Martinho went to work on them as only he could. On those simple minds it would be dangerous to underestimate his powers of sympathetic suggestion. I saw him moving, apparently at random, never in a straight line, from fire to fire, group to group, gathering pollen, alighting with his magic dust, fertilising ears. He made me think of Billy the Bee, of the cartoon character's fat friend, Bumble. This went on for about two weeks. What made it worse was we had nothing to do; literally and figuratively we were licking our wounds.

Osvaldo just ignored it all. He probably felt that it was the sensible thing. I mean he was no moral coward. If I ever ignore things, it's almost certainly for lack of fibre. I know myself that well. Osvaldo wasn't like that – it goes without saying – but it went further: unlike many strong people, he wasn't frightened of *seeing* weak. He had nothing to prove to himself. And it *was* his brother.

Now Martinho knew he had no chance in open forum, as it were. He'd been humiliated once before, through no deliberate design of Osvaldo's. He wasn't about to repeat that little performance. He'd actually been in the right and Osvaldo had been wrong. We should never have gone into the plain at all. Yet the memory of that, in a collective sense, wasn't so much of Osvaldo being pig-headed and Martinho percipient as of Martinho lacking balls. It would have happened again, too. Martinho was in no position to exploit that mistake of Osvaldo's, man to man. It was much more effective just left at the back of people's minds.

The fact that he now had a few real fighters behind him encouraged him to try it another way. Well, it was a typical Martinho failure which went off at half-cock. He was no warrior. I won't say it was half-hearted because they tried to execute it vigorously but they'd set themselves limits, when to succeed you couldn't have limits. It was quite astoundingly childish. They'd decided to jump on Osvaldo and a few others, including X. Ray, overpower and tie them up, and then hector them on their shortcomings before sending a message to the *malais*. It was, I guess, a kind of internal kidnapping. All this to be accomplished without weapons, other than clubs and rope. Martinho was insistent that firearms were not to figure in this little coup. I give him much credit for this. Those not involved in the physical overpowering were to secure the weapons in the camp. There were not a few loose ends here. They couldn't get *everyone's* personal arm, though they could seize the arsenal and most of the ammo. If there was resistance it couldn't go on long, but you can do an awful lot of damage with a G3 and four magazines if you have the mind to do it. I don't see how it couldn't have ended in bloodshed. All this came out later.

I was helping Maria apply a leaf-compress to a nasty splinter wound of the thigh when we heard the ruckus. At first I thought it was the kids playing, then I imagined a real fight was going on between them, the older boys locking antlers. I figured I'd finish the round with Maria, then go and break it up. It wouldn't hurt for them to have the satisfaction of beating on each other a little while; adults intervene too quickly in these things; stop it too soon and the bad blood is still there. It takes, in Maria's felicitous expression, 'one of life's scoutmasters' to know that. Then I heard the Corporal shouting. He wasn't swearing, which in itself was a cause for alarm, but had what I thought of as his 'command' voice on. Apart from anything else, camp life was profoundly monotonous – it was all terror outside and so boring in your bivouac that you missed the fright. We seized on any event that broke the humdrum mould. I wanted to go at once but had to wait for Maria to finish. When we got there, the Corporal had one of Martinho's defectors in a head-lock. X. Ray was held by the arms, two men a side, and he wasn't wasting his energy resisting. He bled very slightly from a cut on the crown; should've been wearing his hard hat, shouldn't he. The main part of the struggle was an octopus of arms, legs, and boots entangled on the floor, rolling violently this way and that, and coming perilously close to the fire. Over all this, the high priest of disorder, Martinho presided at a safe distance, his hands clasped before him in an ecstasy of nervous concern. I had half an inkling already. Then at the centre of the writhing octopus, I discerned Osvaldo's head. He was going purple from where they were choking him – unintentionally, I have every willingness to believe – around the windpipe. He was thrashing around in desperation, probably feeling it was for his life. Jesus, it was an undignified, demeaning little fracas, with that fucking Martinho – the author of it all – holding his skirts (he was actually in camos, but never mind) fastidiously away from the sordid mess. More men were running up all the time and, seeing his squad, the Corporal passed over his conquered assailant to three of his trusties, took a step back and booted him in the balls. Oh God, it was painful just to watch. Then for good measure he kneed him in the face before starting to pull Osvaldo's attackers off him. None too soon, for they'd already broken up the fire and Osvaldo's face was pressed into some embers. He jumped up, slapping his smouldering beard, golden sparks floating away by his ears. I could smell the singeing.

The real FAKINTIL hardcore had all arrived by now, with the exception of the sentries who still possessed the discipline not to leave their posts, however tantalising the sights and sounds of camp. Osvaldo's eyes looked pretty mean to me. The would-be rebels were getting the beginning of a very thorough beating-up, which Osvaldo did nothing to countermand, though he didn't strike anyone himself. I'd never seen him look like that. Martinho, when I turned to find him, was edging away, not with his back turned in flight but still facing the action. He wasn't so much effecting his escape as trying to convince himself that he was invisible. Osvaldo had his attention on the minions, which seemed poor analysis, but then appeared to remember, spotted Martinho, and called, 'Get him!' He was having difficulty controlling his voice, more from breathlessness than loss of emotional control. Martinho held his hands up in horror, that characteristic pious gesture of his, but they grabbed him roughly enough and brought him down. No one set about him, though. Osvaldo looked at him with those eyes. He shook his head and said something to him, I didn't hear what. Probably something more like, 'Well, you really screwed up now, didn't you,' than the sermon the elder brother might have expected.

They tied them all up in a long line, went through their belongings for 'incriminating evidence', and searched them thoroughly for hidden weaponry. Then they worked hard on them: Osvaldo was worried how far the rot had spread, wanted to know who he could trust and what was their breaking-point. In short, we had a little witch-hunt.

It was my turn to have a nasty surprise. I'd always assumed Osvaldo had some special insight into me. Not once had I been attracted by Martinho's blandishments. I'd listened out of politeness, curiosity, anything but agreement. I'd never felt myself compromised, so hadn't worried what Osvaldo might think. When he had me questioned it was as if he'd insulted me; I was wounded. When it turned out that it was to be a full-scale interrogation over days, I had hysterics. It wasn't me and I couldn't believe it was him. Who did he assign to me but X. Ray and the Corporal, with X. Ray in the role of Nice Guy and the Corporal as the Ball-Tweaker of the piece. The version of myself that I had imagined to be in Osvaldo's head was merely an elaborate and fantastical construct of my own devising. For him to imagine that a psychological gambit as blatant and time-worn as that would enable him to penetrate to the heart of me! Really, it was too gross. I wasn't at all frightened. I felt disdain and a cold rage. He'd diminished me and in doing that he'd made himself smaller as well.

Poor X. Ray. He was acutely embarrassed. In his simple, island way he had more the measure of me than Osvaldo. He was so ashamed he couldn't look me in the eye as we went through the charade in the big communal hut. What was my attitude to my comrades with regard to the three FAKINTIL goals of Recovery, Stabilisation, Offensive, followed by Independence? What were my opinions on the useful distinction between FAKOUM and FAKINTIL? Kindly write them down. What were my ideas on Personality Cults? The childishness, the inappropriateness! I was reminded of Canada and the students there. This was the debating society with guns. The same formula games and catchwords but with life and death as the price, the same big words masking petty personal differences. After I'd given X. Ray my piece of paper ('Thank you, Senhor Ng,' he said as he received it with both hands and a bowed head – those little forms of respect and courtesy which matter so much) the Corporal had his turn. And he didn't do his job properly either! I was all ready for a bit of third-degree, but, he, too, the big schmuck, didn't have his heart in it. He certainly had his opinion of me but traitor didn't figure in it. The little games of Russian roulette with the explosives I would purloin from faulty *malai* bombs really had stuck in his mind and impressed him. He thought a quisling couldn't behave like that. This was a fairly naive correlation but then sophisticated intellects are often wrong on these day-to-day assessments of character, where coarser minds can grasp the nettle at once. When they'd finished – and in common with real traitors I didn't get fed for 36 hours – I went to my bower to lie on my face in total chagrin. That little bitch Maria hadn't, to my knowledge, said one word in my favour. I ignored her when she came in, and it was she who broke first – a new experience for both of us, much like her lover-boy was undergoing a novel revaluation of the self. 'Surgery hour, Adolph,' she said, 'time to prepare the bandages.' She cooed this in a manner utterly distasteful to me, as if she were Mom and I were junior sulking in tears on the mattress. Without looking back from where I lay face-down, I enunciated as distinctly as I could, 'You can take the bandages and you can shove them up your ass.' It was no great wit, but it scored, it scored. My type – so you hear – are the masters of repartee but Maria could sting like a Queen bee, too. 'You people like to take it lying down, don't you,' she said conversationally as she left. Ten minutes later I followed her to the sick-bay where, in a complete silence, we ministered to the wounded FAKINTIL heroes. (None of them were under suspicion, by the way, which was a stupid leniency.)

It had been bad enough before. Now as well as fleeing the bombs and bullets of the *malais,* and the interminable search for food, we had a viper in our own bosom to keep a wary eye upon. They were a real nuisance, Martinho and his malcontents. Where could you put them? This wasn't town – there existed no convenient building you could shut them up in. We didn't have iron bars and concrete at our disposal. They had to be bound, hand, foot, and neck at first (an ingenious arrangement contrived by the Corporal where struggling only tightened a noose around the throat) with three armed guards standing over them. They resembled nothing so much as pigs being taken to market. The meaner-spirited and the kids came to jeer at them. One or two bolder souls among Martinho's crew – not the ex-Africa fighters who'd joined him; they were the most daring but also the most ashamed – responded in kind. After a while the adults got bored and went about their own small tasks, but for the brats it was a golden opportunity which they didn't neglect. I knew a couple of the disgraced vets had now and then passed a morsel of food to the juveniles, but this didn't seem to have inspired any feelings of gratitude among the kids, the older ones anyhow, who baited the adults without compunction or embarrassment. Soon, amidst the dirty words – foul abuse dropping out of those young mouths – came pats of mud, followed shortly by actual stones. A couple of the prisoners swore at the kids but they soon learned discretion was in this instance the better part of valour as the hail of missiles concentrated on them. This way and that they endeavoured to duck and dodge, able only to move their heads, these slight movements also sufficing to draw their bonds even tighter. Blood trickled from the crown of one vet – the guy who'd covered my back on the day of the Fence of Legs – but he just looked straight ahead. I felt sorry for him. Martinho sat there, sourly, immobile. No one was aiming for him – that would have been an act of *lèse majesté* that would have been beyond the kids for the moment.

X. Ray came along, spoke sharply to the guards, who intervened. The kids retired to a safe distance, beyond gun-butts, keeping up their taunts much – I thought – like a Shakespearian stage army.

In a few days the sport had lost its interest even for childish minds. The guards sat there, chewing betel, the prisoners scratched themselves. Every six hours they were allowed some exercise in small groups.

Frankly, it was one hell of a waste of everyone's time.

What I wondered, not even in my gloomier moments, was this. Would Osvaldo shoot them?

TWENTY

No, HE DIDN'T. I suppose I was reading myself into Osvaldo, or at least my new up-dated version of him. Probably it didn't even cross his mind. He was no adherent of particular solutions simply because they were inherently more convenient than other methods. Effective, yes. Convenient, no.

The treason, the stab in the back, the cancer within – call it what you like – had the effect of galvanising Osvaldo. He was a man who didn't know when he was beaten, if you'll pardon the cliché. He knew he had to come back hard at the enemy, if FAKINTIL was going to survive. We'd lost the initiative for too long; we'd be rolled up and swept away if we didn't do something that wasn't purely reactive. And, when I think of it now, he surely also wanted to assert himself in his own household. Some coup, some grand success was what he sought, not only to raise the morale of his adherents but to woo the alienated. If he could get us winning again – even for a while – then he could dispense with guards for the prisoners. He could forgive the rebels; they, in turn, would wish to show their devotion with zeal greater than that of the regenerate. They'd be his prodigal sons. Who knows: he might even have slaughtered a fatted calf for them. More likely, a water buffalo. Oh, Osvaldo. So wise and so misguided.

I surmised something was going on from the fact that his confabulations were conducted not only with X. Ray but the

Corporal also. The internal security issue was something he'd share with the trusted and intelligent Xaneros, but the Corporal was strictly on the offensive team. He was there for brawn, not brains; he was at the front of the battering-ram, not at the head of the hearts and minds rectification squad.

Osvaldo's plan had something special about it; the idea was grand, simple, and daring. It conformed also to conventional guerrilla unconventionality. While being in accordance with the classic doctrines on the subject – those principles on which he'd based his early successes – it was also tailored to the specifics of our situation. Hit the enemy at his most vulnerable; attack isolated or outlying detachments; reverse the disadvantage of inferior numbers by concentrating all forces on a smaller, less heavily armed detachment of the enemy; take the initiative; use surprise. He'd dropped the ancient Greek model in favour of the modern Chinese text: Mao, not Macedon. All that was in his scheme, but its boldness and simplicity had something of desperation in it, as well. We were going to assassinate the *malai* pilots.

Note how he went, in his simple way, for the heart of the matter. It was the planes which were making life difficult for us; soon it might be impossible. Aloft, the machines were invulnerable. But, on the ground ... Secondly, the machines were useless without the men who controlled them. It was probably easier for them to be re-supplied with equipment than men. In fact, Osvaldo knew it was. Instructing the pilots overseas – the helicopter pilots were trained in Kentucky, the jet pilots I don't know where – was lengthy and expensive.

We were going to go for both men and machines. Osvaldo thought they'd guard the planes better than the men. Knowing the *malais* more intimately than he did, I had to agree. Their respect for human life was low, even for their own. It was a kind of balancing-out for their contempt of Danuese life. They should have guarded their skilled people as jealously as gold, but with a population of one hundred and fifty million growing by the day it was difficult for them to shake off the notion that everyone was expendable. And the political supremacy of the army gave the air force less influence than was appropriate, considering it was they who were winning the war for them.

Then I had a nasty thought. It only occurred to me because I'd been, as it were, on the receiving end. We were seated in front of the kids' blackboard, in their so-called schoolroom, looking at Osvaldo's dispositions. I said, 'You've done it before, they'll be ready and waiting.' People turned and stared at me. The Doubting Chinaman. They really didn't know what I meant; after three rainy seasons it had been washed out of their minds. I grimaced; didn't want to appear a wise guy. 'I mean when I came here and when Dr Maria came. The raid on Danu, when we tried to get Rebus.' Note the 'we', will you. Someone said, 'Mmm.' It was as if a pit full of stakes had appeared in front of their feet. Osvaldo wasn't fazed, and he didn't appear to resent my intervention. 'It's different,' he said, and left it at that. They all seemed happy to take his word for it. He considered; then expanded on his reasons, though he didn't look at me. 'They'll look after the generals and colonels, nothing special for anyone else. They think we're beaten, so they won't expect anything.' He didn't say more.

I didn't argue.

From our communications chain, our network of spies and informers in the villages, we'd learned the choppers and Broncos were using the old airstrip at Bacalhau. The jets took off from the longer runway at Danu. We didn't want the jets. They weren't the worst of it. And Bacalhau was closer, probably less heavily garrisoned, and had never been attacked before. Bacalhau it was.

Yours truly found himself called to the colours once more. I was required for setting demolition charges: to a bridge that connected the airfield to the new, *malai*-constructed highway and also to the machines themselves. Osvaldo wasn't thinking of putting a few bullet-holes into the planes; he wanted a proper job done. We were to take the last of our medium- and light-AT rockets for this task as well. The attack on the pilots was to take precedence over the attack on the aircraft. X. Ray commanded the demolition squad, the Corporal was in charge of the assassination team. 'Kill as many as you can,' he said, with the typical Danu grin that had neither friendliness nor humour in it, not unlike the formulaic *malai* smile ('Smiling is a national characteristic': tourist brochure).

We weren't many – not for such a task. Five in my group, including X. Ray; ten in the Corporal's hit team. But we were heavily armed – an HK21 general purpose machine-gun to every third man, each of us festooned with hand grenades and criss-crossed with disintegrating-link belt for the automatic weapons. Osvaldo, without saying as much, had learned from the bitter experience of the plain: not all the eggs in one basket, no full frontal confrontation (where there was only one winner). Stealth and invisibility were to be our allies. And, for the first time ever, in the event of an ambush, there were no pre-set RVs. It was every man for himself: we'd scatter 'like a bombshell', divide our pursuers, and get back on our own.

I didn't like it. It seemed a negation of everything Osvaldo had stood for, bulwark as he had been against the excessive Danuese individualism, irresponsibility, panic, selfishness. What he was now counselling might be dignified with a technical military term, but basically it was nothing more than *sauve qui peut*. Nevertheless, I was sensible enough not to open my big mouth again.

The essential thing, we all knew without having to be told (though Osvaldo and the Corporal did tell us over and over again), was not to be detected. We'd be wiped out or, still worse, *captured*, God help us. Yet, the more I thought about it, the more it seemed like a suicide mission, for the hit-team at least. We in the demolitions squad could arrange things so that we had some margin of grace – a big one, believe me, if I had anything to do with the timing – but the people at the sharp end of it, doing the pulling of triggers at close-range, their chances of getting away seemed remarkably poor. 'Kill as many as you can.' That simple adjuration was pregnant with implications. Hovering over it was the unspoken qualification 'before you are killed yourself'. I guessed it would lend spite and urgency to their work. The danger of the mission was underlined by Osvaldo's non-participation. FAKINTIL/FAKOUM could ill-afford to lose its commander. His survival was coterminous with the movement's. His loss would be a blow in both practical and psychological terms from which the cause might never recover. So it seemed to me then. Osvaldo was unafflicted by any false sense of heroism; he appeared utterly unembarrassed by the fact that he was remaining in (comparative!) safety, while perhaps sending his best men to their deaths. I guess he didn't have anything to prove.

Lucky guy, don't you think?

So, once more, we left the friendly forest. X. Ray took both groups out; we had to synchronise final activities and arrive together. I'd devoted some time and thought to the problem of initiating a bang while not being there when the thing went off. Burning fuses, for a variety of reasons, were inappropriate and I was stuck for a while. The answer stared me in the face. Since running out of gauze Maria and I had been dressing wounds and, especially, packing cavities with a fluffy white pith, the discovery of one of the lightly wounded himself, to be found under the pliable bark of a jungle sapling. You could tear regular, manufactured-looking strips out of it. It absorbed liquid to an amazing degree with the capacity to swell four or five-fold from its pristine dry state. The kids weren't above eating it. Well, if you packed a jar (glass for visibility in my first experiments) and put a positive contact on top of an impermeable membrane (the MK 1 leaf) and fixed the negative under the lid, attached a battery to the outside, then introduced water through a straw the positive point would rise on top of the swelling pith and after an interval touch the contact in the lid. Experiments showed six centimetres of pith rose about four centimetres in one and a half hours. Kapow!

X. Ray had looked at me with a strange, uncategorisable expression after my demonstration – when I'd used the current running through the completed circuit to ring a bell dead on midday. It was such a mixture on his face: surprise, admiration, revision of an estimation of someone (namely, me), gratitude, shame for that gratitude. Overtly, though, he confined himself to: '*Ai, bom,* Senhor Ng! You should have worked for me!'

Now, stepping warily on jungle paths over tendrils that might be trip-wires, covering others as they crossed dried river-beds before scurrying over the treacherous pebbles oneself, slithering on my belly over moonlit grass, I could be glad of Xaneros's field-craft.

We got to Bacalhau in 72 hours, a trade-off between stealth and celerity, for while moving carefully was a good idea, nevertheless the quicker we went the less time there was for us to be spotted. Or for tongues to wag in the villages.

The *malai* fliers lived in a compound half a mile from the airstrip. This hadn't existed, that I could remember, prior to the invasion. Sandbag emplacements, arc lights, and a six-metre razor-wire double perimeter fence protected four Nissen huts as well as a large breezeblock building. The airstrip was less well illuminated, with a three-metre barbed wire double fence, but it had a series of guard-houses as well as bag emplacements. Fuel tanks and hangars were inside yet another laager. It was obvious to me, as I regarded the awful brilliance below, that Osvaldo had been wrong about the planes being better watched than their pilots. Both were equally well guarded. And when I heard a dog bark, to be joined by a whole doggy chorus, my despondency was complete.

There had to be an adjustment to the original plans. X. Ray and the Corporal conferred. They got on well, those two; appreciated each other's different strengths. The idea that we could either hit or set-up the easier target before going for the hard one clearly bore no relation to the realities we'd found. It was the two simultaneously or concentrate on just one. Either way, it was an unappealing prospect.

It wasn't just me who had the jitters. I began to contemplate, in a serious way, the imminent prospect of my own extinction. And, after a while, I started to feel more cheerful but in a crazy, hysterical way. The idea of pain was horrific but the kind of animal life we were leading was a great liberator of natural attachments.

After a mere 15 minutes' discussion the Corporal and X. Ray decided to forget about the aircraft and go for the men.

OK. I greeted that with the degree of fortitude expected of the FAKINTIL warrior. It was the next bit I didn't like. I was to stay behind after participating in this first attack, and the very next night breach the airfield security, and destroy the planes.

'Will that be all?' I enquired. This was lost on the audience, the Corporal – and X. Ray, for that matter – being impervious to irony. 'Yes. Then you escape, Chinaman,' said the former. 'How very kind,' I said under my breath.

'You got a question, Chinaman?' the Corporal asked, finally diagnosing terminal reluctance on my part. I shook my head. The bastard could still intimidate me as much as the first night I met him, with his parang in his hand. I looked round at the original hit-squad, of course consisting of the biggest cut-throats and hard cases in FAKINTIL. The roles were deliciously (for them) reversed now: it was me who was embarking on the suicide mission, as the lone Chinese sapper, while they had the comparatively soft option. Funny how everything is relative: it was no easy option at all, being scarcely less dangerous and odds-ridden than my task, though not so daunting because the solidarity of numbers, however small, could boost their morale. Company made them feel better, though dying alone or with a group is still dying. However, we judge according to our neighbour's lot, and the effect of the extra piece of misfortune which had befallen me was to make them count their blessings.

Then X. Ray stunned me by saying, 'Two can do it more easily than one. I stay, too.' I looked at him as if he was crazy, which by my standards – which are the normal standards of the world, no more, no less – he was. The Corporal seemed to think he was quite sane, though, for he said, '*Bom*, then we make sure he does it. Otherwise I think he runs away like a rabbit.' I have to say he had a warped view of the world: not of me – he was 100 per cent right about me – but of X. Ray's reasons for staying. X. Ray didn't contradict him – he wasn't looking for credit – it wasn't his way – plus he would get none from that source. In fact, he didn't even return my look of appreciation.

We spent the day holed up in the roots of a banyan – much better cover than it sounds. A stream ran under this venerable monster. The two leaders planned and briefed the men. I prepared my fireworks, my little boxes of Chinese puzzles. I prepared thoroughly and carefully, actually deriving satisfaction from the manufacture. These weren't the usual land-mines or boobies in which I specialised, so I'd had to improvise new features specific to the purpose. Apart from the time-delay – and as a test I soaked a wad of pith in one of the banyan's pools before connecting X. Ray's torch-bulb to the wires – the method of attaching them to the targets was important. Osvaldo had given me no guidance – remiss of him – but I'd figured I couldn't just place the devices on the aircraft. In the first place, they might fall off; they would be visible, which wasn't quite as bad as with mines but could be awkward if a guard spotted them; and they wouldn't do maximum damage resting on, say, the top of a wing. Of course, I could place them in the cockpit but then I couldn't guarantee it would be open or whether I would be able to open it quickly. Do *you* know how to release the canopy of a ground-attack bomber? Me, I was quite capable of firing myself 100 feet up in the ejector-seat. I determined to place two charges *under* each plane where the blast would not be emptily dissipated: in the cockpit/nose area and under the wings where I believed the fuel-tanks to be located. The method of fixing was simplicity itself. I employed the sticky sap which the kids put on the ends of bamboos to hunt cicadas. This brown, treacly resin was the best adhesive I've ever known; it would stick to anything. By the time I'd finished, the light I'd placed in the roots had been switched on, illuminating the dark recess like a fairy-grotto. I pointed it out to X. Ray, who grinned but didn't neglect to retrieve his bulb at once.

The Corporal had built a surprisingly artistic mud model of the pilots' quarters and defences, which he used to brief us. He was a good soldier. There wasn't much in the way of dead ground on the approaches which we could exploit, except an old culvert which X. Ray very sensibly said we would not use. It had entrapment written all over it. I also had a nasty feeling the space between the fences was sown with minelets and, for questioning it, got the job of wire-cutter and clearer. Thanks, Corporal.

Dusk found us frantically getting our gear together. We had to take advantage of the short space of failing light when we could still see but not be seen so easily. And – to my abstemious mind – with incredible folly X. Ray and the Corporal allowed themselves and their men their first and last smoke in 36 hours. At least they had the cigarettes in one of the banyan's caves. I also left my bombs there. X. Ray accompanied me to the Bacalhau road where I laid five mines in a die pattern in old ruts and two more 100 metres further on. That might buy us time to escape their reinforcements.

To get to the wire took an hour and a half's crawling. It wasn't as bad as I'd thought it would be. After half an hour the nerves settled. I think I was getting more used to these things, becoming a veteran myself. After all, the Africa cadres must once have been raw recruits. My big mouth had got me up the front with the Corporal, earth smeared on our faces and wire-cutters in our hands. I'd worried about electrification, infra-red sensors, but the *malais* had nothing like that, here at least. In fact, most of the lights were extinguished and the arc-lamps were very dim, indicating that the *malais* were experiencing as much trouble with the electricity supply as the colonial government had. The big rolls of tangled, concertinaed wire were difficult but X. Ray had allowed us plenty of time. We'd set out at seven p.m., hoping to get our attack in about nine, nine-thirty, when they'd be replete with their *makaan*. It was a good choice – dawn or three a.m., say, would actually find them more jumpy. I was trailing tape behind me for the others to follow in my steps. As far as wire-cutting went, I was somewhat handier than my abrasive partner, getting through four strands in the time it took him to dispose of one. Within three minutes I was yards ahead of him. The great knots of the stuff between the fences were horrific to look at but not an impassable obstacle for a determined man (which I guess I was), equipped with the right tools. Of course, the best way through was to blow them up with a special charge, a bangalore torpedo, but we wanted to give the *malais* as little warning as possible, get in and kill them in their sarongs. As I got through the final tangle – much like climbing along a giant's balls and trimming his pubis – I heard a tongue click behind. Even in the poor light, I could see the Corporal was hopelessly entangled in the wire, hung up like a snared rabbit. He couldn't even enjoy the consolation of swearing aloud. I shook my head, turned, and cut my last strands with deliberation. In those few seconds I think I paid him back for some of the hard times he'd given me. I mean he was really nailed up there like Jesus. He was bleeding everywhere when I cut him out.

To get through the next bit of ground, I used my wooden paddle. I'd actually crawled some eight or nine metres out before this invaluable little probe came across anything hard in the ground. I put it to one side and felt – a pebble. This didn't make me any less cautious. I kept going slowly, using my fingers now, and a mere body's length later, it was uh-oh. Carefully, oh so carefully, I smoothed the sandy soil away. There it was – an anti-personnel minelet about the size of a tin of shoe-polish. I wasn't sure how to disarm it but I was confident it wouldn't be protected by an anti-tilt fuse or a secondary device and merely put it well to one side. The others would have to make sure to follow exactly in my footsteps. I pointed to the deadly little thing and passed the edge of my hand across my throat to the Corporal, who then OK'd me. Before getting to the edge of an obviously well-trafficked gravel path, I found five more. Two I took the chance of bringing with me. You could say I was intoxicated with myself.

From here on in, however, it was the Corporal's game. He'd brought a loop of wire on his belt that had two wooden toggles on each end. I'd never seen him with it before, but it looked well-used, the wood shiny and worn. To look at this garrotte made you shudder. I was no good – me! – at this cloak-and-dagger stuff, but there were two vets following my tape. They slunk off with the head thug, leaving me to my own devices – pardon the expression. The minelets were incredibly light, considering their power, but I didn't doubt they were capable of taking a man's legs off. I wondered where I could put them, without endangering ourselves: the idea of using the enemy's own stuff against him, turning his home ground into perilous *terra incognita,* appealed to my instincts. Then the vets were back – three sentries disposed of, I guessed from the fingers the Corporal held up to X. Ray. I could see faint shapes moving at the wire; hoped the *malais* hadn't been eating too many pickled carrots.

We were to allow six minutes for everyone to get into their positions. The watch-towers and bagged emplacements were the big problems and we'd agreed the priority was to take them out first. X. Ray and his buddy had crept as near to the biggest emplacement as they dared. I could hear the *malais* talking, maybe wondering what was for dinner. X. Ray threw a metal egg on to their plates, a nasty surprise because they suddenly stopped talking. Then a babble broke out. Just before the grenade exploded, a light anti-tank rocket took the first of the two watch-towers from underneath. They'd taken a risk and got directly below. What a show! Most of the protection was at the sides, with no netting underneath to prematurely detonate rocket-propelled grenades or other missiles. So the whole contents went sky-high, machine-gun, men, search-light, ammo-boxes, a helmet. Shit, it was raining bits of *malai.* Hardly had the debris finished falling when a second missile took the remaining watch-tower square on its sand-bagged side. This wasn't quite so spectacular, but still effective, for the jet of gases from the shaped warhead penetrated the sand and metal sheets they had up there, the blast knocking a *malai* off the platform and sending him tumbling to the ground 15 metres below, where he impacted without a bounce and never moved once again. A hail of automatic weapons fire poured into the tower and either this accounted for the *malais* or the concussion of the anti-tank weapon, for no one stirred up there after that. X. Ray and the Corporal were already leading their men into the pilots' building. A soldier who ran out with a pistol in his hand took rounds from all of them, getting blown straight back through the door again as if you were watching a film in reverse motion. We had one guy remaining outside near the wire with a G3 equipped with an optical sight; he was to pick off any *malais* fleeing from the building, as well as warn us of the *malai* counter-attack. It was inevitable but all we could hope was that it would come later rather than sooner. In all this X. Ray had somehow forgotten to give me a role. Or come to think of it, maybe he (a) didn't trust me (b) wanted to keep me alive for sabotaging the planes. At any rate, I began to feel very lonely out there by myself and rather a conspicuous target. So I ran into the building after the others, which might seem objectively a more dangerous thing to do but was actually just fright on my part. I was in time to see Pedro, one of the more intelligent Africa vets, kick down the flimsy door to a big room (I'd have liked to see him even try on one of the grade-A doors of the O. T. Hotel), throw in a fragmentation grenade, then jump back to crouch and take cover by the frame. 'Down, Chinaman!' someone shouted, but it was too late. The blast assaulted my lungs and ear-drums. No fragments struck me but I was left badly stunned, and the events of the next few minutes seemed to take place in some underwater dream. Pedro and his partner slid round the door on their bellies, firing as they came. From along the corridor came another blast, the pressure waves buffeting my ears again but not as bad as the first time. Upstairs, there was a great burst of fire, three or four single shots, then a huge volume of auto. As I reached the wrecked room, stepping on the door, blown clean off its hinges, with black pock-marks all over its inside face, the two vets were spraying the ceiling with fire. Changing magazines, Pedro fired a short three-round burst into a cupboard which swung open. It was empty like the rest of the room. They ran on, taking me with them, past the other room which had already been grenaded. Its muslin curtains were on fire, the lights otherwise shot out, but in the flicker of the flames I could see bodies on the floor, dressed in the disruptive pattern camouflage of the *malai* military. We bounded up the stairs two at a time, and as we reached the landing three young men in rich sarongs, threaded with gold and heavily embroidered, ran along the railings, grasping the skirts of those impractical garments in both hands. They stopped when they saw us. Before they could turn, the two vets had opened up. The shots smashed them down, exposing the bare legs of one to his buttocks. I kicked a blue rubber flip-flop over the banisters as I passed. A *malai* soldier appeared round the corner of the landing, fired twice, hitting Pedro, and darted back. He had a sub-machine gun but it was on single. Pedro took a step back, and fell on his ass, with his back against the banisters, dropping his light machine-gun across his thighs. His face had gone pale almost at once. He'd been hit in the lungs from the position of the blood-patch. I dropped my G3 and picked up the HK21. I knew the *malai* would fire again from a prone position, exposing as little of his head round the corner as he could. As I glimpsed movement I pressed the trigger, firing off nearly a whole belt into the skirting and lower wall, chewing up the lathe and plaster, dust and fragments thrown up everywhere, and incidentally taking off most of the *malai's* head. The problem with soldiering by the manual is that it makes you predictable. If the *malai* had stood he would only have lost his feet. Firing the gun was delicious; I felt invulnerable so long as I was pulling the trigger and the roaring was going on. We left Pedro where he was – but I cocked my G3, the bolt awkwardly high for a wounded man, and gave it him. Further along the corridor, the whole building rocked to the blasts of two grenades, followed three seconds later by the FAKINTIL machine-guns raking the whole room. X. Ray and the Corporal weren't responsible for this. They were right at the end of the building, examining a door bigger and stronger than those of the other rooms, where they were reinforced by us and the pair who'd been doing the firing.

'Pedro?' X. Ray asked.

I shook my head. 'He's on the landing; he's badly hit.'

X. Ray digested this. Stupidly, we'd been standing in front of the door when we spoke – the only instance of carelessness on X. Ray's part, though he paid heavily for it, because the next instant a burst of splintering holes stitched its way diagonally across the upper panel of the door. One or more bullets hit Pedro's buddy in the head – he'd have been better off to be wounded earlier – and he dropped soundlessly where he stood. Another slug took X. Ray in the upper arm, causing him to drop the Carl Gustav sub-machine gun he'd purloined during the attack. We all jumped back smartly, Xaneros included, despite his wound, leaving our comrade's dead body in front of the door. 'Shit!' said X. Ray, which at the time didn't sound inadequate. The Corporal was on the same side of the door as me, X. Ray on the opposite. X. Ray kneeled to retrieve the sub-machine gun, hooking it with his foot. No sooner had he kicked it towards himself than another burst came through the door. He raised his eyebrows and pursed his lips, as if he was whistling silently. The Corporal motioned to him that he should get ready to fire a long burst through the door, then started to pull a grenade out. I arrested his hand. The last thing I wanted was to be around in close proximity to a fragmentation grenade. The blast would also be somewhat unfocussed for our purposes. I removed an empty ammunition pouch from my webbing, then placed the two AP mines in it, detonators facing the door. X. Ray was readying himself to fire a one-handed burst through the panels when I gestured 'no'. Using the barrel of the HK21, I hooked the pouch strap round the door-knob. We then retired as far as we could – not far, being restricted to the landing and the drop-off to the floor below. I nodded to the Corporal, who banged off three spaced single shots at the pouch. The last bullet did it, just as I was starting to worry. There came a pair of sharp cracks and the door jumped back, still on its hinges, with the lock blown out. X. Ray loosed off his magazine, then kicked the door which yielded a couple of feet. He jumped sideways quickly – but there was no retaliation – and said, 'There's something on the other side.' The Corporal opened up on the door, chewing it up pretty good; then, still firing, probably feeling his bullets were casting a magic mantle round him, delivered a series of stamping kicks which finally levered it three-quarters open. X. Ray, having changed magazines with some difficulty, was in just behind him, me last.

They'd had a table shored up against it.

The one who'd been firing through the door had a Carl Gustav and was wearing a sarong, the off-duty evening wear of the pilots. There was obviously no more ammo in his only mag. The Corporal gave him an economical two-round blurt, sending the boy and his empty gun in two different directions. The sporadic firing that had been going on in the background all this while had ceased. We three looked at the pilots and they looked back at us. One of them lay dead by the window, another wounded in the body, being consoled by his friends who were brave enough to pay us a smaller degree of attention than would have been normal. They'd been picked off by our sniper at the wire as they tried to climb out.

As I say, they looked at us and we looked at them. It could only have been a matter of seconds but it expanded into an eternity and was quite sufficient. We were all thinking: so that's them, that's what they look like, that's who they are. I was struck by their youth – the youngest could have been 20, the oldest not more than 29; by their health and cleanliness, the perfection of their skin, their clear eyes, their short nails. They all had crew-cuts. It was easy to imagine them in Western flying-suits. And they were steady behind their natural alarm; the adrenalin hadn't dissolved them. They were in control of their emotions and their intelligence.

What did they see? Three dirty, bearded, skeletons, clad in stinking rags. God knows what our sunken, red eyes said.

I wondered which ones had bombed or strafed me,

whether they were present or not, or on leave. I wondered if they thought that of me.

All these things flashed into your head, even the dumb-ass Corporal's, I'm sure. It was, I suppose, a moment of group telepathy. Then the Corporal motioned them to the wall. They went obediently enough; you don't argue with a man with a gun and, just like anyone else, for all that they were exceptional, they wanted a few seconds more. Hope, life, anything could happen. They were startled by what happened next. There was a table set with food – we'd crashed into their refectory – and the sight of it was too much for men who'd known what we'd known. The aroma had been in our nostrils for some time, only slightly tinged by explosive fumes, and I found my mouth already full of saliva before my eyes noticed the tempting array of little dishes. The Corporal set his HK21 on the table, unfolding the bipod legs, shoving food into his mouth with one hand, while keeping the other around the grip and trigger. X. Ray and I put our guns down but, while keeping the weapons a few inches away, employed both hands to feed. We shoved the stuff into our mouths. I grabbed a couple of sticks of satay first, then threw the last one away half-stripped from the bamboo skewer before having something more substantial and easier from my right hand: a big ball of rice someone had already moulded. Curried chicken, spiced egg, fried banana, dry beef in thick gravy, all these found their way to my mouth in different fistfuls but got masticated at the same time. It was a cursory chewing it got, I'll tell you. I didn't particularly enjoy it. Very quickly, I stopped tasting the food, beautifully savoury though its smell had been. We had to eat quick, quick: three years packed into 30 seconds. X. Ray only gave us and himself that long. He said to the Corporal, 'José,' – that was his name if you want to know – 'no more.' The Corporal said nothing – all the while he'd been keeping his eye on the *malai* pilots up against the wall – pushing food into his mouth without looking what it was – and now, with a rice-ball in his left hand, he opened fire one-handed before bringing his empty hand down on the front of the butt to control the bucking of the rapid-firing weapon. His cheek bulged with the lump of rice. He was closely followed by X. Ray who worked the other half of the line of *malais,* the belts of bullets slithering across the table-top and the ejected brass cartridges spinning and showering into the sauce-bowls and food. The guns just kept roaring, throwing the *malais* everywhere, gouging out chunks of brick and plaster, showering the wall and ceilings with blood. The firing lasted under ten seconds, I guess, when we were left with a pile of dead and dying that in their native finery resembled nothing so much as discarded *wayang,* shadow puppets. The Corporal had run himself out of ammo, and X. Ray was out, too. We left quickly, though there was still movement in the heap and some quiet groaning. I looked back. The two with their wounded friend by the window had avoided the fate of the others. They stared at me. I shrugged, waved my gun, and ran after the others.

I caught them up by Pedro, who was dead. X. Ray had my G3, the Corporal was stripping a belt of ammo from Pedro's body. I gave them each a couple of rice balls which they put into their pouches without so much as rebuking me. Then it was on and out, fleeing at a breakneck speed, like delinquent kids. We were all ready to be ambushed in the wide hallway downstairs, prepared to lay down a wall of lead at a moment's notice, but there was no one there. Across the path and into the welcome, absolving darkness. To the right a watchtower burned. I shouted to X. Ray: 'To the left, to the left. You're heading into the mines!' He corrected his direction at once. He was a few steps behind the Corporal. In turn X. Ray alerted this latter, who I heard swear before he turned sharply 90 degrees to follow us. To tell you the truth, I wasn't certain about the route myself but my instincts weren't totally wrong as we fetched up some 30 metres from the hole in the wire. We called out to our man and only then did he disclose himself. I guess we were lucky he was a responsible type rather than the trigger-happy, head-collecting Danuese of modern mythology (not unknown in FAKINTIL, as you'll have gathered). X. Ray knew his men in detail – the only contractor who ever got any work done in Danu within six months of deadline. Our sniper had picked off the pilots at their window and one survivor from an emplacement, but there'd been no signs of headlamps coming along the road from Bacalhau. Still, there was no time to be wasted. We crawled through the wire, both X. Ray and the Corporal repeatedly entangling themselves; then ran, with me by no means the slowest. At about 800 metres from the barracks I heard an explosion, the size of a hand grenade. There were no shots, which inclined me to think someone had set off a mine. That was depressing, pardon the pun. I had no particular liking for the Africa cadre but had come to see their good points as well as their bad. We kept on going to the banyan. Half an hour later two more guys came in. About 40 minutes after them one man by himself. And that was all there were to be.

We had a look at X. Ray's arm. I had a look at X. Ray's arm. In the Kingdom of the Blind the one-eyed man is king. They'd have let me cut off his arm if I'd wanted to. He wasn't in terrible pain and from this alone as well as the site of the injuries I surmised the bullet had exited without hitting bone. It was similar to the wound I'd sustained from the Corporal, same round, though I'd caught it in the leg. Some splinters from the door were still embedded, not too deeply, which I removed before disinfecting and dressing the wound. It gave me a great deal of pleasure to do something useful for X. Ray. He had a chew of betel afterwards, the Corporal nodding his head sagely. I guess they were longing for cigarettes.

Everything was now awry. If things hadn't gone wrong, somehow they looked different after our experience – I'd always kind of known they would. X. Ray – so I thought – was hurt and out of further operations. We'd lost even more men than we'd feared. Somehow I'd hoped, going in, that we'd enjoy outrageous luck and come out with a man or two missing. That hadn't worked out. And I'd never liked the idea of holing up an entire day before sticking my neck out again at the airfield. We were bound to be found. If the *malais* didn't have trackers of their own, they'd impress Danuese. Dogs would follow our scent. Not to mention the blood from X. Ray's wound. Forget it.

X. Ray's answer was this: an immediate attack on the airfield. I looked at his pale face. Something told me this was no heat of the moment decision. I could see it in his eyes, steady but guileful, too. He'd planned it this way from the very start, the son of a bitch. He wasn't stupid. I was. He'd never even considered hiding up a tree while a German shepherd barked below, but he hadn't wanted me worrying about the next hurdle while I still had the first to surmount. He knew his man, I have to admit. I guess if any of us had been captured the information inevitably extracted from us would have been usefully wrong.

When I pointed out he was wounded, he dismissed this little quibble. I wished I hadn't been quite so reassuring to him about it: I'd taken the Maria line, though without minimising it in quite such an offensive way. It ended with X. Ray, me, and the Corporal splitting from the others and heading back to the airfield while they fled to the 'safety' of our high ground, our mountain sanctuaries. I didn't want to go back to the planes, I really didn't. I had to watch my tongue the whole time, for fear some sharp, cowardly piece of insubordination would slip from it. Encumbered with my time-charges, I brought up the rear, and the lunatic idea of lowering my G3 and blowing them both away did fleetingly cross my mind. Those strong, unknowing, innocent backs. It would have been so easy. Once or twice the Corporal looked back and scowled, as if he'd read my mind. All round, he was a much lower form of life than Xaneros. Not that I'd have pulled the trigger on X. Ray, but the gunshots would have brought the *malais* down on me before I could have gotten any distance. Slower and slower I went, like Shakespeare's schoolboy except this snail was armed to the teeth and his face was filthy. I could still see them, just, and I wasn't deliberately trying to lose them – I don't think so – but there arrived the moment when the Corporal turned round and no longer saw me. Just to be awkward, I kept still. He was sufficiently unprofessional to swear. X. Ray turned, too. I enjoyed their discomfiture, savoured it a few long seconds. Then I shifted slightly. The Corporal was back with me in five bounds, took me by the shirt, and flashed his parang under my eyes. He didn't say anything, 'Pansy Chinaman,' or anything like that, just glared at me. I said, 'Be very careful. If I drop a bomb, we're all dead.' I was lying through my teeth, of course, but he unhanded me. Not too quickly.

X. Ray said, 'Are you OK?', and I felt ashamed. Him, with his wound. He said, 'You were like a hero at the pilots' place, Senhor Ng. You must go on. It is hard for all of us. Come.' He tried to relieve me of some of my burden, but I wouldn't let him. He was incredible. This time they put me in the middle.

There were headlamps moving up and down the Bacalhau Road. One vehicle had a searchlight which it was using to sweep the side of the highway. As we watched, tracer flared from it, floating out across the blackness. A little later you could hear the deep thumps of the firing. It sounded like 20mm, bigger than a heavy machine-gun. The Corporal laughed behind me. X. Ray halted us. 'I don't think there's anyone out there,' he said. 'They went off the other way.' The heavy automatic kept firing, round after round. Suddenly, there was a huge flash – I mean vast – right under the half-track or whatever it was, an intense burst of white light which illuminated the plain for a split-second. Then it was darker than before as the roar of the explosion reached us.

'Holy shit,' said the Corporal.

Adolph Ng 2 – *Malais* 0, I thought. Someone would have to pay for this night's work. That was my constant reflection. I hoped Rebus would never lay his hands on me alive. Down by the road they were blazing away from their vehicles now, convinced they were under attack from all directions. It was me hurrying the wounded Xaneros along now – there was a window open for us, a diversion, and I wanted to take advantage of it before it closed.

I'd expected the airfield to be lit up like a Canadian football field for a night game – designated daylight in a defined zone. But it was dark as Rebus's ass. They must really have been getting shit from their generator. On the receiving end of all the high tech, we didn't appreciate how inefficient the *malais* actually were; though I was in a better position to judge than most, seeing how many of their bombs failed to go off and, not least, from my contacts with Rebus's goons. It was as if the Americans were giving complicated toys to retarded children.

There was less wire on the airfield perimeter than there had been at the pilots' house, probably because it was a bigger area rather than that they valued the machines less. Osvaldo had likely been right – they'd incorrectly set a value on the planes which was higher than that of the men who flew them.

Once again, it was wriggle, wriggle, snip. It being an airfield, I had a hunch they'd be sparing with their mines, certainly inside the fence. The grass was well-mown. After 20 minutes of imitating a snake, I felt something harder than baked earth under my fingertips. The runway. X. Ray made us go across singly. I thought this redundant. I wondered if the wound was disturbing his judgement – did he think it was a road? The Corporal led the way, me in the middle. As I was half-way across I wondered what would happen if a plane came in to land or take off. The *malais* didn't undertake night flying, but maybe tonight they'd send planes up? I'd end up like a squashed dog on the highway. But the night was silent.

Where were the goddamned *malais*? Surely they couldn't be this inefficient. Two shapes appeared. They became identifiable first as aircraft, then as... OV-10s Despite myself, I raised my head. To see one so close, to view it with impunity! We crept closer. They must have been the ones standing-by for the dawn sortie. The others were tucked up in their hangars. We all, I think, moved almost superstitiously, as if the planes could wake up and attack us, like they were vampires sleeping in their coffins. They were ugly brutes, those machines; all function, nothing beautiful about their lines. When you got very close, they looked like wheel-chairs with propellers. I was struck by the size of the canopy; they really had a godlike view of us fleeing ants. I started, for the first time that night, to feel angry. A saying from student days came into my head: don't get mad, get even. Once under the planes I felt sheltered, which was dumb. They were a focus. The Corporal joined me. He whispered, 'Can I help?' Oh, the privileges and deference paid to expertise! I nodded. He could certainly fix the charges; the more hands the better, in order to cut down our time. I could tell him where to attach the devices, but I had to fuse them. And then ...I just didn't believe it. In fact, I actually clapped my hand to my forehead. How dumb could you get. After all that careful preparation, the thinking that had gone into the design of the fuses... I'd forgotten to bring water. To set the pith swelling, remember? (I didn't.) I wondered how to break this to my redoubtable companions, or whether to do so at all. Maybe we could just place the bombs on the planes without me having to admit to my oversight. They'd never find out they hadn't gone off; if they did, it could be the *malais* who had disarmed them. Nothing could be proved. But I found myself explaining the dilemma to my comrades. They did not berate me. X. Ray had his canteen with him; we others had left ours behind – they had a nasty tendency to rattle – along with the heavy packs. X. Ray's wound had left him thirsty, I think. When he sloshed the bottle it was apparent it was about a quarter-full. He was still going to use it when the Corporal stayed his hand. He was grinning in his nasty way. He took the bomb I was holding, then unzipped his fly, and brought out his dick. Well, he's picked his moment, I thought with some incredulity before I realised. Resourceful didn't adequately describe him. And, of course, I discovered that I, too, so far from having to coax it up had actually been in dire need of a piss for some time. I guess it was nerves. The humour of the situation was not lost upon us, I am glad to say. We giggled like schoolboys as we controlled our streams to the best of our abilities. Wounded as he was, X. Ray acquitted himself manfully. 'Shit!' exclaimed the Corporal as he wet his fingers. 'No, piss,' I said, which sufficed to crack us all up. We might as well have been drunk. We got the charges on to the Broncos, the resin not quite so sticky as when fresh but still very serviceable. Then we wormed our way on to the hangars. Quite why we bothered, I don't know. I mean, we'd been clambering all over the planes like a troupe of monkeys.

It was grass again, after the runway. I was leading now, which was a mistake. With the hangars in sight and not a *malai* around, I put my hand across a wire. The Corporal would have realised what he'd done straightaway. I felt it jerk, thought 'Hell!', but when nothing immediately happened thought I had got away with it. A moment later, *whoosh!* and the flare I'd tripped soared into the night. There it swung by its miniature parachute, and if it didn't turn night into day, it certainly wrecked our night. X. Ray and the Corporal ran at once, followed by me. It was terrible to be out there in the light, worse than being naked in a blizzard for the sensation of vulnerability. The perimeter now seemed miles away; it was amazing how far we'd been able to crawl. We weren't even at the Broncos yet and it seemed we had been running for five minutes. There was so far no response from the *malais*. The area should have been pre-targeted, with machine-guns firing along fixed lines to the spot where I'd tripped the flare and mortars ranged along the known co-ordinates to blast us to a better place. I don't doubt there were. But something had gone wrong, for the parachute flare was dropping lower and still we hadn't been chastised by the *malai* weapons-pits. Our shadows were getting longer; they seemed huge now, crazed and frightening, though we were actually safer. At this point I heard a bang. Then the parachute fell to earth and it was dark again. A few seconds later the Corporal shouted, 'Get down!' I knew enough by then to obey him instantly when he gave instructions like that. Just as I flopped on my belly the second flare I'd heard launched from the mortar went off, shedding a fresh but less intense glare over the airfield.

Now a gun did open up. The awful sound of those rounds cracking overhead – it got no better the more you heard it. Another flare went up. It seemed like midday on that flat expanse. I heard X. Ray and the Corporal calling to each other over the noise. There was no way the *malais* could hear, but I still worried. What if they had sent men out?

'Chinaman?'

'Yes.'

'We move when I call. Run like hell. OK?'

I clawed the ground for better purchase, ready to set off like an Olympic sprinter when the word was given. It was a long time coming. At length he called, 'Now.' Within a few seconds I was ten yards clear of the other two. The flares were almost at the end of their life. No more went up – another *malai* fuck-up; probably someone had put them in the wrong place. Their machine-gun was still going but the tracers were wide of the route we were taking. After a while I stopped and waited for the others. I didn't want to get lost on my own. X. Ray was moving a lot more slowly than the Corporal who was effectively in charge now, but he refused help. As we came to the fence, headlights were visible along the nearby road. Needless to say, we had not found our way back to the hole I had cut. It took me three or four minutes to get through, neither of my companions betraying their impatience by so much as a word. A jeep was moving fast up the road as we crossed. I froze, but the Corporal scuttled across, waving me to stay back with X. Ray. We all hit the dirt on our different sides of the road, clutching our weapons, but the vehicle rolled right past. Our luck held for the next ten kilometres. *Malai* parties were all over the place now but their groups were too big and noisy to surprise us. I think what preserved us was the original choice of Bacalhau as target. They weren't as up with it there as they were at Danu. For them it really was a surprise attack and they'd never had to put any system of counter-measures into practice. As opposed to on paper. Which is a different thing entirely.

A file of *malais,* in somewhat smaller numbers than the others, had just passed in the persisting darkness, we three fugitives down on our faces and hardly daring to breathe, when a distant explosion got everyone's attention, us and *malais*. The rolling echo confirmed it. Not the largest bang I'd ever made, between about a hand-grenade and a tank-mine, but deeply satisfying. It was, of course, the pith-fused charge on the OV-10s. Shortly after, another went off but, disappointingly, no more after that. I never knew what had happened – whether the *malais* had found them, the battery was flat (quite likely with the mildewed cells I had at my disposal), a wire had dropped out of place, the contents of one or other of our bladders had not been up to the task in hand, or if the pith had already been damp and expanded when put in and could rise no more. The *malais* started jabbering excitedly among themselves – from this alone I could surmise they weren't cherry berets, who were a formidable adversary man to man and, at the worst, competent. The explosions way off seemed to make these *malais* imagine we were there too. I could appreciate the subjective conviction which such an equation might carry – it was human nature and apparent common sense after all – but I was a sufficiently experienced soldier now to hold them in some scorn. They must have been new arrivals from their main island. I guess that at their closest they were maybe 10 or 15 metres distant. With the advantage of surprise we could have cut most of them down but it wasn't so much them alone we were concerned about. I could be thankful for my opportune bangs.

They were the last *malais* we encountered. As daylight came we found ourselves in the savannah. Fearful of dogs and trackers – most of all of coerced Danuese – we kept plunging through the high grasses until we reached forest. Three or four planes buzzed overhead during this time but never found us.

Some distance from the old camp we'd left, Osvaldo's scouts intercepted us and brought us into the new base.

Not one of the others had made it back.

TWENTY-ONE

I'VE NEVER THOUGHT OF MYSELF AS A HERO – and you know me too well to labour under that delusion either – but I found myself hailed as one. I am not so pathologically modest that I found it distasteful. I won't pretend that I didn't find it very pleasant, in particular the week's extra food. Admiration from whatever source, even those you may despise, is still something to bask in. Osvaldo held a ceremony. We, the honoured, being the Corporal and yours truly, stood before our leader and the FAKOUM flag, which the washerwomen had run up on a sapling. The female choir sang a specially composed ode, only two days old, but which already sounded traditional in its solemn, rhythmical, reedy melody. Their sweet voices, though perfectly in harmony, en masse narrowly missed a jarring, jeering tone; something to do with the nasal chant which was the distinctive national style. Strangely enough, it had the effect of imparting an undercurrent of truth to all the bullshit, as if I was in my triumphal chariot with the slave whispering in my ear, *Memento mori!* But not a trace of irony existed in those open faces. It was all in my perverted, guilty mind.

Osvaldo said we'd shown bravery of the most glorious kind, courage that would be remembered in the annals of the movement long after we'd prevailed. What we'd done would belong to legend. Remember also those brave men who'd died on this dangerous mission. (He didn't dwell too long on this depressing statistic). I (Adolph Ng) had especially distinguished myself. As I was already at stiff attention I can't say that this surprising piece of information made me sit up but it fine-tuned me. I mean, I was in grave danger of bursting out laughing at anything that came after that.

Of course, Osvaldo was fêting us for his own purposes. It didn't have that much to do with us personally. He wanted to get morale up and, in turn, strengthen his own position. It was important to him to claim what had happened as a success. We had a vested interest in being his accomplices in this distortion or at least magnification of our actions. Note that X. Ray Xaneros wasn't out in the sun hearing an encomium about himself from the lips of his leader. Osvaldo didn't want to exalt his commanders. I don't think because he feared rivals but because he wanted the rank and file to feel they could be as important as the top guys. If it had suited his purposes I don't doubt he'd have had me shot *pour encourager les autres*. It was a joke, me getting the plaudits and X. Ray, his poor arm bandaged, sitting under a tree, smacking his free hand on his thigh. He showed no trace of resentment at all. When I mumbled some shamed words after, he just embraced me with his one good arm and laughed.

And Maria, caustic, clever Dr Maria, did she cut me down to size? Did she hell. Instead of the withering truths she'd favoured me with in the past, I got smiles, caressing words and that closed, false face of the true Chinese. She knew what it was all about, the bitch.

They had the prisoners, Martinho and his crew, out to witness the spectacle of our commendations. They'd tied them all together in a line, hat-less, and made them kneel out in the clearing with the sun in their eyes. To me it seemed somewhat self-defeating, if the ceremony was intended to be re-educative or, alternatively, designed to rub the salt of humiliation into their wounds. The few African cadres who'd gone with Martinho were already full of shame. Martinho himself looked more embarrassed than ashamed – he believed in what he'd done and didn't regret it. The soldiers did.

After the ceremony the camp had three days of holiday, meaning no political indoctrination classes and no weapons drill. X. Ray had a fever but I put aside his dried beans and rice for when he got better.

Osvaldo eagerly awaited his lieutenant's recovery. He had more schemes up his sleeve. You could see him poring over his tattered, mildewed maps, or walking round the table-top on which he'd built a scale relief model of Danu from its own earth (the sea being represented by a mat of overlapping leaves, renewed daily for greenness). God knows what he was planning, some complex schedule of feints and diversions to conceal an attack on Danu.

What had been noticeable for some time was that the skies were empty. I could munch my beans with an easy conscience as I looked at the clear blue canopy. Beams all round from the veterans as I returned someone's thumbs-up sign. The fact that we could chew the grass without being molested by eagles was down to me, Br'er Rabbit. The number of planes we'd destroyed had somehow got multiplied from my first cautious estimate. Camp gossip now had it at nine. I'm not sure the *malais* even had that number deployed in Danu. The most we'd seen together was five, and they could just have refuelled, rearmed, and turned them round in 15 minutes. I let it pass. It would have been bad for morale and would not have pleased Osvaldo.

Malai radio traffic came thick and fast during these days. Their codes would always remain impenetrable to us but the low-level communications were in clear, often just colloquial conversation. They'd had Home on the line to them non-stop since the raid. It wasn't something the Area Commander could keep quiet about. Apart from the loss of their pilots being a terrible blow in its own right, the event had awakened dormant rivalries between the services. The Air Force general blamed the army for not guarding his men properly. Apparently, we had caught the Air Defence corps away and ordinary troops had been guarding the pilots. To match the antics in Danu there was a terrible faction fight going on in their capital. We didn't get this directly. What we heard was the servants' gossip, but then that's always the frankest and most reliable information, isn't it? For our part our operator had transmitted the news to Australia straightaway. Unfortunately, it lost some of its drama. FAKINTIL routinely sent its own propaganda over the sea: this town captured, so many *malai* lorries destroyed, that battalion ambushed and wiped out. To hear it, in the black days we'd just known, you would have thought the *malais* were praying for a truce on any terms. So when we did achieve something substantial, as now, its impact was dissipated. Served us right, I guess, for being as big liars as the *malais*. The operator did his best – but when you habitually deal in hyperbole and boast you effectively devalue the currency of your communication; that's what happens with inflation, with hot air. When we had something real it got obscured in the mists of make-believe.

It wasn't the Broncos who were to chastise us for our latest and gravest impertinence. Nothing so technical. It was a combination of our own failings and *malai* initiative.

The latest camp was sited on a position of great natural strength, with a cliff and a steep ravine protecting two sides and thick undergrowth another. We had decided to remain a while, have a break from the gypsy existence. The approach was surrounded on all sides by high ground. We relied on it overly, we who as so many snakes and rats should have known better.

The mutineers were allowed exercise. Not having dismissed redemption as a working possibility for some, Osvaldo wished to keep his prisoners fit. They were now tied up only on more ceremonial occasions, almost as formal dress. Certainly when they exercised they were freed. Six or seven armed guards kept an eye on them while they marched about on the lip of the ravine. While Martinho's camp-followers strolled aimlessly, the disgraced vets did callisthenics in a squad with their own instructor blowing on a bamboo whistle. They performed with a peculiar vigour, as if their hard work (aimless and unfocussed as it was) might count towards their forgiveness. It was likely rooted in an objective as well as subjective basis: I don't doubt big O. would give them points for it. I'd be up there with Maria when I could. We were going through one of our periodic phases of intimacy, in the steps of that grave and formal minuet which was the history of our friendship, now at a distance that bordered on a chilly detachment, now pressed as close as the lovers we were not.

'It's a little ridiculous, isn't it?' I remarked to her (of the

292

prisoners, stupid, not us).

She looked at me quizzically. 'If you say so. Personally, I don't find anything ridiculous about treachery. It's just shameful. Osvaldo would have been in his rights to have shot them all.'

'Well, the fact that he didn't is what makes Osvaldo Osvaldo.'

She smiled with satisfaction, a kind of indulgence, as if it was an amiable weakness in her lover. *She'd* have had them shot. Raoul, for instance, would not necessarily have found mercy had she arrived in camp earlier. I, as the new FAKINTIL hero, was allowed to have an opinion different from hers without it being held against me. I changed the subject – it was foolish of me to have brought it up – and we spoke of old times, without mentioning the former acquaintances who were now non-persons. She spoke affectionately of our late friend Arsenio (he'd been generous with transport for her clinic), with admiration of old Bill Mabbeley, of Rosa and, surprising me who hadn't thought of her in a long while, Jean Carmichael. 'Jean is one of the best friends FAKINTIL has,' Maria said with a confidence which on reflection I also didn't think misplaced, though not for the same reasons as Maria. Jean was a decent girl with ideals, but her attachment to the movement and Danu would be all the stronger for the fact that she'd been Arsenio's mistress. She'd hate the *malais* for what they'd done and – I'm sorry – she'd also enjoy playing the role of tragic, star-crossed lover without for one minute letting it compromise the pose of hard-bitten journo. Danu filled a gap in her life; we gave her something to be indignant about, and she was the kind of person who liked to be indignant. So I thought, but I kept it to myself. As far as Rosa was concerned, Maria and I were on safer ground.

'What's *she* doing?' I thought out loud. And Maria smiled again to think of her devoted, funny, fat friend. 'She is on top of the situation, whatever it is,' she said. 'She will be looking after the children.'

'Mmm,' I said. I hoped she hadn't suffered because of her

known friendship with us. I suppose that depended most on what Rebus had made of our respective disappearances, whether he thought they were coerced or not, or whether that mattered in his mind. He wasn't logical; guilt by association was the way his mind worked. Bringing the wrong news could be enough. I'd seen it happen. Yes, I wasn't so sure about Rosa, but I didn't want to blight the moment by saying, 'Come off it. She's dead because she knows us.' At least, so I consoled myself, no one had recognised me, or seen my face clearly at close quarters and lived to tell the tale. While we were thinking of old times, Martinho had been walking by himself, hands behind his back, for all the world as if enjoying a post-prandial constitutional at the seminary. That's one guy who doesn't appreciate how lucky he is, I thought; he probably feels hard done by, the *primus inter pares* of peacetime, the prince of our sodality. The prince had taken up smoking, for a clove cigarette spluttered in his hand as he went by, a pernicious habit I'd never seen him indulge before. I put it down to strain and pique. He still enjoyed a few little privileges like this, denied his men. Maria didn't see him; she'd cut Martinho right out of her life, though needless to say we all lived in closest proximity. He was as good as invisible. Martinho now came back, minus clove cigarette. He nodded civilly enough to me, which courtesy I was also sufficiently man of the world to return, discreetly because the tiny, terrible Dr Maria sat by my side in judgement. The prisoners' break was over. The PT cadre stopped its evolutions at the shrill of the whistle. Martinho's degenerates shambled down the hill after him. Although Maria ostracised her brother-in-law (and chief architect of her marriage!), though she behaved as if the prisoners were ghosts, clearly a lot of the fun and interest of sitting chatting on an elevation with me departed with the mutineers. Our talk became desultory. At length, mentioning pins and needles, she indicated we should go.

We'd just washed up preparatory to holding her surgery when the sentries raised a cry. Smoke rose from the hill-top.

The whole camp rushed up there, Osvaldo not ashamed to be with them. The blond grass was well ablaze, you could hear it crackling 50 metres away. Osvaldo tore his shirt off, the buttons wifey had sewn and re-sewn scattering prodigally everywhere. Leading by example, he strode to where the flames were fiercest. X. Ray was organising a bucket-chain – if you could call our stoppered bamboo tubes buckets. We didn't have that much water to throw around, in fact. The washerwomen performed prodigies, the first time I'd ever seen them be useful except in the two obvious respects of sex and laundry (and just laundry in the case of yours truly). But those who combatted the heat with greatest ardour, who stayed in the fray the longest and nearest, to emerge coughing, blackened, scorched, singed, some with their frizz on fire, one or two dragged unconscious away, were the Africa mutineers – Osvaldo's lost legions proving themselves to their hero in a fiery ordeal. Yet in the end it was X. Ray's third group, me among them, unspectacularly cutting down the grass 50 metres away, who put the fire out. I'd thought we were too far from the danger, had felt embarrassed. Personally, I'd have endeavoured to remain nearer the flames and given the impression of working, without ever actually jeopardising my person but X. Ray's conservatism, pessimism, call it what you will, proved justified as the spread of the flames proved too much for the firefighters to contain. As the conflagration sped towards us, out of control, I thought, 'That's a man who always knew the limitations of his people, who knew everything's measure, including his own.' And that was it. The fire died suddenly. One moment there were leaping, cracking flames three metres high, the next some flattened, smoking charcoal underfoot.

I'd crossed the firebreak to speak to Maria, joining Osvaldo's sweating, half-naked blackamoors. When I turned round I saw X. Ray on the unburnt ground in his neat olive greens, a little hot but still presentable. He didn't get much attention, with Osvaldo appearing the hero of the hour. I don't think X. Ray gave a damn worth mentioning.

The camp had been in no danger of burning down; the problem was the give-away smoke. Amidst the general sense of achievement, I couldn't help worrying. I guess I wasn't the only one, but these days you didn't like to be the slightest bit negative; you kept your qualms to yourself. Of course, I had a damned good idea as to what had happened but I didn't broadcast my suspicions. I had that much regard for old times left. And there was self-interest in it, too. Once you start a witch-hunt you're never quite sure where it will end: maybe knocking on your own door. This forbearance did no good.

Some days later I was passing through the weary-looking vegetable gardens – those straggling plants were undergoing a crisis of morale as acute as ours, even the shit strewn on them smelling insipid – when I paused from shepherding my kids' weeding detail to see an undesired sparkle on a high rock. For a sentry to betray his whereabouts by such negligence would be a serious offence. Normally, I would have thought it sunlight hitting mica or some such surface; however, at this time one was suspicious. I kept my eye on the spot. There it went again. Flash, flash, flash. Binoculars, a metal blade, broken glass? It was going too fast, too variedly to be rays catching a discarded object randomly. I said nothing to the kids, kept their heads down in fact and pointing in the whole other direction. They'd be certain to shoot their little mouths off. Leaving stern instructions that no one was to stray from their work, so much as unbend his or her back, I went leaping over the rocks. I was thin, painfully thin, but stronger and more agile than ever before, or since. It took me about the quarter of the time of a fit 'normal' person to reach the scorched plateau. Even so, there was no one there. I guess it's always quicker down than up. There wasn't even any cover left for the culprit to hide in – not that I'd have been tempted to venture into the thick, man-high grasses. What, and get my throat cut for my pains? We lived on top of each other but there were also lonely moments like that. I decided to return the way I'd come. Just then X. Ray Xaneros scrambled up the other side of the plateau, with the kind of expression on his face you didn't often see. He was pretty mad. And the black look didn't clear up when he saw me. He strode on, straight as an arrow. I shook my head. 'It's not me, X. Ray.' The attack was instantly deflected, though he was still angry. I was glad it was X. Ray: not for a moment did he suspect me of doing it deliberately, though carelessly had been a possibility. We poked around the cinders. There were far too many footprints to enable us to follow any trail. We went down to camp. Someone was having a tooth extracted – by the Corporal, not Maria (he would have been my choice, too) – and people had gathered to watch the fun. Perfect alibis for all in sight, especially the cadre with the shard of mirror who held it to the victim's bloodied mouth afterwards. Quite unreasonably – and manifestly incorrectly – I suspected him. A natural reaction. If I was Rebus, I'd have had him tortured. Well, we would have to live with our frustration. All X. Ray could do was make sure sentries were posted on the high ground all the time.

Ten days later the *malai* hit us. X. Ray had taken a fighting patrol down to the plain. This left the camp short of 25 of our best men, yet in the event it was no bad thing as it preserved them.

The event was a heli-borne attack. They came very low, different from their previous tactics, following the contours of the terrain, seeking dead ground and cover, treating the machines almost as if they were ground-bound vehicles. For that reason we had very little warning of their arrival. One moment we were about our normal small affairs, the women working, the kids drilling, me in the sanatorium, the next the air was full of tracer, rocket wakes, and the black seeds from the little grenade-launchers. The Africa cadres on duty had about five seconds to react, which they did as well as could be expected – being the good professionals they were – and we were returning heavy fire within 20 seconds. Yet the *malais* had the advantage; our resistance was desperate but unfocussed, uncoordinated. The gunners on the HK21s thumped away with great, spendthrift bursts, yet I could see

297

the tracer rounds floating away, mostly well behind the whirling tail-rotors. The green bugs danced an invulnerable sequence, inhabiting only those spaces of the air that were innocuous, changing spots with what seemed a superhuman prescience before our gunners' scarlet flurries could drench them with their fire. They lived in thin air, then vacated the shape they'd filled for another empty cut-out as the FAKINTIL tracer clawed at where they'd been. We might as well have been trying to piss on bees. And those bees could sting, more than once. In the first impetus of their assault they'd been excited, too, but as their gunners got their heads together the aerial fire became denser and more accurate. Our big meeting-hall – school-room, ops centre, and court-house all in one – was the first to go up in a dense grey cloud of debris from a quadruple rocket-strike. By chance I followed them from the pod, two-inch rockets they were, in a parallel spread one behind the other. Then the sanatorium and radio-hut got it in quick succession, the first from a salvo of rockets, the last chewed up by a converging stream of tracers from the door-gunners of two helicopters. I watched the flimsy bamboo thatch and walls disintegrate under the blizzard of glowing metal. The sanatorium... I felt sick to my stomach. Those men I'd tended, just lying there. Of course, there wasn't exactly a big red cross painted on the roof for the world to see.

Where was Maria? She'd been talking to Osvaldo near the radio-hut. Jesus Christ.

A couple of our HK21 gunners had got it from a well-directed *malai* burst and, shortly after, a cluster of spinning air-launched bomblets from their grenade-throwers hurled up a pair of guns and their men from another pit. I saw two figures sprinting to the wrecked machine-gun nest ... it looked like the Corporal and Osvaldo. Who else? I didn't have my trusty G3 near and I had no desire to expose myself by running along the clearing like the intrepid pair, who jumped into the pit with the dust-spurts of an observant door-gunner's burst already walking up to them.

Accurate automatic rifle fire from a group of Africa vets,

well co-ordinated by an NCO, forced the helicopter to turn away, with pin-prick holes opening in the virgin green of its fuselage. But our fire was slackening and I knew I had to add my voice to that dying chorus. Besides, I was certain the *malais* would soon put in an infantry attack. Making sure, so far as I could, that the choppers had already acquired targets or were being engaged by us, I dashed across the clearing, hoping fervently as I did that some friend would take the trouble to cover me with suppressive fire should I attract unwelcome attention aloft. I made it OK, but panting far more heavily than I'd thought for such a short run. The weapon I took from the rack wasn't mine, nor had it been cleared prior to storing. There remained a round in the breech (typical piece of FAKINTIL negligence). I slapped in a 20-round box and waited for a target of opportunity to present itself – but nothing that would get me chewed up in retaliation. Difficult choice. I held my fire.

Over my head a volley of rockets shot past. Bangs from the high ground. They weren't air-to-ground projectiles but some of our own remaining 66mm light anti-tank weapons, fired from the hill at the same level as the circling choppers. All missed, but they served the useful purpose of distracting the *malais* and putting their aim off, forcing three of the machines to sheer away. I got off six shots, double-tapping them in sequences of two, but certainly missing with all of them. Osvaldo was signalling, shouting above the din but not making himself heard. He seemed to be telling us to clear out. I obeyed with alacrity, stopping only for my two water-bottles and the personal effects I kept bundled against just such an eventuality.

Six hundred metres distant there shot up a great gout of black and orange *(they* should have been the FAKINTIL colours) followed by the boom. At once a *malai* helicopter banked left and up, door gun still blinking malevolently. I knew at once, with a great feeling of glee, what had happened. That was no napalm strike dropped short but a helicopter landed – deplaning troops – on one of my mines. It sounded like one of the 500 lb bombs. I doubted there'd be any survivors for the rescuing chopper to pick up, more a question of gathering the pieces. It was just the tonic our men needed. I shouted out: 'It's mine, it's mine.' The kids cowering by a felled tree-trunk near me started to laugh. I joined them.

The *malai* pilots had moved off somewhat, maybe thinking we'd downed the other machine with something bigger and better than we really had at our disposal. The fire was a little less deadly, and it was possible to move without getting chopped down in a few seconds. The kids, women, and the wounded (I was stunned by the extent of our casualties littering the clearing) were already fleeing or being carried into the forest. Those who'd decided to constitute themselves the rearguard were laying down a respectable quantity of covering fire. As the choppers came close again the Corporal laid down smoke, beautiful smoke, and we ran, firing backwards as we did so. At tree-top level I could see *malais* – their cherry berets conspicuous – sliding down ropes from a stationary helicopter. I loosed off the remains of a mag, then re-loaded on the move.

At a small, dried-up water-fall I caught up the younger boys and girls, and helped some tiny ones up. I had to sling the G3 across my back to carry them better. Then I gave them directions for a rendezvous. I waited on one knee for the rearguard. Don't ask me why I did that instead of keeping going. I don't know, but wouldn't claim any credit for it. Fugitives started to come now, wild-eyed, their breath rasping. A couple had their good friend between them, his boots trailing, arms across their shoulders: a bad thoracic wound. I told them to leave him with me – I didn't want responsibility for him, but their consciences were afflicting them, I could see, and there was no point two dying for the sake of one who probably wouldn't live anyway. Even as he breathed I could see it was one of those terrible sucking chest wounds. They left him his gun and propped him against a rock with a bottle of water.

Looking down at the camp, I could see people running in the ravine some 400 metres from where I found myself. They weren't *malais*. I didn't need a telescope to see a couple of them were waving white flags. They were, in fact, running in the direction of the *malais*. I screwed my eyes up. One looked suspiciously like Martinho himself: the singularly unathletic movement, the baggy pants; it was him to a certainty. Three or four of them fell down. Then I heard the discharges. My ears had got good at this kind of thing – the direction was from our camp. The crimson of *malai* berets seeded the trees. They also fired on the leading fugitives, putting four or five down, the sharper crack of their M-16s quite distinguishable. The guy with the flag – it wasn't Martinho – waved it frantically. The sound of a whistle carried faintly up.

Scrambling from behind me on the dried-up falls: the face of my beloved leader appeared, with Corporal. They were soaked in sweat, their shirts transparent. I remembered the day I'd first seen Osvaldo, running along the beach from the town to the hotel. Aeons ago.

I said, 'Looks bad, Osvaldo.' He ignored this, got his breath back a little, and – ever solicitous – asked, 'Are you OK?'

'Sure.'

The Corporal swore. 'Look, chief! The sons of bitches!'

More of Martinho's felons were running across to the *malais* who had stopped shooting at them. I thought I could see Martinho himself in the tree-line. The Corporal put a fresh magazine in, wound the sling around his forearm, and lay on the ground. He began firing deliberately, not worrying about revealing our position. I was more worried about this than concerned that he was trying to kill our erstwhile comrades. Settling by his subordinate, Osvaldo sighted through the fancy German scope on his rifle. He added his bangs to the Corporal's, shooting every ten seconds.

'For God's sake, Osvaldo, he's your brother!' I thought he was going to ignore my pusillanimity – it sounded very weak even to my own ears – when after the considered release of another four shots, he said, 'What makes you think it's him, particularly?' *And we all laughed!* Jesus, the strangeness of people. In the middle of this mirth, Osvaldo dropped a cherry beret flat on what was left of his face. By now we were attracting a heavy volume of *malai* fire. It was only a matter of time before they put some mortar rounds down or, still worse, a hunting helicopter returned. The Corporal was still banging away, probably intent on dying a hero's death in that time and place, but Osvaldo tugged at his boot, while ushering me before him. We dodged and twisted along the winding path. Five minutes later the *whop-whop* of rotor blades became audible. We all burrowed into the roots of a forest giant. It was a good feeling. The great curtain of creepers, let alone the jungle canopy way above us, conferred all the protection of 30 metres of water. I still lacked the discipline not to look up. Osvaldo put his palm on my head and gently pushed it down. We stayed put as long as we dared, straining our ears every moment for the sounds of *malais* coming through the trees. Above the sounds of the rotors and engine, we discerned long bursts from the helicopter's guns, giving some other poor FAKINTIL devils a hard time. A hundred metres further on – it took 15 minutes to cover the ground – three kids called to us from the branches of a tree. Poor kids. They were so glad to see their hero. On we forged, Osvaldo the great comet acquiring a trail of followers from boles, caves, roots, forks, grottoes, and trunks. Finally we comprised a party of 20.

The forest became peaceful in the two next hours, raucous not with the screams of injured men and women but the cries of birds and the sawing of insects, redolent not of the stink of cordite or opened guts but the blooms of its own cycles of decay and regeneration. Just as I was starting to think we had got clear the sounds of fighting came from 1000 metres ahead. Osvaldo stopped us. Both he and the Corporal recognised the contact as an ambush, almost certainly by *malais* heli-dropped in front of our line of march. The question was, did we counter-attack the *malais* and help release our people, or did we make good our own escape? It was a hard choice.

Osvaldo didn't even hesitate. We would go for the *malais*.

That was hardly a decision acclaimed with enthusiasm by the majority of us. We thought of our own precious lives. Of course, in the long run we needed to be as many as possible, but it was difficult not to put your own skin first as an immediate priority. Too bad. We followed.

Twice helicopters passed overhead without spotting us. The gunfire became louder but also somewhat less intense. Osvaldo sent orders up to stop the front group. A hurried briefing ensued, at the end of which our main group stayed behind and a recon group went ahead, comprising the Corporal and five Africa cadres, including two who'd thrown in their lot with Martinho. Yes, Osvaldo was giving them a chance. They hadn't run with Martinho's crowd, thus proving their loyalty. Now he was giving them their reward – the riskiest assignment of the moment.

Twenty minutes later a new, smaller firefight broke out closer to us. That was the Corporal running into the *malais'* flank security group. This seemed to be the day the *malais* were not only having all the luck but were doing everything right. We ran and left the Corporal's crew to it, to extricate themselves if they could, and to die if they couldn't. You might find Osvaldo's behaviour inconsistent, but it wasn't really. He wanted to save the greatest number he could: it was a mathematical or rather actuarial calculation with no false heroics in it at all. Honour and shame didn't enter into it at all. Osvaldo had nothing to prove to anyone. He did leave a small reception group at the appointed rendezvous, under my command, with instructions for some basic contingencies. Otherwise I called the shots.

As the last of Osvaldo's people disappeared into the undergrowth my heart sank. I was no safer with the chief and the big group, maybe safer in a small party. But I had to fight my panic. Setting up some rudimentary defences made me feel better. We concealed our post the best we could, settled into it, went into all-round defence, our boot-soles touching, all 360 degrees covered, and... waited. We didn't stir, you know, for some four hours. Indiscipline, fecklessness, and lack of forethought were the Danuese way, but they also excelled at sitting still, being patient, and doing nothing, in a way that would have driven an American or North European stir-crazy. We had to relieve ourselves in this time. If it had been an ambush or a close watch on *malai* activity we'd have had to do our businesses in a banana-leaf, fold it, live with it, and learn to love it. But I bent the rules and allowed my men to defecate outside. About dusk, we heard movement up the trail. I say trail; to any but tribal eyes it was invisible, as impassable as the rest of the undergrowth. I wouldn't have liked to have been the men coming up the trail, whether they turned out friendlies or hostiles; I wouldn't have liked four automatic weapons held by frightened, starving men covering my every movement while I knew nothing about it. And yet that Corporal was a very animal. I'll swear there was no way he could have seen us. We were as well concealed by the jungle and our own embellishment as if we'd been inhabiting a burrow. Yet he stopped, signalled halt to those who followed him, had them cover his advance, and sidled on in a stealthy crouch, all the time looking for trip-wires or disturbances to the soil where he planted his feet. I recognised our issue rifle first, then him. Like a fool, I called, 'OK, it's us.' He stiffened, as if I'd plunged a dagger in his side. As he relaxed, one of his men loosed off a shot, instinct too much for his trigger-finger, the round whirring through the brittle bamboos. That terrible report! The dire, signalling crack which sent birds screeching, the little animals fleeing, and alerted all the *malais* for miles around. The Corporal whirled round, with a ferocious 'Cease fire!', not that it was the fault of anyone except yours truly. As he was stuck in the middle, he had a good chance of being accidentally gunned down.

They'd lost a guy and one was wounded by grenade fragments. I spent a long time patching him up, not because I was feeling particularly kindly but because he'd been leaving a big blood trail, speckling the leaves scarlet with arterial flow. The Corporal squatted on his haunches, drumming his gun-butt with his fingers. But I'd learned that haste didn't make for celerity and proceeded in Maria's methodical way, troubling to suture him in our primitive fashion (too revolting to recount and you would never believe me, anyway).

We left at a brisk trot, settling into the jogging rhythm of the mountain Danuese. There was no call for stealth, not after the sound of the shot; the priority was to put mileage between ourselves and our pursuers. To facilitate this, we used the open, big trails, which every now and then curved out on to a bare elbow of hillside. We should have leap-frogged these, covering each other but just ran in file, weaving in and out of the bushes, dashing across the exposed ground as fast as we could. We never stopped, just slowed to walk when recuperation became a necessity. They passed betel parcels round, to my great irritation. Whilst accepting that swallowing would have made the chewers sick (which was the last thing I desired), I kept having to scuff earth over the red spittle. What was the good of dressing the guy's wound when they went and did that?

We might as well have spared our effort and saved our breath. The *malais* were waiting ahead of us.

As we came to a bluff of rock at the edge of the trees, I had to halt. I had a stitch in my shoulder-blades. Prosaic it sounds, but it made me crave a rest as much as if I'd shipped a slug. The Corporal dropped back, I think to encourage rather than swear at me. The others went round the side of the rock face, then dropped out of sight as they descended the hill. Shortly after, without warning, there came the crack of Claymore mines, followed by a huge volume of fire and two grenade explosions. It was a textbook reverse slope ambush. I don't think our boys, with the wounded man as well, could have stood a chance; they must all have been cut down in the first seconds of that withering fire as they crested the skyline. The Corporal and I looked at each other, then without a word took off downhill. There seemed an extraordinary expanse of open ground to traverse. Tired as I was, I was flying like a goat, heart in mouth. There was a serious risk of breaking an ankle, which I took into account, slowing my demented descent by a quarter. The last thing, the very last thing, in the world I wanted was to injure myself so that I had to lie and wait for the *malais* to get me. Even so, coming off a slope which seemed but a few degrees away from the sheer, I had to speed up to keep my balance and it was then that I skidded on loose stones, staggered, stumbled, and finally fell face-first, the G3 leaving my hand and continuing on down. Fortunately, I'd only scuffed my hands and knees, so I picked myself up, recovered the rifle, and got my momentum going again. The Corporal hadn't looked back – this wasn't the time to think of others. Each for himself was the most efficient way. The whipcrack of a high velocity round overhead startled me, though my exposed back had been dreading it. This was followed by others, all single shots or short bursts; so they were firing at me with the M-16s. I didn't care about tripping now, just ran and jumped for my life. Their marksmanship at this range was not outstanding. Their gunner must have had a struggle getting up to the top of the bluff with the squad weapon, for it was a good minute before I heard the long, deep burst of the M-60.

The forest projected a peninsula of vegetation into the bare hillside. I could see that if I made that I could be under cover until I could melt into the broad mass of the jungle. It was 200 metres off, and the Corporal sharing my fox-like instinct, had veered towards it, being half-way between myself and the trees. More rounds lashed overhead. I retracted my head into my shoulders, moved in a crouch, and started to zigzag. They were shooting for the Corporal, however. The guy with the M-60 seemed the ambitious type: he wasn't going for the nearer target – yours truly – but trying to make sure he got us both by stopping the one most likely to escape, the furthest away, the Corporal. Me, I'd have gone for me. The rounds were falling short and to the right, but he was methodically walking the spurts up to the running man.

'Corporal, Corporal,' I screamed, 'go to your left.' He heard, too, and did it. This spoiled the *malai* gunner's calculation of range as well as deflection, the burst going in front of the Corporal and well to his right. Another line of powder and splinters began, followed a long time later by the reports. The Corporal was moving from side to side in ten-yard legs but the malai was following him. And then he went over in a cloud of dust. Shit. I never felt so lonely, more so because I was now their only target. I dumped my pack – which I should have done a long time ago, though my pathetic possessions were dear to me – and ran till my breath sobbed. I looked to my right and behind, the spurts kicking up to me. Jesus Christ! Then they stopped, though as I say, I still heard the bamma-bamma-bamma of their departure 700 metres away. The malai gunner was slow taking up the firing again. Then as the seconds lengthened, the trees neared, their individual leaves now distinct, it became clear the God-given reprieve was a mechanical malfunction. The machine-gun had jammed. As I came up to the Corporal's prone body, it stirred, then rose. He was grinning all over his ugly face. I was nearly weeping with relief and trepidation combined. My legs had turned to hot jell-o long ago, my lungs and heart rebelled against my bidding. Closer the jungle came. A matter of 20 metres or so. Crack went a single round, way overheard and off direction but definitely an M-60 round and not an M-16. Now we crashed into the trees. I didn't give a damn about the thorns tearing at me, the branches whipped into my face by the Corporal's passage (though my eyes I protected). 'That last one cooked off,' the Corporal gasped. Twenty minutes later we stopped to listen. There was nothing at all, except for the bellows' rasp of our own breathing. That was desperately loud but, frightened as I was, I didn't care. Immediate physical relief came first in your priorities, not the avoidance of a greater future pain or danger. The Corporal had taken over, in the way the dominant member of a pair does, without anything ever being said. I don't mean because he had a rank superior to my own but because he was the natural leader of the two of us, even without the sanctions of FAKINTIL, alone as we now found ourselves.

In this area the forest was not so luxuriant as elsewhere.

In our flight we'd descended 1000 metres or so from the camp, in addition to horizontal distance. This meant we could move faster but, of course, also that it was easier for the *malais* to pursue. We'd been going for around half an hour when the Corporal heard movement to our right. He had ears like a cat. Clicking his tongue to me, he signed me into the undergrowth on the opposite side of the large tree beside which he took cover. A short time later, a stick cracked. Then the foliage moved ten metres down trail from me. These obviously weren't their best troops. More noise and quivering of leaves. Then silence. After ten minutes or so, it became apparent they weren't moving. At first I'd thought they'd somehow sensed our own presence, though we lay as quiet as if we were dead men. Then it dawned on me: they were just lying low, waiting for an opportunity: they'd set up an ambush and they'd hold the position 24 hours or longer. If FAKINTIL refugees passed them, then they'd let the trap go. If they didn't – and by sitting still in the same place there was a good chance someone would cross them – then they'd just pack up and head back, probably by radioing in a chopper. By pure coincidence they'd decided to halt just where we were.

I looked to the Corporal. He held up a WP grenade, then pointed to me. I was to throw one into the bushes. I nodded. Pulling the pin, I closed my eyes momentarily – if I was capable of prayer I'd have prayed then – before lobbing it straight into the now motionless foliage. I heard someone exclaim. Just as I was wondering if it was a dud, the thing went off, showering its fuming chemicals all over the forest. Some fragments fell on my trousers – I was far too close for comfort – and I hurriedly knocked it off with my rifle-butt. It was terrible stuff – sticky and virtually inextinguishable, causing the worst burns you could imagine. Consequently I was late firing, but the Corporal loosed off most of a sub-machine gun mag in a few seconds. As he stopped abruptly – I heard him say 'Shit!' – a wailing *malai*, his back on fire, staggered across the path and I sent a burst into him from hip up to shoulder, throwing him back into the bushes where he continued to smoulder, but motionless. Having cleared the defective round from his SMG, the Corporal finished the clip off and reloaded. Complete silence, apart from the bird screams. We backed off, the Corporal covering me and vice versa, then took to our heels. Within minutes there were helicopters passing overhead, explosions going off in the forest, mortar rounds I think, and we were running for our lives again.

I was dead with fatigue now. I fell farther and farther behind. The Corporal, when I caught up with him, was chewing. He held a package out to me. 'Here, take this.'

I shook my head; even that cost me an effort. By way of reply, he slapped me in the face so hard my eyes watered.

'Do what I tell you, you dumb fuck. Eat it, Chinaman. No, don't swallow it! Just chew!'

My eyes were now watering again, this time from the betel and lime. It felt as if my mouth was on fire – from white phosphorus even. Yet, strange to relate, in about a minute I felt I was treading air, or had become detached from and was floating above my poor terrestrial body. The burning – nearly as bad as chilli – and the odious taste, much like a shit sandwich, I should imagine, soon became a stinging on the lips, then a prickling, and finally numbness. But it was the narcotic, no, the stimulating, effect of the terrible little nut which was its true property. I was still aware of the blisters on my left foot (the boot quarter-full of blood when I came to take it off), my dead legs, my labouring lungs, my chafed nipples (don't laugh, it wasn't funny to me), and the stumbling, reeling exhaustion. And yet, I could now live with those things; they were dissociated aspects of my existence, as if happening to someone else in a dream. I watched myself in a haze of mist (maybe it was the spray of my own sweat!) and I found a steady, almost sensuous rhythm that I could learn to live with. Every now and then, like a flood tide filling a sea-cave, the chamber of my abused mouth would become a satiated receptacle. No more of the production of my own salivaries could it take. What did I do? I spat. Like a veteran – and recollect that in this matter I was a very tyro

– I pursed my lips, turned my head to the side, and expectorated on the run. The bright juice flew. I was still enough myself to try to expel it as far as I could, to do my best to ensure it didn't touch anything before falling, like Satan in his scarlet cloak, to earth; to try to find some hidden place to do it. Some chance.

But I don't think I'd have made it without the drug. Of that I'm now sure. We had to make some serious distance between ourselves and the *malais;* they'd track us anyway from fainter sign. If they mistook the betel splashes for blood they might even slow up, figuring we'd drop of our own accord, the way the Komodo dragons hunted; or, more likely, they'd take it easier to avoid falling on top of us, holed up, dying and dangerous. It was only human nature.

Twice we heard choppers. Then we'd stand next to a tree-trunk, heads down, gasping, before resuming our flight. At last, at long last, the light started to fail. We'd gained some height and got into the thicker growth around 800 metres, so it darkened quicker under the trees. When it was already gloomy in our green half-world, we could look up and see a paler sky overhanging. Soon that darkened as well. We spent the night in the same spot, figuring the last thing we wanted to do was blunder round in the blackness, fall and injure ourselves, get a snake-bite, or walk into a *malai* ambush. Around midnight – there was no sleeping, not with the mosquitoes and we could light no fire – I got doubled over by a stabbing in the gut. It went, then it came again. While I had the message, I knew I should get my pants down, double-quick. When the signal went, I became blasé, as one does. That happened three times. Time four I realised this was the real thing, but I was too late and soiled myself. I sat there cursing inwardly, pretended it hadn't happened, shifted, and felt the swinging heaviness. After quite a surprisingly long while, I could smell it. Some time after, the Corporal sniffed. A few seconds later the warm stench must have got to him, for he swore. I snickered, though I was far from comfortable. A boot thudded into my back. Pansy, pervert, shit-eater were only some of the expletives I was favoured with, not the less intense for being whispered. Well, I did what I could in the dark, scrubbing with handfuls of unseen foliage. I just hoped it was nothing poisonous. Who wants a rash on the ass-hole? I mean getting killed was the problem but there was no percentage itching to distraction, too.

Morning came none too soon. With the first thinning of the darkness, we were moving. I felt like death, my limbs had seized up, I was more fatigued than when I'd lain down. My ass-hole started to leak, in a small way, after ten minutes, not that it was of any consequence in the condition I was already in. It was – time would show – the betel which had this alarming laxative effect upon me. Yet I didn't refuse when the Corporal offered me another chew. The nut had an increased effect upon me the second time. My head spun, I felt nothing of my bodily woes. We did move more cautiously, more slowly than the day before. There were machines aloft, but they didn't over-fly us. We found a spring where we drank and cooled ourselves. The Corporal forbade me to wash my pants in it. For six days we travelled. On the seventh, crawling up to a ridge, we spotted dishevelled green figures below, armed like ourselves. FAKINTIL. I jumped to my feet, shouted and waved; then fell as the Corporal tugged my ankle. I kept waving from my knees. He was a fool – to drop down once sighted would have been suspicious in the extreme. Ten minutes later, he was looking on the face of his beloved Osvaldo again.

TWENTY-TWO

MARIA CURLED UP INTO MY SHOULDER and sighed. I put my hand round the curve of her ass, then ran an impertinent finger between the cleft of the cheeks. It felt like a rattlesnake's tail. At the best of times she'd never been the most rounded of females. She giggled, removed my questing hand, and slapped me on the part of my leg she could comfortably reach. 'Go molest a boy,' she said.

'Oh, I'll close my eyes and pretend,' I said, in the sure knowledge that it would be an act of desperation I could never contemplate. We both sniggered a while.

Maria was ill. Rather she was convalescing. One of the many remarkable things about her was that she'd never been sick before, or at least that she'd never let anyone know about it. However, she'd come down with a very bad stomach complaint, blood in the stool, which had inclined her to diagnose it as amoebic dysentery. We had nothing for that. She'd relied on the traditional pharmacopoeia: ground bones, charcoal, some medicinal herbs. No miracle cure had resulted but she seemed to be improving, if only a little.

This misfortune of hers had done wonders for our up and down relationship – all clouds have a silver lining, don't they say – and we were enjoying our best rapport for months. It was almost like old times on the Praça. The fact that she'd had to surrender some of her responsibilities might have had something to do with it, plus the fact that she'd given me up for dead only a little while ago. Some of the men gave us funny looks as they saw us together beneath the lean-to, but I knew Osvaldo would take no notice. Which was what mattered. I blew in her ear, as it was something she hated, and got an appropriate reaction. But she became exhausted easily and soon stopped her puny strugglings. I spat onto the mud.

It had been merely drizzling for the last half hour. Now, without warning, it came down in winding sheets again. I loved the coolness, the drama of the spectacle; more than anything, I liked the protection it conferred. You knew the Broncos and the choppers couldn't hunt in this, that the *malais* would never get up here in any strength. And, Jesus, we needed the break.

There were 67 of us left. Of that, a quarter were kids of ten or over; no toddlers survived. Most of the washerwomen had lived to tell the tale, having been a little distance from camp at the time of the *malai* attack. I don't know if I wouldn't have changed them for a smaller number of better pieces if I was a chess grandmaster, like Osvaldo. In the

312

euphoria of deliverance, it was easy to forget that we'd lost our gardens, such as they'd been. All that seed-grain we'd deprived ourselves of! We might as well have eaten it! Thus did the meanest brain in the camp – yours truly's – torment itself. There still existed the old gardens, that is the scattered plots we'd left around the mountain-sides and forest clearings from our old encampments and the allotments we had established, like provident squirrels, for just such a contingency as this. The garnering expeditions we sent out departed with great enthusiasm, far greater than for killing *malais*.

But our outlook was terrible. I didn't think we could see the year through again. The roots and the grubs – I could take no more of those.

Osvaldo was thinking on the same lines as me. Losing the gardens was a worse blow than the 30 per cent casualties. He was training the washerwomen at small arms intensively now, so we could have a certain number of replacement eyes behind rifles. Food couldn't be conjured up with sleight of hand like that.

So I thought.

I was one of those commanded to teach my old foes, the washerwomen. How the wheel had turned full circle. From the public menace I had become the competent instructor. Practice makes perfect, experience is all. I strutted before the blackboard, demonstrated the safety precautions first, the catch, how to cock and clear in the port arms position, the need to show the empty breech when handing the gun in and to check it when the weapon had been out of your sight, and not least never to point it at anyone. I loaded the magazines with practised dexterity, making sure the rounds were properly inserted to avoid jamming, rotated the rear sight of the G3, demonstrated the magazine release, the fire selector/safety, the two trigger pressures (some hope of ever using them on weapons of this type and in our combat conditions), showed the different shooting positions – prone, sitting, kneeling, standing – how to hold the butt tight into the shoulder to minimise recoil, the inadvisability of bone on bone contact for support, the trick of leaning into a standing shot, how to judge distance and the different points of aim on a target at varying distances, how much lead to take for deflection shots. Field stripping the rifle was a mystery reserved for later. Well, I'd thought it simple enough but the women were worse than I'd been. Conceive of my exasperation to find my pupils aiming with both eyes open, in one case even banging the magazine with the flat of the palm under the impression that this was the manoeuvre which made the gun go off. No, I'd never been so stupid.

This was the dry-firing.

To give them real practice with live rounds seemed essential but, alas, problematical. To me, anyhow. We didn't want to attract attention, even under the cover of the rains. Osvaldo turned it to advantage. We'd go ten miles away and practice there – that way the sound of our rounds would act as a distraction from where we really were. But it turned out to be a sodden, futile exercise which always left me savage as hell by the time we returned, skidding and falling through the jungle with leaves plaited over the stumpy muzzles of the G3. X. Ray came on one trip with his little camera, darting ahead to photograph us as we approached in single file. I didn't think at the time it would make much of a snap and, in my ill humour, squirted a tracer-like burst of red across his perch of rock. He didn't notice and the rain washed away the spit in a few seconds. I had them firing three five-round groups at 100 metres, from which I'd average a mean point of impact and zero each markswoman's sights accordingly. Six or seven of them weren't bad, I'll say that. As for the others, Holy Christ! They'd be able to make a noise to put the *malais* off, that was about all.

He had a purpose in mind, being Osvaldo. And if his tools weren't the best, they were easily adequate for the task in hand. A few weeks after, he formed up the women and some of the older kids, all armed with the big rifles, put them under X. Ray's command, with me as assistant, and ordered us to go to two villages 50 and 60 kilometres away and return with food.

Well, this was a big step. We'd always behaved correctly to our own people. Of course, there'd been a few incidents, some instances of coercion. The cattle slaughtered for Maria's wedding, for instance, but generally FAKINTIL had been a model of propriety. It was straight from the Chinese, Mao. We needed the support, good-will, information. Besides, they were our own people; at least, they were their own people to the native Danuese.

Osvaldo had obviously spent time thinking about it. In the first place he wasn't sending a FAKINTIL regular unit but one composed of women and children. That took the sting, the overt threat out of it somewhat. It also showed need; and it showed the villagers FAKINTIL were like them and not an armed mob. And, of course, the women would have a better idea than a hood like the Corporal of where food could be secreted around a house. To that add the natural inquisitiveness, suppleness, size, and genius of children for worming into small places.

X. Ray and I walked into the village as civilians, in plain-clothes if that's the right expression for costume as fancy as the mountain tribesman's. I felt half-naked out of my *malai* boots and long pants, to be walking – the last part – in my bare calves and with toes squelching in the mud. But under our rain-cloaks we had something to make us feel dressed for the occasion: I had a pistol and three fragmentation grenades, X. Ray a prize capture, a little Uzi sub-machine gun and three mags stuck in his sarong. It was certain that there were no *malais* around – Osvaldo wouldn't have made trouble for the villagers with reprisals; however, we were to assess, or as Osvaldo put it himself, 'appreciate' the situation.

The village seemed empty, but I could feel the eyes in the darkness of the straw-roofed huts. And then I wondered if Osvaldo was losing his grasp. Did he think we were strolling in, lost among the market-day crowds? Wrong season, buddy. We took shelter from the drizzle under a blacksmith's eaves. X. Ray started to interrogate the man: there were indeed no *malais*. The man kept his eyes down, wouldn't look at us. But

X. Ray kept talking in his friendly, persistent way and, at length, the blacksmith lost his reserve. We admitted who we were. We disabused him of the notion – put around by the *malais* – that Osvaldo was dead. We lied about how many of us were left. We did not mention Martinho. We promised a big offensive at the change of seasons. In return for this mendacity we expected – and I think got – artless truths as to *malai* activity (a ten-man patrol five weeks previously) and what they'd heard from the plain and town. After ten minutes we departed, yours truly spitting with a facility that would have deceived any lurking *malai*.

An hour later we were back, at the rear of the armed FAKINTIL detachment. Of course, this was to keep our profile low, minimise the soldierly involvement in what was about to happen. It was a device so transparent, so blatantly insulting to the intelligence of the recipient *(why* did Osvaldo, that complex and subtle man, resort to such basic subterfuges in his dealings with others?) that I felt embarrassed. Nevertheless, looking at the way the women were handling their guns, over and above natural Danuese carelessness some intrinsic female awkwardness manifesting itself, not just because it was those black male symbols spitting their seeds of death, but as with, say, the way Maria used to return a ping-pong service with faultless accuracy and speed but also with a strange and ungainly angle of the wrist and elbow that belied its effectiveness, I was glad to be behind their barrels. They managed those weapons with intimidating incompetence. I feared for people's safety, I really did. What if they blew away a villager by mistake? As if reading my thoughts – Chinese thoughts they were – X. Ray smiled at me. 'The guns are empty,' he said. As I looked at him with a quizzical admiration, and he could see I comprehended instantly, he elaborated, just to prolong our mutual amusement, 'The G3s aren't loaded. I emptied the mags and cleared all their chambers before we set out.' This I savoured before having second thoughts, which he forestalled. 'They've got live rounds in their spare magazines, don't worry.'

The head washerwoman was talking to the village chief in what I'd call the jokey Danuese way. That was broad smiles, a bit of tee-heeing, not very sincere really. He was saying they didn't have any food at all. What he meant was they barely had enough for themselves. I had no doubt if there'd been even the tiniest surplus we'd have got it. They were a tough, frugal people and they hated the *malais*. FAKINTIL were *their* champions. But it's not human nature to give your sustenance away when you're starving.

Things moved on from the laughing stage. Our women got serious, the headman's face lengthened. He looked like a hurt and injured child; with his roundening, watering eyes and miserable expression he reminded me of the monkey Chico when it was night and the dogs had got his bowl. Three of our women had surrounded him and were starting to scold; the others were also talking at the tops of their voices to their best friends six behind them in the file (smart move of X. Ray's to separate them), to themselves, to their neighbour. Meanwhile, village, kids, me, headman, were all getting impartially muzzle-swept in a way that was alarming even when you knew the guns were safe. The headman was exposing his upturned palms to the sky: not a grain of rice, not a single tuber anywhere. The women broke ranks. In separate groups, probably the same as those gossip rings in which they'd laved yours truly's shirts and briefs, they moved purposefully to the huts in which the villagers lived, to all intents and purposes habitations of identical construction to those in which they'd passed their own peacetime lives. They held no mysteries for them, no secret corners. Looking to neither left nor right, marching with stiff, short strides on their calloused heels, a goose step that had no military derivations but was the same indignant locomotion employed to lynch a seller of bad meat or an adulteress in the old days, they stormed into the houses, rifle-butts scraping on the earth as they dragged them by the sling, muzzles jabbing into the derrière of the harridan in front. Within seconds I heard screams of triumph: in one hut there was a flapping of wings and squawking before a grinning washerwoman emerged with a chicken by the feet; non-human squeals and oinking from another dark interior and three black porkers fled from the door under X. Ray's feet with ears back and hooves clicking. I grabbed one but it squirmed from my arms, dislodging a grenade from under my cloak which rolled on the earth. Fortunately the pin didn't come out. The chief washerwoman and her cronies found the village's rice barns bare – they were mini-replicas of the ornater houses, raised on stilts against the depredations of pests, small pests – the headman in close attendance, shrugging and gesticulating to say, what did I tell you? But they weren't fooled. Within ten minutes they'd located the subterranean stores, tearing the grass mats away to reveal the ears of corn, the boulder-like tubers, and even some rice. How the village women wailed then! How devastated the old headman looked!

It was X. Ray's turn. He stood on the steps of the empty rice-barn to lecture the entire village. They listened to his homily of need in an uncomfortable silence. It wasn't bitter, it wasn't sullen, it was despairing. X. Ray wasn't being a hypocrite – I don't think – he really seemed to believe what he was telling them: how FAKINTIL wouldn't do this if they weren't compelled by utter necessity. How it was necessary for everyone to make sacrifices. He finished by saying that promissory notes would be given to be redeemed by FAKINTIL as soon as it could.

Our women had been stringing pigs and chicken up, packing grain into containers, chuckling to themselves over their booty.

The village chief could control himself no longer. 'We'll starve,' he cried. 'Give us our food back.' Now X. Ray got mad. He started shouting at the chief, calling him a stupid ass-hole who couldn't see beyond his own nose, a traitor to the cause. You didn't often see X. Ray go off on a short fuse; it was that he'd convinced himself of the propriety of his actions and that, like many inarticulate men, he was angry that he hadn't been able to convey his sense of the rightness of what he was doing. The typical FAKOUM spouter would never have lost his temper with the populace if his rhetoric had failed to work. The headman shook his grey frizz; he was in tears. X. Ray pushed him aside, called the women to order, and we made to set off. Five minutes from the settlement I thought to check the women for their arms. Three, and not the most heavily burdened with provisions either, had left their rifles behind. I ran back – ran as well as the unaccustomed sarong would allow, stumbling two or three times, risking shooting myself in the balls – to find the villagers clustered around the biggest of the magazines we had excavated. What was my surprise to discover that under the layer we'd opened there was about half a metre of earth, then further mats concealing yet another stratum of food, much like the expensive box of chocolates I'd once bought my friend Annie Laval in Canada. The fools had opened it to check, I guess; to reassure themselves. I saw two of the G3s straightaway, where those dumb women had left them on the dirt by some pots. A couple of villagers turned round and saw me, amid cries of dismay. It was by no means a pleasant moment. Without rushing, I picked up the two automatic rifles. The poor old headman was shaking his head, quite overcome; worrying, I'd imagine, that I was going to spill the beans, literally and figuratively, when I rejoined the other plunderers. I just couldn't locate the other gun. The villagers were all round me now, the women babbling away; it was difficult enough for me to understand the dialect, never mind there were 30 voices. At least I've got the rifles, I thought, which meant 40 rounds. Then I remembered the goddamned things were empty. Jesus. At this point a young man came up and presented me with the third G3, for which I rendered thanks that were sincere. He wasn't to know it was unloaded. X. Ray had sent two woodchucks to wait for me, whom I met on the edge of the village. They received the G3s with puerile alacrity, putting in the charged magazines X. Ray had given them. We caught up the main group and I kept my mouth shut, for the time being.

Well, I needn't have troubled with fine or noble feelings. Osvaldo's master-stroke was to come yet. We didn't have a feast or anything like that, just a decent meal which left you vaguely hungry but not feeling like you had a load of crap and pebbles in your stomach. After that he held a torch-light ceremony in which people were presented with awards or promoted in rank, mainly to fill the shoes of the dead or missing. Corny, corny, but the cheap theatricality worked even on me, the flames bending in the slight wind, the tarred twigs crackling and hissing as a prickling drizzle began. In the torchlight faces you knew from every day assumed a supra-normal quality, like statues come to life.

I think that light suited Osvaldo best.

That wasn't the master-stroke, by the way. A day later Osvaldo took me, X. Ray, the Corporal and a squad of the vets to the village. We were carrying a couple of pigs and about one-quarter of the roots and grain. And the village was *not* pleased to see us. In fact, there was a little group of them, armed only with traditional weapons but armed nonetheless, who blocked our way down. Poor, angry, determined people, with their parangs and skinny spears. It was for show, of that I'm sure; they wouldn't have offered more than a token of resistance, and not just because we possessed firearms that could have cut them down in seconds. However, it didn't even come to scuffling and hard words. Osvaldo obviated all that.

You see, he hadn't come to take more. We'd come to *return* some food!

The perversity was awe-inspiring. I mean, even the vets were shaken. I don't think the rest of the camp had known; the surmise was that we were caching an emergency supply somewhere secret. The Corporal looked at his Leader as if he'd taken leave of his senses. X. Ray smiled quietly. The headman and his boys thought it was a typically reptilian trick of city folk; they eyed us with even greater suspicion.

But Osvaldo led the way down, talking kindly to the little headman who came up to his chest pouches. With the sacks of grain and two pigs on their poles laid before him (those intelligent beasts probably as mystified by their reprieve as the villagers) Osvaldo resembled Santa Claus with a big black beard. He started going on about how FAKINTIL was the friend of the people, their protector and their best hope for a free and peaceful future; how any accommodation with the *malais* was illusory and would only lead to more misery. I was interested to see he wasn't giving them the better dead than unfree stuff of his Praça days. Then he said FAKINTIL would only take from the people what it needed: a bare minimum and no more. They'd taken too much from them and he was now returning it.

Shit!

I think he'd planned it all along, from before he'd sent the washerwomen. Whatever they'd brought back, he'd have given back a quarter. It was some conjuring trick, it really was: he was stealing, yet he was making it seem he was bestowing a gift on them. People remember the most recent thing: what they'd recall was the donation, not the robbery. And, I'm cynical enough to believe also, he wanted to be known as Osvaldo the Just, Osvaldo the Protector. It strengthened his position. Of course, the fact that it was soldiers generally who were making the restitution was good, but he came out the best.

The headman sat down heavily. He was nonplussed. But the boys with the parangs and spears grinned with delight. They gave us a guard of honour out of the village (us!) and a kind of farewell cheer.

What we had taken, what we had stolen, kept us alive in those rains. It was the bridge to a renewable future. I've often thought about the pangs of those days and of how one existed. It never got to the stage – I'm being serious now – when cannibalism was a serious possibility. I believe you would have to have nothing for that. I believe you'd have to be living in a social vacuum. One ear of corn, one rat between you would push that dire possibility to the edge of the conceivable. There was always the chance of turning up something in the forest. The stab of joy one felt as he or she turned up some of the edible insects of Danu for frying among the members of their messing group was unimaginable. And snake or giant lizard was a gorgeous delicacy, chased recklessly, stone in hand, from rock to rock, and to hell with the bite. It would have been a big jump from there to the transgression of the ultimate taboo.

There was plenty of time for thinking. What principally exercised me was the fate of Martinho Oliveira himself. Such had been the turmoil since the day of the *malai* attack that I'd been able to think only of Number One. Now I began to reflect on the fate of my old friend. Had he gone down in the first confusion of fire, hit indiscriminately by the *malais* or his brother's men? No, I thought he hadn't. And the *malais,* what had they done to him? That was less certain, and somewhat of a disturbance to my peace of mind. I mean, had they executed him out of hand, an hour after capturing him, put him on his knees and terminated him, like they had Bill Mabbeley? I wondered if they'd ill-treated him before that, the rifle-butts going into the kidneys, the boot in the ribs. That was the least you could expect, the very bare minimum.

But I didn't think they'd finished him on the spot – or if they had, some junior officer was going to pay for his rashness. I thought Martinho was useful; I thought Rebus would value him. That frightened me. It might have been better all round if he'd got cleanly eliminated in the cross-fire. What they'd do to a FAKOUM committee member, and the brother of Osvaldo, didn't bear thinking about. They'd keep him going for weeks. I had to make an adjustment here to think how Rebus would see Martinho, not as the conscience-stricken doubter and do-gooder he was to me, but as a ringleader of the national resistance.

And then… and then I thought of Osvaldo, lying on his belly, peering through the telescopic sight of his rifle, shooting not as a combatant but like a huntsman, squeezing the round off with voluptuous expertise, and I wondered if it had been the final expression of his love for his brother, his regard for his comrades, the beneficence of his ultimate mercy, the crashing, painless oblivion he could bestow upon them? And when in my own pettiness I'd shouted, interpreting according to my own capacity for spite, I'd misattributed his motives entirely.

There was also, which I tried not to be consciously aware of, my own vested interest in the fate of Martinho. I really tried hard not to be explicit to myself about this.

What would they do to me if I surrendered myself to them?

My will was eroding. Having the penitents around us had been a great stiffener of resolve. To look at those miserable outcasts of Martinho's gave you a sense of superiority which encouraged you to endure. Not only could you see someone worse off than yourself in a material sense, you also felt all the mean-minded triumph of the Puritan or witch-hunter. There was a visible reward and confirmation of your membership of the elect. Every society needs its criminals, its scapegoats. The position now was that they were either dead – in which case they were no longer of account – or actually better off than those who'd felt morally superior to them. Perhaps to be dead was also to be better off. There was the slimmest of chances that they'd landed in clover, that they were being well treated, getting plenty to eat, and decent medical care. Were the *malais* that smart?

The answer came a month later. By then we were clear of the heaviest rains. There'd been a renewal of aerial activity to pre-pilot assassination levels – so much for that brilliant success – planes trolling the hillsides with a methodical, terrible patience. It fell to a patrol I was leading to discover the first leaflets. We came upon them on a bare stretch of hillside. Strewn over the red earth, mud-smeared and crumpled, they resembled nothing so much as a pile of ass-wipings. And it was shit they had on them, too. Postcards from Martinho and the boys. Wish you were here.

I won't trouble you with the exact details of the wording. Suffice to say that I detected much of the reverend Martinho's own handiwork in it, with a minimum of dictation from the *malais*. It began with forgiveness on high for us rough, wicked men, alluding lightly to our misdeeds towards him and saying, basically, that there were no hard feelings. He kindly told us, also, that we hadn't a snowflake's chance in hell. He said we should put personal pride behind us. Danu needed peace and unity. We should work to rebuild – under an 'armistice'. The *malais* would accept our surrender; we would not be harmed or ill-treated. There would be food: he and his men ate meat twice a day. That was a nice touch and Martinho all over: the noble and the base, the appeal to highest sentiment and the belly as well, without the smallest shred of embarrassment or sense of incongruity. Finally, he said, the *malais* promised to withdraw after a period of reconstruction. We could have our Independence, if the fighting stopped. He'd personally spoken to their commander. He had been able to clear up certain misunderstandings and misconceptions. Misunderstandings! That took the breath away, even coming from the *malais*. I looked forward to having my comprehension of the true inner significance of cluster-bombing villages clarified.

What was noteworthy, which only struck me after a while, cutting through undergrowth on the way back to camp with a sheaf of the leaflets in my webbing, was that Osvaldo's name was not mentioned once, even for vilification.

He wrinkled his nose as he perused them, probably thinking they looked like what I'd thought but too mightily polite to say so. (He had that much of his brother in him.) His lieutenants stood around him, X. Ray grinning, Corporal scowling. Osvaldo raised his eyebrows once or twice, but didn't say anything. He let Maria have one, without comment. The Corporal started swearing as he got to the end, about 20 lines behind the rest of them. 'You should have shot them all, chief, when you had the chance,' was his wise owl contribution.

Osvaldo asked me, 'How many of your men read these?'

'Everyone who knew how to read,' I answered truthfully. He looked displeased, which I thought was very unfair. You could see him thinking.

Maria said, 'Let everyone see. Read it out to those who can't read.'

Osvaldo stared at her. She said, 'You have to be quite open with them. There will be more dropped. Otherwise...'

She didn't need to go on. The Corporal looked somewhat perplexed. I think he was all for executing any waverers from now on. But, as usual, Osvaldo knew when he was well advised by the little doctor. The camp was given the full FAKINTIL treatment, one of the offending papers pinned to a tree by a bayonet while Osvaldo paced up and down. He didn't castigate our former comrades, but reserved his contempt for the *malais*. He said it was a trick fit only for children, stupid children, not the smart kids of FAKINTIL. He got appreciative laughter from the juvenile section of the audience – no reaction, if it's favourable, is too low or too cheap if you happen to be the speaker. He said their former comrades had been tortured into giving those details of our common life which gave the touch of verisimilitude to the leaflets; he wouldn't be surprised if nearly all of them had been shot by now. Me, I wasn't so sure. Like I said, I detected the authentic voice of Martinho in the words. But I kept my peace. It was wise to. He had them all going by the end. We finished with 'O, Mighty Mountain!' – a long time since we'd done that.

And a porker, precious pig.

That wasn't the last of Martinho and his *malais*, not by a long way.

About three weeks later the camp was struck by a mystery illness, or rather, specific portions of the camp became victims of a peculiar affliction. The sanatorium was empty at the time – not because we were all particularly well but because (a) there'd been no campaigning in the rains and (b) our notion of health had been revised drastically downwards. Mere fever no longer got you the attentions of Dr M. Three men were violently sick one morning, and their vomiting did not appear to alleviate their nausea. They looked a nasty, grey colour I'd never seen before. I realised something was very wrong when they refused their day's ration. By evening they were in the throes of excruciating stomach cramps, with a bloody, odourless flux from the bowel. At first Maria was unusually sympathetic. The symptoms passingly resembled what she had been suffering on and off and, cold professional though she still was in despite of all adversity, she could more readily identify with her patients in this instance. It was like pitying herself.

Well, charcoal and bone dust failed to work their limited remedy. A couple more men went down. They were making lots of noise, these tough guys, worse than others I'd seen gut-shot. The hours went by. Someone's hair started falling out. That was weird. I started to worry. My stomach didn't feel so great either. 'You're imagining things, Adolph,' Maria told me crisply, absolutely refusing to countenance the possibility her assistant could become affected as well. Osvaldo looked in – he was concerned, too. He tried to joke with his men, but they were in too much pain. Another fresh case came in, clutching his gut. Then Osvaldo exclaimed, 'They're all from the same patrol!' He sent a boy off for X. Ray and the Corporal who were trying to get sense out of the radio-set, which had been badly damaged in our flight while we had all this time imagined it was merely thwarted by the wet season atmospherics. His subordinates confirmed Osvaldo in his analysis. From that patrol of two days previous there was only one man still fit – and lo and behold, he came in with a grey face and a crab in his belly just a few moments later.

Osvaldo began to question them seriously now. The debrief of 48 hours ago had been quite normal.

At first he thought of chemical weapons, nerve gases and powders. He asked them if they'd noticed any itching or irritation of skin and eyes, discolorations on leaves, dead animals. 'They'd have eaten the dead animals, chief,' joked the Corporal. Osvaldo ignored him. He looked earnest, urging his men to remember anything that could help, that would give us a clue. He gripped the squad leader by the arm. This guy only shook his head and groaned the more loudly. To me, accepting the reality of his malady, he still seemed to be exaggerating. It was the frequency of his moans, not their intensity, which was suspicious. You didn't fool the Corporal easily, either. Not with things like malingering, which this wasn't, or acting it up. The leaders' mood was changing; you could feel it. Through their pain the men looked increasingly uneasy as well, furtive, guilty. Suddenly the Corporal stomped on the squad-leader's stomach. 'Tell the truth, you son of a bitch!' he shouted. Well, the guy just jacknifed, clutching his abdomen and folded in half like a caterpillar. There was no acting about his groans this time. X. Ray didn't check the Corporal or rebuke him, which was how I could tell that he, too, sensed something in the wind. Osvaldo said, 'Tell us everything, don't leave anything out, even if you think it's unimportant. That way we can help you.' He was the least aggressive of the leaders. Even X. Ray was starting to act sharp. I thought of the Corporal's earlier jest about them eating dead animals and how quickly things had changed. And then I, the Chinese booby-trapper, knew what had happened. The realisation spread slowly through my mind, ramifying from the one tiny point at the centre of my intuition through all its external details to the periphery. You didn't get it all in one flash, is what I mean. So instead of looking surprised, the electric bulb of the idea lighting up in the cartoon balloon above my head, I grinned to myself as if I had something pleasurably melting up my ass.

Osvaldo said, 'What is it, Adolph?'

I replied, 'I think I know what has happened.'

'So do I,' he said. 'Now, come on, make a clean breast of it,' he told the squad.

I never knew whether he'd been bluffing or not, but my own hunch turned out to be correct.

They'd been combing the forest according to normal practice, nothing out of the ordinary, no signs of *malai* activity, the various traps all unsprung, when they had come across a sight which had made them doubt their senses; it was hallucinatory, so close was it to our universal fantasy. It was like a mirage in a desert, an oasis of palms and tinkling waters shimmering before a man perishing of thirst in stony wastes, except that we had more rain than we wanted. Starving men dream of ... food, and that was what the patrol saw strewn before them, with a promiscuous carelessness that was all the more alluring for its accidentalness, two long containers still depending from the cords of the parachutes which had snagged in the branches ten metres above. A third had hit the floor, spilling its innards over the leaves and dirt, and it was this cornucopia of gleaming tins, and paper and plastic sacks, and boxes, and cartons, some with their contents of rice, and sugar, and beans and powdered milk burst over the ground like snow that enticed these malnourished men like North American children into Santa Claus's enchanted grotto. They said they'd just looked at it for five minutes before they'd touched anything, and I did believe them. Then they'd gone for it.

'You stupid fuck!' the Corporal shouted. The squad leader grimaced under a particularly bad cramp.

'You didn't think it might be poisoned?' Osvaldo enquired gently. The squad leader nodded. 'We only ate from the cans.'

'There were openers?'

The squad leader nodded again.

'Think you're clever, do you, you piece of shit?' The Corporal was beside himself with fury. I had to prevent him from kicking the guy, in the face this time.

'Chief, I'm sorry,' the squad leader said. He was both ashamed and in agony – a difficult combination. They'd decided to keep quiet about their find and hoard it to themselves in a secret place. I couldn't find it in myself to be indignant about this, in the way the Corporal genuinely was, about them letting their buddies down, 'mateship' as Bill Mabbeley used to call it down at the Lusitano bar. I guess I'd always been pretty fouled up. Osvaldo, though, didn't seem to be angry with them, and I don't think it was cynicism but something bigger than that.

He had a word with Maria in quiet, yours truly in attendance. She didn't think it was ordinary gastric upset from too much and too rich food, and nor did I.

'It's poison,' she said. 'What exactly I don't know, but it's nothing good.'

We speculated on it. It had taken 48 hours to show, which

328

was no doubt deliberate; so that had we tested it on guinea-pigs, like the king's food-taster of old, the precaution would not have preserved the majority. 'I don't know if it's a question of a cumulative dose, like arsenic,' Maria said, 'or if it's the type of poison which is slow acting. I'm no toxicologist.'

In the face of this illness we were more than usually powerless. But it was not in her nature to sit by, abandon hope, and do nothing. (By the way, there was no question of Osvaldo ordering us to abandon them as a punishment for their selfishness and treachery.) We were all too aware that the poison was already in their systems but Maria still went ahead and prepared an emetic. There existed plenty of those in her repertoire. Poor men. They were already miserable enough. The effect of our potion was merely to add to their nausea and twist the knife in their guts one turn more. The groans and retchings were genuine enough now. I felt sorry for them, really sorry. It was my idea to give them a lot of water, on the principle that it might dilute the evil in them and flush it out. But that came fountaining straight up again. It was bad for morale, the whole spectacle. None of us gained any satisfaction from watching these capable men suffer for their one lapse, a lapse any of us might have been inveigled into committing. Not even the merciless kids got any pleasure from it. In the end all but two of the patrol died within the next 36 hours. Osvaldo announced the survivors had been the reluctant ones, who'd taken only a slice of bully beef out of misplaced solidarity with their greedier and more ignoble comrades. I wished I believed him – the apportioning out of just deserts by such a neat physical measure answered to a need for law, for logic and for fairness in all of us, in our bust-up dispirited community. But I think Osvaldo just said that for the sake of the men, to ease their passage back into the fold. They certainly weren't likely to contradict him – their saviour and now their co-conspirator.

Looking back on those days, I don't believe that at the time I had the glimmer of a suspicion that something was about to end. That a period in my life was to terminate, I mean. The struggle for daily survival, the routine of patrolling and foraging, dulled the reflective edge; you were kind of so shoved down into the minutiae of everyday life that you didn't get your head above water for long enough to do anything other than gasp. Remembering is what gives significance; the shape is never there at the time.

I have now to recount the meaningless death of my dear friend.

We had taken up the notion of travelling to all the villages within a week's march of our new base. This was not to requisition food but to give aid. Such aid as we could give. It was Maria's bright notion. We would give medical aid. God knows it was primitive enough, but it reminded me of the old days of setting out for the mountains from town, driven by Rosa. We'd come full circle.

Osvaldo gave the proposition his blessing – it was, to be cynical, good public relations after the demands we'd made on our fellow Danuese.

This went well for a while. The marches were without incident, the villagers suitably grateful. In some instances they even gave us presents: a carved betel-box for me, a gay blanket for the doctor; memorably, we once got six eggs: half a dozen eggs. We ate those at a decent distance from the village. 'They will only break,' Maria said firmly. 'Or go bad,' I said. 'And there are only six.'

We had them boiled. The three-minute egg – one of the earliest products of man's culinary inspiration. We declared our good fortune when we arrived at camp again. X. Ray laughed.

We had men with us on these excursions. You had to watch them carefully in the villages. We didn't want them stealing – something to eat – or molesting women. But I couldn't keep an eye on them 100 per cent of the time, not when I was assisting Maria. They were meant to be standing around us, not to protect but for the guns and FAKINTIL camos to be associated with good works. I'd look round after dressing a bite or helping Maria stitch, to see the glorious FAKINTIL number diminished by half. The most difficult thing in the world is to keep together a group of more than three people surrounded by distractions.

Excursion eight seemed no different from the others. We were going to a village for the third time. We'd built up a friendship with the patients, some of whom actually appeared to be getting better as a result of what we were doing. Even Maria didn't seem to believe that was wishful thinking. This particular hamlet lay at the end of a small fold in the hills; it would have been pretentious to dignify it with the name of a valley, but the way to it was still overlooked by ridges of higher ground on both sides. I had sent two men in, 1000 metres ahead of the rest of us, though I was still not expecting much *malai* seasonal activity. They had gone round the village and all appeared OK from our distance when the whip-crack of two high velocity rounds overhead made me flinch. The thumps followed a little over a second later, with me rapidly calculating the shooting as coming from some 700 metres distant. I imagined they were not using squad weapons but specialised sniper's rifles. There was an echo off the high ground, which could readily be discounted as such, so I wasn't confused. Amazing how survival sharpens the wits of the dimmest city boy. Three more rounds went overhead. We'd all scattered. There was no cover to speak of. I scanned the opposite hillside intently. Two more rounds, very close. No one seemed to have been hit. Then I saw a puff of dust, near the top of the ridge, where his muzzle gases had disturbed the chalky ground. I told the first team to put down deliberate fire, giving the clock direction and the range. We others withdrew. It was no use calling for smoke – we had no more smoke grenades, and the small stock of white phosphorus was now reserved for offensive purposes. We began to retreat, scurrying with heads down – ludicrous, useless but absolutely natural. The reports from the G3s did morale good if nothing else. I doubted very much if they'd hit anything at that range and at that elevation. Looking back, I could see that three who should have gone with us had remained. My group were all zigzagging without being told. 'Down,' I called. They began to shoot, very indiscriminately, in the general direction of the hillside. There were obviously just a few *malais,* not using automatic weapons. The first group started towards us. But the three remained on the ground – when I looked at them now, it was obvious they'd been hit. In fact, I would have bet they were dead.

Maria was holding her green canvas satchel to which, as a small act of pedantry or vanity, I'm not sure which, she had stencilled a red cross on a white background. She'd led the flight. Now she ran back to me. 'There are three hit,' she said. What she meant was: go back for them. Of course, I was going to already. I didn't say so, though. I'd got beyond the point of having to justify my actions to Maria as my conscience. I ran back, meeting the retiring group half-way and ordering them to take over from the others. There hadn't been any shots from the ridge for a while, so our fire couldn't be so ineffectual if it was making them keep their heads down. Our people looked very deceased to me. We were by the first one, shot through the chest with a big exit hole in his back. Maria was a little way ahead of me, going to our second casualty. I could see it was going to be a waste of time, and I was not going to risk more men retrieving the bodies, never mind the Corporal's insistence we always did so. Exercising my authority I called Maria's name. She never looked round, just ran on. The next moment she was flat on her back. One moment she was there and upright; the next she was dying on the ground. Maria there as a person in one instant and flopping extinguished on her back the next. That's long-range fire for you. Did I run off? I didn't even think of it. I went to her in a straight line. She'd been hit in the middle of the chest, probably right through the heart and spine. Her eyes were open, fluttering. I think she was conscious for that small time, aware of who she was and who I was. She couldn't speak. After a little while her eyes rolled up and she stopped breathing. I'd been kneeling – I'm not stupid – and I tried to send a message to her, I really did, concentrating all my thoughts. Does it count as a prayer? At least a requiem for the brave. Maria, just lying there. If anyone could suddenly sit up, talk, come back to life, it was her …Two bullets kicked up the earth, one in front in perfect line, another to the side and just behind. There was no percentage in sharing Maria's fate – I could imagine her scornful voice. What I could do was bring her body back. She felt absurdly light; must have been even in peacetime days. I ran at a respectable pace, not neglecting to jink from side to side, even though it put me in greater peril from my own people while they were firing so enthusiastically. As I reached them one of the youngest woodchucks got up and ran back. 'Don't do that,' I shouted. 'You come here.' But he'd gone to retrieve Maria's satchel, slinging it round his thin shoulders, and scampering back with two misses cracking by him. The thumps of the discharges, reaching us a second later, were almost friendly, innocuous. I made a mental note to commend the boy to X. Ray. It was good, practical thinking. We needed Maria's box of tricks and to leave it would tell the *malai* many things. 'Good boy, Arsenio,' I commended him. 'Right, we go.'

In ten minutes we were outside their range. Then we were ascending once more. I had forgotten about our two men in the village. And when I did recollect, I behaved like a Danuese and shrugged, speaking metaphorically.

Both of them were already in camp when we arrived.

Well, it was from the frying pan into the fire for yours truly. I had the worst of all worlds. Osvaldo had been alerted as to the fact that we had been bushwhacked but not given precise details of casualties, if any, or the number of the enemy. Most important, he had no firm news of Maria. He'd had time to worry – not being a robot – but no time to prepare himself for the worst. It would have been easier for me if either I'd been able to come in unannounced or if he'd heard of Maria's death an hour before.

Just outside camp the men put down the improvised stretcher on which we were carrying Maria's body. It was their unsolicited gesture of consideration and respect for their commander. It also forced me to walk to camp by myself. I dreaded telling Osvaldo, and even then I wasn't to

333

know how unreasonable he was going to be.

He was wearing a pistol, which was not a good sign, though I ruled out summary execution. The Corporal was with him. Neither of them asked 'What happened?' They just waited for me to speak first. 'Osvaldo,' I began. I shook my head and paused. It wasn't that I was at a loss for words, I just wanted to show proper respect. Osvaldo didn't need this. 'Just make your report, Chinaman,' the Corporal said.

'Maria's dead,' I said. 'We got hit on the way in. I think it was three or four snipers.'

'Shit!' said the Corporal. 'You think!'

'Where is she?'

'We brought her back, Osvaldo. I'll get the bearers.' I badly wanted to get away even for a moment. But they were already bringing her in. I could hear the cries of lamentation from the women. People were crowding round the stretcher. By the time it reached us, more or less the whole camp was there. A trickle of blood had dried by the corner of her mouth. Her face had gone the grey colour we'd both seen in others, strands of her coarse hair still stuck to her forehead by sweat. Her shirt was stiff with blood; the entry hole with the fabric glued to it was something like a large black sore. I just couldn't hardly believe it was Maria, it was so much like a wax doll of her in bad taste. What would I look like? Like that, too? And then I thought, well, my darling Maria, at least you're out of it now. No one can hurt you any more. We could burn you and it wouldn't matter. And then something strange happened. My eyes filmed, the moisture pooled, and a tear ran down my cheek, just one. Which was weird, because I didn't feel at all sad but only concerned for myself. It would appear the body is nobler than the mind, its chemistry more simple. Osvaldo touched the corpse, the way anyone would, and I think felt the anguish of its coldness the way anyone would. The Corporal took me by the arm in an uncomfortably hard grip and we went off to the communal hut. I wasn't sure whether I was being debriefed or prosecuted. He extracted the tale of the ambush from me very easily. There was no point lying. There had been too

334

many other eyes. And it was back in time again, to the days when I could do nothing right. I don't know how to put it exactly but there's a certain practical bent of mind which delights in finding fault, which relishes its own pettiness as meticulousness, which exhibits low cunning and thinks it's clever, which mistakes mockery for humour. It was deeply Chinese, but the Corporal had it. Nothing I'd done was right. I should have put the doctor at the rear with the (non-existent) flank protection group until I had completely checked out the village for myself. Was I crazy to put a big group of us all at the same time into a position overlooked by higher ground? Why hadn't I sent scouts up on to the ridge to cover us in? And I'd done nothing short of abandon my two men in the village to their fate. On and on in this way.

Well, I am no longer in a position where I need to justify myself to anybody; so you will not account me guilty of special pleading when I say that the Corporal was talking through his hairy ass. No one did anything by the book. It could have been any of us who got caught with their pants down. Osvaldo, X. Ray, had some special sense, some animal inkling, that would have left the neck bristling, that would have cried danger, and pushed them into taking precautions without them ever being consciously aware of it. But to reproach me with being plain Adolph Ng was ludicrous; it was monstrous. Half-way through all this, Osvaldo came in. I looked at him with a mute appeal. Why I persisted in believing that we had some mutual understanding beyond the others, in the face of all the continuing evidence to the contrary, I don't know. He made eye contact with me – his look never slid away, under the most atrocious circumstances – but he looked straight through the other side of my head. I felt a shiver go down my spine. His brown eyes looked black. 'Osvaldo, I did my best,' I beseeched him. 'She was my friend, too.' I was going to say 'before she met you' but decided it would be best not to enter into competition with him. 'If I fucked up, I blame myself worse than anyone.' Now he focussed on me, the person he knew, instead of looking right through the pawn he might use or sacrifice.

'Tell me from the start,' he commanded. That was my chance. If I could get my mouth going, I could manipulate them. There was some magic in the words; by just talking I could weave a spell which would facilitate my escape, hold them bemused until I had disappeared in a manner of speaking. I couldn't tell falsehoods, but I could make them see it from *my* viewpoint – perspective was a powerful weapon.

He only interrupted me once. 'Was she killed immediately?' he asked. I hesitated. 'No, no, she was still conscious when I got there. But,' I hastened to add, 'she wasn't in pain.'

'She wouldn't be, not with her spine shot out,' the Corporal said grimly. This was not the kind of interpolation I welcomed. I ignored him and said, 'Maria said your name to me. She wasn't able to go on. Then she smiled and she seemed to go.' I didn't actually have the brazenness to put it directly: i.e., she died with your name on her lips, but I came as close as I could.

Osvaldo said nothing; he betrayed neither pleasure nor pain in this terse but, I trusted, evocative account of his lover's death. 'I did what anyone else would have done, Osvaldo,' I said. 'Maybe you or X. Ray would have done it differently. I don't think anyone else could have.'

Flattery, craven flattery. At this moment I was not above the lowest subterfuge. Something occurred to me. 'I take the responsibility,' I said, 'the blame. But it wasn't all bad,' and I proceeded to recount the actions of the boy who had run back for Maria's little satchel. I praised him lavishly. Why? He deserved it, but I probably wouldn't have made a big thing out of it normally. Somehow I felt it would help get me off the hook – anything to distract attention from the inadequacies of my own actions, a psychological transference of some kind; that would fix on something positive rather than negative, courage and clear-thinking from an unexpected quarter, instead of cowardice and

336

incompetent leadership; and I could more safely blame myself if I praised the boy at the same time. I would appear noble instead of a stupid fuck who'd got his oldest, dearest friend killed.

Well, it worked. Note how much more sophisticated, how much less crude my ploys were than Osvaldo's own employed on me, at the time of the witch-hunt against the Martinho tendency. I mean, I have to admit, his style and Rebus's worked in their simplicity, but they left the victim aware of what had been practised upon him; my subjects didn't have an inkling. Osvaldo was like putty; but the material had to be warmed initially to make it pliable. Otherwise it would break in your hands, the crumbs left as incriminating evidence. I don't believe Maria would have wanted me punished, even moderately, on account of her; I think she'd have smiled to see me wriggle, to watch me manage that strong man the way she had. I think I knew her better than Osvaldo ever did. Who was he to hold her death against me? Nothing I did in this respect could be accounted unscrupulous. My conscience is clear.

For a while I was not given any positions of responsibility. This suited yours truly. Did I seek a bullet in the head at the front of a FAKINTIL column? Did I want to do chores? The spunky, quick-thinking boy, on the other hand, got a rifle of his own, G3 No.19 from the armoury. He was as pleased as if... I don't know ... he had been made head of the church choir in normal times, or he'd been given a shiny bicycle for his 14th birthday. As I was armourer and quarter-master he received this token of manhood from me, not unfittingly. He held the worn, black weapon with more awe than pride. The rifles were getting venerable, they had the look of top-class antiques: beautifully oiled, polished, repaired, and maintained but surfaces distressed from daily use, corners smoothed from the laying-on of hands. The magazines especially were knocked about. 'On your way,' I said, with all the gruffness I could muster, 'make sure you get one *malai* for every bullet in the box.'

In the end, of course, the Corporal and Osvaldo had to

use me again. The qualities of the Chinese shopkeeper were not readily found in the FAKINTIL encampment. I was playing my old parts again within less than a month. As for Osvaldo, he never showed his feelings much. He was a Japanese at heart. Yet I guess his loneliness turned into a greater ruthlessness. Maria had stepped into the gap left by Arsenio Remedios's death; you could say she'd been even better for Osvaldo than Arsenio – the strengths and weaknesses of the two men had been identical almost, while Maria offered a complementary set of qualities. She'd kept him in touch with the weaker in the camp, ensured his leadership was not a dictatorship. Now he had the chance to become ever more aloof, savage, and arbitrary. I don't say he succumbed utterly – even on the secondhand evidence I was to have – but as they were forever saying in Toronto, the yang that was in him began to get the upper hand of the yin.

These days I thought I'd stopped caring whether I lived or died. A numbness set in, a novocaine of the soul. This was the onset of the reaction to the loss of Maria. I began to realise how much I'd taken from her, even during the times when we were not on speaking terms. She was the only one I'd consorted with as a friend and equal in the normal days. We'd had memories that acted as an anchor of a kind, however far we were carried by our destinies. Her spite was better than the stupidities of others. She had a sense of humour; I appreciated her malice. She was never a hypocrite – she was a much better person than she allowed herself to seem, a reversal of the normal mode of self-presentation. And now she was gone.

Of course, this abandonment of mine, this wish for death, was sheer self-delusion of the kind Maria herself had despised. No way did I wish to be extinguished. I'd run in terror from the prospect of any threat. As you'll see.

During this time X. Ray showed me numerous small kindnesses. For the others, Osvaldo had annexed Maria completely. And the monopoly of bereavement was to be his, too, in their eyes. But X. Ray had the empathy, the magnanimity to include me. Do you know, I have no recollection of him from the Praça days, other than as my building contractor. He couldn't have seen me arguing with the sharp-tongued little Chinese doctor over our glasses of black coffee in that over-crowded square. Yet he alluded to incidents from those days at which he could not possibly have assisted. Had he noticed, weaving his way through the throng on his motor-bike? Or had his policeman brother been spying on us, reporting back to the metropolitan governor?

An unworthy thought, that. His unforced firmness, the unseeking hand on my shoulder, the willingness to sit and talk with me about my dead friend, saved me from the perpetration of many foolish excesses. Wherever you are, X. Ray, bless your kind, simple heart, and your courage.

I was now the camp doctor. God help everyone. In a way that did me no credit, I enjoyed the position. I was not perceived as inferior to Maria by the ignorant. I inherited her mantle – it was thought I could do what she had done, that there had been some magical transfer of powers. This opinion I did little to discourage. I wanted to be thought valuable, I desired respect. Privately, I dreaded the first rejoining of serious hostilities, the groaning or unconscious men who'd be brought to me for the butchery from which little Maria had never shrunk. When I looked at her instruments I quailed. Those cruel, shiny clamps and cutters. The saw! Oh, Jesus! It was – how may I put it – their functionality, the simple, efficient purpose in which their special horror consisted. That I'd seen her use them, placed them in her hand, at critical moments had to employ them myself, did not lessen my dread. I would open the case, contemplate them for half an hour on end, while people passed the sanatorium, grinning encouragingly, doubtless believing me to be mentally rehearsing my skills. In the end I decided that if it ever came to it I would leave those I couldn't help – probably most of them – to die without adding to their suffering. I guess if I ever had reason to congratulate myself in those last days it would be on that score: that in the end I never had to take responsibility for the FAKINTIL wounded.

We were still letting the *malais* know we were there, the activity mostly in the form of mining and sabotage. Occasionally, we'd attack a *malai* outpost, but nothing big. My bet was Osvaldo would come back with something worthwhile once his depression had lifted. I realise that is a word so inadequate as to lead to accusations of bathos, but I can think of no other description for his state of mind. Gloomy would fall so far short as to be funny; grief-stricken would be excessive. I don't disparage his true feelings for Maria. He did grieve, but he had the ability to put away what he wanted from the forefront of his mind. If he wanted to brood about it a while, it wasn't a luxuriance of weakness, a wallowing, but I should say more of a deliberate stimulation. These black ruminations were a mental chewing-over, which could produce an irritation and then an anaesthesia of the emotions far in excess of what betel could do to the body. I judged it best to leave him to it.

As you may well imagine, I was somewhat gun-shy during my first patrols. Every stick cracking, every flapping and screeching of the birds was an augury of the stealthy *malai* presence. I wouldn't travel by paths. I had my scouts hundreds of metres ahead. When we had to make crossings of open ground or over the jungle thoroughfares, my irresolution became terminal. We dithered, we became separated; I was more of a menace than I had been before getting myself ambushed. People started to notice. There was jockeying to get out of my assignments. 'Leave him to the doctoring,' I heard one of the vets say. 'We don't want to lose the Chinaman anyway.' Well, the Chinaman agreed, but X. Ray and Osvaldo kept sending me out. I guess they knew best.

I came to Osvaldo in mid-adventure. I arrived at a moment of no special importance. I departed also at a juncture of little significance. On both occasions, I had no prior warning as to the turn my fate would take. Of how little consequence we are. And how difficult it is to accept that startling fact. The great meteors, and I call big O. a great meteor – their fates are bound up with history, their petty accidents act on the levers of events, but the likes of the Corporal, me, even Maria ... we could die and nothing would have changed.

I was in charge of a work-detail, going to one of the straggling, half-wild gardens which we'd seeded in another time to pick up the fruits of our historic abstinence. The way lay through very dense jungle at a lower level, then took us up again. I eschewed the 'trail' – which could be remarked only by Danuese eyes – for a way even more obscure that took us against the grain of the hills, up, down, up, down. I was not popular. To compound this, I forbade the use of cooking-fires by night. Thus we took four days, instead of one and a half and had sore bellies. (Heat was necessary to denature the rinds and seeds to which we resorted.) At length we arrived. Weeds, wild creatures, birds had levied their toll, but something was, indeed, left to us. After posting sentries I set the women to work.

They collected with a will. Once you set Danuese to a task they weren't too bad. It was the before which saw all the inanition, the fecklessness, the fucking around. Of course, they had an incentive: the rumbling in their painful bellies. I strode around the unkempt clearing, checking my dispositions with the anxiety I hadn't been able to shed. I was glad it was overgrown; there would be less harvest but also smaller risk of it having been spotted by the *malais*. When I thought about it, I wished I had studied agronomy in Canada – tropical agronomy, to be specific – that would have proved remarkably useful. I might have been so valuable that, like Maria, I wouldn't have had to fight. On the other hand, look where it had got Maria: one and a half metres underground while thugs like the Corporal still ran free. It was in your stars, had to be.

I was becoming increasingly uneasy; hence, I would say, the morbid train of thought. Like a dog, I was registering sounds above the usual thresholds of the human ear; picking up, as they were always saying in Toronto, on 'vibrations'. Except these weren't psychic vibes but real, physical ones that palpably disturbed the air. My garnerers were labouring

341

in rhythmic unison, humming quietly to themselves the songs I had forbidden them to sing, when the co-ordination of backs and arms became ragged and at length faltered as two or three of the more acute straightened to cock an ear. It was there next instant, the sound you wanted to disbelieve even as you registered it. 'Choppers!' the cry from the scouts. We'd become coded for the correct reaction; it was so ingrained, you didn't have to think – the legs moved for you. One moment the clearing was full of industrious ants, the next they were scattering into the trees, the majority not neglecting to take their bundles with them. We were desperate for the food, I tell you. The habit of unassuming command hadn't yet established itself in me, not by a long way. I wasn't helped by my sense of guilt over Maria, and because I was scanning the deserted clearing for anyone who'd tripped and sprained their ankle, I was the last out. The first helicopter was already coming down and forward, seven, six hundred metres away. They could close in a blinking of the eye, once you'd heard them. However, I wasn't going to get hosed down with fire, for I just made it into the trees. I even had the presence of mind to pick up a dropped rifle magazine when the earth humped itself under my *malai*-issue boot and I was thrown skywards as cleanly as if I'd trod on a huge spring or as if a giant had clasped his hands under my sole and heaved me like a kilted Scotchman does his tree-trunk. I must have turned a complete backward flip for I landed on my face, with the hole in the earth smoking before me, one leaf still dropping a spark or two. The ringing in my ears told me of the bang but I hadn't heard it as such, nor could I hear anything else – shots, rotor-thumps, nothing. I was too stunned to realise I was stunned, i.e., in bad shock. I felt a deep peace. That lasted about five seconds. Then my right foot started to pain me like hell. Goodbye deep peace.

I knew what had happened. I'd trod on an Adolph Ng special – the bullet boxed above the tack. If it wasn't one of my own, lifted and employed against me, then someone had violated the patent. As I started to gather my wits, I rolled over on to my back. Two choppers were hovering a few metres above ground, the troops preparing to jump, while another circled overhead, the door-gun streaming brass behind in the rotor wash. I pulled myself in to some bushes. They were thorny; so much the better. It would dissuade the *malais* from taking a close look. It was as if my ripped, bleeding palms belonged to someone else. The two choppers took off, blowing dust and leaves everywhere and incidentally somewhat thinning my cover. I lay there, breathing heavily. After a while, I turned on my stomach. I felt better able to meet my fate on my back, but I knew I would be less visible this way. I suddenly felt a ball-shrinking dismay. My gun, my G3! It had left my hand where I'd trodden on the booby-trap. I'd become sufficient of a soldier to rely on it. I might not be able to evade the *malais* but it offered another kind of escape to its possessor. You could be killed while you had a loaded gun, as the Corporal liked to say, but you couldn't be abused. That was, you had control still; there was choice. What they did to your bullet-riddled corpse was no problem of yours.

I still couldn't hear a damn thing. This spared me the horrible anticipation of the search party drawing nearer. Then I saw a pair of boots, exactly similar in all respects to my own – except my right one was a mess I didn't like to contemplate too closely. I wished I wasn't wearing them. These boots were parallel to the line of my own body. He went past. Shortly after, a pair of unmilitary boots. Then two soldiers: boots and gaiters. They didn't see me either. The leaves parted and I saw the dull metal of a bayonet. Next moment: the exultant face of the hunter and his opening mouth. I shut my eyes, but then opened them again just as swiftly. I had to look. His buddies joined him. Four M-16s covered me. I saw the soldiers wore red berets. I began to cry. One came in and dragged me out, by my good leg. Someone kicked me in the ribs. Then a gun-butt came down on my head. Above my eyebrow there was a minor explosion. I felt it go outwards, not inwards from the force of being hit. I felt glad in a way that it had begun. Maybe they would just shoot me there and then, like Bill Mabbeley. The men gave way to an officer, very young. He pulled at the flap of his pistol-holster. Now I did close my eyes. Five or six seconds passed. No shot. I opened my eyes. Martinho was standing over me.

PART THREE

PART THREE

TWENTY-THREE

THE FIRST TIME I SAW MRS COLONEL GORENG she was in *that* jeep. Skimming along the water-front with the peculiarly flat ride jeeps give when they're not lurching on one wheel over lumpy terrain. She was chauffeured but was otherwise without a military escort. She wore a scarf over her head and dark glasses. It was a green scarf but let me quickly say that it was bereft of religious significance. She was in fact a Christian, not a Muslim. The scarf was simply to protect her hair-do in that open vehicle as it bowled along at a business-like 60 kilometres per hour and, with the sunglasses, conferred upon her a touch of the Jackie Kennedy chic to which she was innocent enough to aspire. Like all the other officers' wives she wore a uniform of their own devising, pale-green skirt and shirt. It wasn't compulsory by any means – there was nothing to prevent them wearing civilian fashion – but they chose to advertise their solidarity with their husbands, to demonstrate *esprit de corps* and, as it happened, even at home in *malai* land as well as here in occupied territory, it was to their advantage to show who they were. Prices came down in the street and as for having a purse snatched, well, such things didn't happen to army wives.

She was throwing back her head and laughing. Now you may find that unremarkable, but in the context it was startling. A woman by herself, laughing, in public, sharing a joke with a menial. Any one of those things would have been unusual in itself; jointly, and in a humbler personage, it would have verged on the scandalous. I can remember staring after the fatal chariot until it was a dot on the new road. The mount for the .50 calibre machine-gun was still on the vehicle but the *malais* had found a use for the Browning elsewhere, I think because they also used the jeep to drive foreign journos around and it would have vitiated the claims to have pacified Danu if they'd left it on. Mrs Goreng was safe anyhow.

Later, I asked her if she wasn't frightened to ride around

like that. She laughed the same way as when I'd first seen her. 'No, Adolph, not with a dangerous guerrilla like you to look after me.'

'I mean before we met, my lady.' (I have to translate in this clumsy fashion and to the best of my limited ability the native title of respect by which, on my own insistence, I addressed her.)

She showed her beautiful teeth again – perhaps one of the reasons why she liked to smile so readily. 'I am a brave woman who is frightened only of the dark and her husband.'

In fact, she did possess mettle, though going round alone in the jeep was – I believe – just feminine carelessness, like the terrible state she'd leave her room in for her maid: powder everywhere, pink for face, white for body; her long, strong, glossy hairs in the sink, so you would have thought the orang-utan had been availing himself of the facilities and not a pretty young woman of 31. But... like all *malais* (do forgive me for this) her backside had been innocent of paper all her life. It was the left hand and a ladle of water. (You didn't pour the contents of the ladle down your crack – that was for getting the shit out from under your nails.) I think it was one of the reasons why you didn't see so many *malai* women with long fingernails. She still liked to type, so they would have got in the way of that, anyhow.

Mrs Goreng, the wife of Colonel Goreng, had been ... a journalist. This took me aback somewhat. The only representative of the species I'd met till then had been Jean Carmichael, with her hairy legs, head for hard liquor, and golden heart. Mrs Goreng couldn't have been more different. But she hadn't been a hard-nosed grubber after facts (or compiler of falsehoods, for that matter). Even if *malai* society had allowed such a role to the female, her family would never have permitted it. She'd worked on a woman's magazine. She liked to show them to me about every three months, each time as if it was the first. Knowing who was servant and who mistress, I entered into the spirit of the farce. I felt embarrassed for her. The cheap paper and poor colour of this tawdry imitation of the *Ladies' Home Journal* or *Harper's* were so plainly unworthy of her. She'd written about a new restaurant or hotel in one of the issues, a 'puff' being the expression, I think; gone on an inter-island cruise; star piece, always shown first, was her interview with their president's wife. This was a slavish, mind-numbingly trivial recitation of clichés and banalities about family and nation. The photograph of her with the older woman was well done, though. Mrs Goreng came from an aristocratic family. They'd been minor royalty in some petty, pre-Independence kingdom. It didn't really mean a lot. But she'd spoken a different baby language from her husband, the Colonel: a kind of upper-class malay with 30 different words for 'you' and 'me', depending on the grade of the person speaking and their mutual relationship, that kind of thing. Colonel Goreng, a rural thug with ribbon on his chest and scrambled egg on his cap, was somewhat in awe of the antecedents of his young wife. Which enabled her to get away with many things.

She was very bored. What an undesired posting it must have been! Away from the traffic-jams, the night-clubs, and chilly, marbled hotel lobbies of the *malai* capital, its metropolitan glamour, such as it was. She'd enjoyed a wide circle of friends, a coterie of the bored wives of the rich, except that when together their collective boredom was no longer ennui but just time-wasting. We would flick through her photo-albums, moments of conviviality glassily preserved. There had been a trip round Europe. This class of *malai* never did anything by themselves but always in a party of at least ten. To judge by the photographs, on this occasion it had been as many as 20. Rome, Vienna, Frankfurt, Paris, Barcelona, London. Neither she nor the Colonel had paid a cent. There was a rich woman who picked up the check for her friends – in short they were an entourage. I bit back the word. 'Oh, she is a very kind woman,' my mistress said. 'She makes all her friends so happy.' I looked hard at the photograph. The generous friend's eyes were red because of the flash. She looked Chinese to me.

Mrs Goreng had been in Danu ten months, every one of which seemed a year to her. There'd been no women before

349

then, in the sense of a community. Girls for the brothel, yes, recruited from *malai* land. They'd not favoured local women for security reasons. But there had been no families. The men made a six-month tour of duty. Now they spent a year and the officers were allowed to bring their wives. This was part of the policy of 'normalisation' for the territory, which they'd begun as they started to register decisive military successes. The other prong of the fork was 'Danuisation' of the war – of which more later.

The Gorengs made their home in the former diplomatic quarter, the area which had, to the glee of the Chinese in the Toku-ru warehouse, been accidentally shelled by the *malai* navy on invasion day. I'm not sure whose house it had been. It was not far from where Raoul's father had lived, the same kind of two-storey place with a walled garden, ornamental trellis gate, and roaming dogs. (Colonel Goreng kept three German shepherds.) I was officially the gardener, but had come to fulfil also roles of secretary, comptroller of household, translator, interpreter, and stool-pigeon (which they had always intended me to be). Finally, I was also paid companion and professional flatterer. I'm not proud.

There were distinct advantages for me in the relationship. Apart from the obvious one of self-preservation, I'd had nearly four years taken out of my life. That time was a black hole of nothingness. I had been an animal, not a reflective human being. Of the outside world, I had more or less no knowledge. The 'man of the world' had become if not a rude caveman, then a sorry Rip Van Winkle figure. My physical hunger could be quite quickly assuaged, my mental starvation was a different matter. That's why I was quite happy to peruse my lady's jottings. In the middle of the trivia, the stuff that could easily have been 1930 or 1960, there was information for the gleaning. It wasn't by any means a straightforward process. The articles of direct newsworthy interest in her magazine were as few and far between as the flecks of gold in a prospector's pan. What you had to do was listen for the echo – not the report itself. So there would be stray references and allusions in the feature articles to events of great consequence or intrinsic interest of which even the bird-brained wives of the garden suburbs of *malai*-land were cognisant but not I, Adolph Ng, BA (Hons) Toronto. Thus I learned that Chaplin was dead and so was Elvis (I'd thought the former long since gone but this intelligence of Presley startled me), that Iranians had held Americans hostage, administered show trials and televised humiliation; that a geriatric cowboy had become President of the mightiest nation on earth – all in all, show biz news. I couldn't, even with my mistress, be seen reading their newspapers or turn the radio on. Mrs Goreng, I think, guessed at this hunger of mine, but would tantalise, only dropping the knowledge a fragment at a time, like mother bird stuffing nourishment down the throat of fledgling. She was a journalist, but she was also a tease.

There were only nine or ten other wives; most officers had chosen not to bring their spouses to what was still a danger zone. Mrs Goreng was by no means the youngest but, unfortunately, the women of her age were married to officers of a rank far junior to her own husband and – therefore – herself, while the youngest colonel's wife was 43, as I ascertained. She'd far rather have enjoyed the company of her contemporaries and, in fact, Colonel Goreng didn't forbid her consorting with them. What happened, though, was he ordered one of the captains on a dangerous mission – just how dangerous I knew – on which he'd been wounded and the young wives hadn't forgiven her for it. The older women were kindly souls, as maternal as their husbands were ruthless murderers, but honestly they weren't much fun for Mrs Goreng. So I was something of a godsend for her.

I was always her property, but I could make an evening, or an afternoon for that matter, swing for all the ladies. Swimming? I knew the best spots. The fact that we had an armed guard lowered no one's spirits; made everyone feel a lot more comfortable, including, if they only knew it, the ex-FAKINTIL chief sapper himself. Mrs Goreng would take off her jazzy (does that word date me?) little halter and shorts to reveal a swimming costume underneath whose intrinsic modesty was in inverse proportion to the daring of the shorts and top as relative items of apparel. That was her all over: the tease that failed to deliver. The other wives would tut-tut, taking sidelong glances at me. (The soldier in uniform they didn't consider as other than a walking rifle.) Well, don't concern yourselves about *me*, ladies, I thought. I'd walk off to a respectful distance – I had no desire to listen to their conversation, there was nothing useful to pick up from that babble. About the third time we went to the beach (I took them to the one known since 1945 as 'Staging Post B'), as soon as I rejoined the group I realised she'd told them. Bitch. No, I didn't care. What was it to me? Their smiles, the slight but palpable sense of relief, the failure to meet the eye, the stifled giggling, all told me they knew I was not a threat. Next time all but the fattest felt free to wear their costumes. Then mah-jong parties became all the rage. Two of them knew how to play already. I taught the others, hanging discreetly round the table to advise the tyros. They didn't appear to mind me playing a double game, allying with each in turn, then becoming their opponent at the next round. Of course, I had an eagle's eye view of developments, knowing far, far more about their strengths and weaknesses than they individually could. Sometimes, I'd have to take a turn if someone failed to arrive, enthroning myself at the green baize table and stuffing myself with shrimp rolls and pickles, me, the killer who'd lived on bugs. If we heard the Colonel's car draw up, of course I had to drop my bricks and run. It wouldn't have done for him to see me there.

TWENTY-FOUR

I OWED MY LIFE TO MARTINHO. The *malai* junior commanders in the field were not of the smartest. It was nearly impossible to get them to accept a surrender. We'd known that in the mountains and in due course I was to see it myself from the other side of the fence. The bloodthirstiness of the *malais* only helped FAKINTIL and, in particular, Osvaldo. They'd have had four times more FAKINTIL deserters if they'd shown as little as a quarter extra clemency. To leave the enemy without hope is to make him more dangerous in the way that a cornered rat, the kind of vermin that robbed our granaries, will leap a fantastic height into the air to sink his incisors in your cheek. Rebus, belatedly, had realised that, but the message had never truly been absorbed by the lieutenants and sergeants at the sharp end. They'd seen too many of their comrades tread on something nasty or gut-shot in a FAKINTIL ambush. And even those captives who'd got back to Danu, the town I mean, had been merely mice – helpless and squeaking – rolled this way and that as the cat pleased. So they had been theoretically rehabilitated, set at liberty – some mere shells after interrogations as fearful as one's most perverted imaginings might devise – only to be pulled in again just as their taut nerves had said, yes, they were free of the cord. The neighbours would hear the truck draw up in the middle of the night, the rattle of the tail-board, the despairing slurry of the prisoner's feet on the dirt. And some just disappeared, vanished never to be seen again, taken who knew when or where – though by whom was no mystery.

Rebus was no longer on the island. That ogre of FAKINTIL demonology had been recalled. I liked to think it was because they thought he'd failed, that our survival in the mountains had been his humiliation, but I would have to admit this might have been mere wishful thinking. The *malais* believed in quick rotations for Danu. He had no successor, in the sense of someone doing an identical job. His functions were now split between several officers who specialised in counter-insurgency. Had he been around at the time of my capture I don't believe I'd have made it very far.

I owed my life to Martinho. There was no question of that. Looking up into his concerned brown eyes, I had felt an inexpressible sense of relief. This wasn't the flawed, haggard Martinho I'd latterly known but a clean, composed, god-like creature, the perfect Martinho of the peace-time Praça. He bestrode me like some stalwart saint of old, defending my prone body with buckler and flaming sword. The *malai* lieutenant, a firebrand six months out of officer training school, shouted angrily at him. He still had his pistol out. Martinho didn't budge a centimetre. The *malai* shoved him in the chest with his free hand but he pointed the gun at the ground behind him. Martinho shook his head. 'This one is valuable,' he said firmly. 'You don't touch a hair of his head.' The *malai's* men were crowding around now, with bad intent. Martinho kept his head. He said, 'Colonel Goreng will require this prisoner. You are responsible to him for your actions.'

Well, even then, not knowing Goreng and with two toes blown off as cleanly as if the surgeon's knife had done the job, a mangled calf, and shrapnel resident two centimetres from the balls, I could recognise Martinho had played a masterly hand. So did the *malai,* for he pulled up short. Martinho was, as I learned later and surmised then, himself vulnerable – he had his uses, and therefore power and influence, but as soon as he became dispensable he'd reap the consequences of any ill-considered actions, such as this. In short, he'd become a Chinese. The *malai's* face showed his predicament. There was no way he could risk incurring the wrath of a superior but he didn't want to lose manhood in front of his uniformed thugs. *'Tuan,'* I said, 'please do not kill me.' An NCO answered this plea by stepping on my foot. I screamed, of course. There was nothing in the least feigned about this howl of anguish. But at the same time I revelled in the unlovely sound because it might be the saving of my miserable life. For the more I yelled, the lower I made myself and the greater the sense of mastery and control the *malais* around me could enjoy. Kids, the cruel little monsters, like to poke Teddy in the gut, don't they, to hear him squeak? I gave them a good show, with my writhings and moanings. Martinho, too, sensing what the rules of disengagement from the deathbed were going to be, allowed them to have their fun, or – the priestly hypocrite he'd been in the jungle – got his kicks out of the spectacle, what he might regard as my just deserts for my equivocal behaviour toward him in those nightmare days. After a while the lieutenant stopped things.

He wasn't particularly sadistic, for a *malai,* though he would have lost no sleep that night if he'd terminated me. I figure he thought his men would get out of control if it went on any longer. I was frisked, my belt and Seiko taken from me, and, as an afterthought, kicked in the ribs. Which was almost a relief after the agony of my abused foot. When I gave them a grenade they hadn't found, I got another kick. It was one of the tiny, egg-sized types, but it was still careless of them. After that, they put me into Martinho's care.

Well, in the next few weeks I sang like a canary. I wasn't proud, not me. I knew I'd give in under whatever duresses Goreng had up his sleeve for me, so what was the point of resisting? That wasn't my notion of myself at all. Nor did I need to buy time for anybody. I knew my former comrades would be long gone from the latest of the encampments before the *malais* ever got near them.

It was recent history Goreng was most avid for. Martinho had told them of everything up to the time of his own escape. They got his version constantly; he was a walking thesaurus on FAKINTIL. Now I became the second edition. Every day for three weeks I'd be taken from my cell in the old colonial prison, from the cool, noisome darkness into the harsh day of Danu. Three or four times they varied the system to pull me from my palliasse at a dead hour of the morning – about three-thirty or four a.m. I'd say – and interrogate me in the cell itself with shouted, rapid-fire questions, punctuated by slaps in the face and, just once, hair-pulling. You couldn't help but contradict yourself from time to time. They deliberately looked for inconsistencies where they basically knew I'd told them but two aspects of the truth, in the hope that I'd blurt out the real truth about something else in my fright and confusion. I could see the primitive method; that didn't stop it from being effective. The main sessions took place at Goreng's HQ, which was a new tin-roof construction which post-dated my departure from Danu. At first I had the blindfold and loud noise treatment but that pretty soon stopped. They realised I told a better story when I was composed. They put me in the same category as

Martinho. In some ways the *malai* could be deeply caste-conscious, a souvenir of the days of the Hindu kingdoms. For the most part they were nominally Muslims now but they appeared to have an idea of torturable classes. Being an intellectual or bourgeois didn't help that much in itself but those of their own journalists and professors they'd sent to the remote prison island of their archipelago, Guru, hadn't been systematically tortured; just neatly excised from society for 20 years or the stay of their natural existences. In their eyes Martinho had some mystique, as well as usefulness. He'd survived where they had eliminated some of his followers because they took him at his own estimation, a man of the cloth. And the fact that I was Chinese, like many of the top brass's personal financial advisers, for once helped.

Yet I was careful to ration what I told them. Like Scheherazade, I always had one more tale, one more piece of information, to titillate the imaginations and jaded appetites of my Islamic captors. It was Arabian Nights in the mountains, my 1001 relations of the exploits of the great Osvaldo. And, unlike most story-tellers with an involvement, I was at pains to minimise my own part; the last thing I did was boast. How many machine-guns did we have left? Mortar tubes and bombs? Where were the main gardens? Who was Osvaldo's chief assistant these days, X. Ray or the Corporal? Who was Osvaldo's rival? Were there different cliques? These were Goreng's constant questions.

And, 'How's morale?' Martinho suddenly asked one afternoon. 'Everyone happy, are they? Getting enough to eat?' I caught his eye. Dangerous as it was to betray the smallest complicity before Goreng and his goons, we both started to laugh. I said, 'They'd surrender many of them, if they knew they wouldn't be shot or mistreated.'

Goreng said, 'You're alive, aren't you?'

I said, carefully, 'There's what happens and there's what they think will happen. Some of them are only fighting because they think they've got nothing left to lose.' I waited a little and after weighing it in my mind continued, 'They think if they're not shot at once, then they will be when they're no longer useful. That's what keeps them fighting in the hills.'

Goreng said, 'Then they're right.'

Knowing him for the hard-hearted son of a bitch he was, I was still shaken. I don't think Martinho liked it too much, either. After that I got us on to less dangerous ground, and I gave him a few tit-bits of intelligence, which was probably what he'd been after.

Twenty-three of those who'd escaped with Martinho still survived. In the indiscriminate gunfire of that day, more had died. Martinho said the *malais* had very quickly stopped shooting at them and that most of the casualties had come from our own fire. Goreng had been with his forces that day. Martinho had had to do some quick talking but none of them had been executed on the spot. It was afterwards. As I say, the *malais* had this habit of letting people go home, then pulling them in six weeks to six months later. Five of those who'd come in with Martinho had disappeared subsequently. None of us slept very easily, I have to say. We regarded ourselves as more hostages than prisoners.

A few months after my return Goreng found a use for the less obviously subtle or versatile of his captives, which while turning them to material advantage also catered for a certain desired degree of planned redundancy. He didn't mind the natural wastage, at all. Martinho's men were to form the nucleus of a Danuese battalion which would take the brunt of the war against FAKINTIL. That is, they would have the worst jobs, occupying the positions of most danger against their old comrades. I believe it was canvassed as a first stage towards total 'Danu-isation' of the conflict, internalisation of the war. The *malai* propaganda machine had always lied about the scale of casualties in our earlier Civil War. That way they could minimise the extent of their killings, particularly those on invasion day and the month afterwards. If they'd murdered 4,000 Danuese but said 3,999 had been killed by ourselves in the Danuese Civil War, then it meant they had killed only one. It was that kind of statistical perversion. And it worked, it was something to say in the international talking shops. Now they could claim that Danuese was fighting Danuese again, with their assistance. I believe that they were also becoming concerned about the steady casualties they were taking. Their country was overpopulated; the leadership had little care for life. But it was becoming a political factor. They were nothing if not astute, those mild-seeming old men with their erect bearings, gentle manners, and hands reeking of innocent blood, their own victims at home as well as the Danuese.

While the surviving ex-guerrillas occupied the positions of responsibility, the rank and file were drawn from their old IP opponents of the Civil War, those who had no reason to love Osvaldo. That was one way of looking at it – modern political opponents. But, of course, overlaying and underlying this transparency were the old tribal and family feuds and enmities which had put most of the followings into the rival camps in the first place. Ideological opinions had been modern luxuries for the leaders. Martinho had lost no time in recounting the true details of Osvaldo's moment of weakness, the point at which he'd flipped his lid for the first and last time in his career, that murderous aberration which had been the doom of old friend and new foe alike. Rebus and his successors had not been aware of the true details of this massacre of prisoners.

About four weeks after Martinho's capture – or his escape from Osvaldo, whichever way you like to look at it – he'd taken Goreng to the spot. It had been a big thing, photographers, *malai* officers, local chieftains, city Danuese of all walks and classes, dogs, trackers (for sign that was five years old!), cherry berets, and helicopters making self-important passes overhead. Goreng had been worried it might be a set-up – paranoia, dirty tricks, and distrust were that army's staple – and he'd assured Martinho that he'd be the first to go if that was the case. Poor Martinho, almost his portly self again, had spent the whole time with at least one gun in his back. 'I tell you, Adolph,' he confessed, 'I was sweating.' The most nerve-racking part in the end had been

358

to locate the site of the graves. It had been a long time ago and the jungle had reclaimed its own. Martinho had led them from one identical spot to another, sure each time it was the place, blundering through the heat and humidity with a fresh excuse burbling from his thick lips. Boredom took the place of apprehension in Goreng's mind; he began to take it out on people. Martinho was beside himself with anxiety and frustration. 'It's here, Colonel,' he assured Goreng. 'It was here. I haven't made it up. I swear the bodies are somewhere near here.'

'They had better be,' Goreng said. 'Or there will be new ones.'

Soares was one of those along. He'd lost a cousin and some good friends in these reprisals. *He* believed Martinho OK. He'd taken the lead up here – fear of ambushes or not – poking the roots with his chieftain's stick of authority. And in the end it was he who turned up a bullet case (7.62 mm x 51 and therefore probably FAKINTIL). The dogs did the rest.

Well, it wasn't as gruesome as it might have been had the bodies been five weeks rather than five years old, but it hadn't been a pretty sight by any means. The *malai* photographers had made a good job of it, this genuine FAKINTIL atrocity. The skulls and one complete skeleton in rotting clothes had leered out of magazines. Those of the dental classes had been identified by their records, Soares's cousin included. 'And Raoul?' I asked. 'You found him? His body I mean? You reburied him?'

Martinho shook his head. 'I didn't trouble with that,' he said with decent honesty. 'It was a long time ago. What good could it do?'

In any event the find had been the making of Martinho with the *malais*. He hadn't looked back since then. As for the Danuese battalion, the Sons of Death, as they called themselves, a few still had revenge on their minds. The others didn't want to know and, in fact, soon after my capture, a whole platoon deserted to Osvaldo under an Africa cadre, complete with their 5.56 mm automatic weapons. For this, Goreng shot three of the other cadres, definitively encouraging the others. He had it done in front of Martinho and myself in the courtyard of the prison, the men made to kneel rather than shot upright against a wall. I trembled for hours afterwards, so Goreng's medicine was effective. It concentrated my mind at our interviews again; I'd been relaxing. Just before the men were shot – they'd had two weeks inside so their beards had taken on something of the authentic rag-tag FAKINTIL glory, as opposed to the clean-shaven image they had presented in their neat *malai*-issue camos – one shouted out the name of Osvaldo. The youngest of the trio – he was a 27-year-old ex-seminarian who had been greatly under the influence of Molloy before going to Africa – began to sing, in a terrible, faltering voice, probably the most unmelodious I ever heard from a Danuese, what sounded like the first lines of 'O, Mighty Mountain!' The gunshots soon ended that. The awful, abrupt finality of a man pitching forward, so easily, so arbitrarily terminated – the convenience of it to the killer: they were things to which I could never become habituated, however many times I saw it. I never got hardened, that way. As we left, Martinho whispered angrily, 'The fools! They just showed Goreng he was right to do it. It only makes things more dangerous for us!' When I had recovered from my immediate repugnance, I had to concede he was merely correct. It did show Goreng what all Danuese thought, deep down. But then he would have had to have been more obtuse than he was not to have known already.

I met the Colonel's wife while I was waiting for Martinho outside church one sunny afternoon. I had a mouth full of red betel juice. Not desiring to defile the wall of the consecrated place, I went round the corner to spit into the gutter. When I came back Mrs Goreng was coming down the steps with her chauffeur, who was a one-armed sergeant with a pistol. I hoped for her sake he had been naturally left-handed. She was immediately recognisable, though she'd had the scarf on as she sped past me the only other time I'd seen her. I took my hands out of my pants pockets and bowed, expecting her to go by. She didn't. 'You are Japanese, are you?' she asked. Taken aback, I could only stammer, 'No.'

'Ah,' she said, 'it's just that they bow a lot.' The armless NCO glared at me as they went past.

I don't know why women like to taunt me, but they seem to grow fonder of me by doing so. If I had done Mrs Goreng a favour, she'd have forgotten me speedily enough. Because I'd been the butt of her wit she remembered me. I guess Colonel Goreng would rather his wife had been less unconventional. It might have made for easier dealings with superiors and a better example for juniors, but then it was a major part of her sexual thrall over him. The irritation was dissipated by the balm of her bedroom personality. I guess it made a stimulating change for him not to be surrounded by fawners and flatterers the whole time. Maybe she tied him up and gave him soft whip. Who knows? I do know she was the subtlest of nags. It took about three months for me to realise how she did it. The Colonel wouldn't know in a lifetime. She undermined his private notion of himself. The flattery and deference of his subordinates and his entourage (two different groups) didn't count; he wasn't enough of a fool for that. Like many men, deep down he was unsure of himself. He didn't have that steadiness or grasp of the self of Osvaldo, X. Ray, or, I am sorry to say, Rebus. She exploited that. By looking for faults in his behaviour, by constantly diminishing him with little criticisms – he neglected their boy (at school in Randung), he was cold, he was selfish, he was an inadequate and clumsy lover (did she dare), he never listened to other people, he had no sense of direction because he was always getting her lost in foreign capitals – she made him feel a kind of leper, different from and inferior to the run of men. There was no objective standard for him to measure himself by – there never is in this kind of case, either you have the confidence in yourself, or you don't – all he could do was see himself reflected in her eyes, and it was not a pleasing portrait. The deference of his courtiers did nothing for this – that was a piece from a different jigsaw puzzle he had already solved. Alone with her, he floundered; she kept pushing him under water, teased him with planks that didn't float. That merciless, bloody-handed *malai* (and he was a good and ruthless professional soldier) was subject to the slow water torture every day of his life. I watched with interest – it was like observing the gyrations of an alien species, a praying mantis or something. It made me glad to be what I was. Of course, in front of his associates, before subordinates, she treated him like God.

She, therefore, recognised me when our paths crossed once more. By then I had been released to the Toko-ru on my own recognisance, that is an abject willingness to betray my comrades and help the *malais* in every way. I was lending a hand in the store of one of my compatriots; for which I received a miserly stipend and a corner of a room in the warehouse already occupied by two young Chinese. I was accorded a degree of respect appropriate to a man who had been under arms, which was as well as, after rumours of my predilections spread through the warehouse, there were not many willing to share with me. They needn't have flattered themselves.

Mrs Goreng was returning a hand-held blow-drier to the shop which the proprietor, an elderly Chinese, had had the temerity to refuse earlier from her house-boy. When he saw Mrs Goreng disembarking from her jeep, he at once made himself scarce, retiring through the back of the shop to his living-quarters and instructing me to deal with this dissatisfied, difficult, and, in all likelihood, dangerous customer. Something told me not to get ruffled about Mrs Goreng. In any case, I had already decided to give her a refund *and* a new drier. They weren't my goods.

She only took her sunglasses off when she was inside the dark little shop but even then it took a few moments for her eyes to adjust. I had the advantage of her for that much unobtrusive study. I saw nothing that made me dislike her. A little arrogance, yes, some petulance, but nothing extra that went beyond what her position in that place and at that time would have encouraged in her. You would have had to be superhuman not to be a little corrupted by the power she had. I didn't see spite. More than anything, I thought I

362

discerned boredom, intelligence, and energy denied an outlet. Then she was able to see again.

'Ah,' she said, 'you again.'

'We Japanese are everywhere,' I said. You know, I had to say something clever – to win her, to set me apart, to make her see me as an individual – but wit is normally aggressive. I had to say something humorous without being a smart-ass or putting her down in any way. My feeble little quip was self-diminishing, it might raise a smile, it paid a homage to her own earlier remark, and it gave us a shared history. And it worked. Mrs Goreng's laugh tinkled round the shabby store. We exchanged a few pleasantries; I used words which would give her an idea of my station without patronising her. I could watch her face as she made repeated revisions of her assessments of me of only a few moments before. Surely a storekeeper in this barbarous place wouldn't have a vocabulary like that? Even a Chinese storekeeper. My dear Mrs Goreng, I felt like saying, you would have been surprised to come across a *hotelier* who'd read Thomas Mann. We got about six sentences too deep in our conversation for her to institute personal questions about my background, without appearing offensive (she had to treat me as a person now and not a *peon)*, even for Asians who delight in asking pertinent questions as to age, income, etc., unthinkable for more backward Europeans. Well, finally she left, and I saw her to her jeep with the new hair-drier which I found I had to press her to keep. The old Chinese now came shambling from the kitchen, agog to hear everything. I was distant with him.

Mrs Goreng was back a couple of days later, with some excuse about a plug malfunctioning. She was bored, poor girl. This time she started to interrogate me from the very beginning. Me, I was forthcoming with the details.

'And what have you done since your hotel closed?'

I told her and her hand flew to her mouth as her eyes widened. Yes, I enjoyed startling her. Under the fear of death, the shadow of the disappearance squads, I still drew pleasure from causing an effect. The queen in me, would have been poor, dear, dead Maria's acerbic comment. Well, we spoke some more after that but we stayed clear of FAKOUM and FAKINTIL. Next time I saw her, she was with the Colonel, this time in his sedan, leaving the old diplomatic quarter. I saw her speak to her husband, clearly about me. He turned, and I bowed, ever so humbly, an innocuous (I trusted) figure receding in the minor dust-storm of their exhaust wake.

I got the job in the Colonel's household a week later. She must have gone to work on him, probably saying he'd get more out of me that way. I was very glad of the protection. By going to the household I was kind of taking the salt; I was realistically enhancing my prospects of survival. And I made sure I blabbed a bit to her, even contradicting in inessential details some of the earlier recitations to the Colonel, so that he might think he was getting better quality intelligence this way. It was a gamble between being bumped off for lying earlier or allowing him to think he was gaining no advantage by my presence in the household. Either way the consequences were terminal for yours truly.

TWENTY-FIVE

No ROSA. Of my old crony there was not the smallest trace. Soon after my release from the old jail I'd gone looking for the crèche in which the Organisation for Working Danuese Women had made its home. There'd been a lot of changes under the *malais*, I'll give them that, even if most of the development was for reasons of military necessity and accomplished, like the Japanese for whom they had more than a sneaking admiration, with forced-draft labour. I thought it might have amused X. Ray to see it and hoped one day he would, but not under the hostile circumstances in which I had the misfortune to discover myself. Going out to the outlying part of town in which the crèche had been situated you now travelled along a metalled road. Not only that, it was lit by electric lamps. Of course, this wasn't simple philanthropy on the part of the *malai* military, although there was the element of impressing locals and making propaganda with such foreign visitors as there now were, but a tactical requirement. It happened to lead from the old barracks (still used for housing a garrison) up to the hill pass above the town. They needed a strengthened carriageway for their armoured personnel carriers and lighting to make sabotage difficult, not that the demoralised citizens had the nerve to inflict mass reprisals upon themselves. I looked down in some wonderment at the shiny blacktop, therefore, nevertheless noting that unevenesses were already manifesting themselves. I felt like someone out of a pop song, revisiting the haunts of childhood, going to see an old sweetheart, not knowing if they would still be there or not, hoping against hope that they might. I hadn't asked for Rosa, that was for sure.

I'd tried waiting for the natural course of events to bring me the way of the crèche, some errand Mrs Goreng might send me on, but it hadn't worked out that way. After some while I got tired of waiting. My curiosity I could check, but not the little notions my brain threw up, such as: she *will* be dead before you get to see her. And it was true, over the long term you were finished if the *malais* took it into their heads that you were the wrong kind of Danuese. You might get through a few months, gross good luck see you to a year, but from then on the odds against survival lengthened considerably. See Rosa while you can, said a little bird to me. And I was eager to see her, the desire built itself up from nothing, as desires do. I could not endure the irony of missing her now.

I invented a task for myself, which would take me that way. I'd get wild orchids for the garden, I told Mrs Goreng, knowing some had grown near Rosa's. She clapped her hands.

'It will please the Colonel to see them at the breakfast-table in the morning,' I said. 'But we won't tell him until they have established themselves in our soil.' I was also smart enough to wait three weeks, so it was at her request I departed in the end.

I needn't have troubled. Limping down that glossy road, the yellow brick road to my fantasy land of the past, I was consumed with an expectation which would have been delightful save for the physical effect of breathlessness. I could see the place some way off. Smoke rose from the yard, which encouraged optimism within me. The building was still occupied, then. As I got nearer, I saw they were young people, mostly in their late teens and early twenties. This caused some puzzlement. I mean, surely the waifs and orphans, not to mention the *bona fide* seedling sons and daughters, could not have sprung into these young oaks in such a relatively short space of time? It was well under a decade; they'd still be kids. Yet whatever common sense suggested or arithmetic dictated, I half-believed these were the children of the women Rosa had tried so hard to have live up to her Spartacist ideals. I wanted my old friend to be there; I prayed for nothing to have changed. And as I drew nearer I steadfastly rejected any contrary observation, the persistent negating evidence of my own senses: the lack of older women, the mound of rubbish Rosa would never have tolerated, the general air of apathy and neglect. I could see the people lounging in the yard now. Strangely enough, for such a filthy place, there was a lot of washing on lines; at least, they didn't look like the mere rags one might expect. The smoke I'd seen earlier was from a bricked-in fire under a cauldron, in which more garments appeared to be bubbling. Eager for information as I was, I was careful not to stare, looking at the roadside straight ahead, or at the sea from time to time.

'Senhor Ng!' someone called.

Well, I cringed at the fellow's stupidity; my neck went right into my shoulders. 'Senhor Adolph!' There was no ignoring it. I turned with what I hoped was an innocent smile on my face.

'Remember me? I'm João, from the hotel.'

Well, I didn't, not at all. And if I'd known he was going to turn out a stupid and objectionable youth I'd never have employed the foolish boy. I looked at him closer; trusted that he was not one of those (not so many) that I'd pleasured myself with. No, I would have had to have been snatching them from the cradle then. 'Ah, yes,' I lied, 'how could I forget? But you have grown so tall and handsome.' I could see his friends grinning among themselves; probably there were more who had better cause to remember me. 'And what do you do now, João?'

'We're the laundry,' he said in surprise. 'We launder the soldiers' clothes.'

'Ah,' I said. Yes, I could now see most of it was olive green, with the odd camo suit. I wondered if blood was hard to get out. 'It must be hard work,' I said, neutrally. He grinned vacuously. I think he was a good-natured but very unintelligent boy. I offered him a slice of areca and we both, uh, masticated with enjoyment. After a while I had to spit. Life being life, the wind blew (it was a good drying day for them) and a large red splotch appeared on a *malai* vest. A girl ran up angrily, removing it for fresh soaking and ignoring my apologies. João kept grinning.

'You can see how old I am,' I said. 'I remember this place when it was the next best thing to an orphanage. Now what was the name of the woman who ran it? Rina? Rinaihi?' João did not cue himself in. However, a few of his friends came by. Young people have always liked me. After a while João got told to go work by the angry girl. He still wore his expression of vacuous merriment, which must have been habitual rather than assumed in my honour. Following the usual exchanges I enquired how long they'd been there. More than three years came the answer.

'Oh, what was before then?'

A kind of club.

'For soldiers?'

No, for women. They started to wear that blank face all us Easterners are so good at assuming when we are uneasy. Yet I persisted.

Had it been closed by the authorities (I used that word, not 'the *malais*')? They didn't know. Well, what I knew was I would get no more. After further inconsequential chat, which I deliberately spun out to 15 minutes, I made my excuses. Fifty metres down the road, I heard the insecure flap of rubber sandals. It was the girl I'd annoyed with my carelessness.

'You forgot your areca-box.'

'Many thanks,' I said, genuinely grateful. She waited, instead of turning straight back as I'd expected. Then she said, 'The woman you knew, the one who ran this place, you won't find her.'

Tears came to my eyes – truly surprising me. I blinked.

'But she had a baby.'

For a second I was hopeful – Rosa with a child! No, never! It must be someone else she was talking about. She must have seen my surprise, for she then used a native word for an unwanted or deformed child. It had a shock effect on me. 'They keep the children on a prison island.' Then without a backward look she nodded and returned to her piles of steaming clothes.

I continued aimlessly down the road for a while more. I could walk as fast as I ever did but I tended to roll my shoulders and turn my three-toed foot in as I did so. A group of burly *malai* soldiers came jogging in full combat gear from the other direction, the little sergeant who was trotting beside them bestowing on me a suspicious glare. That brought me to my senses. I didn't feel like passing the laundry once more – don't ask me why. But it was difficult to return by another route. I tried going through the undergrowth and looping round – my sense of direction had far improved from peacetime – but the saw-toothed grasses left me bleeding like a scored steak. Then I spotted them – superb orange orchids of a kind I had never seen in Danu. Gently, I extracted them from the soil with the trowel I'd brought more as alibi than implement. Then I packed moss and earth round the roots. A banana-leaf from a fruitless palm accomplished the rest. By the time I passed the old crèche again it was getting darker and the insects were out. The launderers were at their evening meal – I could see their backs at the windows. I started to worry about the curfew.

Even if, as a servant of the Gorengs, I could likely avoid punishment, there was a real risk of being shot on the spot by some itchy-fingered *malai*. I did not appreciate the irony of being knocked dead on my back with a bunch of flowers clasped to my chest. It was OK, though. I got in through the back gate without being challenged.

Colonel Goreng was already home. Mrs Goreng had missed me. She came out of their lounge with irritation written all over her; I think if she hadn't liked me she would not have been annoyed. She had got bored by herself – and, if I flatter myself, there was a tinge of concern for me. I put my finger to my lips and widened my eyes. I beckoned her to the kitchen. The orchids were in a pot with some water. Her annoyance vanished and we became conspirators.

'But you are bleeding, Adolph!'

I shrugged, as if I thought them honourable scars to be gained in my lady's service.

'We'll have to see if they live or die,' I said. 'If they live, we can transplant them into the garden. If not … he won't know.' She touched the flowers, looking at them with the steady, close, and intent gaze that Annie Laval also reserved for such an occasion. Was it a weakness intelligent women allowed themselves? Maria had worn them in her hair at her wedding. 'Thank you, Adolph,' Mrs Goreng said.

Whatever the ups and downs of life in the Colonel's household, I was spared the ordeal of coming under the fire of my old friends. Serving in the Danuese battalions was a living hell. At least in the hills with FAKINTIL the enemy was obvious and you had your freedom. We had no compunction about killing *malais*. But I understood that many in the battalions – some of Soares's people apart – soldiered even more poorly than their already mediocre training and leadership might have led an expert onlooker to anticipate. If they possibly could, they avoided contact; their shots went wide – high I think they already would have been. As I said, Goreng had to shoot some after a desertion so large that it could not possibly be ascribed to the category of MIAs.

Oddly enough, the *malais* were not at all eager to admit that the desertions in twos and threes were such, preferring to list them as missing presumed killed. I think the Danuese battalions were the idea of someone high up at home and they didn't wish to offend him by indicating that his brainchild was, as Mr Burnett would have said, a white elephant. It was bad for Martinho's people, caught between Osvaldo and the cherry berets.

Whether it was the reluctance of the cannon-fodder or FAKINTIL's growing weakness, engagements became increasingly few. A big probe, Operasi Dragon, failed to encounter large-scale FAKINTIL resistance. The *malais* began to think a triumph was just around the corner. Goreng's superior was coming to the end of his tour of duty. He badly wanted to believe he had beaten FAKINTIL – it would have eased a move into their crony politics for him. The pressure came on to Goreng from above. Normally he would have been too shrewd. In turn, the heat was applied to Martinho and then myself. Martinho wanted to please them, so he passed the buck to yours truly. I said, 'The bandits will not be beaten until you have Osvaldo's dead body.' That was about as welcome as a stick of shit in the tub-water. Martinho blanched. The General glared at me. Goreng looked at me in some surprise. He was about to say something; then decided not to. The General said, 'Then my men will bring it to me.'

I said, 'It is only a matter of time, *tuan,* but maybe the time is not quite yet.' I was treated to the full force of the General's disapproval, which was not negligible. Just out of the line of his sight, Martinho mouthed furiously at me. The General said: 'I shall know who to blame if treachery helps the bandits.' In English the words sound weird, but – believe me – it was the logic which was bizarre. Did I say they were a subtle people? I got the message OK. I just shut up.

On the way down the corridor Martinho hissed in my ear, 'You want to get us all shot? Let him think what he wants.' He was mightily pissed off with me; perhaps he wished he had just let them shoot me on the ground. I said, 'Martinho,

I'm sorry. I was thinking of both our heads. And I was thinking of the future.'

'Think of now,' was his terse retort.

What I thought was: 'You are very like your brother in this one respect, my friend. You *only* think of here and now.' But I left it at that.

Things continued quiet for some while. Sweep after sweep came up with nothing.

The Broncos would return with guns unfired, their ordnance dumped at sea or on top of old FAKINTIL sites, notoriously long deserted. Word spread: Osvaldo had died of malaria; he'd been shot in the back by X. Ray; he'd fallen down a cliff. Or – this was a really good one – he had fled to the Northern Territory by boat sent by Australian sympathisers. Someone claimed to have heard him on the radio from Darwin – but it was always someone at a third-hand remove; someone who had heard it from someone who had heard it from someone. I can truthfully say I never believed it. I would not be at all surprised if the story had been put out by Goreng or his superiors. Morale rose in the Danuese battalions. Teixeira, the old IP leader, tried to get put in command of them, having up till now succeeded in putting as much distance between himself and those dangerous embarrassments as he could. He wanted control of guns. He had seen what had happened before when FAKOUM had enjoyed this and he hadn't. He wanted some greater degree of power for himself, always within a political reality where the *malais* ultimately called the shots. Yet, strangely enough, it was Martinho the *malais* appeared to favour. It was clear to me that they had spared him in order to groom him for their own uses. He was a weaker and more intelligent man than Teixeira. That suited them.

One dank afternoon I was summoned to the Gorengs' lounge. Mrs sat behind the Colonel. From her encouraging smile I realised she had suggested me for something. I was unable to smile back. I just hoped whatever it was would prove to be neither inconvenient nor dangerous.

'So, Chinaman,' the Colonel said, 'how stupid are you? Very or only a little?' I looked to Mrs for guidance; she looked amused, so I surmised it was not the inception of a punishment for my earlier and inconvenient frankness. 'I am a smart fool, *tuan*,' I said, with my eyes on the ground.

'I think you are too clever for your own good,' the Colonel said, 'but my wife says otherwise. And a wise man listens to his wife. We will be having visitors shortly.'

'*Tuan?*' I said, wondering if I was being told to make A. Ng a scarce commodity. 'Not now, silly,' said Mrs. She and he laughed. I was happy to be the butt.

'There will be journalists coming,' said the Colonel. 'From many countries.'

'All from the West,' Mrs interrupted. The Colonel nodded; he seemed not to mind. I was at once interested but I did my best to suppress the instant flicker in my eyes. I did not succeed in evading the notice of either of them as they had the advantage of knowing what would come next. It would have been better just to let the natural reaction show through. 'See?' said the Colonel to Mrs. 'The Chinese don't show what they're really thinking.'

She waved her hand. 'I know what Adolph thinks.' (I thought this very over-optimistic on her part but let her persist in the delusion.) 'We need,' she said, 'an intelligent Danuese to talk to these newspaper people. And I thought of you.'

But how kind, I thought. I decided not to say so; it might sound ironic.

'There is Mr Oliveira, of course, and Mr Teixeira, and maybe another one or two, but you could play a part, too.'

'Thank you, nonya.'

'You see, you are not involved directly, like the others. You haven't got... what is the expression?'

'An axe to grind?'

'I don't know that. But your testimony will be a good one. You can tell them the true way things stand.'

I thought that was one thing I'd better not do.

'Don't get any clever ideas,' the Colonel said. 'We'll tell

you what to say. And you say what we want to hear, or you take a long walk. The Australians can't take you with them, you know.'

'Whatever pleases you, *tuan*,' I said.

So that was it – an extended press conference on the grand scale! They'd answer the outside world by giving their own authorised version of the intervening years. They intended to make a prophecy that would be self-fulfilling in its entirety. By saying the war was over, the territory pacified, they would make it so. It wasn't just hot air – it was a blow against FAKINTIL that was as deadly in its way as a Bronco strike. If all the press reports chimed the same note at the same time it would be a brave and stubborn fool who would go against them. What they had in common would become irrefutable, objective verity, the stock-in-trade of general knowledge for the educated and interested (few enough in all conscience) of the metropolises of the West. Where they contradicted each other in inessential points there might be room for debate and uncertainty. The *malais* weren't fools – they knew no one would buy a uniform screed. A few minor inconsistencies and divergences would give the appearance of verisimilitude. And it also served to draw stings: it ensured the main issue got cloaked in unimportant wranglings. Get people talking *round* a subject. There's nothing like it for losing sight of the real point.

Whose idea was it? Maybe it went even higher than the Generals. What I did know was that I discerned in the detail the cynical hand of the practising hack. Maybe not even cynical, maybe just female practicality which can stoop with clearest conscience below the level of the lowest stratagem. Yes, I think Mrs had a guiding part in what she called 'these media arrangements'.

We had about two months to prepare for the seven of them; a period useful not only for the co-ordinating of the PR assault but also, I believe, a safety gap, a firebreak, a time in which the military could take stock, an interval in which Goreng could see if there was to be a resurgence of the lost FAKINTIL in the hills. The cherry berets did the scouting; they didn't trust the Danuese battalions with this.

Meanwhile Mrs hatched her plans, abetted by the man of the world. How we'd house them, the way to pamper, what facilities to offer. Mrs Goreng had the ideas; I put them into practice for her. And was that not my destiny, with my past of libraries and hotels? That was what I had come to. Mrs Goreng read herself into her visitors. The fact that she had expected to be cossetted by the subjects of her own journalistic attentions in the past had made her no warier of the reporters she was inviting. You couldn't say the free food and drink or the luxuriously appointed cabins had bought her, but it had affected the tone of her pieces. I guess it was like the primitive interrogation techniques both *malais* and FAKINTIL were not above resorting to: you could see the stratagem but that didn't stop it from being effective.

Booze we had in abundance. The majority of the *malais* were Muslims but that didn't stop the senior military enjoying their glass of whisky – Bourbon rather than Scotch, for the notorious *malai* sweet tooth extended to tastes alcoholic as well. Mrs Goreng used her husband's influence to impound every bottle on the island, as well as a stupendous quantity of crates of beer. The Colonel was a little surprised, amused too. He said, 'This is like Al Capone.' (He could surprise you sometimes with the bits and pieces of his knowledge.) 'You think they drink this much?'

Mrs smiled at her husband. 'They are as bad as sailors, Colonel,' she said. He liked that one. I agreed with my mistress. I remembered those sessions at the Lusitano with Jean Carmichael. They drank like fishes, those guys. Bill Mabbeley was the only one who could keep up with Jean. Funny how it had been *malai* policy to murder him and, earlier, the young men in the television crew, and now it was policy to stand them, or their kind, a round at the bar. And, I was forced to admit, both times it was the correct policy for them.

Mrs Goreng laid on a school, a rally, a football match, the army hospital, and a model village for the journalists. This was liberally interspersed with launch picnics, swimming, the services of a chef flown specially from one of the *malais'* five-star hotels back home, and 'ethnic entertainments'. I got more of a role in the whole thing than the Colonel had figured on – I don't know if my mistress had intended it from the start. As the idle beings they were in a group, the *malais* were used to last-minute arrangements and alterations, spontaneous changes and improvisation; so it wasn't as big a deal as if he'd been, say, an Israeli or a German officer. Still, it was lucky for me everything went well. I could easily have become a scapegoat.

Maybe that was what Mrs Goreng intended all along.

Driving to the sterilised zone in which the *malais* had reconstructed a thatched Danuese village complete with miniature rice-barns one of the two Americans turned and said to me: 'Sir, tell me, truly, do you think the Integration has been a good thing for your country?'

The dumb fuck! Of all the ass-hole questions! I guess he thought it safer to ask me there over the noise of the engine and in the babble of conversation than in some quiet spot alone, where we might be bugged. If so, he was right. But did he think I could give an answer? Did he want me to eat shit or the words stick in my throat and choke me? What he really wanted to do was show what a smart, concerned guy he was. The question didn't pertain to me; it related to him. He asked me in a very slow and serious voice, looking at me with solemn eyes. He was asking me to respect him for an astute and informed observer, an impartial and honest man. It was one step up from small talk; it was aggrandisement. *'Tuan,'* I said, very slow and serious, too, 'it is a good thing, but the cost has been high.' He nodded sagely. I could see the nape of Mrs Goreng's neck in the front seat; she'd put her hair up. I hoped she could hear.

They'd chosen the journalists very carefully, of course. Rather, they'd selected newspapers which, while endowed with authoritative reputations, were sympathetic to the *malai* government – in a nutshell, quality right-wing newspapers which weren't soft on Communism. Mrs Goreng depended on the editors to send the right people. For her to have vetted the reporters on an individual basis (which would have been the first instinct of the *malai* military left to their own devices) would have caused offence to the point where the exercise would have been counter-productive.

The day after their arrival they got a full-scale historical briefing on Danu. There was a lot on the early history, less on recent events. Mrs Goreng was able to make it sound quite romantic – good copy for the female journo from the up-market US ladies' magazine – so we heard about the Spice and Sandalwood Trades, the black Portuguese, and then an interracial love story which Mrs Goreng had invented herself. She told some lies about the close relations between the old *malai* half of the island and ours which had, she said, made them indistinguishable for all practical purposes: for example, it was not an invasion but a reunion. Jesus, it was one island, that was true, but the terrain made the halves more remote from each other than if they had been two islands separated by a sea channel: you couldn't skip across our jungles and mountains in an outrigger. There was a common inheritance of language and culture, she claimed. That was baloney. A whole series of lies about the Revolution, FAKOUM, the IP and the Civil War followed, centring on the deaths caused by the IP – FAKOUM conflict which she magnified by a factor of one hundred. That was nothing, membership of the *pro-malai* party she increased by thousands.

Not that the journalists let her get away with quite everything. They were not incompetents, I'll give them that. The German asked about the atrocities on invasion day – these were known abroad. Mrs Goreng had something up her sleeve for this. She admitted there had been excesses. She said they were deeply regretted. But war was war. Sometimes men get out of the control of their officers. She shrugged at the American woman – it had happened in Viet Nam. Then she looked the German squarely in the eye. 'A whole nation does not have to carry the guilt of a few wrong-doers into perpetuity,' she said. The guy flinched.

I don't think a Chinese could have taught Mrs Goreng anything about the black arts of dissimulation. The honest confession on top of the bag of lies was masterly. She gave the impression of candour, of surrendering a point. But that point was indefensible anyway. She turned weakness into strength, for if she had tried to dismiss those accusations it would have made everything else she said suspect.

She'd wanted to keep the army out of it as much as possible. She was wise enough for that and so, I think, was Colonel Goreng. But the General wanted a piece of the action. I guess he'd seen American officers on TV the whole time during the Viet Nam war. He didn't want Mrs Goreng's husband stealing all the glory. The cruder stuff was his idea. Like the crowd at the airport and in the main street of Danu waving the *malai* flag of red and white. These were strictly extras; he didn't even trust the IP people not to make a demonstration of some kind; these were non-Danuese from a couple of *malai* islands 100 kilometres north-east. Would the foreigners know the difference? Would they, shit! Even I wouldn't realise until they opened their mouths – which was only to sing the *malai* national anthem. And, in fact, at the airport standing at Mrs Goreng's side – me, this time, already returned, waiting to greet *other* people arriving, the emissaries of the greater world – yours truly didn't understand the deception for some time.

Mrs Goreng was on safer ground with the schools. Native Danuese kids – if their parents wanted them to go to school at all, and they were mostly IP big shots – had to study the principles of the *malai* constitution, bow to the flag, learn the kitchen malay which was the official language throughout the *malai* islands. They wore the same red and white of *malai* children all over that archipelagic state. There was nothing wrong with the noble creed they were taught – it was just that it played no part in the actual operation of the military dictatorship. Well, the seven journalists went round the classrooms, looking at the well-scrubbed, well-fed, well-clothed children. The 'teacher' was one of the younger army wives – not so classy as Mrs

Goreng but not bad. She had her arms round a boy and girl, who were regarding the open book on her lap. As we came in, she brought her head close to the little girl's. I watched the strange smile on the American woman's face – like the smile students wore in the movie-house at Toronto when they were watching some particularly syrupy moment from a corny trailer, extorted smiles, full of shame and self-consciousness, but the suppressed emotion sincere enough and shown unguarded in the darkness, except I was playing the voyeur. That's what the feature-writer from the American ladies' magazine looked like – she was no fool, but once again crude and simple was the name of the most effective game.

At the hospital, it was more of the same. *Malai* military doctors treating Danuese, again mostly kids. For me, it was the hardest thing to watch. My eyes filled with tears, that took me as unexpectedly as one of the Corporal's ambushes. And I cursed my weakness, dashing the back of my hand over my traitorous eyes, for I saw the American woman look at me. She thought I was moved by the kindness of the *malais!* Oh, Maria, my darling! How you would have despised me!

Mrs Goreng didn't miss this. As we stepped into the street, behind the others, as grateful for the iced Cokes in prospect as they were, she whispered to me: 'You are doing well, Adolph. Keep up the good work!'

It was a strange moment, and I had to grapple with conflicting sensations. In fact, this was the only spectacle which Mrs Goreng had not had to contrive for the benefit of her guests. The *malai* army doctors really did hold a little surgery for our children. Not for a moment must you imagine that this philanthropic gesture was anything but calculated on the part of the occupying military. It was about the only piece of hearts and minds they did. But the fact remained, the doctors were a different sort of person from the regular army officers; they wanted to do the good works they did; that they would have done it anyway, without being ordered, is my certain opinion. Within the material

378

constraints of the situation they did what they could for the kids. And it *was* in their spare time – they didn't get leave from the official rota. At a personal level it was noble; professionals plying their skills without a thought of personal advantage. They were decent people, the *malai* medicos.

I guess, if he'd known, Osvaldo would have made it a priority to kill them all.

Mrs Goreng came up with a good one. The American lady was fumbling for words. She was wanting to describe the nature of the *malai* government but didn't want to use the first words which came to mind, which were 'military dictatorship'. Mrs Goreng came to the rescue. She nodded. 'The army,' she said helpfully, 'plays an important part in our national life.'

I was hard put to know what I thought about our guests – I mean since, as well as then. The senior American, and the New Zealander, were right-wingers of a purity I'd thought extinct, little imagining that the vogue for radical chic – which had been the orthodoxy of the day in Toronto – was now no more than the memory of an ebb tide. Before I'd been salvaged by Martinho and Mrs Goreng they'd had a Frenchman and a Philadelphian about three years previous who'd written uncomfortable stuff about starving kids, flattened villages, and summary executions. This time the *malais* were especially careful about the New Zealander and the American. Apart from their views, these two had in common a great physical height, towering above average mortals, let alone the diminutive peoples of the Orient. I called them De Gaulle and Wellington. Wellington, the Kiwi, never actually troubled himself to speak to me during his stay. He was the defence correspondent of his paper and I wasn't surprised to hear he'd served in the military. I think he might have been a security man of some kind, although I couldn't prove it to you. He wore a blue suit of safari cut, a non-military colour but a safari-suit nonetheless. He was constantly taking notes – on a special pad which didn't disintegrate in the rain, a feature of some interest both to yours truly and his colleagues. I heard him refer to the Danuese as 'natives' and myself once as a 'Chinaman'. He had a very loud, metallic voice, a little like Arsenio's in a strange way. The others were wary of him, and slightly intimidated. His views were simply and inflexibly held. He justified everything the *malais* did because FAKOUM had been terrorists. Martinho encouraged him in this opinion – he liked to make out that the organisation had been moderate until hijacked by extremists who believed in violence. With his vowels short as his hair, it was easy to mistake Wellington for an Afrikaner. I believe he had friends in that community. He had an argument with the American lady on the subject. She disagreed with the system of apartheid. Wellington's riposte was that she had never been to South Africa, while he had and was therefore in a position to judge properly. The woman said, 'I've never been to the North Pole, Mr MacKenzie, but I know it's cold there.' This was the only time I heard anyone get the better of Wellington.

De Gaulle was an altogether subtler animal, with a good intellect, equal to the better teachers at Toronto. At least I'd say his reasoning was good but the conclusions suspect. He was, like Wellington, well over six feet tall but where the New Zealander emphasised his height with his erect bearing, De Gaulle stooped slightly. You wouldn't have caught the late French President doing that, even when being shot at, and my De Gaulle also wore spectacles all the time, but the nose and toothbrush moustache were the same. His brand of conservatism was more cerebral than Wellington's temperamental and instinctive belief in hierarchy, although, as with all of us, it was emotion and not reason at the bottom of it in the end. It was De Gaulle who asked me the dumb question in the van – his condescension brought him down to what he imagined was my level. He did have more of an interest in what was going on around him than Wellington. What he saw wouldn't change Wellington's thinking: it hadn't in 50 years, so why should it now? But given three months, I flatter myself I could have modified De Gaulle's thinking on the *malais* and Danu. As it was, the week he spent on Mrs Goreng's tour confirmed him in the ideas he had brought with him. He was a means justifies ends man. The author of what I later discovered to be a scholarly, if tendentious, account of US foreign policy since Korea, he expressed a fastidious regret for the instruments America had to work through but justified the excesses of the client governments by reference to the worse alternative of Marxist dictatorship. I thought it dishonest – comparing facts with a hypothesis. However, even if I'd had access to the book at the time – he gave a signed copy to Mrs Goreng when he left and another to the American woman journalist, which I accounted a waste – it would not have been wise to argue.

I think De Gaulle was an OK guy. At least, at the personal level there was some decency about him. It was just that he had strange ideas which took him into bad company. With Wellington, much of it was showing off – he liked to antagonise, to shock the liberal lobby back home. De Gaulle, I think, regretted alienating people.

The journalists were granted an interview with His Grace, the Bishop of Danu. This was no longer the wily old ecclesiastical politician from the metropole who had first closed down Martinho's seminary news-letter and then later, seeing which way the wind blew, had made an unholy, if tacit, alliance with Caesar in the shape of Osvaldo. He'd gone home after about a year of occupation. This wasn't because he didn't care for a hardship see, or because the *malais* had intimidated him. Danu had never been that easy for him, even though the people had taken to the saints and images of Catholicism with the usual zeal of the pagan at heart. He was a tough old fellow when it came to it – his older brother had been an artillery colonel – but his health was failing and I guess he felt a younger man would serve his flock the better in the iron times to come. Typically, he didn't care that the abdication might be interpreted in terms that were not personally flattering. The new man was a Danuese, Monsignor Teixeira. And he wasn't – how can I put it? perhaps best in the terms of FAKINTIL – a substantive bishop

381

but an acting one. He was the bishop designate, in expectancy of the see, but Rome hadn't confirmed him. How clever of Rome. In fact, the anomalous status gave him greater leeway. From his pulpit thundered the most extraordinary denunciations of violations and abuses. The position was clever. He did not attack the *fait accompli* of *malai* occupation. He merely condemned the actions which preserved that regime, and then only the worst. At the beginning, the *malais* had wiped out whole villages. Monsignor had not compromised. Not only did his broadsides provide the only small check there was against wholesale *malai* excesses, they alerted the population to what would have been kept secret. His pulpit was the only source of news in Danu. And he was fed the information from myriad channels, to be dispensed with the holy water on Sundays. Every month he'd read a list – it was a list of names of young men, and some women, who'd vanished from the face of the earth. In his strong voice, redolent of anger just kept in check, he'd read those names, among which had figured that of my friend Rosa Soares, christened Maria. And the list grew longer every time, for he didn't just read the new names but began with the first and proceeded to the newest, the tension in his cathedral growing as he reached the end of the litany of those whose names were already familiar and, without pause, added those of the latest. Many who had no belief, I among that number, packed into the house of God to hang on the words of his servant.

The *malais* dared not harm him.

It was the visitors who pressed for the meeting. The *malais* would never have initiated it. Mrs Goreng walked right into the German's trap – he'd wanted to pay her back – when he'd asked her as they walked down to the edge of the beach for a post-picnic swim, 'And are the people religious?' 'Oh, yes, very,' she answered, eager to inform on a harmless, non-specific matter, to say the Danuese were really good people, and to look down on them jointly, since she already knew Herr Speich was an atheist.

Kapow!

The journalists then wanted to talk to the 'Bishop', as he was such a vital figure.

Mrs Goreng had back-tracked desperately. He wasn't available.

Why not?

He was ill.

Then they would see his deputy.

No, he didn't want to receive them.

They'd like to ask him themselves.

Really, he was very hostile to foreigners.

Oh, we are quite thick-skinned, the journos chorused.

It became apparent they weren't quite the compliant, bought and paid for hacks the *malais* hoped they were. The more Mrs Goreng tergiversated, the greater grew the ardency of the reporters for an interview with the Monsignor. From being shifty Mrs Goreng started to become nervous and then irritable. 'Why you want see this stupid man?' she snapped, her grammar deteriorating with her temper.

'But Mrs Goreng,' the German said with a mild surprise that only a paranoiac could think assumed, 'you don't have to ask, surely? You are also a journalist.'

Well, she had to bite the bullet. They got what they wanted.

Monsignor was only too pleased to receive them. I went along for the ride; Mrs Goreng needed moral support and a straight guy to conduct an emergency dialogue with, if the need arose. The journos were all on their best behaviour, the American woman in stockings and a long dress, the men in long shirt sleeves. Going up the seminary hill to his Residence – I don't think one would be justified in calling it a palace, gracious old house that it was – I felt giddy. Not with height, but the changes I'd seen, not just in my own life but in the fortunes of Danu. We had to put the vehicle into second gear most of the way as we proceeded slowly but with great steadiness and sureness up the steep incline, the hill Arsenio and Osvaldo had walked to their lessons as boys, up which Martinho had run to Fr Molloy the day they burnt the FAKINTIL files while Danu lay concealed in smoke below, the hill Rosa claimed with scorn never to have walked in her life, except she was strongly there, too, in spirit.

The Bishop designate's secretary received us and asked us into his presence. He was a very small, very dark man, with straight hair, not at all mestizo-looking. I saw the American woman kiss his hand; so she was an RC, too. No refreshment was offered, not because Monsignor wished to be inhospitable but because he didn't feel it was appropriate to the place and time. He didn't trouble with small-talk, or asking if the visitors were comfortable, or enjoying their stay. He didn't talk about the weather. He began by saying that people were starving to death, and it got more pessimistic from then on: the resettlement camps, the ensuing dislocation which meant people could no longer grow their food, the dying children. Finally, Mrs Goreng could bear it no longer. All her hard work was coming down around her ears. 'Monsignor means the people are *spiritually* hungry,' she said with a bright and desperate smile. I winced – inwardly, of course; my outer expression was that of the adeptly dissimulating Chinaman, i.e., nothing showing. But Mrs Goreng then got help from an unexpected quarter; although maybe not totally surprising. Wellington, the New Zealander, said, 'That's right, padre,' and I again winced, 'you talk a great deal about material things. Wouldn't it be more appropriate for you to concentrate on the spiritual welfare of your people?'

Monsignor Teixeira said simply, 'If your belly is empty you think of your hunger, not God. Man cannot lead a spiritual life unless he is free of his body's demands.' He betrayed neither irritation nor sharpness.

Wellington said, 'Well, that's a novel piece of theology, Father. I don't know if it's the view of the Church, though.'

A silence followed. I could see the American woman was angry, but she didn't come to Monsignor's support. Monsignor indicated he was prepared to answer questions. Some desultory queries followed, the more intelligent ones from the German. At length Mrs Goreng terminated proceedings by saying, 'Well, we have taken up too much of Monsignor's time already.' Her whole manner said, 'told you so.'

Monsignor looked grim. He nodded to the journalists, putting his hands behind his back. As we were clattering down the worn red tiles of the corridor, a junior aide bumped into De Gaulle, apologising with great profuseness. I think we all felt more relaxed outside. Somehow – God knows why or how – it had turned into a victory for Mrs Goreng.

There remained another two nights of their stay. Colonel Goreng was to entertain them at home that evening. The Colonel was many things, but he was no hypocrite. He knew who he was and what he stood for, and he was not ashamed of it. He was himself before the journalists = which the General hadn't been – and because of that he came over well, that is unaffectedly. He unaffectedly frightened yours truly.

After a buffet *rijstafel* of gargantuan proportions – 30 dishes concluded with a chewy sweet much beloved of the *malais* which resembled nothing so much as toenail pie – the Colonel served Tia Maria which he and his wife thought the last word in cosmopolitan sophistication. The scenes of destitution which the journalists could not be prevented from glimpsing – it is impossible to put someone in a hermetic bubble all the time, even for ten days – had not apparently impaired their appetites. Each new delicacy was greeted with mock consternation and genuine appreciation – 'What *more*?' – but finally we retired to Colonel Goreng's 'den'. I'd never been in this room before. He kept it private; I liked to imagine for showing his cronies stag movies, but probably just for men's talk. In we filed, yours truly with some hesitation. This beast's lair was lined with the heads of beasts – tiger, rhino, and other exotics interspersed among the more usual deer trophies. Wellington's eyes lit up. He began to talk to the Colonel with animation I'd not seen before about hunting deer from helicopters in the South Island. He'd used an Armalite semi-auto on the creatures as they stampeded from crag to crag. Colonel Goreng smiled. I kept my face still. They don't shoot back at you, my friend, I thought. Not that a rifle round could beat gravity sufficiently to threaten a helicopter at 500 metres. The Colonel was thinking along the same lines as me. 'Hunt men make more interesting,' he said, with a smile.

The American woman was looking at the rhino. 'You've been to Africa, Colonel?' she enquired. He shook his head. 'Shoot at home,' he said. They all looked incredulous. Mrs Goreng was able to volunteer them some (absolutely correct) tourist information. 'We have tigers and rhinoceros in our country,' she said. 'We do not have to go to Africa.'

'Very small rhino,' the Colonel said. We examined it in detail. It was indeed small, as a species rather than because it was a young animal, but unmistakably a genuine 100 per cent authentic rhino's head. The German raised his eyebrows, but the Colonel didn't notice. After a while Mrs Goreng led the American woman out, leaving us males by ourselves. I don't think the female journalist would have gone if she'd known, but by the time she realised it was too late. The Colonel broke out whisky, which I wasn't offered. Wellington encouraged him to talk about his hunting exploits, not to flatter but out of genuine interest. Going to a locked cabinet, the Colonel pulled out a handsome rifle with a telescopic sight. I'd never seen a weapon like that before – only military rifles. The journalists, Speich included, hefted it with appreciation. 'English gun,' the Colonel said politely. He turned to Wellington, 'How many animals you kill?' Wellington hesitated. I guess he didn't actually know his bag. Colonel Goreng said with an earnestness that took away all boast, 'I kill 2,000 more.'

We digested the information.

Speich said gently, 'And men, Colonel? How many men have you killed in your life?'

Colonel Goreng said without hesitation, 'Seventy-nine.'

'With your own hand?' This was De Gaulle.

Goreng held up his right hand. He wagged his trigger-finger. 'This my own good hand. And two with knife – our knife.' He pulled open a drawer in which a dozen antique krisses were displayed. They really were beautiful objects. The foreigners all exclaimed. 'Magic knifes,' the Colonel said. 'Kill many men, make more stronger.' He shut the drawer and turned the key. Unlike the British rifle, these were not to be touched.

Speich said, 'You have killed for pleasure or necessity, Colonel?'

Goreng looked him in the eye. 'The same,' he said.

De Gaulle laughed nervously. 'Would you kill us if you had to, Colonel?'

Goreng looked him in the eye, which was the answer. It was a crass question – and an honest answer – but then there is nothing to say that very clever people can't be stupid when it comes to everyday human exchange. I stood by the door, making myself inconspicuous. I could sense the Colonel had got himself into a capricious and dangerous mood. I thought of him as the rhino: myopic, short-legged, thick-skinned, not too bright but with a mean temper, a surprising turn of speed over a short course, and, above all, a keen sense of smell. The Colonel gestured to me: I was to refill the glasses. No one refused. The Colonel started to talk about 1965-66, the terrible slaughter of Communists and Chinese by the army and their thug friends in sarongs. He said it was in response to a coup. A handful of Muslim Generals had been assassinated by the radicals – he himself, a captain then, had narrowly escaped such a fate when a gang with knives and spears had broken into his home. He had climbed over two garden walls. I thought the whole thing had been a set-up – to get rid of the old President and his Communist allies. But I kept my big mouth shut.

The Colonel was getting loquacious, relating his part in the anti-criminal campaign in *malai*-land two years back. I'd been in the jungle then. They'd targeted known hoodlums, sent plainclothes snatch-squads round – who wore cherry berets – and 'disappeared' the culprits.

'No more social problem,' the Colonel grinned. I was surprised he knew those words; he must have acquired them from his wife. Salon talk and murder.

In his pleasure at recounting his hunting exploits the Colonel had become indiscreet. The analogy was there to draw between what they were prepared to do at home and what they might contemplate doing out of sight in a subjected territory. I started to feel very uneasy. Speich, the German journalist, it had become clear, was the best at his job. He chose to sit still and let the Colonel run on. Any interruption might stop the flow, and if it gave the Colonel pause for thought, and the brain behind the little piggy eyes a chance to work, it might result in an enraged charge. Colonel Goreng was moving away from the details of the operation to talk about the Western concept of 'human rights', to mock it, to say what a ridiculous shibboleth it was when it stopped you defending the rights of those who weren't criminals, when Mrs Goreng knocked on the door. Had she guessed? Did she know her husband well enough to come to rescue him from the consequences of his own indiscretions? She could certainly see his face was flushed with liquor, in that typical Asian way. 'Oh, Colonel,' she said, 'Mrs Frewin is getting bored and so is Mrs Goreng.'

They all laughed, rather more heartily than the drollery warranted; so I was not the only one who felt awkward. We went into the garden, where Mrs Goreng showed them her flourishing orchids. 'But Adolph is the gardener,' she said. I did my level best not to look shifty.

'Where did you find them?' the American woman asked, expressing gracious interest. 'Oh, around,' I said.

'He doesn't want to give away his secrets,' Mrs Goreng said.

'You are right, *nonya*,' I answered.

Well, the evening dwindled into an exchange of inconsequentialities, skirting the more dangerous topics. At a relatively advanced hour, our guests were driven back to their hotel, probably alarming the Danuese in their beds, for the sound of motors in the curfew never augured well.

Next morning De Gaulle had a bombshell for Mrs Goreng, or what he thought would be a bombshell. We generally got to their place just as they were finishing breakfast. They'd be on cup three or four amid the toast fragments, still relaxed but just beginning to wake up to the day's promise, when Mrs Goreng and myself would join them for what was left of the luke-warm coffee. Today Mrs Goreng had bestowed her usual dazzling *malai* smile of white teeth on the Danuese teenager who had brought her a clean cup when De Gaulle said, 'Mrs Goreng, may I have a word with you?'

'Yes, of course, Dr Smithson,' she replied. 'What is it?'

Well, Mrs Goreng had a pretty good grasp of English – and her French was improving, too – but she was not well versed in the nuances of behaviour. De Gaulle meant, as you would realise, that he wanted to take her out of earshot and have a whisper. Naturally, he wanted to impress his colleagues, set up a little *frisson,* as he'd have put it. He was the kind of guy who liked to appear remote; aloof but capable of pulling strings. He must have enjoyed it when he was scoring off his pupils in his days as a college professor. He could, for instance, quite easily have taken Mrs Goreng aside later in the day and no one would have noticed. Now he tried to smile a discreet and ironic little smile. You could see he had altered his plan and would get her to herself later. The details of it all were a little mundane to him and he did not necessarily want to be implicated in them. But his colleagues had their curiosity whetted; they wouldn't let go. Most people wouldn't – what can be more tantalising than a secret mentioned then withheld? It's one of the things that don't change from childhood to adulthood – but worst of all for De Gaulle, his companions were, unlike him, real journalists. Speich, for instance, was a genuine investigator with some coups behind him, and they had the scent of something hot now. The pack wouldn't let go. 'Okay, okay,' De Gaulle said. He handed a twist of paper to Mrs Goreng. Speich barely restrained himself from grabbing it out of her hand. She held it this way and that, frowning. I knew she had this little vanity that she didn't like people to see her with her spectacles on. 'Adolph,' she said, 'I cannot understand this. Can you read it?'

'With pleasure, my lady.' And then I, too, found myself squinting and peering at it, turning the scrap this way and that.

'*Ja, ja,* permission.' Speich snapped the paper out of my fingers. His eyebrows rose. After a while he said, 'However, it is in Latin.'

De Gaulle was starting to enjoy himself again. He had an inkling he was the only one who could decipher the code. But aid came from an unlikely quarter. It was Wellington. It turned out he had had the rudiments of classicism flogged into him as a schoolboy. He said the first verb he'd learned was 'to love' and the first noun 'a table', bizarre beginnings to a vocabulary with no connection between the parts.

'Oh, I wouldn't say that,' I thought to myself, but kept quiet.

'Okay,' said Speich impatiently. 'But you can read this for sure?' Wellington was quite laid back, for him. He didn't say, 'Get lost, Kraut,' but just asked if he could borrow Speich's note-pad and ball-point. (Someone, probably a junior *malai* officer who knew the jungle, had stolen his impermeable paper earlier.) 'The secret is to be logical,' Wellington said.

'Like all empire-builders,' I couldn't resist adding. He ignored this. 'If you can find the subjects for the verbs, then their objects, everything else will agree with them, or not as the case may be.'

And to aid this he began numbering the main verbs. Ten minutes later we had a garbled appeal to the outside world from a Danuese patriot, mentioning injustices, famine, and the burning desire of a people to be free.

'Who gave you this?' Mrs Goreng asked sternly.

De Gaulle said, 'It sounds like Tacitus or Polybius, doesn't it? Strange how some things don't change. I like the list of happenings.'

'Dr Smithson, you must tell me who gave you this.'

De Gaulle smiled. 'It was given to me by someone who feels deeply on the subject,' he said.

Mrs Goreng was in no mood for intellectual badinage. She was a woman; she was a third worlder. That is, she was pragmatic by sex and had no time to waste on cerebral subtleties. De Gaulle obviously expected her to say something like: 'So much is evident from the content.' Instead she said grimly, 'Where did you get it?' He just grinned again.

Speich said, 'Mrs Goreng, you know that a good journalist always protects his source.' Speich was serious – being German – but he was also serious because he could see what was coming over the horizon looked like a storm. Mrs Goreng was relentless. She knew what she wanted and intended to get it. She ignored the games of men, of clever men from the world where they indulged in mind games for the sake of them. Her needs were basic and true.

'Who was the man who gave it to you? Was he maybe a woman?'

De Gaulle was starting to look a little harassed. He'd been stupid enough not to expect anything so crude, or so relentless. He didn't get much help or sympathy from the others. After a while Mrs Goreng seemed to drop it. You could see De Gaulle fervently hoped it wouldn't be broached again. Some chance! Mrs Goreng was just thinking, and her thoughts were hard and mean.

They were scheduled to pay a visit to another model resettlement village that morning – their last official tour. The *malais* attached a lot of importance to the foreigners going away thinking these places of starvation and imprisonment were little paradises of plenty and contentment. As the others were climbing into the van, Mrs Goreng said to De Gaulle, 'Colonel Goreng will grant you an interview.' Those were the words she used. 'Grant' and 'interview'.

Well, I saw De Gaulle's eyes widen in panic. What flashed through his mind? Did he think they were going to terminate him? Pull his fingernails out? 'I... ha...,' he actually stammered.

'We have a car here,' Mrs Goreng said. 'Adolph will guide your colleagues. We can all meet for lunch together at the beach.' If De Gaulle was expecting help from the others, he was deceived. I think he was thinking of saying something as bad as, 'Please don't leave me.'

Speich said, 'But this is not to be fair. He gets a scoop!' He laughed nastily. He didn't like De Gaulle at all. Why he said that, it wasn't as a protest; it was to land De Gaulle in the shit. They all got in, quite quickly. De Gaulle was too embarrassed to make a scene of it. I mean, people generally are. It's only the immediate, definite prospect of harm which will dissolve inhibition. If men with guns had come up to seize him, he'd have cried out shamelessly in his terror. But, real though his dread was to him, he was unwilling to make a fool of himself quite yet. I sneaked a look behind as we went off in a cloud of dust. Mrs Goreng was talking to him quite normally.

To cut a long story short, they did rejoin us at lunch-time, De Gaulle no longer looking shit-scared so much as downright shifty. He and Mrs Goreng sat down to the *alfresco* buffet without volunteering anything. But they weren't going to let him get away with it. The lady journo said, 'Come on, what happened, buster? Share a little news with your friends.'

Speich said, 'The Colonel has been showing you his human heads, yes?' (I didn't find that so funny, though no way was I going to tell them about how this least amiable aspect of Danuese traditional warfare had been continued by FAKINTIL.) De Gaulle grimaced. Mrs Goreng, instead of keeping quiet, said, 'The gentleman has not abused his position as our guest and we are grateful to him.'

'We are all the guests of your government, gracious madam,' Speich said, 'and we do not forget that fact.' He looked slyly at the others, 'How could we?' After a week the first cracks were appearing within the group and between the group and its organisers. Which was just why Mrs Goreng had not made the trip any longer. She knew. She'd done it. After a while – pleading the heat – she abandoned a sketchy meal for the shade of the beach hut reserved for senior *malais* and their friends. That gave the journos their opportunity to hound De Gaulle without restraint. It began half-jokingly, then turned unpleasant. Finally, Speich said, 'It was from one of the priests, I think without doubt?' De Gaulle reacted like a sullen schoolboy; the august professor had gone for a while. 'Think that if you want.'

'So I am correct?'

'That's not what I said, and you know it.'

But Speich's arrow, fired I won't say in the dark but certainly the gloom, appeared to have hit its mark. De Gaulle looked agitated.

'You told them who gave the note to you?' the American lady asked in a tone of high disbelief. Speich had decided to do a double act with her, for he remarked, 'Ja, that he has done. So why the big scruple to tell us? We don't shoot him.'

'You bastard,' she said, 'you *bastard.*' She got up and walked away. Speich went with her. After a while all of the others, except Wellington, followed. Wellington always had a large appetite; he'd piled fruit simultaneously on to his plate with the meat and rice, instead of having it separately as a dessert. And he kept chewing, though he didn't look at De Gaulle. I kept my head down and pretended to be consuming the scraps left on my dish. I don't believe Wellington stayed to give De Gaulle moral support. He wanted to eat and he didn't give a damn two ways anyhow.

De Gaulle had, indeed, incriminated one of Monsignor's aides, the one who had knocked into him. I guess he'd picked De Gaulle as the most sympathetic and scholarly-looking. He would have done a lot better with Speich, but the burly, moustached German didn't look very sentimental. They could have done without De Gaulle's sentiment. He'd told Colonel Goreng everything in under five minutes. Well, why? I tried to figure him out; he was by no means the worst of the bunch. I didn't come up with a theory immediately, though I had hunches which were difficult to put into words. There were two separate actions: disclosing the note and then informing on its author to the *malais,* though the young priest was doomed the moment he selected his man with his eyes. I think De Gaulle produced the note because he was bored, firstly, but mainly for self-aggrandisement. He wanted

393

to be the centre of the group's attention. It was a dramatic gesture, a revelation; it put him in a position of power, if only for a moment, but he liked that position and his primacy had been denied in that group of irreverents. You might think I'm adumbrating the psychology of three-year-olds in the kindergarten. Believe me, intellectual age has little to do with emotional maturity. The behaviour of the clever is far from complex; it's simple, if you see through the glosses. As to snitching on the donor, he excused himself to the others later, in my earshot, by saying his loyalties really were to his hosts. Besides, he was against Communism. I buy that, to an extent. He was also intimidated by Goreng – especially the previous evening. I knew how it worked. The subtle mind used against itself by the simple mind. Maybe the Colonel had intimated how easy it was to have an accident on the awful Danu roads. And the *malai* Colonel, with his dead animals and knives and his talk of the men he'd killed, was scary. Goreng had dominated him with his will.

Funnily enough, De Gaulle was one of the better behaved of the gang in all other respects. Group comportment had deteriorated by the day, with yours truly bearing the brunt of the collective delinquency. In a nutshell, they behaved like spoiled kids. Mrs Goreng had been too kind to them in the sense of what to expect. It wasn't New York; it wasn't the Florida Keys, but they expected the standards of those places. Complaint after complaint I had to deal with: the bed too hard, the air-conditioner whistled (me, I was surprised it worked), a spider in the goddamned bath. If she had taken a tougher line with them at once, they would have known where to stop. But granted total freedom, they made pains in the asses of themselves. Individually, they were mature, intelligent human beings; collectively, they were the fifth grade in Disneyland. And I was not in the position to show the sternness which would have nipped it all in the bud. They'd just have complained to Mrs Goreng about me, and then there would have been hell to pay. I would have been the scapegoat for anything bad they wrote afterwards. I just had to grin and bear it.

So I was not sorry to see them go. De Gaulle, who had never murmured about leaking taps or malodorous drains, remained somewhat out of favour with the group for the short time remaining. He bore his unpopularity with the stoic dignity of a Consul discovering himself amidst epigones in a barbarous province.

Just before they left, Speich called me to his room. He had been unhappy about efflorescent damp. But this time it was to shove US$50 into my hand.

'Tuan,' I said, with unfeigned feeling. I forgave him instantly for changing rooms three times.

'You like me to take a letter to any friend? Or a message for anyone – anyone you know?'

I knew what he was saying. I did trust him; I thought he was tough but straight. But I didn't like the terrible risk. 'No, tuan,' I said. He looked at me and understood. I didn't think I saw condemnation in his eyes. I turned at the door and said, 'Just write the truth, tuan Hans, that will be the message.' It was what I'd said to Bill Mabbeley.

Speich said, 'Truth is relative, Mr Ng. Like beauty it is in the eye of the beholder.'

TWENTY-SIX

ON THE SEMINARY HILL A STRANGE EDIFICE had been constructing over the last previous months. First to be built was a concrete block-house, reinforced with metal struts, which it soon became apparent was a large pill-box to protect whatever it was that was going to go up. They dug solid foundations, spending a lot of time pouring concrete into four pits. I found it odd that they were building on the most exposed and inconvenient site on the hill, though the view was no doubt prodigious. Then a lot of girders arrived, by the monthly cargo ship, the Lumba (meaning 'dolphin', though there was nothing in the least sleek about its ugly, orange-streaked lines). The lorries toiled steadily up the hill, occasionally shedding part of their loads. One girder sailed straight over the sheer drop at a bend where Rosa used to make my heart enter my mouth, plunging for all the world like some bolt of Jehovah's vengeance a metre into the earth of the football field below where its shaft stuck up angrily for some days. Yet, barring the little mishaps, always a feature of Danu life, the work progressed. After a while we realised that the girders were not a skeleton for something fancier but the thing itself. It was some kind of an observation post or mast. By the half-way stage it was apparent to the dimmest Danuese that it was a communications antenna. The man of the world was not as interested as he should have been; I had become quicker in some respects, mostly practical, but the price for this had been to lose the ability to make other connections. I thought it was military – to allow the top brass at home a more direct control. Other Danuese, particularly the ex-FAKINTIL in the *malai* battalions, thought it was to help planes to home in more accurately. And we were all wrong.

It was a TV mast.

The General had decided to put *malai* transmissions into the island. At a stroke he was lifting the ban on radios and newspapers. No half-way house: from silence to incessant blare.

Mrs Goreng passed the news on to me. She was plainly delighted. 'Civilisation, Adolph!' she said. 'We are bringing Danu into the 20th century.' Now where had I heard that before? But I humoured her; and, in truth, I was a little pleased myself. I guess it was kind of a bribe to the populace from the *malais;* most important, it was a sign of normalisation, of assimilation.

Martinho was not pleased. He saw it as a deliberate insult to the Church, a kind of Satanic Cross on the hill. Nor was he at all anxious that 'corrupting' programmes be beamed at the impressionable population of Danu. He thought it a punishment for the note the young cleric had tried to smuggle out via De Gaulle. Not that he harboured any sympathy for that foolish act. He said to me, 'It's all over, Adolph. We have to make the best of what we have.' That summed up my attitude, too. On the other hand, unlike him, I was not proud of the motto. It seemed a poor thing to have descended to.

I knew the completion of the antenna would not go unmarked by a celebration. By nature the *malais* were heavily into festivals, and this was a landmark in the history of their presence. It was the extent of the thing which surprised me.

They were still security conscious, but it wasn't possible to disguise the progress made on the mast. I mean, you could see it going up on the hill above you. They couldn't put a cloth over it, you know, like I had that night when the Corporal rushed, parang drawn, into my room at the O. T. X-Ray.

Some five days after the last girder had gone up – it was more than 50 metres high – Mrs Goreng came to me, eyes alight and finger on her lips. 'Adolph, *he* is coming! The big man!' After a few seconds' thought I realised that she meant their President, that is the former General who was dictator with the continuing consent of their other commanders. Well, thought I to myself, isn't this something. That put the cork in the bottle, so far as the Danuese were concerned. Mrs Goreng said, 'It's a secret, Adolph.' I could see she was feeling she shouldn't have told me, but I knew she trusted me better than anyone else. More than she did the other army wives. '*Nonya*,' I said, 'you can rely on me.'

'Oh, I know that, Adolph,' she said, half-apologising for hurting my delicate faggot feelings. It was a strange relationship we had, half-slave, half-best friend and confidant. She went the whole way now: 'He'll pull the switch for the first television transmission to Danu, and that will also be the moment Danu is absorbed into the republic as the 58th province. The whole proceedings will be filmed here and transmitted simultaneously all over the archipelago.'

'Holy shit!'

'I beg your pardon, Adolph?'

'Nothing, *nonya*, I was just surprised a little.'

'Things are changing, Adolph. You know, something can begin badly but end well. Everyone makes mistakes.'

Mistakes! The atrocious deeds they'd committed! But I remembered who and where I was. What she'd said was the nearest to regret and apology I ever heard from a *malai*. So I bowed my head.

They couldn't keep it airtight, of course. The extra security alone showed that an important event was brewing. Personally, I'd not have made any heavyweight preparations but avoided giving any clues until the last moment. But that was just the way I'd learned to think in the mountains. I didn't think like a *malai* regular.

Two days before the President's visit they began to dress the mast like a Christmas tree. Long strings of coloured bulbs wound back and forth through the girders. They fixed a podium, stands, and some banners. The day of the opening of Danu to the emissions of the outside world, a couple of ancient boats gurgled alongside the wharf, bearing a crowd of stage extras from the outlying, historically *malai* islands. They were making a bundle of money these days, one way or another. The Danuese allowed to participate were few in number and rigorously selected, mostly the same 'chiefs' who had voted for assimilation into the *malai* republic in the show referendum of a few weeks back. Well, they marched them to the top of the hill and they marched them down again. And when they were down they were down, and when they were up they were up, and when they were only half-way up they were neither up nor down. It was nothing; it was a bluff; it was a dress rehearsal. It was all of those things.

I doffed my cap to Goreng and his superiors. They had wanted to lure FAKINTIL into showing its hand. And nothing had happened. They weren't quite so stupid as to believe wholly their own propaganda. This had been a safety-check.

Thirty-six hours later the Big Man himself arrived by Air Malai DC-10. No announcement. We saw the big white bird bank over the town, and then land at the new military airfield. I don't believe Mrs Goreng had known either, until

398

she saw the jet. You never saw such a frenzy as her frantic rush to dress herself, me pulling outfits from the wardrobe, she rejecting them as fast as they landed on the bed, trying on and discarding until she stood there in a stew of irritation and indecision in nothing but bra and panties. Well, that was one for the album: the ex-FAKINTIL sapper together with the *malai* Colonel's wife, half-naked in her boudoir. Finally, she left for the airfield in a pale-green safari suit, which marked her a soldier's wife but distinguished her from the lesser spouses.

'You look fine,' I reassured her.

'Only fine?' she remonstrated, half-seriously.

After she had roared off, it was one of those days when I had the house to myself. The other servants were at market or running errands. On these days I never snooped. The idea of breaking into the Colonel's den never occurred to me – it was just too plain terrifying. Instead, I cut back some of the more boisterous forest plants in my garden. It was a riotous success now. You expected Tarzan to come swinging through the bushes after Jane. I guess I was fairly content – bored sometimes, but happy to be alive and eating properly. All that would change.

I wasn't on the hill that evening but Mrs Goreng sent me to one of the big communal TVs they had set up on poles in the Praça. I half-hoped, half-dreaded the mast would go up in sparks and a bang when the Big Man pulled the lever; that FAKINTIL had found a way to wrap half a dozen shearing charges around the legs. But no; watching in the big square, simultaneous with the lights suddenly sparkling like unsupported, autonomous constellations way above us, the fuzz of the TV screen resolved into the big, broad, beaming face of the *malai* President. There were three *malai* personnel carriers in the centre of the Praça and a company of troops at one end. But the revelation of the Big Man's round features above us might have been the full moon appearing to a pack of wolves, for the bolder souls watching started to bay abuse in Danuese. This was incomprehensible to the *malai* captain, though he was left in no doubt of the crowd's sentiment, for he frowned and fingered his white baton. It was a difficult choice for him. A year earlier and maybe even yesterday, he'd have been more likely to fire into the crowd than order tear-gas or a charge. But tonight of all nights they had to act against their immediate inclinations. Firing in the square below would not have impressed the President overly. And the General and Goreng would likely have shot the itchy-fingered culprit themselves. Crowds possess great wit; the group throws up nicknames of an aptness and ingenuity the clever individual by himself could never invent. So it was now. We knew we were safe, so long as they couldn't spot individuals and target them for later, and in the darkness the Danuese let the *malais* know what they thought of them. Someone sang 'O, Mighty Mountain!' And other voices joined her.

It wasn't until two a.m. that I saw the Gorengs. I didn't spoil their evening by mentioning what had happened in the Praça. She was glowing; bright-eyed and excited. I think she'd had something to drink. And the Colonel was smiling. The President had congratulated him. The First Lady hadn't been there or Mrs Goreng would have been reintroduced to her. But she had flirted with the Big Man. At least that's what she hinted to me. And the Colonel had grinned and encouraged it. 'What about you, Adolph? Did you like the TV?'

'It was wonderful, *nonya*.' I was lying, of course. Most of the transmission had been pictures of *malai* soldiers back home in *malai*-land, strumming guitars in their uniforms, singing with their arms round each other, carrying kids, helping old ladies. It made you want to puke.

'So that's the first time you've seen television? It's the first time he's seen television, Colonel.'

Now I could tell she was really quite drunk. I wasn't even offended; just disgusted with her. The pictures others carry of you – it's not even funny.

Well, the TV we had wasn't our own. We were just picking up the *malai* national programme. There was no studio in Danu, not even for a little 15-minute slot on

Sundays. I know Martinho had been hoping for a religious programme. He didn't even get that. Every evening there'd be jostling in the Praça to get the nearest pitch to one of the big sets. This wasn't North American type viewing in the privacy of your own living-room but a communal participation. The audience no longer heckled the *malais* but enjoyed the programmes, calling out comments, arguing with each other. And the *malais* on duty, in white helmets, white gloves, and white gaiters, they also hung around the back of the crowds to sneak a look, instead of doing a beat of the whole square. What a great success it all was.

Three weeks later the Gorengs' son arrived. I believe the Colonel now thought things so pacified that it was safe and expedient to bring his oldest child out for a vacation. It put his dick where his mouth was, if you'll be kind enough to excuse the expression. He hoped it would be his last sharp-end posting; that he'd get a nice political appointment with the chance to make a lot of bucks. Before then, he wanted Junior to see Dad's moment of glory. He wanted him to see his Father in a shooting war. Goreng, I should have said, in common with his peers, lagged 50 years behind the rest of the century in his sense of the male sex. I'd realised that long ago, but it took the arrival of the boy to truly bring it home.

We flunkeys were all at the front door to receive the family from the airfield. Master Goreng was eleven and a half-years-old.

'This is Kaptan, Adolph,' his mother said. 'And, Kaptan, shake hands with Adolph.'

The Colonel looked indulgently on all this.

'Is he a servant, or what?' Kaptan asked and, in *malai*, I said, 'I am the servant of your father and mother, Kaptan, and your servant, too.' When I say that 'Kaptan' did not mean 'captain' but meant 'hawk' perhaps I have told you all you need to know about the Colonel's attitude to his son's upbringing and his expectations of him. If those primitive attitudes hadn't also been the determining factor in my own fate I would have found it as ludicrous and pitiful as I do now.

401

In fact, Kaptan was not such a bad boy. It wasn't his fault that powerful and doting parents had systematically brought out the worst in him. He was as capricious and manipulative as his mother could be on her bad days and as violent and arbitrary as his father. Then, at moments, he could also manifest his child's natural sweetness. As Raoul would not have been ashamed to put it, he was like a wild young colt. However, these were not to be total days of vacation for him. Both the Colonel and Mrs were insistent that he do well at school – his father had the elite military academy at Randung in mind for him and maybe America later, too. Mrs, for her part, didn't want a culture-less idiot for progeny but someone she could talk to as an adult: i.e., she didn't want someone too like his father. The homework lessons he'd brought with him didn't find a great deal of favour in her eyes. There was quite a quantity of useless crap in there, based on the *malai* five constitutional principles of justice, tolerance etc. Mrs Goreng didn't want Sonny wasting his time on that nonsense; *she* knew it was a pile of meaningless shit, though she couldn't actually say so. Kaptan was to apply himself to something useful.

I would give him English lessons.

Mrs Goreng presented the idea like she was doing me a big favour, giving me the chance to teach the future *malai* President.

'What's wrong?' she enquired, noting my lack of alacrity. 'You don't want to?'

'Oh, no, *nonya*,' I hastened to say, 'I would be honoured. It's…just that I don't think my English is so good any more. It was years since I was in America.'

'Nonsense. The American lady told me it was perfect, much better than Herr Speich's or even the New Zealand gentleman.'

Did she now, I thought.

'Anyway, I thought it was Canada where you studied.'

'You are right, *nonya*, it was Canada.'

So that was how I came to sit at the Gorengs' dining-table with Master Goreng and Longman's standard conversational texts before us. Mrs Goreng had not wanted Kaptan to learn American English.

'Don't worry,' I said, 'I was taught by a Balliol man.'

Mrs Goreng didn't ask what that was, and I am damn sure she had no idea.

At first, Kaptan was unwilling to give his attention. He threw one of the books on the floor. I resolved to assert my authority from the beginning, or I would be trampled underfoot by even this most junior member of the Goreng clan. 'Pick it up,' I said.

'Why? You can't tell me to.'

'Because if you don't, I'll tell your mother.'

Kaptan did not look impressed. I thought again. 'You pick it up, or I'll say you wet your bed.'

'But I haven't.'

'No, but I'll make it wet.'

'I'll tell Ma.'

'She won't believe you. And I'll also let a spider into your room. There.'

Kaptan digested this. Lies and blackmail, overt blackmail, were new to him from an adult. So, after all, I was educating him. I said, 'Be a good boy and we can do our lessons at the beach. Now pick the book up. That's right. Then we have made a new start.'

I got Mrs Goreng's agreement on the lessons, after an initial wavering. 'It's *conversation*, *nonya*, not grammar,' I argued. 'Let it take place in a natural environment.'

'All right, but don't tell Colonel Goreng. And Adolph...'

'Yes?'

'You must not, you know, touch Kaptan.'

'*Nonya!*' I exclaimed – and my outrage was genuine.

'Oh, all right, I'm sorry, Adolph.'

So to the beach Kaptan and I would go, or walk around the garden, pulling out weeds, me trimming back the undergrowth while he handed spare tools up the ladder. All the time we would talk in English. 'The men *who* bring the water, Kaptan. Not the mens which bring the waters.' He'd grin and refuse to repeat the correct words, but he'd get it

403

right next time he used them. That wondersome facility of the young. Later, I heard Mrs Goreng coaxing Kaptan to say a few foreign sentences in front of his father. 'You see,' I overheard her say through the half-closed door, 'I told you he could be useful.' This semi-audible remark made me uneasy – that there had been debate at all on my utility – so much so that I wished I had never heard it. I tried to convince myself that she had said, 'I told you *it* would be useful,' referring to the accomplishment rather than the teacher. I wondered if it was so smart to allow Kaptan to make such good progress. There was another problem: he was becoming quite attached to me, in the way that children – especially the privileged children of the East – do become attached to their servants. It is more common with female servants and younger children but far from unknown with older kids like Kaptan. I think the problem was he couldn't get close enough to his father at an important time in his life; he was frightened of the Colonel, and I don't blame him. He was at that hero-worshipping age. He particularly admired his mother's one-armed chauffeur. This soldier had let him load his pistol and point it empty. I thought how Kaptan would have loved Arsenio. Now that would have been interesting. But, in the absence of anyone more suitable, he transferred his attachment to the unlikely figure of yours truly. What was it Maria had called me? 'One of life's scoutmasters'? I was Unca Donald and I had a new junior woodchuck.

TWENTY-SEVEN

THE MAST HAD BEEN UP THREE MONTHS and Kaptan still had one week of his vacation left when Osvaldo made his move. True to form, he attacked at an unexpected moment. He chose daylight. Six years ago he'd attacked the town by darkness, the night he'd stolen Maria and me. I guess he figured the malais would be less alert in the torpor of the mid-afternoon, while darkness was still not so far away that it couldn't cloak his escape. I don't know if he realised it either, but the Danuese would not have taken kindly to having their programme wiped off the air-waves midway through.

Mrs Goreng was at a mah-jong party at the General's residence. At half past three Kaptan and I should have been reading from one of the textbooks but, in fact, I was lying in the Colonel's hammock while Kaptan, with his inexhaustible energy, was trying to catch frogs. Four sharp explosions rent the air overhead with their tearing cracks. I had my feet on the ground as the echoes came back. I hadn't had to think. The old reactions died hard, if they would ever perish at all. And I knew at once what had happened. I ran into the house and upstairs into Mrs Goreng's dressing-room, which commanded the best view. On the seminary hill was no more mast. Just a settling cloud of dust. It looked as if it had gone straight over the side and into the valley. 'Cordtex,' I said to myself.

'What is that, Adolph?'

'Nothing to concern you, young Master.'

I began to think of other things. 'Come away from the window, Kaptan.'

'Why?'

'Just do as I say.'

'Is there going to be fighting?'

'I hope not.'

'I hope so.'

The other servants were twittering like Danu sparrows downstairs. I ordered them to fasten all windows – much good that would do – draw the curtains, and stay out of sight. Myself, I peered out of the front gate, and acknowledged the two white-helmeted sentries in their box. They looked on edge. I decided to keep away from them. Then I let the dogs off their chains. A few minutes later came the first gun-fire. It was some distance away. I found the staff lying on the floor. Kaptan was wearing a plastic GI's helmet and putting a roll of caps into a toy gun. I took the hat off his head and placed the gun in a drawer. 'Stay quiet and everything will be all right,' I told the staff. I fervently trusted that would be the case. As usual, the sound of the shooting gave you no clear picture of what was happening; the bursts, however heavy, and the ragged, irregular intervals between them were quite meaningless. I thought that if FAKINTIL were confining themselves to bringing the mast down, then they would be just escaping now, shooting their way out of town. But the reports were getting louder. I hoped it was my imagination.

There was nothing imaginary about the shooting which erupted in the street outside. We all stuck our noses that much deeper into the Colonel's Sumbanese rugs. The maid crept under a wicker sofa. There followed an explosion, and another a few seconds later. The windows shook. Grenades, I was certain. The firing stopped. I could hear the gate being kicked. It seemed to resist. Three evenly spaced single shots. It creaked open, and the sound was worse than the bangs. I lay like a fool, my heart pounding into the floor. The front door opened. I had forgotten to lock that. Then I became angry. And even as I did I was astounded at myself. I wasn't angry with the attackers, not with the *malais*, not even with my stupid self but with the whole situation. I knew that if I did not act, things were set so that we would be annihilated with no time for questions or replies. The grenade would come in and then they'd spray what was left of us. I got up, without excessive trepidation, and opened the door of the room. The others just looked at me as they lay. I called out quickly, 'Don't shoot, don't shoot. There's no one armed. I am a Danuese.'

Silence followed. I could imagine them looking at each other. I said again, my voice a little higher, 'There are no *malais* here, just us servants. Don't hurt us.'

From just round the corner of the hallway, probably by the teak chest on which Mrs Goreng kept a vase of orchids and three US *Vogue*, a voice said, 'Show yourself.'

I said, 'Well, don't shoot me.' My lips were dry now.

'Come slowly and your hands in the air.'

'I am coming now. Please don't do anything. I'm a Danuese.'

And as I rounded the corner there were three human skeletons waiting for me, wicked imps from the centre of the earth, eyes glowing like the demons of *malai* puppetry in the grizzled mass that was their beards and hair. I had never seen human beings so emaciated. They hardly seemed able to bear their weapons. They were not dressed in the remnants of FAKINTIL olive but sarongs and dirty T-shirts. The leader said, 'You look fat, Chinaman.'

It was the Corporal.

I looked at him as if he were a zombie. He looked like a famine victim or someone from a concentration camp. Had I looked like that? But it was one of them who said, 'We thought you were dead.'

'Not yet,' I said.

'Who's here?'

'The house belongs to a *malai* Colonel. But there's no one here, just the servants. Have you taken out the guards?'

The Corporal nodded. But he told one of the three, 'Go to the gate and keep a look out.'

I could now see his two men were very young, though not quite boys, then that they were two of my old woodchucks. The Corporal went into the lounge. The servants were still on the floor. He looked at Kaptan. 'Who is he?'

I didn't answer.

'Come here, kid.'

Kaptan looked blankly at him. It was plain he didn't understand Danuese.

'This is the big *malai's* kid, right?'

'Yes, but he's just a boy.'

'So are my boys.'

The Corporal pulled Kaptan to his feet. Kaptan looked very scared. It had stopped being a game. I followed them out. The young guerrilla waiting looked anxious. I could see he wanted to get the hell out of it. I accompanied them into the street where they rejoined the boy who'd been standing look-out. The sentry box was burning on its side from the phosphorus grenade they'd posted into it. There were two bodies, one helmet, still pristine white, lying in the road. We trotted along the side, under the shelter of the trees. It was still a very pleasant suburb. The Corporal had Kaptan by the arm. Once Kaptan turned to look at me, his eyes full of appeal, but he stumbled and the Corporal pulled him roughly up. Dumb kid. What was I supposed to do?

We were heading into town again. I caught the Corporal up and pointed this out. He was a Bacalhau man, of course; didn't know this part of Danu at all. 'Bear right here,' I told him. My breathing was not too good – I'd led a soft life these past months. 'You can get to the high ground this way without going into town again.' The two boys agreed; they were very nervous. In their place I would be, too. It was strange to see them grown older, and more familiar with the Corporal, whom they'd always feared, than me, their old mentor. Now I led the way – which was not so bright, after all. I'd be first to catch it. And I hoped the Corporal had noticed I'd said '*you* can get to high ground' and not 'we can get to high ground'. I now knew the last thing in the whole world I wanted was to go into the mountains again with FAKINTIL. I'd rather be a slave in comfort than endure those conditions of freedom. Until now I'd never consciously posed that choice to myself. I might even have griped about my existence with the Gorengs and thought wistfully of alternatives. That life seemed sweet enough now.

The Corporal and his boys were armed with M-16s, not our old G3s. I guess they must have used all the NATO calibre ammo by now and have replenished with 5.56 mm weapons, either supplied by deserters in the Danuese battalions or captured. More likely the former. The Corporal was also carrying his trusty parang. I figured they'd infiltrated into Danu in ethnic costume, though their appearance was that of wild men from the outer reaches. The bizarre thing was, I don't think they realised this.

There was no one around. The townspeople had learned the hard way that curiosity killed the cat – you stayed indoors if there was trouble. We padded through those quiet, leafy roads in utter silence. There'd been no shooting for a long while. That I didn't like.

A little further on the quiet was broken by the rumble of a truck. We scrambled into the drainage ditch. 'Kaptan,' I whispered into his ear, 'please stay quiet.'

'That's right,' the Corporal growled, not understanding the words but knowing very well their import, 'keep your face shut.' He put his dirty hand over the frightened boy's mouth. Kaptan resisted, because it was unpleasant, but I shook my head and he subsided. The vehicle passed the end of the road but it didn't turn toward us. It was an armoured personnel carrier with a 20mm weapon-fit in a turret. We came out of the ditch, moving now with a lot more urgency. Very soon after, a file of *malai* troops passed at the other end of the road. We dove again. I was starting to get that unreal sense, the dream feeling I'd had on invasion day all that time ago; the idea that it wasn't really me who was going through all this. For sure, I was terribly confused. With all my heart I hated the *malais*. Yet I didn't feel part, either, of this desperate band, fleeing through these quiet suburbs. I wanted to find myself a quiet corner and curl up in it.

Just as we scrambled out of the ditch again, one of the woodchucks dropping his black rifle and barely managing to grab the sling as it slid back into the foul water, a straggler from the *malai* patrol crossed the road 150 metres away, looked to his left and saw us. He didn't react at all strongly. In fact, I think he was turning to look the other way. Maybe the disguise was better at distance than I was prepared to believe. Unfortunately, the boy who had dropped his rifle now brought it smartly to his shoulder and loosed off three shots, incidentally missing with all of them. The *malai* jumped a mile – you could see he'd nearly had a heart-attack – before heading for the ground, shouting our number and whereabouts to his friends. As we tumbled into the ditch again, half the contents of his magazine went overhead, knocking paint, rust, and sparks off the gate of the house behind. We scurried along the ditch, doubled over. It was good protection, but for how long?

The Corporal stopped, ordering the boy who'd fired to go

back to the spot and engage the *malais* as they came down the road.

You got us into this, was my uncharitable thought, now you hold the fort while we climb out of it. The boy looked shit-scared, but obeyed. From the other end of the road came a truly dismaying sound: the powerful motor of an APC being revved. The Corporal's face said it all.

I wasn't prepared to die in a ditch, though. I shouted, 'Over the wall, on each other's shoulders.' Behind us, the boy who was our rearguard had opened fire, in well-schooled three-round bursts. I pushed Kaptan up the bank with my palm in the seat of his pants. Under the circumstances I think his mother would have permitted it. We were at the corner of an 'L' formed by the two roads down which the *malais* were coming. I could see the boy holding the post would be flanked by the APC which would be able to put in fire straight down the line of the ditch. I took the Corporal's rifle and crouched down. He was extraordinarily light on my shoulders. His black toes flexed and he was up. It was a good thing there was no broken glass embedded in the concrete. I passed his M-16 up. Then Kaptan baulked at the wall. I shook my head: 'Your father's people can't see who you are. They'll shoot you, too.' He hauled himself up, refusing the Corporal's arm.

I was damned if I was going to be last. I gestured to the remaining woodchuck to crouch. He staggered as I clambered on, but stayed upright. The Corporal was still on the wall, all credit to him, legs astride as if he was riding a motorbike. He offered his right leg to the woodchuck. The firing from our rearguard had stopped. Holding the wall carefully, I leaned across and saw he was not dead but changing magazines.

'Please, Senhor Ng.'

It was the boy under me. I took his rifle. I was surprised he remembered my name. He took a run at the wall and missed the Corporal's leg. Panic welled up in his eyes. The Corporal swore as only he knew how. 'Run up the wall, son of a bitch, and grab my foot.' The boy's run up was limited by the ditch behind, but this time he managed to plant a foot on the wall and grab the Corporal. As he came to the parapet, the APC turned down the road. I dropped off the wall. Simultaneous with that, the *malais* opened fire, hitting the boy still on the wall. The impact of the rounds knocked him over on top of Kaptan. I could hear Kaptan whimper as he pushed the dead woodchuck frantically from him. When he stood there was blood all over the white shirt his mother had dressed him in that morning. Still sitting as if he was in the saddle, the Corporal loosed off a defiant burst, then swung over and down to us. He'd timed it right, for the whole of the top of the wall then disintegrated in a shower of fragments and dust. The noise of the 20mm cannon was deafening. We made it round the side of the house, unlocked the back door and got into the street behind. No *malais*. I was aware of the firing in the road we'd left, mostly the muted thunder of the APC's automatic cannon drowning any small-arms fire. I was leading now, the Corporal hopelessly lost. I put 50 metres of road behind us, then turned left down a footpath, figuring the best thing was to jink cross country, not lay a straight path. I looked behind. The Corporal had two M-16s by the carrying handles in his right and was holding Kaptan's hand with the left. It looked like Father taking Sonny for a walk. I slung the woodchuck's rifle on my own shoulder. It was so light, compared to the heavy-duty G3, that I'd been able to forget I was carrying it. It felt familiar – the reassurance of a weapon on the shoulder. I assumed there were a few rounds left in the magazine. The firing behind us had stopped. I guess the boy had been no match for the APC. Into a garden we plunged, across a low wall, into another. 'Where are we?' the Corporal asked hoarsely.

'There is a main road soon, which goes up to the pass, but it has no cover.' The Corporal digested this. I had a closer look at him. He didn't look well, his eyeballs were an unhealthy yellow. I wondered if he had hepatitis. The era of Maria was long past for them. But I thought also – this is not the first time I have fled for my life with this man, who is brave and loyal if he is also stupid. Kaptan seemed in better shape than either of us. 'You are doing well, Kaptan,' I told him, which was a strange thing to say, when this was no co-operative venture but a kidnapping in which his complicity and enthusiasm were hardly assured. But he brightened at these words of encouragement, for their kindly tone more than their meaning.

The Corporal said, 'We will have to lie low and wait for dark. It won't be long.'

'Here?'

'Why not?'

'No, OK, it just seems strange – someone's garden.'

He shrugged. I don't think he had any idea what I meant. Cover was cover. I was glad to stay and rest at first, but after a few minutes I became unbearably nervous. Movement acted as a kind of therapy. When we heard dogs barking the Corporal's nerve cracked too. Away we went, the Corporal talking about getting into a drainage ditch to hide our scent.

Bad move. The roads were swarming with *malais*. We were now on the glossy blacktop that led towards the army laundry, Rosa's old crèche. We got under a flat little concrete bridge that was the driveway into someone's garage. From its shelter the Corporal and I stuck our snouts up. A squad was coming our way. We got into the shadows. The Corporal was gasping. For some reason he was more scared than I was, and I was very frightened. I guess the surroundings were more familiar to me. He held the parang to Kaptan's throat, drawing a finger across his own. I could see his diseased eyeballs glowing in the gloom. Poor Kaptan. I heard the *malais'* boots overhead. We held our breath. They went on, without breaking step. After a few minutes we all started to move along the ditch. The sun was now down but there was still plenty of light. We crawled out of the drain, saw the coast clear, and ran down the road together. Rosa's old place was a couple of hundred metres away. After that, it was straight on and up to the hill pass. We trotted on. Just as we were coming up to the laundry, Kaptan broke free of the Corporal and ran down the side of the building. The

Corporal was after him at once. There was a lot of washing on the lines, which they had to dodge around. Kaptan tripped on a green hosepipe, and went flying forwards on his face, and the Corporal, trying to stop too quickly, also skidded and fell on his side, the two rifles he was carrying sliding across the bald lawn. He drew his parang, lining Kaptan up with his clenched left fist for the blade blow with the right. I was behind a dripping blanket folded in half over the line. I shouted, 'Stop!' and almost immediately pressed the trigger of the M-16. Nothing happened. The Corporal looked at me in amazement. I also froze. Then he dropped the parang to fumble in his sarong. I looked for the bolt of the gun desperately, ham-fisted with the unfamiliar weapon.

The Corporal drew a pistol and fired twice. The bullets thumped into the wet blanket in front of me, making it jump like there was a bear inside. I cleared the gun and fired at the Corporal, the burst hitting him in the chest and knocking him backwards into a line of sheets which he brought winding down around him.

My hands were shaking. I put the gun down and passed my hand over my eyes. All the birds flew screeching out of the trees as the shots echoed over the wasteland. I stepped round the side of the blanket – there were no holes in it – and picked Kaptan up. He was crying. I put my arms around him. 'It is all right now,' I said. 'It is all right now.' Over his shoulder I looked at the sheets covering the Corporal, the bloodstain widening. He lay motionless.

There were running feet. As I knelt, I put Kaptan in front of me, holding him round the waist, my chin on his shoulder.

'Tell them who you are, Kaptan. Be quick.'

And he didn't let me down.

As the *malai* officer ran round the side of the building, Kaptan shouted, 'I am the son of Colonel Goreng – don't shoot!' I think he was pretending we were in a TV movie.

We were lucky it was the officer. He was quick with the situation, turning round at once and checking the men behind. Otherwise we'd have got blown away. Even so, the cherry berets threw me to the ground, kicking me in the ribs as they frisked me for weapons.

'Don't hurt Adolph!' Kaptan cried. 'Don't hurt him!'

'I've saved the boy's life,' I said desperately. The answer was a kick on the eyebrow which I almost mistook for being shot.

'No!' Kaptan cried. He broke free of the lieutenant and threw himself on top of me. I was on this side of consciousness, just, feeling very sick, with a huge head. 'He saved me!'

The cherry berets pulled me to my feet. I said thickly, 'Help me, Kaptan, tell them.'

The lieutenant was leading him away. 'Don't leave me, Kaptan,' I begged the little boy. The lieutenant turned and he said, 'Bring him.'

They were the best two words I ever heard in my life.

TWENTY-EIGHT

SO MUCH HAPPENED SO FAST IN THE NEXT FEW DAYS. I'd thought I was going to rest on my laurels. I thought we were in for some stability. But that had just been the beginning of the turmoil. Physical disruption, fear, the adrenalin events – they were only part of it. What was more disturbing, and could never be truly exorcised, was the way a whole history of friendship, a lifetime of amity, could be nullified in a moment. It seemed what mattered, what defined, was the acute moment at the end, not the long, unfeigned relationships which had subsisted before. I am, as you know, not a religious man, but my version of a prayer is to contemplate those placider days, as if by doing it often enough, telling the beads in my mind, I can confer upon them a greater significance, sufficient to obliterate the terrible moment. The moment, I guess, of a powerful but partial truth.

I was taken straight back to our house. Kaptan insisted we go there. The *malai* officer had wanted to take us to a superior. He wanted to pass us up the line of responsibility.

But Kaptan would have none of it. The pettish, wilful side of him came out, the Colonel's spoiled son. I was very glad to see that side of him again, I can tell you, and gladder still that I had not succeeded yet in eradicating it. Lost in the *malai* chain of command, shuffled round from captor to captor, I would not have given a great deal for my chances. They'd have terminated me just to get rid of a nuisance. 'You take us home,' Kaptan said stoutly, 'or my father will be very angry.' His mother, too, the formidable Mrs Goreng, I thought (but was too wise to compromise my chances by saying). She'll rip you to pieces if you keep her cub from her one minute longer than necessary. Eventually, the young officer weighed up the pros and contras and made the correct decision, for him and for yours truly, by delivering us to our front door. There was a roadblock set up with no less than three machine-guns. We got through this in no time. As we skimmed along the last 100 metres, I said to the lieutenant, '*Tuan*, have you something the boy can put over his shirt? His mother will faint if she sees him like this.' You know, I didn't give a shit what fit Mrs Goreng would throw. I wanted to make certain I was leaving the jeep with Kaptan – I wanted to establish my connection with the family, give a hint of trouble I could solve (without making it look like a threat), and put myself into the frame without a hint of asserting myself. The lieutenant thought a bit, then nodded. He had a hard, ruthless young face. I think if I'd opened my mouth to say something irrelevant or personal to myself I would have been in jeopardy. He passed over a camo poncho, which I told Kaptan to put on, after I removed his blood-stained shirt. I could see the boy was thrilled. I held on to his hand as we went through the gate.

Mrs ran through the door. She flung herself on him. 'Oh, Kaptan, Kaptan,' she kept saying. I thought she could have been a little more original than that; I mean, she was a journalist.

The Colonel came home briefly, just before midnight. She'd got through a call to him on the radio-phone that Kaptan was safe. He hadn't had to suffer as much as her – I don't so much mean that, like fishes, his pain threshold was higher than a human being's (although I don't doubt that was the case) as that he'd been aware that his son was missing for a shorter period than his wife. Mrs had got home in her jeep with just chauffeur and one extra bodyguard, defying the pleas of the other wives, some half an hour after Kaptan and I had left with the Corporal, but she hadn't been able to get the Colonel on the military net for nearly two hours after that. Whether it was the high volume of radio traffic, FAKINTIL sabotage, or his underlings keeping it from him, I'll never know. Mrs, I think, suspected the latter and it showed in a permanent coldness to them thereafter. So he had only had to cope with the loss for slightly over half an hour. I was mean-minded enough to wish it had been for longer. He wasn't so effusively grateful as I could have wished. Mrs, my friend, Mrs Goreng was all over me after she'd sobbed a bit over Kaptan. He had to tell the story umpteen times, getting a little further into the tale each time, whereupon she'd ask to be taken from the beginning again. By the time Colonel Goreng brought us into his den, we'd got quite good at telling it together, feeding each other cues and lines. I liked it when Kaptan described his moment of deliverance, the point at which I tried to shoot my old comrade in arms in the back, then the desperate fumble to see who'd get their shots off first. 'Ka-prap!' went Kaptan, imitating the snarl of the M-I6 and spinning sideways to the carpet. I wanted the Colonel to hear that; he couldn't hear it too many times for my liking. How I had gloriously saved his son and heir. I was even glad now I'd had trouble with the M-16; didn't want him thinking I was too handy with weapons.

'So he shot at you first?' the Colonel enquired, trying to get the whole picture straight to his satisfaction. I didn't want him thinking I'd only fired in self-defence. I explained how I'd attempted to fire at the Corporal as Kaptan lay on the ground and how the gun had malfunctioned; it would be more accurate to say I'd been first to aim but the Corporal had got his shots off first. It sounded like some cowboy duel. Most of all, the Colonel was intrigued that the wet blanket had absorbed the energy of the pistol shots. He made a *moue* but said, 'No, I believe you. Allah was with you.'

'He was with me,' I agreed.

The Colonel could only spend half an hour with us. When he went he shook my hand.

That night I didn't sleep too well. It wasn't just adrenalin. I wasn't allowing myself to think too much, but below the conscious level all kinds of adjustments were going on in my head.

A great deal worse was to come.

In the next two days everyone in Danu was put under terms of strict confinement. No one was allowed out. The cherry berets made meticulous house-searches, even digging up the floors of some places, going into roof spaces with torches. Everyone had to produce an identity card, including those actually in the internment camps! I was in some doubt as to whether the Corporal had stumbled upon us accidentally on his way out of the town or if he'd been deliberately tasked. If he'd just been trying to clear the hell out, then it meant there were probably other FAKINTIL escapers at large who hadn't been able to make it back to the mountains either. I had a feeling they'd been blocked off by the *malais* and hadn't been able to go by the quickest route they wanted. I didn't like to ask the Colonel, even with the credit balance I'd now established.

The attack had happened Thursday. Monday, the Colonel came back to lunch with a big grin on his face. He couldn't hide his satisfaction. But he shut the door of the dining-room, so we flunkeys couldn't hear what he said to his wife. He also sent Kaptan out of the room. Kaptan, big-eyed, tried to eavesdrop like the rest of us.

That evening a jeep, *that* jeep, came to the house. I will tell you I was not happy to drive into the night. Still less to see the flood-lit walls of the prison. I thought: surely even he wouldn't kill the rescuer of his son? Two cherry berets took me through the first gate. As we went down some steps and along a dark passageway, open to the sky, I recalled Maria's visit to this terrible place, the night they'd had Raoul here, the night Arsenio had wanted to kill Raoul and Osvaldo had forgiven him. I wondered who would forgive Goreng.

I blinked in the big exercise yard. It was like day, except for the silveriness of the light. There were three APCs in the yard, with their light cannon trained on the far wall. There also stood four machine-guns fixed on sustained fire-mounts. All this bristling weaponry was aimed at a line of about 40 men standing against the wall. Goreng was with some junior officers at the side of all this, talking to a captain who had a clip-board, with corded pencil dangling. More than the heavy weapons, this banal accoutrement of a rudimentary accountancy scared me shitless. I knew what I'd witnessed last time I'd seen one of those in the possession of a *malai* officer. I then received two shocks in quick succession. From the open door of the nearest APC, three white men emerged. They were dressed in military olive greens. Despite the heat, one of them, who had bright red hair, wore a sweater with cloth patches on the shoulders and elbows and still shivered violently. None of them had headgear or bore any sign of rank or unit. The one in the sweater looked pretty sick. After them came Rebus, the Devil himself.

Well, I'd say seeing the white men was the biggest surprise and Rebus the worst shock. My heart seemed to stop beating, then kick reluctantly into life again, like those temperamental old generators of colonial Danu. I put my head down, slowed my walk to try to put my escort in front of me. Very foolish, as it merely postponed the inevitable and could serve only to irritate my guards. Martinho came out of a door in the 'administration' wing of the prison, walking very quickly. He was wearing dark sunglasses; why, I don't know. Behind him came the General and his staff. Goreng said to me, 'We can use your help tonight.' When Rebus joined the group I began to tremble nearly as badly as the red-haired foreigner. Rebus didn't appear to recognise me; but that didn't mean anything. Goreng said, 'These men are going to approach one at a time. If you know them as FAKINTIL you will identify them at once.'

'Where have they come from? Are you sure they are FAKINTIL?'

'That is for you to tell us,' Goreng said. He was less severe with me than he would have been normally, but I saw I could not expect great leniency from him. I imagined they'd picked up their prisoners in sweeps of the town. Anyone without ID papers was in serious trouble. 'By the way,' Goreng said, 'there will be two of you on this parade.' He gestured to Martinho. 'You will be checking on each other.' I looked uneasily at Martinho, who no doubt wasn't too happy either, except I couldn't see his eyes.

I thought we were going to walk down the line of men, touch them on the shoulder maybe, like some cop programme on TV, but that wasn't it at all. Martinho and I were separated, then put back to back at about 20 metres, very much like pistol duellists from the old time. In fact, for one crazy moment I thought this was what Rebus had in mind. The suspects were then brought up by number, a single man at a time (and as I heard them begin with 'one', the skin of my neck tightened in anticipation of gunfire which never came). Martinho saw them first, before they came along to me. That way, you see, we couldn't collude (assuming we wished to) in passing through people who were known to us. We had no way of reading the other's mind. And if one identified someone the other had let through, the culprit was doomed. To be safe, you had to finger everyone. And, it occurred to yours truly, even then you weren't safe; for you might genuinely forget a face the other was able to remember. Still worse, he could imagine he recognised a face which wasn't a FAKINTIL man at all. I began to wish it wasn't Martinho who was my partner in this deadly game of doubles. I didn't trust his nerve. His imagination might start to play tricks on him. And in all this system, these rudimentary ploys, these crude but, oh, so effective mind games, I discerned the hand not of Goreng but of Rebus.

From behind, the first prisoner was brought up. He was an old countryman with a betel-ravaged mouth, the cancerous tongue sticking helplessly out like a crimson prickly pear. I shook my head. The cherry berets dragged the bewildered old montagnard away with a brusqueness which inspired no confidence in me for his future prospects. Next up was a hard-looking fellow I remembered as one of the surviving Africa veterans, a prodigal who'd been seduced by Martinho but had redeemed himself by daring and sacrifice under Osvaldo – I was surprised he was still alive. From his demeanour, fierce and uncompromising, I knew he'd already been denounced by Martinho. I nodded, and he spit in my face. The *malais* removed him without punishing him especially; I guess he was permitted to spit on me. The next was a city man, a former civil service clerk who'd been in FAKOUM from the early days. He looked scared to death, and he had reason to be for he was doubly identified by both of us. And so they processed, the defiant and the hopeless, the resigned and those who pleaded with a silent desperation. At length I heard urgent but whispered conversation to the rear. I was able to resist the temptation to turn. A tall, luxuriantly bearded man, with steady eyes stood before me. It was Osvaldo.

'Who is this?' Rebus asked. For him, that was a mistake. His eagerness betrayed him. If he wanted a real, 100 per cent unprejudiced check he should have kept quiet. I knew from this that Martinho had already identified his brother. Then Osvaldo startled me. He said, '*Bom dia,* Adolph.' In other words, 'Hi!'

I said, 'Hello, Osvaldo. I am sorry.'

He said, 'Don't be.'

I was stunned. He'd thrown away his last hope, flipped his cards brazenly on the table.

The *malais* had him securely. Rebus had the same smile as when he'd repossessed the Hotel Oscar Tango X-Ray and its flush toilets. Goreng was on the fringe. He wasn't unhappy by any means, but not quite so pleased with himself as Rebus. I suddenly realised they didn't like each other; that they were rivals. Martinho was watching, with that 'I've got nothing to do with this' look that he put on when he'd fucked things up good. It was the same expression he'd had when backing away from the struggle around the campfire just before Osvaldo – his beard still smouldering – had put him under arrest. Osvaldo stumbled – I watched him intently – although he appeared uninjured and the *malais* weren't noticeably ill-treating him. It wasn't a casual roughing-up Rebus had in mind for him. The two cherry berets kept him up; then I saw Osvaldo hook his bare foot round a *malai's* boot and the two of them went down. Osvaldo came to his knees, holding with his tied hands his groin, which was wrapped up in his grubby, checked sarong. He groaned. Martinho hurried up. I believe Martinho thought he could secure his brother a position not unlike his own; save his life at least. I doubted that.

Rebus then grabbed Osvaldo by the hair; he looked disappointed in his prisoner. Osvaldo came up as he had to, his face contorted with the tearing pain. He stood close to Rebus, looking down on the smaller man, fixing him in the eye. Then he started to say something. Rebus's face changed; he recoiled in horror, but Osvaldo had his thumbs hooked in the *malai's* belt. Osvaldo never finished his sentence. In the next instant came a great flash. I threw myself backwards but those around the exploding grenade had shielded me. I was not conscious of hearing the blast, but my ears buzzed. Rebus and Osvaldo had been blown away from each other some three metres. Their bodies were the worst mutilated. Most of Rebus's face had gone. Osvaldo had lost both arms to the elbows and the stumps of his arms lay outspread. He was on his back. Martinho lay on his side. After a while he got to his hands and knees. He began to crawl uncertainly around. His shirt had been as cleanly stripped from him as if he had never been wearing it, although his skin appeared uninjured. That was the freakish effect of blast for you, so powerful, yet capable of being deflected by the flimsiest thing, always choosing the line of least resistance. His shades had gone, however. His mouth kept opening and shutting as if he was trying to say something. Goreng had escaped injury entirely, being just outside the radius of harm. The two cherry berets with Osvaldo had been quite badly chewed up, though one still moved. People started to run up. A gunshot went off, stopping them all in their tracks. Then one of the machine-guns opened up, hurling five or six of the prisoners against the wall, flinging their limbs around as if they were scarecrows and as they fell in a heap that was what they were. The line wavered like a branch in a breeze. Goreng screamed 'Cease fire!' The captain with the clip-board ran over to the offending gun-team, yelling abuse. I reached Martinho, my friend. He was whimpering with pain, moving on all fours into the line of gunfire. I dropped beside him. 'Stop. It's me.'

'Oh, Adolph, my eyes! I cannot see!'

When he put his head up to the sound of my voice I could see the mess. 'Try to be still, if you can. Movement will make it worse.' I put my arms around him. He fumbled for my hand, which I gave him. 'Where is Osvaldo?' he asked. I hesitated; I didn't want to add to his shock. Then I said, as gently as I could, 'He is dead, Martinho. I am sorry to say Osvaldo is dead.'

'What?' He was still deafened.

I told him more loudly this time. Then I bent close to his ear and said in as big a voice as I dared, 'He's taken Rebus with him.' Martinho's hand tightened on mine. I squeezed it back. I was jumpy. Things looked very tense – as if they could swing either way. It was the nasty period when it wasn't quite certain yet. The white men were talking to Goreng. It was the sick one – exhibiting all the symptoms of the fevers which used to cut such a swathe through the FAKINTIL encampments – who actually appeared to be their leader. I should dearly have liked to know whether they were Europeans or Americans, but I couldn't hear the accents. They appeared to be arguing. I hoped the white men weren't telling him to eliminate all witnesses because I don't believe it would have needed much persuasion. However, I think these guys didn't carry the weight with Goreng they should have done because they were Rebus's associates. Rebus, I now suspect, was part of a plot by a faction of military intelligence to usurp credit for the suppression of FAKINTIL from the regulars. And these foreign spooks, these non-existents on the pay-rolls of any Western army, were part of that scheme.

I wanted to get close to Goreng. Right then I thought that was the safest place to be. But Martinho, through his pain and his panic, the horror of being unable to see, said, 'Don't leave me, Adolph.' It was what I'd said to him, near enough. I didn't want him to hear the reluctance in my voice, so I squeezed his hand again.

Goreng was giving the captain orders. These turned out to be to take the prisoners into the cells. The corpses they threw into the APC. You could see the prisoners looking back at the two bodies in the centre of the carnage; there was a lot of blood now, spreading in pools. I was amazed each time by how much. They didn't want to look back; they knew it was dangerous; but they still did.

Goreng went away with the foreign advisers. I had wanted to enjoy the protection conferred by his proximity, but I was very, very pleased not to be drawn to the attentions of the spooks. I contrived to get Martinho beside Goreng's jeep and laid him against a wheel. Then we waited. Martinho didn't complain or fret, just sat there, only gasping a bit now and then. I found him a clean scarf to hold over his face. When Goreng emerged half an hour later, he troubled himself to take Martinho to the military doctor.

I believe he was in a very good mood.

There wasn't much they could do for Martinho. If they could have restored his sight I am sure they would have. But the damage to his eyes was irreparable. I saw the look the *malai* doctors gave each other and I knew then he would never see again. As I have had reason to observe before, the *malai* medics weren't such bad guys. They didn't tell Martinho what the situation was for a while, and then they preferred to get me to break it to him. Martinho had the air of a man who was permanently waiting for a question to be answered. I don't mean for his fear to be confirmed – that he was sightless; the unspoken query which hovered over us for those few days. I mean the way that thereafter he would cock

423

his head, slightly sideways. He had to make greater use of his sense of hearing in order to compensate. In an awful way (you didn't even like to think it) this improved him, made him less superior.

So far as the *malais* were concerned, it also made them like Martinho more, in the political rather than personal sense. It was the nearest thing they could get to having a castratus; he was already a political eunuch, him and Teixeira both. Now he was quite helpless, yet still alive and still Martinho. Nor had the *malais* done the damage to him, but his own side, his own brother. He stood for damaged Danu; he got your sympathy. They thought he could be used at some time in the future even better internationally than locally.

I spent a lot of time with him. Mrs Goreng had no objection – if she did, maybe the Colonel overruled her. Even now I don't account it time wasted. I was glad to do what I could for my friend, the only survivor of the Praça days. Martinho was a good man and remarkable in his way; the time and place were wrong for him, that's all. He was very quiet; I did most of the talking. When he did speak, it was mostly of the very distant past, remembering his brothers as boys. The youngest three brothers he hardly knew; he hadn't grown up with them. He had already been a first-year seminarian when Eduardo was five. He said Osvaldo hadn't seemed special as a boy. Joaquim, the next oldest after Martinho, had been the leader in their various scrapes; even Rogerio (who had died with Joaquim on the pillion in a motor-bike accident) had seemed more remarkable than Osvaldo. Osvaldo, said Martinho, had only really bloomed in his last year at the seminary and – truly – in Africa.

I said he shouldn't derogate Joaquim and Rogerio; maybe they really had been more gifted than Osvaldo and we would never know. I said how surprising it was that even in a small society like ours we should be able to throw up any number of superior people to replace those lost in the normal or abnormal attrition of life. There always seemed to be someone else to hand over to. 'It gives you faith in human beings,' I said.

Martinho corrected me. He said, 'You are mistaking the hand of God for the work of man.'

I couldn't say anything to that which would not have been construed as offensive. We sat in silence for a while, but a friendly silence. Then Martinho started talking about the seminary journal. I got the impression he regarded his editorship as the high point of his life.

I encouraged him to talk about those days, to focus on something positive. I thought it would be beneficial for him. I didn't want him becoming morbid. Obviously, that was in his interests, but I have to admit it was also in mine. Did I want to be brought down? Call me selfish, but life was hard enough as it was, without someone else demoralising me. I guess I didn't want to realise how depressed he was. He bore his affliction with a great dignity. I was happy to admire this. There wasn't a shred of self-pity there. You could say at the last he had his brother's fibre, but it was manifested in fortitude instead of daring – which is a more admirable thing. I thought he'd find a way for himself in the end. How self-centred I was.

Colonel Goreng broke the news to me, making no effort to cushion the blow. If things had been otherwise, perhaps that's how he would have liked to hear of his son's death.

'Your friend is dead,' he said. 'He hanged himself yesterday evening.'

I closed my eyes for a second. Then I took a deep breath. Goreng's face gave me no clues; there was no information there; sympathy I didn't expect. Then he made a big concession. He said, 'You can take it from me – he hanged himself. That's what happened.'

I mumbled, 'Thank you, *tuan*.' I believed him and I still do. Apart from anything else, he wouldn't have bothered to lie.

Martinho would have accounted his act a mortal sin. Of that I have no doubt, but I am equally certain that it was his own hands which fastened his belt around his neck and fumbled for the window bar. And I believe his motivations would have encompassed things other than his own predicament. I do believe it wasn't just inability to cope with a terrible handicap.

He didn't say anything of great consequence the last time I left him. I said, 'I'll see you tomorrow.' 'You will see me tomorrow,' he answered, and we shook hands as we had taken to doing.

About a fortnight before that, and ten days after the night at the prison, I had been passing along the road, with my arm through Martinho's, when I had cause to do a double-take on a group of beggars by the roadside. Goreng had given us two guards – whether to protect us or to stop us getting up to mischief I'm not sure: maybe both. These soldiers dogged our faltering steps. I halted, before realising my mistake. The guards, being *malais* as well as red-bereted killers, were quite nonchalant for the moment, but they'd start getting suspicious and edgy after a while. I pretended to take a stone out of my shoe. (I could no longer wear thongs.) As I knelt, I looked up. I hadn't been wrong. I was looking at Xavier Ray Xaneros himself. And I think behind him had been one of the older woodchucks and João the electrician, except they'd made themselves scarce commodities. But X. Ray stood his ground, regarding me with his usual grave and steady expression. He saw what had happened to Martinho. I dropped my eyes to my foot, straightened out the tongue, and stood up. I apologised to our escort. Then we walked on, at no brisker a pace than we had come. I knew far better than to turn my head, but I had the feeling my old builder stayed squatting by the roadside. It has always been my hope that he didn't trouble to bestir himself even when we had gone out of sight.

Martinho never asked why I'd stopped. I think he had no inkling at all, though I stared at him. I could do that without his noticing, of course.

As we walked, I was quiet. Martinho let me think. He could be considerate like that. I was trying to put myself into X. Ray's head. Had he expected me to shout and betray him? Did he stay still because he was resigned? Martinho and I must have seemed a bad pair to him. Or did he know what my inclination was? (Then he knew better than me.) Perhaps he relied on our personal friendship to override whatever my political views or personal interest had become. Whatever it was, he'd served me with his final invoice and I'd paid it in full.

And then I thought again of Osvaldo, of what he'd said in the silver light of the prison yard, his smile and the *'Bom dia!'* with which he had favoured me, knowing even then the terminating choice, the course that lay before him. There was that difference in their characters, the imperturbability of one, the charisma of the other. X. Ray stayed quiet because he had a chance, as would Osvaldo in his place. But there was also the question of Osvaldo's grace on that evening, his special calmness; his natural generosity and his ruthless decisiveness in tandem at the very last. I think he wanted to get Rebus closer, for he was his primary target. He saw the excitement of the *malai* and he exploited it. Bound, starved, beaten, he was still the master of himself. That was his primary motive. But final though the action was, it was no abdication either. He thought of the future which no longer contained him but which he could still control. He knew what happened to men and women whose notion of themselves had become degraded; he'd seen how traitors worked with a special spite, with a fury that was reserved for themselves as they twisted the knife in the wound. He didn't want to waste yet another that way; he didn't want to make me a betrayer; he wanted to keep me, as far as he still could. And so he made it easy for me. He denounced himself. And if in the flamboyance of the act, the studied casualness of the greeting, he found a certain bitter amusement, why, he was still able to relish an irony and a situation. That was Osvaldo Oliveira and his greatness. And at the last Martinho participated in it.

TWENTY-NINE

AFTER KAPTAN HAD RETURNED TO SCHOOL, Mrs Goreng became the victim of anti-climax. She stayed in the sitting-room a lot, reading in the cool shade with the french windows to my garden thrown wide. She was not the only one.

In the town the populace was subdued. The death of Osvaldo was a devastating blow to all Danuese patriots. It took something away from everyone, whether they'd been IP in the past or not. Even if they had never contemplated the smallest act of resistance themselves, the notion of FAKINTIL in the hills with their leader had offered the possibility of freedom one day. It had been a remote possibility, but it had existed. And this possibility had been closely identified with the figure of Osvaldo himself. To eliminate him had also been to destroy a dream. And now they didn't even have TV.

I had a dream as well. But it had the presumption to concern myself.

Eighteen months previously I would have been content merely to be alive. To have enough to eat was a luxury of extravagant proportions. But we grow discontented in Eden, which Danu was not. My expectations rose with the quality of my life. I hardly dared formulate my ambition to myself.

One morning I saw Mrs Goreng's chauffeur grinning as he went about his chore of servicing the jeep. He had a kind of surf-board on roller-skates which he used to lie on to slide under the chassis, propelling himself with his padded stump. As his usual expression was a scowl, particularly for me, I was interested. We used to feud about the oil-leaks which would drain down the side of the little courtyard and get under and into my flower-pots. I would have to bite back my angry words – that better men than he had driven the jeep but that I knew he would share their fate. It was pitiful. Did I think they were *my* flowers? Did he think it was *his* jeep? I had acquired the true menial mentality.

He whistled, this piratical chauffeur, while he shot back and forth under my feet like a stiff in a mortuary drawer. The whistling had a peculiarly aggravating quality. When I went into the house, the domestics refrained from looking at me. The truth dawned. Everyone knew something yours truly didn't. I went off to milady's boudoir. 'What's going on?' I demanded. Note I didn't say, '*Nonya,* what's going on?'

'Going what?' From her flustered expression and the fact that I wasn't instantly told to mend my manners, I knew she felt guilty 'Come on,' I said. 'Everyone else knows. Why don't I?'

'I don't know what you're talking about, Adolph.'

Well, the queen sulked after that. He didn't want to brush milady's hair, or put flowers in it. Finally, Mrs said crossly, 'All right then, have it your way. It was meant to be a surprise. We're going to Dili. Are you happy now?'

I kept my face blank. Dili was the *malai* island of romance, the most beautiful spot in the archipelago. It was a place to associate with bare-breasted maidens, the bohemian European artists of the 30's who immortalised them, floral garlands, towering cloud-capped peaks. Many a Hollywood blockbuster had been shot there. It had also been the scene of the worst communal massacres of the sixties, and parts were now an Aussie-designated budget-tourist hell on earth.

'*Dili?*'

'You'll like it. It's only a temporary posting for Colonel Goreng. You could say it's a reward.'

'Dili,' I said to myself. I didn't like it at all. You might have thought that, in the abstract, the immediate prospect was attractive.

But it wasn't, if you cared to put yourself in my position. I didn't even have to think about it to dislike the idea; my repugnance was instinctive. Here, in Danu, I had a meaning; it was where I had been born and lived. Not through choice, not by a long way, but it was where I'd made my destiny, even if as an alien. And, most importantly, it was where Colonel Goreng had a use for me. Outside Danu, I was nothing. I'd be retained purely as a servant, subject to the whims of an above averagely capricious employer with a short memory. Only my wiles as a courtier would preserve me, and I'd prefer to have something between me and the Colonel's wrath that was more substantial. Put it this way: in Danu, even with FAKINTIL on the way out, with my history it was like I possessed a personal qualification: doctor, lawyer, accountant, except I was not one of those but a traitor. Let me put it poetically: in Danu I was a garden plant with roots in the soil that would sustain me indefinitely. Removed from my natural environment, I was a cut flower in a vase of water. I might be interesting, I might be decorative, my exoticism might be diverting, but sure as hell my span was finite.

And so I looked at my uneasy mistress with an anxious and angry eye which she was unable to meet. I think she, too, had an inkling.

But she continued, 'It won't all be a holiday for you.' She turned from the mirror now, with a smile on her face and I wondered if her unease had just been an illusion of my own. 'You can help the Colonel with business dealings. I've told him how clever you are. Can you speak Chinese as well?' Her smile had a kind of crazed brightness about it. I didn't take offence, nor did I think her last question the *non sequitur* of a schizophrenic – Chineseness had everything to do with financial acumen – but she was treating me with the politeness she would accord a stranger who was her equal. I couldn't put a name on her treatment of me, no word existed for what she was trying to do, but I knew I was being manipulated under the guise of deference and consideration. '*Nonya*,' I said, with what I trusted was dignified reproach. I left the room.

Well, things were quite advanced by now. Mrs Goreng had no reason to conceal anything from me any more. She walked round the house, planning what she would take: this ornament to be packed in a shoe-box stuffed with wood-shavings and placed in the top drawer of that chest, that cane-chair to be left behind for the benefit of the Colonel's successor, those curtains to be carefully arranged when the time came, with not more than one fold. Yours truly followed, notebook in hand. 'What about the sofa-covers, Adolph?' she asked. 'Will they go with the red and grey marble? That's what the floors of the new place are, you know.' I suddenly realised that she *really* didn't want to lose me. I'd tried to safeguard myself by worming my way into her heart and confidences. And I'd succeeded all too well. She depended on me for company; I was a better companion than Colonel Goreng. If I was honest with myself, I liked her, too. In a better place and time, we'd have been friends. (She'd have appreciated Maria, if not Rosa.) But now she was a ball and chain around my ankle. I said, 'Not all interior designers are queers.' She sighed. We went on compiling the inventory. After a minute she grabbed the notebook and pencil from me. I turned and stalked away to the servants' quarters. My few possessions mocked me. I was going to garden for some active therapy but when I got there I thought better of it. With deliberation, I pulled up all my orchids and threw them, strewn with crumbs of earth, into the wheel-barrow. I left them there for her to see. Let her make of it what she would.

I think my plan was to make her like me less. I was not altogether explicit about it to myself at first, but the tactics clarified themselves in my mind. My relations with her became cold, but correct. She bore it with a little smile of amusement that began to enrage me. I'd meant her to lose control and give me an opportunity, but it was proving the other way around. This went on for two weeks. I had no idea when we might be going to Dili, so I was unable to time my campaign, to know when to bring it to a climax, to know when I could afford to cool things down, to be nice to her, for I didn't want to be thrown out of the house there and then, did I? I was operating in the dark; I was deprived of intelligence. And we know what happens to commanders bereft of good intelligence.

But one morning she came into the bare-looking garden to say, 'We're going on Sunday.' That was in two days' time. 'You and Sogono are going,' she said. Sogono was the armless chauffeur. 'The others will have to stay.'

'I am not going,' I declared. Now she did lose her temper. She stamped her foot. 'You are a fool. Where else can you go? If you stay here you will be dead in a year.' That was the first time she'd acknowledged the truth of the *malai* presence; we'd never mentioned the disappearances. 'You can be safe with us. Am I so bad to you?'

'No. You are good to me.'

'Well then.'

'It's not that,' I said. I decided to try to be open for once in my life. I would be frank, say directly what I wanted, and to hell with it.

'What can it be then?'

'Ely,' I said (that was her name and the first time I'd ever used it), 'I want to be free.'

She looked stunned. I don't think she'd considered this. It was like a trap-door had opened at her feet. Then she looked embarrassed. I could almost feel sorry for her, she had gotten herself into such a false position. It never pays to treat servants as people. Look where it had got her now. She said something about no one being free, it was all relative. I just looked her straight back in the eye, as if to say, 'Don't give me that bullshit.'

'It's just not possible, Adolph,' she said. 'I would like nothing better personally.'

At last I had to say it. 'I saved your son,' I said. 'Does that count for nothing?'

She shrugged, not dismissively but as if to say she was helpless. I was a fool now; I was gambling. I, who was so prudent, was recklessly throwing all my cards into the game. To mention Kaptan was to devalue the exploit. It could be used once. I said, 'You *malais* are all the same. I should have let him shoot the boy.' My bitterness was real, but I had not spoken wildly; the words were uttered with calculation. I had never used the word *malai* in her hearing; now I'd applied it to her. I wanted to hurt and shock. I succeeded. 'You are all the same,' I had said – reducing her from an individual to a stereotype, lumping her in with the worst of the cherry berets. I turned on my heel and left the room.

If she'd been in any doubt as to the strength of my feelings, she had no excuse any longer. As I started to cool down, I didn't regret what I had said. I was sure she would not denounce me. I was certain there was very little risk on the downside, whereas the prize was great.

I was right. She had a conscience – or rather she had what was an Asian's limited version of a social morality, the strong sense of a favour done and an obligation to requite. She couldn't pass over that. The bad side of it was all the things which afflicted the *malais:* nepotism, corruption; the good side of it was the desire not to show ingratitude. 'Do unto others as you would be done by' was a more positive social prescription of societies like Toronto but 'Scratch my back and I'll scratch yours' was a workable Asian substitute.

She came to me, quite timidly for her, as I was cleaning the mirror in the hallway that afternoon. 'Adolph,' she said. I ignored her. I didn't believe she had anything to say to me – not anything that I'd want to hear. She was just saying something, anything, my name, to establish communication. I glared at a fleck in the mirror, dabbed at it, then wiped furiously. After a while she went away. I kept looking at myself in the glass. It wasn't such a young face any more. Maybe it was the hardship in the mountains. At least I had a good head of hair, even if one or two were gray. I wished I could get it permed again.

In the evening she sent her maid for me. She was in the lounge, with one of the ancient US *Vogue* in her lap. She had an almost beatific expression on her pretty face. She was perfectly genuine in her feelings but expressing them by playing a role – I think maybe Bette Davis nobly renouncing a married lover. Not specifically our situation, you will appreciate, but the same range of feeling. 'Adolph,' she said, 'I understand things better now.' I inclined my head in acknowledgement; I understood that the terms of the game were that she was the one with the power, but I was the one being wooed. 'I will help you with all my heart, but you must be patient.'

'I have been patient a long time, *nonya*.'

'And you must be patient a little longer, my dear Adolph. It is not simple. You have to come to Dili with us. From there it will be a lot easier to arrange things.'

I thought about it. She was speaking the truth. An exit from Dili would indeed be a lot easier.

'Help me to help *you*, Adolph. You must come with me.'

I decided she was right. In any case my nerve was going. Did I really want to be left in Danu without a protector?

'I agree, *nonya*.'

She left the sofa and embraced me. I felt her spearmint breath on my cheek. Without wishing to be over-familiar but not to be stand-offish either, I put one hand on her shoulder. We looked at each other from a very close distance. I was reminded of Annie Laval. She smiled, disengaged herself and patted my cheek. 'You will see, Adolph. Everything will turn out just right. Trust me.'

Well, in the short term things were not quite how I imagined. The Gorengs flew to Dili, courtesy of the *malai* air force, in the relative comfort of an old Russian turbo prop. We saw them off at the airfield, we being Sogono and myself. Up to virtually the last minute I'd assumed that we, or at least yours truly, were going on the plane as well. Not so, my friend. We were to go by sea. This wasn't even by the rusty old tramp which brought stores to Danu once a month, but on a smaller wooden vessel, captained by a cut-throat old Bugi from Makassar, whose bilge pumps were perpetually squirting a drooping arc of water from the sides. It stank to high heaven of salt-fish and shit, the aforementioned by far the more offensive. When I saw her my heart sank. 'You little bitch,' I thought, referring to Mrs Goreng rather than the *Patna*. The Gorengs' effects made the sea-passage with us; or rather we made the passage with the effects, for that was the whole idea. She didn't trust the captain, so we were there to ensure her vases were carefully loaded and no pilfering went on. I chewed betel with the barefoot skipper in his wheel-house until, as the old tub began to roll in the outside channel, I realised that had been a mistake. I was as sick as a dog. And while I was leaning over the side, Sogono tapped me on the shoulder and said, 'How many soldier you kill, Chinaman? How many?' and kicked me behind the knee. I didn't even notice the pain. And before the nausea anaesthetised me, did I feel nostalgia, did I feel regret, did I feel the sense of something ending as the island slipped below the edge of the sea? No, I did not. I was too bound up with the problems of the present moment to enjoy the luxury of retrospection.

There was a ten-ton truck supposed to be waiting for us at Dili but it wasn't there. When we got in touch with the Colonel – a surprisingly easy task, the military communications network superbly efficient – it turned out we had been landed at the wrong port. Sogono and I sat on the dock beside the cargo – the crafty old Bugi way out to sea – before restoring ourselves on sticks of shrimp satay and bowls of turquoise ice, yellow maize, red beans, and syrup. Having emptied my stomach into the Banda Sea, I had a raging hunger. I was a little anxious as to payment, which would have been only a few coppers except we had none. Need I have worried? The question never arose. The vendor didn't even look for remuneration. Did I refuse to consume the food gained by the uniform and gun? I did not. I was quite happy to reap the benefits of being a fully fledged *malai* killer. At length the big green truck arrived and we were bumping off to an anxious reception from Mrs G. Anxious about her fragile porcelain, I should say.

She was childishly excited about their new place. Of course, it was much better than Danu as postings go. And their house was really grand. She was thinking of houseboys in a saffron uniform she'd design herself. When I looked at Sogono, in his olive greens and boots, he looked a fish out of water. I thought his days were numbered. There were also some wealthy French in a villa further down the hill. I would encourage that particular connection; I wasn't at all jealous.

For a while I kept quiet. I'd let her settle into the new surroundings – that way I'd seem more supernumerary. I was also a little curious about the place myself, to tell you the truth. After three weeks I broached the subject. She was evasive. I could read her like a book. She had genuinely meant to facilitate my exit from Dili; at the time she'd made her little speech to me she'd been perfectly sincere. It was just that in the intervening period she had changed her thinking a little. I threw a carefully modulated tantrum. Several, in fact. I moved her nearer the point again. This time she had a gambit. 'Adolph, *I* would like nothing better than to give you the chance to start your life again, but Colonel Goreng … he's the cautious one. He's worried for you.'

I was completely certain she'd never mentioned anything of the kind to the Colonel, but quick as a flash I said, '*Nonya,* I know you've done all you can. Now let me try the Colonel.'

She wasn't fazed by this. 'Oh, of course, Adolph. But I don't think you can change his mind very easily. He is very obstinate.'

'I'll do my best,' I said, and then I made her bite her lip in vexation for I said with a smile, 'And I'll tell him you're all in favour, if I may.'

'Oh, yes, of course, Adolph.'

It took some balls to beard the Colonel in his lair. I spent three days plucking up the courage. He raised his eyebrows but he didn't actually skewer my hand to his desk with his favourite kris. He shook his head. 'No.' I tried to go on. 'No,' was the answer again. I was on the point of surrendering when I thought that it would be more dangerous to resume the subject on another occasion; I also didn't trust my nerve. I might not ask again until it was too late; my native caution would betray me just as effectively as Arsenio and Osvaldo's natural daring had subverted their judgement. The Colonel waited for me, really with amazing politeness. Whether he thought it would be more unnerving than a show of rage or whether he imagined he owed me civil consideration, I was uncertain. I guess mild irritation would have been his best bet as tactics for A. Ng: sufficient to intimidate me, but with the prospect of worse to come. 'Colonel,' I said, 'I know that if it was within your power and it was up to you, that you would free me.' He nodded, the merest inclination of the head, to say, well, he didn't necessarily commit himself to agreeing but that he wasn't ruling it out as a might-have-been either. At this stage I don't think he saw what I was leading up to. I said, 'I know things are difficult. There are people who make things difficult.'

Colonel Goreng said, 'There are people who make things difficult.'

This was good – this was the closest we'd come to meaningful exchange. It was a little like talking to a wooden puppet. A devil puppet. However, I was going to try to pull the right strings. I said, 'These people can sometimes be taken care of.' I paused meaningfully. I wondered if he was too obtuse to pick up what I was driving at; he was a simple soldier, after all, serving his country to the best of his ability, etc., etc.

'Yes?'

No. I needn't have worried. Seemed that *malais* had a sixth sense, a special antenna for propositions of this kind; it was absorbed in the mother's milk. 'These people can, uh, be induced to step aside.'

His antennae were quivering now. 'How do you mean?'

That was an invitation. I said, 'With these people anything is possible with money.'

He shrugged. 'You have to have the money.'

I said, 'Well, that would be my problem.'

We said nothing more after that. Things had gone far enough for then. During the next few days I went about my duties with propriety and correctness. Mrs Goreng had been befriended by the French lady down the hill, who was an amateur painter; so I was no longer required continually. I didn't mention my interview with the Colonel. What was possible with him was not proper with her. I knew it was for me to approach the Colonel again, rather than vice versa. So when he brushed me aside brusquely the next time, I knew everything was OK. Politeness and kindness would have constituted a refusal. I let a fortnight elapse. This time he didn't send me away, but he went on annotating a report on his desk, without looking up.

I said, 'There is money abroad, which would be enough to satisfy these people. But I would need your help.'

'What money?' he asked, still waiting.

'It is money which belonged to my father. It is in an American bank,' I told him truthfully.

'Yes. How much?'

I had decided to be vague. 'I am not sure. But enough for this kind of person. A few thousand dollars. Do you think you could speak to them on my behalf?'

'Maybe.'

'Colonel, I do not like to remind you of this, but I saved your son's life. Please take the money and speak to these people, as a favour to me.'

God, the sonorous hypocrisy of it. He knew I knew he knew I knew.

For nearly a minute he said nothing and I had the sense to keep quiet, too, looking down at the top of his head. He said, 'I could pass the money to them. But then they may take it and do nothing.'

I said, 'That is why *you* must do it for me, Colonel.'

He nodded and he looked at me for the first time. I said, 'Thank you, Colonel.' He said, 'I do it for my wife and for my son. I don't do it for you.' But he let me kiss his hand. He entered into the spirit of the farce.

I won't go into the reneguing, the disappointments, the false optimism, the anti-climaxes. I won't go into the third-person mind-games and transferences. The only easy part was the telegraphic transfer of the funds into the Colonel's Singapore bank account.

Four months later I was in New York.

THIRTY

Cedar Avenue
Don Mills
Ontario

Dear Adolph,

It was really a pleasant surprise to have your letter. My mother forwarded it me the day she received it. Of course I remember you. In fact, I have often wondered what became of you. I did recall you were from Danu, so when I first read about the troubles there I became somewhat anxious on your behalf. At the time (I know it was seven years ago because that's when I left for Edmonton where I met Michael) I would always make sure I read the foreign page to see what was happening in Danu. The articles were quite big at first, then got smaller until they were maybe only one or two paragraphs long, then they stopped at all. It must have been scary for you. You said you got caught up in the fighting, my husband Michael said he'd love to hear more about that. I always remember your joke at the North and South Club when you told the Jamaican guy those things that he got mad at you that you didn't have a black belt but you had a yellow streak at Origami! Seriously though, it must have been a bad time. You must be glad the terrorists have gone away, even if it was at a terrible cost to your country. When I first met him Michael already belonged to the Unification Church and I do as well now, so we are aware of the threat from Communism in all its forms.

We have two children, Emerald and Brandon, Emerald is four and Brandon will be two in November. On account of my grandfather leaving me this house we moved here from Edmonton. Michael is a sculptor and a poet, as well as a

*feminist. When 1 met him he was co-manager of a jazz cafe
in Edmonton. No, I do not see any of the people we knew
back in school. We all seemed to split up and go our separate
ways afterwards. I did hear Ras Mohammed, the Ethiopian
who kept to himself pretty much, got to be a big General but
maybe you didn't know him. I think I did get a letter from
you in Danu when you got back first all those years ago, I
remember I gave the stamps to my nephew. I am sorry if I
did not reply.*

*Well, Adolph, it certainly was a real pleasure to hear from
you after all these years. They seem a very long time ago
now. Write when you have a chance and I will too, if you
pass through Toronto look us up. You are in my prayers and
thoughts,*

Your friend,
Ann (Laval)

No, I never wrote again, and nor did she. I sent the letter
across the Atlantic from the metropolitan country. I'd hoped
to go to Australia, a mere couple of hours by jet, but the
Colonel was too clever to allow that. Away to Europe I went,
out of controversy's way. If I had wanted I could have
shouted there, too, but the noise would have got kind of
muffled. You shout loudest into the Anglophone. I had no
relatives left behind for them to blackmail me into silence –
that had been the biggest obstacle. Without the Colonel I
might never have got through; they preferred you to leave
someone dear behind. Then, if you began to sing, they'd tell
you your mother, your brother, your children even, would
catch a cold on your behalf. All I gave was my solemn word.
They thought it meant nothing; but I have tried to keep my
promise.

That way, they might be readier to let someone through
again.

The Home Country could not detain me long. It held no
allure for me. On my first evening, my body still believing it
was morning, I wandered up the maze of cobbled alleyways

to the city's most venerable quarter. This was the old world, and you could keep it. I thought Macao had greater sophistication – certainly the casino hotels offered a more ambitious modern architecture than anything I could see in this furred heart of a moribund empire. This wasn't where it happened; this was a backwater, too. I read reports of food shortages in the countryside, though there was no clue as to this in the windows of the truly excellent restaurants. It was a pity I detested both sea-food and olive oil. The lights of the city twinkled below me. That, anyhow, was different from Danu. I could see the black of the river estuary and the car lights, all red in one direction, all white in another, sliding over the big bridge that was the most impressive thing in the city. It dwarfed, for instance, the monument on the river bank to the Renaissance explorers and circumnavigators who'd set the tiny country on the path to greatness. I imagined they must have been bold generals like Arsenio and Osvaldo, pathfinders like X. Ray, stalwarts like the Corporal, boys as eager and facile as my woodchucks. For them, the time and the place had been right. The Vascos and Fernandos had been no greater than Osvaldo. From a cafe a guitarist broke into one of the wild, melancholy laments that were the typical music of the country. Too much. I laughed.

Going down the hill, I heard furtive steps on the stone stairs behind. I could make out four men. I didn't have to think – I was leaping downhill like a goddamned goat before I'd summed up the situation: which was they intended to rob me. Being the casual criminals they were, they didn't persist long in the chase. I am accustomed, I thought with scorn, to a greater degree of perseverance from my pursuers. I mixed among the crowds strolling the avenues. Safety in numbers was an illusion. I spotted a gang of bag-snatchers, sizing up a tourist. Why couldn't everyone else? I had no pity for these complacent victims.

The good thing about the Home Country was its passport. Poor and shrunken though it was, no longer a power with an empire, half-way to being a third-world nation itself in material terms, the place was still an Atlantic civilisation. It was a passport of Europe. And soon, so the official who interviewed me said, it would be a passport of the full community; it would be a key that could unlock the gates of Paris, Rome, of London, even. It would become a magic talisman. His eyes gleamed; he smiled as he recited what it would do one day. And I smiled in appreciation.

But in the meantime I had no interest in remaining, not in what I found an ossuary of the spirit. Yes, I'd come back. But now I wanted to be somewhere that had a future and no past to carry. Not too much of one anyhow. I didn't care if it was raw, if the pangs of birth were ugly; I wanted to be somewhere I wouldn't be defined by what I'd been, where I could fashion a new notion of myself and impose it on others as the truth. I decided to go to Brazil.

Don't think it bizarre. I was not alone in thinking it a splendid plan. The case-officer assigned to deal with me thought it a gift from the gods – I could see that, though he did his best not to show it. He'd speedily seen I wasn't the typical Danuese. I had no religion for a start, though I had developed respect for the Church through knowing Monsignor. I'd kept my involvement with FAKOUM and FAKINTIL and in particular my personal association with Osvaldo and Martinho to myself, but he smelled a rat. I had no intention of giving trouble or offence to anyone, not me, but the case-officer discerned in me the potential for terrible trouble.

'A very sensible idea, Senhor Ng,' he said, and if he could have applauded he would. 'You'll be out of my hair there,' was what he didn't say. He did say, 'You can make a whole new life there. We will do all we can to help.'

And he did, he was as good as his word.

I never had problems with Brazil all the time I was there. You could say it was a big, peacetime Danu. My Portuguese, of course, was as excellent as my English (no, I lie; it was nearly as good as my perfect, my Balliol English). The metropolitan accent conferred a touch of distinction, which was not unpleasant to me. Chinese I knew there would be, that petty diaspora of restaurateurs and storekeepers. But I had other, nobler plans for myself. I knew for a start that there were more than a million Japanese there.

I was to be interviewed in New York, en route to Rio, by an agent who specialised in placing people like me. I was warned before I left not to do anything silly, like becoming an illegal immigrant, a runaway. Momentarily, I was offended. That was something quite below my dignity. I wished he could have seen that. It would not have been the act of the person I had chosen to become.

As things turned out, I had a week to cool my heels in New York. The agent had unforeseen business to detain him. I hoped the US authorities were giving him a hard time. During this time I browsed the book-stores, and resisted the temptation to steal two or three interesting volumes, among them De Gaulle's foreign policy monograph. I was surprised to be able to stand and read as long as I liked without feeling a hand on my shoulder. I'd forgotten the indulgences of that world. I strolled down towards Greenwich Village, sat in the dismal gray square outside the university. I looked at the faces; the man on the bench next to me was talking to himself. His eyes looked insane. I knew this had been a place of elegance, had been sanctified in literature, but it was not that kind of place to me.

On my fourth day I went to visit the United Nations. It had started to snow, the first I'd seen since leaving Toronto. The building looked as impressive in actuality as it did in magazines, though the Hudson somewhat less so than the river I'd just left. I was unable to spot the *malai* flag anywhere, which cheered me perversely. I was wearing a blue woollen sailor's hat as disguise. I had the feeling that this was the kind of place no one would want me going to, although it was a perfectly innocent visit of curiosity. I'd changed subway trains unnecessarily three times in order to check no one leapt out with me as the doors slid shut. No one had. I guess I was afflicted with delusions of grandeur. I removed my flake-laden pom-pom inside, dashed it on my knee, and stayed bare-headed a while, so that I wouldn't appear like a nut bent on an assassination mission. I joined a tour.

As it was finishing I saw a man who was familiar. I looked longer than was wise or discreet. Our eyes met. It was definitely Joaquim Lobato, the ex-FAKOUM Minister of the Exterior. He had been abroad on his support-gathering tour at the time of the *malai* invasion. I had thought him the luckiest man on the FAKOUM Central Committee. He was certainly one of the only three still living.

But he didn't think so. He accounted himself the unluckiest man alive. He almost wished he'd shared the fate of his friends. So he told me in the diner to which we resorted for coffee and blueberry pie. Over the plastic-topped table with its mustards, ketchups, and sugar-shaker we exchanged stories. I told him mine first. It was a comprehensive and truthful account, save for my name. He had already heard Osvaldo was dead – the *malais* had wasted no time in letting that be known – but the circumstances had been different. They'd said he'd been caught in a heliborne ambush and killed in hand to hand combat by a *malai* captain. I disabused him of that notion.

Then I heard how he lived hand to mouth in the Bronx, lobbying whom he could at the talking-shop. There was a resolution he tried to get passed every year, condemning the invasion and calling for a withdrawal. He lobbied as hard as he could – he seemed tireless and undaunted even to me – but it was an uphill struggle. So far he'd got sympathetic countries to 'deplore' the *malai* act of aggression, which was not the same thing as condemning it, he said. Small verbal distinctions mattered in this world. That was the high- or low-point of his annual calendar. He did his best to see that his phone wasn't disconnected at that time – he lived, as I say, from day to day.

The waitress came round and blackmailed us into buying another cup of coffee. I let the Minister know I'd pay.

'It's funny sitting here,' I said, 'talking about Osvaldo, so remote from Danu.'

'*Remote?*' he cried. People turned to look at us. I gestured to him. I wanted to go to Brazil, even if he didn't. He lowered his voice. 'This isn't remote,' his voice shook. 'This is where it's determined; this is where it began; this is where it will end.' I looked at him; I thought it was forgivable, egocentric but forgivable. Then he changed my understanding for ever. He laughed bitterly and he said, 'Do you know what it was all for? Do you? I mean, do you really?' I waited. He said, 'There's a deep-water channel off Danu. I don't suppose you ever thought about it, did you?'

'I knew the sea was deep there. It changes colour to deep blue.'

'Exactly, it changes colour. Well, they didn't want it turning red. That channel is one of only three in the whole archipelago that will allow a nuclear submarine safe passage. Only three in two thousand miles. Otherwise, if they take the long route, it adds ten days going from Guam in the Pacific to Diego Garcia in the Indian Ocean. Is that a nice little geography lesson?' He smiled; there was rage and misery in that smile. And I understood at once the implications of what he'd been saying. That was why it had all happened. 'So we are as vital as Panama to the US?'

'No. But still very important to their global projection. They didn't want a new left-wing government sitting on the canal-bank. Oh, there was a reason for it. It wasn't just mad *malai* Colonels looking for action. And the oil for the Australians, of course. Do you know the American President and his adviser were in the *malai* capital at the time?'

I shook my head.

'They left the day before the invasion. Nice timing, don't you think?'

The waitress hovered meaningfully by us. After a minute, she wrote out the check and placed it on the table. Joaquim Lobato said angrily, 'I did not ask for that.' She ignored him. He said, 'I'm talking to you.' I wondered if confrontations like this gave him strength and relief; anything that would help. I didn't think he was so lucky now. We sat there, defying her. Lobato gave me his telephone number. That was when he told me it was often disconnected. 'You'd think they'd keep it open so they could go on bugging me,' he said.

I could see a somewhat bitter sense of humour was what kept him going. I told him I would contact him in a few days, but never did. We shook hands in the snow. Then for some reason we embraced. I looked back at the corner and he waved. I don't think he thought I was a *malai* informer.

That night I took a stroll around the expensive quarter. I played with the notion of bombing it. I'd have done it with minimalist technology; say, beans swelling in water and lifting a diaphragm and bare wire to a contact for the time-fuse. That would be the check I'd present them. But such spite was not Osvaldo's legacy. He'd been a dinosaur in a world of pettiness. I felt ashamed of myself.

The Brazilian agent saw me the next morning. He asked me if I had any special skills.

'I have experience in the hotel industry,' I told him. 'Also the construction industry.'

'That's an interesting combination,' he said. 'You could build it and then manage it.'

As he was the one with the power, I smiled.

'What was your expertise in the building business – quantity surveying or cost control?'

'Neither,' I said, 'blasting.'

'Well, let's go for hotel. The construction is mostly in the interior, and I don't think you would like that, malaria and Indians. What name would you like to use?'

This was something I hadn't thought of. I was gratified. 'Call me… call me, Mr Kawasaki,' I said, and, like my old generator, my heart skipped a bound.

That was neither an end, nor a beginning. If I thought I could unmake my old self so easily I was a fool. I could not terminate Adolph Ng so conveniently. I was trying to accomplish within my own small person what the *malais* hadn't been able to do to a nation. An identity and a history cannot be obliterated with a switch of a name or the stroke of a pen. I arrived in the vastness of a new country as what I thought a *tabula rasa* but there was writing underneath, the coded determinants of what I was and always would be inscribed in (what shall we say?) acetic acid or lemon juice which gradually browned and showed in the revealing action of sunlight. For the first days, weeks even, I carried on in a light-headed and even giddy way. The scenery – nothing remarkable – the very banalities of the vacation industry, sea, city blocks, beach, bronzed androgynous bodies, was nevertheless sufficiently different not to trigger associations of the past. I didn't have a solid grasp of myself – I depended on other people and surroundings to cue me. So I wandered bizarrely, often with that feeling of standing outside myself as a separate and dispassionate watcher, that I had experienced the day the *malais* had invaded Danu but this time without the terror. I'd repeat my name – and as I got really far from shore I'd say 'Ng' or 'Adolph' – to try to bring me back inside myself. But it didn't work. I realised who I was OK – I just couldn't live inside the envelope. One is given to understand that it is a perfectly common psychological state which has afflicted nearly everyone at some time.

But the surroundings grew familiar, a routine established itself. I made acquaintances, I met partners – that special freemasonry of glances – and gradually I saw my features reflected in the iridescent circumstances of Rio. It was a countenance I'd seen before; only the mirror's frame was more ornate. I learned to accept it. I was wearier, I was more tolerant, that was the only difference and that change only enabled me the better to accept what I'd always been. The invisible writing, the lineaments of me, which had been there beneath the surface all the time, became manifest. I accepted myself again. I even wrote to Lobato, before tearing the letter up.

Well, it was a conclusion, not the start of anything new. And if I couldn't make away with myself, how could the *malais* make away with a whole nation? Before the invasion there were 700,000 Danuese. Now there are less than half a million. If that isn't genocide I don't know what is. But I know something else – you can't kill everyone. It isn't over. They might have caught up with X. Ray by now; Martinho might have done away with himself. Yet I still believe what I said to Martinho, as he cocked his blind head towards me before talking of the hand of God: there's always someone else who'll step forward. Even a tiny society like ours had the capacity to throw up any number of superior people. There's no such thing as a hero – only ordinary people asked extraordinary things in terrible circumstances, and delivering. The Danuese might have thought they'd lost their leaders, that there was no one else, and that's the moment a frizzy-haired messiah will choose to come upon the scene. X. Ray's unshowy steadiness was right for the low time in which he newly found himself – he could put the fire out. Even if X. Ray was only the Baptist to some little woodchuck's saviour, I do know that nothing died with Osvaldo except his own faults. (I think of him in some tropical Valhalla, rejoined with Arsenio. They are not swilling from horns of ale but chewing betel.) The *malais* might have put the torch to the field, they might think they've exterminated all the creatures in it, but there'll always be one woodchuck left. There always is.

THE END